'A novel I long to live in, a vivid evocation of the famous female-owned Parisian bookshop . . . Heroine and shop owner Sylvia Beach shepherds seemingly all of the great writers of the 20th century with an appealing blend of warmth, wit, frustration and understanding. Kerri Maher writes a love letter to books, bookstores, and booklovers everywhere'
Kate Quinn

'Absorbing and beautifully written . . . transports you to 1920s Paris – and keeps you utterly captivated with its vivid cast of characters'
Heat

'A story about Paris and bookshops was bound to find a place in my heart but this one has the pièce de résistance: the character of Sylvia Beach. I was completely enthralled . . . a fascinating rendering of Paris's glory days during the 1920s and 30s, this novel will transport you as only the best historical fiction can'
Natasha Lester

'An intriguing story, beguilingly told'
Mail on Sunday

'A worthy homage to Sylvia Beach and a love letter to all bookstores, libraries, and the passionate and committed women who run them'
New York Journal of Books

DISCARDED

014459501 7

'In a novel exuberant, bittersweet, and reflective by
turns, Maher explores the life of Sylvia Beach ... readers
will emerge with sincere appreciation for the artistic
spirit and courage of a remarkable woman'
Historical Novel Society

'A compelling coming-of-age tale, in addition to
an impressive piece of historical fiction'
Culturefly

'A compelling and fascinating look at the world-changing
mavericks who bonded, bickered and triumphed
in the realm of literature'
Nuala O'Connor

'Intelligent, fierce and filled with reverence for a fascinating
epoch in literary history ... a delight for readers and writers'
Whitney Scharer

'A compelling portrait of a remarkable woman, who steps from
the pages in all her charm, courage and vulnerability. It's also a
colourful snapshot of literary Paris in the 1920s, with its glamour
and gossip, ogres and egos. Meticulously researched yet above all
a page-turning story, this is historical fiction at its best'
Gill Paul

'A paean to Beach, and a love letter to bookstores and libraries'
Boston Globe

'Maher vividly reimagines the indomitable Beach,
who struggled for years to get *Ulysses* published'
Washington Post

'A book for the bookshop lovers ... an absorbing novel about the life changing nature of our favourite reads'
Belfast Telegraph

'A beautiful ode to Sylvia Beach, the renowned Shakespeare and Company owner, a real-life heroine who has left her mark on us all'
Marie Benedict

'Lulls you into an interwar Parisian dream where love – be it romantic, friendly or even for a book – can be found on a quirky little street in the 6th'
Kaia Alderson

'Wholly immersive, a literary romp through Left Bank Paris ... an enchanting glimpse of the storied lost generation through a female gaze'
Toronto Star

'Come for the love of books and Sapphic passion and stay for the frequent cameos by the likes of Ezra Pound and Ernest Hemingway'
BuzzFeed Books

'A fine tribute to a tireless and selfless champion of literary genius'
Kirkus

'Recommended to fans of Paula McLain's *The Paris Wife* and anyone who enjoyed Hemingway's *A Moveable Feast*'
Booklist

TITLES BY KERRI MAHER

The Kennedy Debutante

The Girl in White Gloves

The Paris Bookseller

THE
PARIS
BOOKSELLER

KERRI MAHER

REVIEW

Copyright © 2022 Kerri Maher

The right of Kerri Maher to be identified as the Author of
the Work has been asserted by her in accordance with the
Copyright, Designs and Patents Act 1988.

First published in the USA in 2022 by Berkley
An imprint of Penguin Random House LLC

First published in Great Britain in 2022 by
Headline Review
An imprint of HEADLINE PUBLISHING GROUP

First published as a paperback in Great Britain in 2022 by
Headline Review

1

Apart from any use permitted under UK copyright law, this publication may
only be reproduced, stored, or transmitted, in any form, or by any means,
with prior permission in writing of the publishers or, in the case of
reprographic production, in accordance with the terms of licences
issued by the Copyright Licensing Agency.

All characters – apart from the obvious historical figures – in this
publication are fictitious and any resemblance to real persons,
living or dead, is purely coincidental.

Cataloguing in Publication Data is available from the British Library

ISBN 978 1 4722 9078 6 (B format)

Offset in 10.23/14.6pt Adobe Caslon Pro by Jouve (UK), Milton Keynes

Printed and bound in Great Britain by Clays Ltd, Elcograf S.p.A.

Headline's policy is to use papers that are natural, renewable and recyclable
products and made from wood grown in well-managed forests and other
controlled sources. The logging and manufacturing processes are expected
to conform to the environmental regulations of the country of origin.

HEADLINE PUBLISHING GROUP
An Hachette UK Company
Carmelite House
50 Victoria Embankment
London EC4Y 0DZ

www.headline.co.uk
www.hachette.co.uk

Pour mes amis—near and far, old and new.
You made this story possible.

Paris is so very beautiful that it satisfies something in you that is always hungry in America.

—Ernest Hemingway

THE
PARIS
BOOKSELLER

PART ONE
1917–20

Famous people, they were not born so.
One always begins by being unknown.

—Adrienne Monnier

CHAPTER 1

It was hard not to feel that Paris was *the* place.

Sylvia had been trying to get back for fifteen years, ever since the Beach family had lived there when her father, Sylvester, was the pastor of the American Church in the Latin Quarter and she was a romantic teenager who couldn't get enough of Balzac or cassoulet. What she remembered most about that time, what she'd carried in her heart when her family had to return to the United States, was the sense that the French capital was brighter than any other city she'd been in or could ever be in. It was more than the flickering gas lamps that illuminated the city after dark, or that ineluctable, glowing white stone from which so much of the city was built—it was the brilliance of the life burbling in every fountain, every student meeting, every puppet show in the Jardin du Luxembourg and opera in the Théâtre de l'Odéon. It was the way her mother sparkled with life, read books, and hosted professors, politicians, and actors, serving them rich, glistening dishes by candlelight at dinners where there was spirited debate about books and world events. Eleanor Beach told her three daughters—Cyprian, Sylvia, and Holly—that they

3

were living in the most rare and wonderful of places, and it would change the course of their lives forever.

Nothing had compared, not making posters and answering phones and knocking on doors with Cyprian and Holly and Mother for the National Woman's Party in New York; not adventuring in Europe solo and reveling in the spires and cobblestones of many other cities; not her first longed-for kiss with her classmate Gemma Bradford; not winning the praise of her favorite teachers.

But here she was now, actually *living* in the city that had captured her soul.

From the rooms she shared with Cyprian in the staggeringly beautiful if also crumbling Palais Royale, Sylvia made her way down to the Pont Neuf and crossed to the other side of the Seine, breathing in the wind from the river that whipped her short locks of hair across her face and threatened to extinguish her cigarette. She stopped in the middle of the bridge to look east and admire Notre-Dame Cathedral, with its symmetrical Gothic towers flanking the rose window and the precariously dainty buttresses whose strength still dumbfounded her—they'd been holding up those gargantuan walls for centuries.

Soon she was winding her way through the narrower streets of the Latin Quarter, which were still familiar from her adolescent wanderings. Though she got a tiny bit lost, it was happily so, because it gave her an opportunity to admire the Église de Saint-Germaine-des-Prés and ask instructions of a pretty French student sipping café crème at a sidewalk table at Les Deux Magots. At last she stopped at 7 rue de l'Odéon, the location of A. Monnier, bookseller.

The facade of Madame—*ou, peut-être, mademoiselle?*—Monnier's little shop was painted a pleasing shade of gray with a pale script bearing the proprietress's name above the large picture windows. When Sylvia pushed open the door, a single bell jingled cheerfully. A scattering of people stood here and there among the floor-to-ceiling shelves stocked heartily with books; they were reading and browsing spines, but no one was talking and so it was as silent as an empty church. Feeling suddenly shy about asking her question, Sylvia looked around and postponed her request.

She was glad she did, for she discovered some beautiful editions of her favorite French novels, and read nearly an entire short story in the latest issue of *Vers et Prose*, and as she did the shop stirred to life around her. Customers made register-clanging purchases and chattier couples entered, filling the place with sound.

Plucking the book she'd come to buy off the shelf, along with the journal she'd been absorbed in, Sylvia went to the desk with the big brass cash register, where a striking woman of about her own age stood smiling with her slim lips and Mediterranean-blue eyes, the contrast of her dove-white skin and raven hair making her impossible not to look at. In her mind, Sylvia heard Cyprian criticize the woman's outfit as old fashioned, with its floor-length skirt and the blouse buttoned all the way up, both overly modest barriers to the voluptuous figure beneath, but Sylvia liked everything about the look of this woman. She seemed like the kind of person one could talk to. There was something more, too, though; Sylvia felt such a strong urge to stroke the woman's smooth cheek.

"Did you find . . . your heart's desire?" the woman asked in heavily accented English.

My heart's desire? Sylvia smiled at the typically French passion in the woman's plainly spoken words, then replied in French, "Yes, I did, though I'm disappointed you knew I wasn't French." Languages were something of a gift to her; she spoke three fluently. She was gratified to see that as soon as she spoke, the woman appeared impressed by her accent.

"Where are you from?" she asked, in French this time, using the formal *vous*.

"The United States. Most recently Princeton, New Jersey, near New York City. My name is Sylvia, by the way. Sylvia Beach."

The woman clapped her hands together and exclaimed, "Les États-Unis! The home of Benjamin Franklin! But he is my favorite! I am Adrienne Monnier."

Sylvia laughed, as it somehow made perfect sense that this pretty girl in the outdated clothes should so admire her own favorite founding father. Mademoiselle indeed; not madame in the slightest. "Pleased to meet you, Mademoiselle Monnier. Your shop is very special. And I like Ben Franklin, too," she admitted. "But have you read any Hawthorne? Thoreau? What about *Moby Dick*? That's one of my favorites."

And they were off. Sylvia learned all about what American authors had and had not been translated into French, and also how difficult it was to come by English-language books even in cosmopolitan Paris. "And anyway," Adrienne admitted with a demure flicker of her lashes to the floor, "my English is not good enough to read the great literature in its mother tongue."

"Perhaps not yet," Sylvia assured her, feeling her heart grow and glow in her chest. Something was passing between them, and it was more than just books, she was sure of it. Her hands felt clammy with it.

"There you are, Adrienne," sang a lilting and lovely voice from behind Sylvia.

She turned and saw a stunning waif of a woman, with a thick and wavy mane of reddish-blond hair piled atop her head, who wore a similar ensemble to Adrienne's, though it fit her slight frame entirely differently. Her fingers were long and slim and moved airily, as if they were not entirely under the control of the woman who possessed them. But when they rested on Adrienne's shorter, thicker hand, Sylvia could see the intent there and knew immediately the two women were lovers.

And there she'd been thinking that she and Adrienne were flirting. Already, they'd slipped into using the familiar *tu* instead of *vous*.

The warmth and admiration in Adrienne's smile at this woman, who now stood shoulder to shoulder with her, opened a painful fissure in Sylvia's heart. These two women had something here, together and in the store. Something she'd been looking for a long time but hadn't known she wanted—*needed*—until she saw it. Was this something she could make happen, for herself? What was *this* anyway? Sylvia felt suddenly disoriented, knocked off balance by her surroundings: the store, the women, the books, the baritone hum of the other patrons.

"Suzanne," said Adrienne, "Please meet our new friend Sylvia Beach, of the United States. Sylvia, this is Suzanne Bonnierre, my business partner."

In an overly enthusiastic gesture, Sylvia thrust out her hand, which Suzanne appeared amused to shake. "It's a pleasure to meet you, Mademoiselle Beach."

"Sylvia, please," she said. "What an amazing store you have here. It's so cozy and inviting, and you stock only the best." Though she did wonder why Suzanne's was not part of the name of the store. Well, Sylvia supposed, Monnier and Bonnierre, however charming they looked and sounded together, might have been a bit too obvious, liberal as Paris was about such things. Just the other night, Cyprian had stuffed Sylvia into a pantsuit and donned a sequined dress herself, then enveloped them both in full-length cloaks for the metro ride to a new bar on the rue Edgar-Quinet where the clientele was entirely women, half of whom wore monocles and spats. The establishment looked like any other local watering hole from the outside, with a small awning simply labeled BAR, but once they were inside, the loud, jazzy openness of the place had made Sylvia uncomfortable. She'd told herself to relax and enjoy the fact that she was living somewhere such an establishment could prosper, somewhere she could be entirely honest about her attractions and a woman in a tweed suit and cap could sing Billy Murray tunes; it was even protected by the law because same-sex relations had been decriminalized in the French Revolution. But she didn't enjoy feeling like another piece of fruit in a market. The reader in her preferred the quiet and subtlety of A. Monnier.

"Why thank you," Suzanne replied. "I have never been to your country, but I have heard and read many wonderful things about it. It has been quite an inspiration to France, of course."

"There might be many excellent things about my country, but I'm glad to be here instead," Sylvia replied, her mind going straight to the rise in censorship under the Comstock and Espionage Acts, the long and precarious slog to women's suffrage, and the outrageous idea of an alcohol prohibition that was spreading like wildfire. It seemed like ideas that had once seemed fringe, too strange to contemplate as serious, had taken root in America while good, strong ideas that would help the country progress into the new century were languishing away.

"We are also glad you're here," Adrienne said, beaming.

"You must come to the reading tonight!" Suzanne exclaimed. "Our dear friends Valery Larbaud and Léon-Paul Fargue will be there. And Jules Romains. You know these writers?"

"Of course I do! It would be an honor to meet them." The prospect also set Sylvia's stomach churning. *Jules Romains? Vraiment?* What could she possibly have to say to him?

"Come back at eight. We pay no attention to the air raids anymore."

Well. There was simply no concentrating on her Spain essay after that. Sitting at her little desk in the Palais, Sylvia kept catching the scent of dust and lavender that reminded her of A. Monnier—the shop and the woman, both—and every time she buried her nose in her sleeves to find the source of it, she found it was always elusive.

She couldn't help thinking that this distraction was just one more sign she was not destined to be a writer, despite the fact that after all the reading she'd done in her life, everyone around her, from her parents and sisters to her oldest friend, Carlotta Welles, just assumed she would be one.

"There's a Walt Whitman in you," her father told her every time she brought home another high mark on a school essay. "I just know it."

But essays were not poems, or novels. When she tried her hand at verse or a story, it came out all wrong. She adored Whitman. To try to be anything remotely like him—or Kate Chopin or any of the Brontë sisters, for that matter—almost seemed an insult. It didn't help that as she grew older, she began to prefer the writers she saw successfully continuing Whitman's legacy, singing so startlingly of themselves and the world that she would sometimes complete one of their works and lie awake half the night wondering, *How do they do it? How do they reach inside me, put their fist around my very soul, and rattle it in its cage?* It had been like that with Chopin's *The Awakening* especially, and also with James Joyce's *Portrait of the Artist as a Young Man*. Oh god, she felt a roiling stew of lust and admiration and jealousy thinking of both those novels. The exquisite honesty with which they wrote about bodies and their cravings, and the guilt and consequences of those cravings, using words strung into unsettling sentences that embodied the very nature of the character's inner turmoil, made Sylvia sweat in her sheets.

Could she ever write so bravely, knowing her minister father, whom she loved dearly, would read every word? It was one thing for him to quietly accept her spinsterhood, and perhaps even her discreet sapphism—for he'd never encouraged her to marry and he'd never questioned the friendships she'd had with women, which after all had run the gamut between entirely platonic and, rarely, heart-wrenchingly intimate—but it would be quite another thing for her to write about her desires with the kind of honesty she admired in the new writing she was starting to see in the more progressive journals.

Could she write about her own deepest longings with abandon, without abandoning herself? Could she help fill the pages of her favorite journal, *The Little Review*, which its editor Margaret Anderson had boldly left entirely blank in 1916, publishing twenty-odd white pages with only an editorial saying that she was no longer willing to publish *good enough* writing; everything she published had to be true art. Art that would remake the world. And Sylvia believed with all her heart that this *was* the purpose of art—to be new, to make change, to alter minds.

She recalled her mother's reply to her father's suggestion about Whitman: "Or maybe she'll be the next Elizabeth Cady Stanton." Why did her parents have to pick such big shoes for her to fill? Was it their fault she was secretly jealous of Cyprian's success in acting?

In some ways, Cyprian was the reason they were in Paris at all, so Sylvia supposed she ought to be grateful. Her sister had a recurring part in a popular weekly film called *Judex*, which was so well known that the two of them were regularly stopped in the street and asked for autographs; occasionally, someone would even ask Sylvia for her signature, assuming she was some sort of up-and-comer hanging around with the glittering, gorgeous star. Sylvia would sigh and reflect that it had always been this way between her and her younger sister. Even at thirty years old, Sylvia was still riled that Cyprian could rely on her arresting *looks* to get attention, while she toiled in libraries and at desks, hoping her words and ideas might be discovered someday.

"It's always adolescent boys and little girls, though," Cyprian would complain after signing another napkin or cardboard coaster. "Where are the *ducs* and other admirers of means?"

"You know they exist, sister darling. They're the ones sending you Veuve and Pernod at the Ritz." *And anyway, you only want the male attention for the status of it.* Cyprian was more willing to attach herself to a man than Sylvia, who'd entirely sworn off the idea of marriage, even a marriage of convenience that could provide her with some camouflage when she needed it. Joining her identity with that of a man, even one who preferred sharing his bed with another man, was simply not appealing. For joining, she'd noticed, almost always meant subsuming. And even though Sylvia was one of very few people on earth who knew her sister preferred the affections of women, Cyprian liked to act parts that flattered her, and helped her afford Chanel dresses and Italian shoes, indulging a taste for finer things she'd inherited from their mother.

"If I could just get a part *onstage*, they could send flowers to my room" was her familiar lament.

When at last it was time for her to return to the rue de l'Odéon, Sylvia took the metro and then paced the cobblestone courtyard in front of the Odéon Theater up the street for half an hour, chain-smoking and rehearsing possible topics of conversation to have with *famous writers*, before she told herself she was being silly and marched into Adrienne's shop.

In the summer twilight, the lamps were soft and the conversation bright. Adrienne and Suzanne swanned about the room, pouring drinks, touching backs, inciting laughter. Adrienne especially—the other guests competed for a chance to wave her over. A veritable Hestia of books, she was otherwise engaged in deep and serious conversation with a small group when Suzanne introduced Sylvia to Valery Larbaud and Jules Romains. Both men kissed her on each cheek as if they'd known each other for years. "Monnier has been telling us all about you," Romains informed her. "That you are a reader, and that you enjoy the American transcendentalists. I wonder if you also like Baudelaire? Of the same period here in France?"

"Oh, of course. *Fleurs du mal* was important on both sides of the Atlantic," she replied, and basked in the warmth of his approval. They went on to chat for some time about nineteenth-century literature, a conversation that flowed seamlessly into others about recent novels and poetry, the end of the war, and the prospects for literature in France.

Well. Maybe all that reading is finally paying off.

The tickle of a hand lightly touching her elbow made Sylvia jump and slosh a little wine out of her glass. *Adrienne.* Sylvia turned from Larbaud and Romains to her hostess, who smiled and kissed her on both cheeks, a greeting Sylvia reciprocated, though with overly firm lips.

"Are you having a good time, my friend?" Then, without waiting for Sylvia to answer, Adrienne fixed her eyes on the two men and said, "I trust you've been making our new American friend feel welcome?"

"Very welcome," Sylvia rushed to assure everyone.

"And as usual, Monnier," said Larbaud, "you have added another treasure to this bounty."

It seemed impossible they were talking about her. Or that she'd been so nervous just an hour before. Sylvia felt at home there, as if she'd been stopping by this shop all her life. And yet, it was also thrilling like a new adventure, a fall headlong into the unknown.

"Do not blush, dear Sylvia!" Adrienne laughed. "I knew you were a treasure the moment I laid eyes on you."

"Well, my sister is an actress, so I'm afraid I've rather gotten used to her being the treasure."

"An actress?" Romains cocked an eyebrow. "Anything we might have seen?"

"*Judex*. It's a weekly."

The two men laughed uproariously, the wine they'd consumed making the apples of their cheeks red.

"Pay them no mind," said Adrienne, playfully patting Romains's arm as he got hold of himself. "They are the worst snobs. I love the cinema myself, even some of the regular dramas. I have not seen *Judex*. Perhaps we should go."

There it was again. The *frisson*. Why did the French have the best words for attraction?

"We should. Cyprian would be thrilled."

"Suzanne will love it, too."

Suzanne. How could I have forgotten?

And yet, there she was again, as if summoned by their conversation, with a loose, lingering kiss on Adrienne's cheek and a hearty, familiar greeting for the men—reminders that Sylvia was the newcomer, the outsider, that no matter how warmly she was received, none of this was truly *hers*.

CHAPTER 2

⤢

D ay after day, though, she was drawn to A. Monnier, as if by Sirens.

The French writers were deeply curious about the American and English writers she'd read, and Sylvia found herself lending out her own copies of Wordsworth and Whitman as well as older issues of *The Dial* and *The Egoist* and *The Little Review* that she'd picked up on her last trips to London and New York. She wrote to her mother and asked her to send more volumes from the library she kept in her childhood home in Princeton.

Sometimes Cyprian would accompany her, and the two of them would smoke and whisper on the sidelines, which gave Sylvia just a little extra confidence around Suzanne, whom Cyprian referred to— very quietly, and only to Sylvia—as *la crapaudette*, a variation of the French word for toad. Originally, she'd called her a toady.

"But she's not," Sylvia had protested, though she jealously and thoroughly enjoyed her sister's uncharitable criticism. "The shop was as much her idea as Adrienne's."

"Then why isn't her name above the door, too?"

"I suppose because it was Adrienne's parents who gave her the money to open?"

Cyprian shook her head. "I'm telling you, Sylvia, there's more to it than that."

If there was, no one was talking about it. The well-circulated story was that the two women had been friends at school in Paris, and then they went to London together, where they hatched the idea for the bookshop that they opened in 1915. Sylvia wasn't sure what about their relationship she envied most: the easy, daily partnership, the sisterhood of books, or the obvious physical intimacy. How long had it been since Sylvia had so much as kissed someone? And though she'd had one or two short-lived romances, she wouldn't say she'd ever been truly in love. Certainly she'd never been as close to someone as Adrienne was to Suzanne; they were practically married. As married as two women could be, anyway. They did not kiss in the store, but if one of them was invited somewhere, it was assumed the other would accompany her.

Sylvia hated herself for her jealousy, especially when Suzanne was nothing but kind to her. It was she who'd rounded them up one Sunday afternoon and said, "They are playing the archive of *Judex* today. Let's go." And armed with pockets full of licorice and brandy, she and Adrienne and Sylvia and Cyprian had sat in the dark theater getting tipsy and marvelously lost in the melodrama. At the intermission, Suzanne and Cyprian excused themselves to the ladies' lounge, and Adrienne leaned in close to Sylvia and said, "Your sister is almost as brilliant as you."

Good lord, the heat those words in her ear produced in her chest.

"That's nice of you to say, but also utterly ridiculous."

"Not every star is like the *étoile polaire*, *chérie*. Some are more elusive, more subtle. But they are no less brilliant, no less important."

"Thank you." There was so much more she wanted to reply—that

Adrienne herself was like the sun, the brightest star of them all, bathing everyone in her warm light. But that hardly would have been appropriate with Suzanne coming back any minute from the toilet. Convinced she was blushing furiously, Sylvia glimpsed Cyprian returning to her seat and told Adrienne it was her turn to use the loo.

When the foursome emerged from four hours in the theater, it was dark outside and Cyprian said, "Well, that was mortifying, but thank you for buying tickets and paying my salary."

"You were wonderful!" Adrienne and Suzanne exclaimed together, launching into a list of their favorite scenes with Sylvia's sister.

"You're very sweet for saying so, but I need a drink. What about the place on the rue Edgar-Quinet?"

Sylvia's breath caught, as many things occurred to her at once: though she'd assumed Adrienne and Suzanne knew she was a lesbian, she'd never confirmed it; clearly her sister thought it needed confirmation; none of them were dressed properly for the place, where everyone showed up in a suit or spangled frock, so it was plain to all four of them what Cyprian was doing.

Neither Suzanne nor Adrienne batted an eyelash, however. With a theatrical yawn, Suzanne said, "I do love an aperitif at Lulu's place, but it's such a *production*, and I don't really feel like changing clothes, do you?"

"No," Sylvia quickly agreed. "I'm too tired for that as well."

So, Cyprian's gamble had worked, and if there had been any unspoken questions among them about each other's sexual preferences, they were now answered.

Still playing, Cyprian pouted out her lower lip and said, "You're no fun."

"Another night, *chérie*," said Adrienne. "I know a place close by that does superb sole meunière."

"I'll hold you to that," Cyprian said.

As they tromped down the road to the bistro, Cyprian and Suzanne took the lead, while behind them, Adrienne laced her arm through Sylvia's and she leaned just a little heavier than necessary on the bookseller's ample, soft form.

❦

The air raid sirens had just started after they'd cleared away the empty bottles and jumble of chairs that had hosted guests for a reading by André Spire early in the autumn. As was their tradition when the sirens began, Suzanne held up a bottle with a little Bordeaux still in it, clinked it to a nearby bottle, and finished the liquid in an enthusiastic swig.

She coughed. She'd been coughing more and more as the days became shorter and a chill crept into the air.

Sylvia was ashamed at what Suzanne's coughs did to her. The coughs and the darkening purple shadows beneath her eyes. No one had said it, but Sylvia suspected Suzanne had tuberculosis. Consumption. Somehow it was the perfect malady for this Dickensian beauty and her equally Victorian companion.

Though she was reluctant to admit it, even to herself, Sylvia started coming to the shop when she knew Suzanne would not be in, for the coughs were driving her to a rather *grand "petit somme"* every afternoon.

"I live more among books than people," Adrienne said one of those lazy afternoons as she and Sylvia shelved a recent shipment of new novels.

"Yes, as do I!" She and Adrienne smiled at each other in mutual recognition. It was a relief to hear that this goddess of the Odéon, whom so many great minds sought out, also preferred the company of words to that of people.

Looking around and seeing the store empty, Adrienne fixed those aquamarine eyes on Sylvia and said, "But even I need a break from books now and again. It's almost closing time anyway. How about we take a run through the impressionist rooms at the d'Orsay? I haven't visited *Olympia* in too long."

In an hour, they were standing before Manet's magnificently nude prostitute, who gazed brazenly out of the picture at Sylvia and Adrienne.

"She started it all," said Adrienne. "All the other paintings, the Morisots, the Monets, the Renoirs, and Bonnards, the Cézannes. They owe it all to her."

Sylvia narrowed her eyes at the alabaster figure, the way she was held together with the loosest of brushstrokes, her African maid merely suggested in the dark background, the arrangement of flowers she held suspended beside her mistress, done in the same paradoxically pure colors. Sylvia supposed she ought to find *Olympia* titillating, as the scandalized first audience had nearly sixty years ago, but today she viewed the painting more through Adrienne's appraising eyes, and what she saw was the very beginning of modern art, a progression that was still evolving that very day in the works of Picasso and Matisse and Man Ray, as well as the writers who were experimenting with the literary versions of the painters' techniques: the preoccupation with the properties of language that paralleled the painters' obsession with the properties of paint, their mutual determination to represent "modern life," as Baudelaire had called it, in all its glory and grotesquerie. For modern life was indeed the stuff of gods, as Manet's name for his prostitute-model plainly said.

"It must have been incredible to grow up with these paintings in your own city," said Sylvia. "To know that your country *started* one of the most important art movements in centuries."

Adrienne stuck out her lower lip as she continued looking at the painting. "No more incredible than knowing your country's revolution inspired others."

Sylvia laughed at the comparison. "That is ancient history. This"—she held her hand out to *Olympia*—"is still happening."

"Rome is ancient history," said Adrienne. "The American and French Revolutions were just yesterday. At least to a Frenchman. This painting was shown in 1863, less than a century after your Declaration of Independence. And it owes something to that declaration. All of this art would not have been possible without independence, I truly believe."

Sylvia inhaled. Had she ever had such conversations before? With a beautiful woman, whose skin and eyes and mind she admired so much? In this city she adored? Everything about the moment had a too muchness to it. And yet, despite the pressure it produced inside her, she wanted it to go on forever.

Alas, a guard approached to tell them the museum would be closing in ten minutes.

"Adieu, *Olympia*," said Adrienne. Then, tearing her eyes away at last and looking at Sylvia, she said, "And now it is time for you to sample the finest hot chocolate in Paris."

Oh thank goodness. She didn't want the day to end, either. "Lead the way."

⁂

"You're in deep trouble, you know," Cyprian said on their way home from the shop a week later.

"What do you mean?"

"Don't play dumb; it doesn't suit you. I'm talking about Adrienne. I don't think a ménage à trois is your style, big sister. Nor do I think it's Suzanne's. I'm not so sure about Adrienne. She seems . . . imaginative. And her sister Rinette is clearly sleeping with both Fargue and her husband."

Sylvia sighed. There was no point in denying anything her sister said. "I know, I know. I . . ." *I'm falling in love with Adrienne. But wait.* "You really think Adrienne would have a ménage à trois?" Sylvia didn't even want to think of such confusing couplings. She'd heard stories of what went on in the apartments of bohemian Paris, but she had yet to see or experience any of it herself. And she definitely didn't want to think of Adrienne in that light; Sylvia would much rather Adrienne remain true to Suzanne, much as that pained her.

"Adrienne strikes me as a woman with appetites, who might get bored easily."

"Just because she is an indulgent gourmand, Cyprian, doesn't mean she's profligate in her love life. That sounds dangerously like Madame Bovary–style thinking." She hoped that referencing their mutually least favorite Flaubert novel, in which the title character is one-dimensionally incontinent in everything from her spending to her sexual habits merely because she's a woman, would help her sister see she was wrong about Adrienne.

But her sister merely shrugged. "Maybe not."

Cyprian could be so infuriating.

Still. Sylvia was glad of her sister's continued company as she tried to figure out what to do with herself next. Her Spain essay was going nowhere, and she was thirty years old. She needed a *purpose*. She couldn't just assist in Adrienne's shop, unpaid, forever. Especially not given the way her feelings were developing.

No sooner had she begun to despair about her aimlessness than an idea began to take shape in Sylvia's mind.

A bookshop of her own.

A place that would attract the same sorts of people that Adrienne's did. But at a distance from this shop she loved so much, from this woman she was beginning to love too much. New York was far enough away to protect her heart.

Yes, a bookshop! A place of her own. The idea grew roots inside her, and she couldn't help mentioning it to Adrienne and Suzanne as they prepared for a reading, setting out chairs and bottles of wine. Sylvia had looked for opportunities to say something to Adrienne alone, but Suzanne always seemed to be around.

"I've been thinking about opening a French-language bookstore in America," mused Sylvia, trying not to betray too much of her own enthusiasm.

"What a marvelous idea!" Suzanne's exclamation cost her immediately, and she doubled over with coughing.

Adrienne rushed to her side, putting one hand on her arm, and the other on her back, which she used to rub comforting circles between Suzanne's shoulder blades.

What would that feel like?

"It is a wonderful idea," agreed Adrienne, her eyes on Suzanne as she righted herself. "But what will we do without you, here in Paris?"

Sylvia's heart burst at the notion that she would, could, be missed. "I'd miss you all, too."

"But your home is America," Adrienne went on, with—*was it?*—a lament in her tone.

"I'm not so sure of that. I've felt happier these last months than I can say."

"You've made us happy as well."

More coughing, more rubbing.

Sylvia's heart hurt. *New York*. Was it far enough?

⁂

She knew she should leave Paris for the sake of her heart, but she wasn't ready to abandon Europe entirely and start working on her New York bookstore yet, so when she saw the poster in the Red Cross office requesting volunteers in Serbia, excitement flooded her. She'd never been to Belgrade, and she wanted to help the war effort. "The call to service is as noble as the call to God," her father had always said, and she had helped before, in 1916, when she'd volunteered to help farmers till their soil in rural France. It wasn't bandaging wounds or ambulance driving, but it was hard, rewarding work, and she craved that kind of purpose and cleansing physical activity.

Thus the end of 1918 found her in khaki trousers nearly two thousand kilometers east of Paris, backpack laden with tin cups and a few precious volumes, among them Joyce's *Portrait*, which she'd lately felt a hankering to reread; she found such solace in his character's quest for a more authentic way of being in the world. She saw herself in Stephen Dedalus's search for meaning through intellectual inquiry and found a kind of vicarious release in his description of lust, which for merciful moments obliterated the overactivity of his mind. *What would that be like, to be so consumed with passion I could forget my other troubles?*

For the moment, it was only through focusing on the needs of the people in the villages outside Belgrade, pushing her body to work long, hard hours, that she was able to obliterate anything. Though the armistice was signed shortly after her arrival, the land mines were still very much alive, and the bad feelings on both sides had hardly been put aside. As a result there were still skirmishes that resulted in gunshot and shrapnel wounds that needed tending, and everyone, young and old, needed blankets, clothing, shoes, soap, and food. She acted as nurse, auntie, dispensary, sock darner, story reader, letter writer, hand-holder, and anything else the people needed.

Anytime there was a loud noise, even if to her ears it was perfectly obvious that it was as benign as a door slamming or a motorcar sputtering, Sylvia noticed that the young men around her—whether in hospital beds or taverns or markets—would crumple, wince, or even hide, crouched, sometimes in an upended garbage can if he could fit. It was remarkable what these poor traumatized boys could fit into when they folded themselves small enough.

Sylvia tried not to think about the way her work with frozen fingers made the skin on her hands crack and bleed until a kind Hungarian girl gave her a tin of salve that smelled of sheep piss but protected her hands through the worst of the cold months. Before she knew it, the labor became hard work she did with sweat pouring down her back. But the effort was welcome. At the end of the day, she'd light a candle and read on her hard cot. *Portrait*, yes, but it was Whitman who sang her to sleep most nights. Her softened, much-loved volume of *Leaves of Grass* was like a prayer book that brought her comfort and companionship. Though his words sometimes made her yearn, too, as when her eyes lingered on the lines in "From Pent-Up Aching Rivers," "O that you and I escape from the rest and go utterly off, free and lawless, / Two hawks in the air, two fishes swimming in the sea not more lawless than we." She longed for her own lawless hawk mate, though she knew that Whitman himself didn't have just one. He'd never married, nor had he settled into a partnership like the one between Adrienne and Suzanne. He clearly knew closeness, and felt the mating impulse. But it was his poetry—his *work*—that had been his seed.

The idea that work could be a life's great fulfillment took hold of her. She thought of it as she sewed buttons and rode in trucks over dusty roads to deliver cans of food; she used it to push away romantic thoughts of Adrienne that snuck into her mind. Much as she valued the kind of work she was doing in Serbia, however, it wasn't the work of her life. There was too much of her mother in her, too much affection for Paris, for glittering conversation and delicious meals; Cyprian would gloat if she ever admitted that aloud, and Sylvia couldn't help but smile at this notion.

A French bookstore in New York. *Yes—that had to be it*. A. Monnier had shown her that a life for and among books was not just possible but *worthy*. In quiet moments or during mindless tasks, Sylvia arranged the shelves and furniture of an imaginary space in her mind. A little place on a leafy street downtown, perhaps in a brownstone where she could live above the store. It would be warmly lit, and she'd serve tea on cold winter days. She would host dinners with professors of French literature from Columbia and Princeton, as well as local writers familiar with Flaubert and Proust, and they would eat sole meunière and boeuf bourguignon and drink wines from Burgundy and Bordeaux while they discussed new literature and the state of the world after the Great War. Important literary people would come to her store; perhaps Margaret Anderson of *The Little Review* would become a regular. Perhaps she could find her own Suzanne in New York, where women could live together quietly in Washington Square without neighbors looking askance. Perhaps she didn't need to pine for a raven-haired lost cause in the Latin Quarter.

Unfortunately, her mother, who loved the idea of her daughter opening a French bookshop and was enthusiastically scouting locations in Manhattan, reported that it was turning into something of a wild-goose chase. In one letter, she wrote:

> *One almost wishes there had been no armistice, as the war was apparently keeping rents down. Now everyone is full of optimism and cash runs through the city like the last of the legal gin, inflating the prices of every last thing.*

Her mother's pessimism gave Sylvia pause but didn't deter her. She was meant to run a bookstore. If New York didn't work, maybe Boston would. Or Washington, DC. She refused to give up.

Her sister Holly wrote a letter that reminded her of some excellent news, and of the power of persistence:

> *Suffrage is now the law of the land! Everything we worked for! I can hardly wait to cast my first vote, and I don't care what anyone else says, but I think it's even worth it that the female vote came with a price—Prohibition, which as you know, so many of our sister suffragists were in favor of. I sometimes thought, especially at the end, that women were more eager to make their men stop drinking than they were to change the country by voting. The kitchen table, it seems, continues to rule the lives of our sex.*

Only one letter disturbed Sylvia, and it came from Adrienne.

> *Suzanne has married the son of a friend of her father's who has been in love with her for years. Well, who wouldn't love Suzanne? They are content, though I missed her during their wedding trip. But happily, as soon as they returned to Paris, she returned to the store, and things feel much as they were.*

Sylvia reread the passage so many times the words began to swim in front of her. The marriage had to be some sort of convenience, for she didn't think Suzanne was like Cyprian, able to enjoy the pleasures given by men, and she'd never heard so much as a whisper of a beau. She just didn't understand who was gaining what. What were the bride and groom—to say nothing of the bride's mistress—getting out of the arrangement? Did it have something to do with Suzanne's health? Adrienne didn't say and Sylvia didn't ask.

When her contract with the Red Cross was finished, Sylvia knew it was time to begin the next chapter of her life. First, though, she had to make one more stop in Paris. It was calling to her, another Siren distracting her from that next stage.

It had to be a Siren.

Why, then, did it sound more like Odysseus's Penelope, a loving voice summoning her home from across the vast that separated them?

CHAPTER 3

꧁ ❦ ꧂

I n July 1919, Sylvia alighted at the bustling, stifling Gare de l'Est and squinted up at the long skylight above which was a clear blue sky. Rows of arched windows on both sides of the cavernous station flooded the space with more daylight, and as she hoisted her bags onto her shoulders, Sylvia listened to the harassed announcements of the conductors and the gleeful screeches of children and loved ones lost and found—and she very nearly wept. It was relief she felt, but also a brimming sense of mystery and adventure. *There is so much to do.*

Without bothering to bring her meager belongings to the hotel she'd booked near the *école*, since Cyprian had vacated their shared premises at the Palais when Sylvia had gone to Serbia, she went straight to A. Monnier, and was greeted by an exhausted-looking Adrienne who nonetheless threw her arms in the air and shouted welcomes and endearments as she crossed the store and enveloped Sylvia in a tight embrace right at the entrance to the store. *"Mon amie! Sylvia, bienvenue! Dieu merci!"* Sylvia returned the embrace, and almost immediately, Adrienne's euphoric laughter turned to sobs.

The three customers in the store, all strangers to Sylvia, who'd gotten to know the regulars well, politely looked away.

"Can you escape a few minutes," she whispered in Adrienne's ear.

Wiping away her tears with the back of her hand, Adrienne nodded and sniffled, then pulled a well-used handkerchief out of a pocket in the folds of her skirt and used it to mop her face and blot her nose.

In the little back room of the shop, an adolescent girl was unpacking a box of journals, and Adrienne shooed her to the front of the store, shut the door, collapsed on the box, and put her head in her hands.

Sylvia knelt before her, putting her hands on Adrienne's knees, feeling the soft, tight weave of the muslin skirt under her calloused hands. "Tell me," she said.

Adrienne fixed her watery, red-rimmed eyes on Sylvia's and, fighting the tremble of her chin, said, "Suzanne died. Last week." Adrienne exhaled, then drew in another deep breath too quickly and it choked her.

Sylvia's hands found Adrienne's and gripped them tightly. "I am so, so sorry. I know how you loved her."

Adrienne shut her eyes and nodded, fighting to breathe.

They stayed like that a long while, holding hands while Adrienne took ragged breaths. Sylvia's own heart throbbed but she was determined to stay strong for Adrienne. She couldn't help but wonder what this might mean. Was it possible that the voice she'd heard calling her back to Paris hadn't been the city's, but Suzanne's dying plea, asking that Sylvia come back to take care of Adrienne?

Dear Lord, she pleaded to her father's god, whom she didn't even believe in, feeling a bit like Joyce's searching, guilt-ridden Stephen Dedalus, *let it be so.*

✿

"What if instead of a French shop in America, I open an American shop here in Paris? There seems to be a hunger here to read more works in the original language and no shop or library to supply them." Sylvia had woken that morning with this idea, like a lightning bolt thrown at her from the heavens, and then she'd spent the whole day working up the courage to share it with Adrienne.

Now, over a dinner of Adrienne's miraculous roasted chicken and potatoes with rosemary, was the time.

Adrienne blinked, then broke into a wide smile. "*Oui!* It is a perfect idea. And it would allow you to stay in Paris," she said excitedly.

Hearing Adrienne say this made Sylvia feel lighter, as if her sails had suddenly caught wind. "Paris feels like home," she said.

It was August and Adrienne had stopped crying every day; even better, she was finding herself again in the shop and in her beloved kitchen, to which she invited Sylvia nearly every night for supper. They ate and read and talked for hours, very often about serious artistic matters like their conversation at the d'Orsay, but also sometimes about playful subjects like the new confiserie in the neighborhood.

"*Pâtes de fruits* are still my favorite," Adrienne said, sinking her teeth into a chewy, jewel-toned square. Then, with her mouth full and smiling, she mumbled, "These are exceptional."

Sylvia nibbled on a flaming red square. "*Cerise.*" She shrugged. "Cotton candy is my favorite sweet of this nature. Otherwise, I'd rather have chocolate."

"They have the most wonderful candy floss at the Eiffel Tower!"

So the next day after closing, they took themselves to the vendor with the green cart and shared a pink spun cloud bigger than either of their heads, the sugar melting on their tongues as they gazed up at Gustave Eiffel's remarkable monument. "It opened three years before I was born," said Adrienne.

"Have you ever been to the top?"

"All those stairs? Heavens no! I think my heart would give out by the tenth floor."

Sylvia wasn't sure if Adrienne was referring to the bit of weight she'd gained since they'd met. Sylvia liked the way it filled out her face and made her bosom that much ampler, and she loved how un-selfconsciously Adrienne enjoyed food, unlike her mother and Cyprian and so many other women who pecked at their meals like birds, but she wasn't about to say any of that out loud. "Surely your heart is sturdier than that."

"I do enjoy a nice long walk, like we have around my parents' cottage in the country, but on a gradual incline. Among wildflowers. I have to sit down any time I take all the flights up to Sacré-Coeur in Montmartre."

"The long walk near your parents' sounds lovely."

"I'll have to take you sometime. They'll love you. And you'll love our dog, Mousse. He's practically a bear, but entirely gentle."

"I'd love that." Sylvia stuffed another puff of cotton candy in her mouth to keep from saying anything more or smiling too broadly. She wasn't entirely sure that Adrienne returned her affections, and she felt it was wise to give her as much time as she needed to grieve for Suzanne.

It seemed that every evening they spent together would begin at eight and become one in the morning in the blink of an eye. Sylvia would walk the few empty blocks between Adrienne's apartment at 18 rue de l'Odéon and her hotel, smoking all the way, sometimes hearing the sonorous bell of Saint-Étienne-du-Mont ring in the ungodly hour, and she didn't feel lonely—she felt full, of Adrienne's food, her ideas, her voice, her scent of lavender and olive oil. Of Adrienne.

She wasn't sure how Adrienne did it, but no matter how late she'd been up, she was always in her store by nine, awake and smiling. Sylvia sometimes didn't drift in until eleven, at which time Adrienne would cluck her tongue at her, then give her some task to complete: invitations to readings, book ordering, bank account balancing, shelf organizing. "You'll need to know how to do all of this when you have your own shop," she said, and Sylvia would marvel that the other woman was five years younger than she was. No matter what she might say about staircases, Adrienne had boundless energy. And bravery. And fortitude. For goodness' sake, she'd opened a bookstore in the second year of a world war and kept it open through the end. At twenty-three years old!

More and more, Sylvia had the sense that their friendship would become something more. Was she imagining it, or did their hands brush each other's more often lately? Had Adrienne truly sat closer to her on the sofa the other night?

She shoved these thoughts and feelings away. *Be patient. She's still in mourning.* But the fog left by Suzanne's death was dissipating. The remembered presence of Adrienne's former partner had become like that of a patron saint whose taste and ideas they would refer to, and often replicate with reverence, and even sometimes salute with a cup of tea or one of her favorite macarons from the patisserie the next block over.

Then, without so much as a whisper of Suzanne's name, Adrienne found an ideal location for Sylvia's new shop around the corner of the Carrefour de l'Odéon at 8 rue Dupuytren. The laundress who'd let the space for decades was retiring to the country.

"It's perfect," Adrienne told Sylvia when she learned it was available. "The only thing that could make it more perfect would be having it on the same block as my store."

"Maybe someday," Sylvia said brightly, because *it was happening*—a bookstore of her own, in her most favorite of cities.

"I also had an idea," Adrienne said, sounding surprisingly shy.

"Go on."

"I feel that perhaps I should change the name of my shop. To signify a new beginning."

Sylvia smiled and tried not to betray too much of the elated hope Adrienne's idea stirred in her. "If you think that's the right thing?"

Adrienne nodded firmly. "I do. I was thinking La Maison des Amis des Livres." She pronounced the name slowly, with some fanfare as she moved her hand above her head as if stamping each word on its new place above her shop doors and windows.

"The House of the Friends of Books," Sylvia said in English. Then, back to French: "That's certainly what it is. *Meilleurs amis.*"

"*Bon.* I shall hire a painter to change the name tout de suite."

Sylvia's grin made her cheeks hurt. *A new beginning.* "I admire your decisiveness."

"I don't see any point in equivocating."

"Well, it's easier when you know what you want."

At her friend's desk later that evening, Sylvia sat down to write a letter to her mother saying a space for the store of her dreams had become available, and if there was any assistance her family could provide aside from sending her all the books from her room in Princeton, she'd be eternally grateful. She hated having to ask, but no one she knew in postwar France had any money to spare, and Adrienne had been an inspiration: she had already paid her parents back in full for the money they'd given her to open her store in 1915. Sylvia intended to do the same.

Her mother wrote right away to say the books, as well as some other literary surprises, would soon be on a ship, and money, too, was on its way:

> *I always knew you'd find your calling. To show my faith in you and your idea and your good sense, I shall be sending you the contents of my own savings account, from before I was married. And secretly I'm glad you will be in Paris instead of New York, as it gives me all the more reason to visit you there. Enjoy yourself, dearest. I am so proud of you, as is your father. I shall visit as soon as I can.*

Sylvia wiped tears from her eyes and missed her mother more than ever.

At the first golden signs of fall, Sylvia booked passage on a ship to London, where she planned to troll the best publishers and shops looking for bargains with which to stock her shelves.

"I'm jealous," sighed Adrienne the night before Sylvia was to leave. "I love London, and the bookshops there are unrivaled." Sylvia wished she couldn't hear the nostalgia for her London days with Suzanne in Adrienne's voice, even if she didn't sound melancholy at the memory of her first love.

"I'll miss you," said Sylvia. "But I'll be back before you can say Shakespeare."

"Shakespeare," Adrienne joked.

Sylvia cocked an eyebrow, and both of them laughed.

"Hurry home, *mon amie.*"

What was that she saw in Adrienne's cheeks? A blush? And was that a kind of longing that thickened her voice?

"I will. I promise."

Maybe it was because of that last conversation with Adrienne that Sylvia replayed so many times in her mind on the train and then the ferry to the English capital, or maybe it was because names for bookstores had been much on her mind since Adrienne had renamed her own, but by the time she lay in bed her first night in London, she knew the perfect name for her shop: Shakespeare and Company.

After all, Old Bill had never, as far as she knew, gone out of style.

London was rainy and exhausting. Sylvia went to Elkin Mathews's famous shop on Cork Street, taking care not to shake any of her wet hair or belongings on his books, and asked him for the latest by Ezra Pound, James Joyce, and W. B. Yeats, whom she'd heard was his neighbor. Curiously old-fashioned in his frayed jacket and snarled muttonchops, he was genteel and friendly.

"You like the new writing, it would appear," he observed as he set ten volumes on the table between them.

"I do. My friends in Paris are hungry to read more by these writers, and in my new shop, I aim to always stock the latest and greatest by American and British writers."

With creased forehead, he squeezed his monocle between his cheek and furry eyebrow. "An English-language bookshop? In *France*?"

She nodded vigorously.

"Goodness."

"I know. I'll be the first."

"I hope you have a secondary plan."

"I think things will go swimmingly."

He continued to look at her with a puzzled and avuncular expression of concern, so she added, "I'm also stocking some classics. But since I can't afford all new editions, I'm looking for those secondhand."

"Very wise."

"My secret wish, though, is to find some William Blake drawings. You know, the ones he made to accompany *Songs of Innocence and Experience*?"

Holding up the index finger of his right hand in silence, he turned and went into his back room.

Back rooms of bookstores, thought Sylvia with glee. *Soon I'll have my own!*

After a bit of audible rummaging and one *CLANG!* Elkin Mathews reemerged holding two small pictures in slim wood frames painted black. Slowly, he turned them to face her, and she saw, unmistakably, two of Blake's drawings. The color was excellent, hardly faded at all.

Her stomach churned. "These are marvelous," she effused. "But I suspect I can't afford them."

"Blake's out of fashion." Mr. Mathews shrugged, then told her how much she could have them for.

This is meant to be. Shakespeare and Company will be a success—it must, with serendipitous beginnings like these. When she stepped out of Elkin Mathews Ltd., heavily laden with bags and packages, the rain had stopped—as if by the same magic that had conjured the Blake drawings—and the sun began to shine on the shiny, wet city. A week later in Paris, when she opened a package her mother sent containing three precious original Whitman pages from the family attic, Sylvia was convinced she'd been struck by the same current of enchantment and generosity.

While a carpenter built shelves to her specifications, Sylvia and Adrienne visited every secondhand bookstore in Paris, returning to deposit bags and bags of volumes at 8 rue Dupuytren, their arms and legs becoming more and more sore with every trip. But it was worth it, and the wine they sipped in celebration at the end of the day seemed to wash away the twinges. As in Adrienne's shop, the used books would be part of the lending library. Sylvia would sell the new books until she only had one left, at which point she'd lend that one out until a new shipment of the title arrived. For furniture, she couldn't be too fussy, though she was determined to make the space cozy and inviting like Adrienne's; after true antiques proved too dear, church sales and other stores of jumble and bric-a-brac yielded some charming, if tippy, tables and chairs.

Soon all the back-and-forth down and around the carrefour, and knocking on doors, and making sure one of them was home when all the other one wanted to do was drop off a bag of books, got to be too much to juggle. So Adrienne handed Sylvia two keys tied to a red velvet ribbon. "The silver one is to La Maison, and the brass is to my apartment. Come and go as you please."

"Are . . . are you sure?"

"Why wouldn't I be?"

Adrienne's openness was hardly guileless, which made it all the more remarkable to Sylvia. "Thank you. And wait." She went to the drawer of her desk and took out the skeleton key to her store and apartment that she'd been waiting for the right moment to give Adrienne. Pressing it into Adrienne's smooth, strong hand felt right and electric; she felt their touch in her thighs, knees, breasts. And Adrienne's hand lingered under Sylvia's just long enough for her to believe she felt it, too. This was more than an exchange of practical necessities; she was sure of it.

Later, as they shelved books after La Maison had closed, Adrienne said, "I believe it is auspicious that Shakespeare and Company will be opening on the eve of a new decade." Their backs were to each other, as Adrienne was in the poetry section of the lending library, and Sylvia in the novels area of the shop.

"Goodness, a new name for your store, a new decade," said Sylvia, turning around. "You seem preoccupied with newness lately."

"Not *new*, exactly. Reborn. As is necessary after the war. The 1920s will begin everything again after the hunger and destruction of these last years." Adrienne slid a book between two others and then faced Sylvia, who did the same in the same moment.

"One does sense that everyone is ready for something different, for experiences that will help them forget," Sylvia said. Thinking of the buoyant, popular melodies of the Original Dixieland Jass Band, she added, "For example, the music on the radio is positively cheerful."

"The hemlines are more flirtatious."

"The embroidery on coats and hats is whimsical. And goodness, the colors of the feathers!"

"The flavors of the cocktails are more and more outlandish. And delicious."

Thrilled at the confirmation that she and Adrienne had been noticing the very same changes around them, Sylvia added, "And the journals here and in New York and London are bursting with it. Margaret Anderson would be hard-pressed to publish a blank *Little Review* these days, what with the avalanche of great writing by ambitious new voices all around us."

"New." Adrienne winked at Sylvia. "Perhaps I am not the preoccupied one?"

Sylvia laughed. "Yes, new. I wonder what we'll be saying in 1929."

"I am glad we cannot know. It preserves the sense of adventure."

"I agree completely." For Shakespeare and Company, 1920, Paris—all of it—felt like an adventure, and the intensifying closeness with Adrienne compounded the exhilaration. And the tension. Sure as she was of her own feelings, Sylvia was leaving it up to Adrienne to make hers clear first. Sylvia wanted to know, in every corner of her heart, that Adrienne had chosen her.

And so she waited.

Nearly every day, well-wishers from Adrienne's shop stopped by to admire Sylvia's progress.

"I cannot wait to procure my own lending card," Jules Romains said.

"I shall beat you to it," said André Gide.

Still, Sylvia could hardly believe these great men of French letters were her friends. Soon to be her first patrons.

One afternoon in early November, mustachioed but still somehow baby-faced Valery Larbaud brought Sylvia a precious clutch from his beloved collection of toy soldiers, which he arranged with great care among hand-built houses, trees, and other landscapes in his bachelor apartment on the rue Cardinal Lemoine, about a ten-minute walk from her store. "These will be your protectors," he told Sylvia as he presented her with the figures. "And if you don't feel *you* need them, think of them as the books' guardians."

"I am honored, Larbaud! And Shakespeare is grateful for the protection."

They laughed, and he stayed to help shelve books and drink tea.

Cyprian stopped by as frequently as she could, though her new film schedule kept her very busy, as did a dalliance with a monocle-wearing weekly tabloid editor whom she'd met at the bar on the rue Edgar-Quintet. "If it wasn't for her, I'd be more mad at you for avoiding me, big sister," she told Sylvia.

Sylvia grinned, though she did feel bad that she'd seen so little of

Cyprian since returning to Paris, what with the whirlwind of opening the store. "The companionship's done wonders for your disposition, sister darling."

The closer she got to opening day, the more restless she felt. She woke before the sun, which was ridiculously early given how late she was always up with Adrienne, but there was a fire in her veins that wouldn't let her sleep on either end of the night. She'd get up and stalk the streets, studying shop windows, smoking, and making notes of ideas in a little leather-bound notebook. When the boulangeries opened, she was first in line so she could wake Adrienne with a crusty loaf that smelled of yeast and heat. Though Sylvia slept on a small bed in a tiny studio—little more than a room with some cupboards, a gas stove, and an ice chest—behind the official bookstore back room, now that she and Adrienne possessed keys to each other's buildings, they came and went so freely between them it was almost like living in three places: 8 rue Dupuytren, and 7 and 18 rue de l'Odéon.

On one of those mornings at the start of the second week of November, Sylvia purchased two apricot croissants in addition to the baguette—a little celebration of the fact that her store would be opening in only a few days' time.

When she pushed open the door at the top of the stairs and entered Adrienne's apartment, she smelled coffee already made, as well as milk scalded just as she liked it.

"*Bon*," Adrienne said, taking the baguette from Sylvia's hands. Their fingers grazed one another, nearly interlacing around the bread, and Sylvia felt a shiver run up her arm. "Our little ritual continues."

"I couldn't resist these as well," Sylvia said, handing Adrienne the wax paper bag with the pastry.

Adrienne peered inside, then smiled widely at Sylvia. "My favorite!"

I know.

"I have a little gift for you, too," she said, hurrying out of the kitchen to her bedroom.

Sylvia felt nervous. The croissants were hardly a *gift*—she'd been contemplating the perfect *petit cadeau* for Adrienne to thank her for all her help, but hadn't been able to come up with anything even remotely appropriate.

Adrienne bustled back into the kitchen holding a book-size package wrapped in brown paper and tied with a white ribbon.

"I should be the one giving you gifts," said Sylvia, embarrassed.

Adrienne waved her hand, and said, "This is something you *need*."

She took the package and saw that the brown paper wrapping was stamped by Maurice Darantiere, a printer in Dijon whom Adrienne used occasionally to publish slim volumes of Larbaud's lectures, Paul Valéry's poetry, and other short works by a handful of her favorite writers under the name Les Cahiers des Amis des Livres.

The bow of the ribbon came undone with a gentle pull, and Sylvia kept its slippery length between her fingers as she tore open the wrapping to reveal a stack of heavy stationery cards with the words Sylvia Beach embossed at the top, and Shakespeare and Company, Paris, just below.

She opened her mouth to say something, but no words came out, and she felt a mortifying hot flush of tears come to her eyes.

"Darantiere was Suzanne's favorite, and she'd have wanted you to have the best."

"Would she?" A whispered prayer to the patron saint.

"She would." Adrienne nodded, smiling, appearing amazingly cheerful at this memory of her lost love.

"Thank you," Sylvia said, as much to Suzanne as to the woman standing in front of her. She clutched the smooth paper in her hands, hoping she wasn't ruining it with her sweaty grasp.

Adrienne put her hands on Sylvia's, stepped forward, and touched her lips to hers. Sylvia set the stationery on the kitchen table, and used her right hand to touch Adrienne's cheek, as she'd wanted to do when they first met and on countless occasions since. Adrienne closed her eyes at Sylvia's touch, and Sylvia coiled her fingers into Adrienne's hair and pulled her close enough to feel her breasts against hers. Flooded with desire, she kissed Adrienne harder and tasted milk, coffee, jam. Adrienne's tongue slid over Sylvia's lips, and she reciprocated as she moved her hand down Adrienne's back.

Just as Sylvia thought they would each lose themselves in the moment, the way she'd read about but never truly believed could be hers, Adrienne moaned quietly and stepped back. "Not yet, Sylvia. I want you, but . . . soon."

Though every nerve seemed to be on the outside of her skin, chafing against her clothes, against the *air*, for crying out loud, Sylvia said, "Okay."

Soon. *Soon.* She knew, like she sometimes knew what would happen on the next page of a book, and the anticipation was an exquisite torture.

Adrienne took Sylvia's hand and squeezed it. "I am so glad you are here. You are like the phoenix that has emerged from the ashes. You give me so much hope."

Sylvia couldn't help her burst of laughter. "You flatter me, Adrienne."

"Sometimes a world has to end before a new one can begin," she said, and this time Sylvia was sure Adrienne was talking about much bigger things—her long affair with Suzanne, the war, and now their two stores, the whole vast expanse of the future sprawling out before them, between two short blocks of Paris.

CHAPTER 4

"**W**ear the bloody shoes," said Cyprian, shoving the red leather pumps at Sylvia.

"They're too . . . *red*."

Cyprian sighed and rolled her eyes. "Oh for heaven's sake, Sylvia, you're opening the only English-language bookstore in Paris. You've worried endlessly for weeks that no one will come to the store. And now you pretend you don't want people to *notice* you?"

"It is ironic, isn't it?" She did want people to notice her. But not for her shoes.

"Clothing is armor, big sister. You might need a little of that today."

Sylvia looked at the shoes her sister was dangling between them and remembered how much she'd always admired them on Cyprian's feet. What would it be like to wear them?

With an exaggerated sigh of her own, she took the shoes and slipped them on. They were surprisingly soft and comfortable, and she wished she had a mirror in her little bedsit at the back of the shop so she could see how they looked.

Lighting another cigarette in satisfaction, Cyprian said, "Now that's more like it."

"You'll come by the store tomorrow? For the party?"

"How many times have we talked about this? *Stop worrying.* I'll see you very soon. Try and get some sleep."

Which was laughable advice. Sylvia tossed and turned all night and couldn't string together two consecutive hours of dozing, let alone real sleep. Finally, at six in the morning she gave up, bundled herself against the November chill, and went out in her trusty walking shoes to find a café crème and a croissant. No sooner had she sat down and lit a cigarette than Adrienne was standing at her table. Heat rushed to her cheeks; it had been three days since their kiss, and Sylvia had felt shy around Adrienne ever since, the word *when* pulsing through her mind like a distracting mantra.

"I thought I might find you here," she said.

Sylvia smiled. "I didn't want to wake you so early."

"I couldn't sleep."

"Neither could I!" *When?*

"I made five dozen macarons," Adrienne said as she settled into the wooden chair across the table.

Sylvia gasped. "Last night?"

Adrienne nodded. Sylvia pushed her coffee toward her friend. "You need this more than I do. All I did was toss and turn."

"I had to do something with all the nervous energy. And I thought we could serve them at the party."

Adrienne had already cooked and baked up a storm for the opening party; Sylvia had no idea how any group might eat so many mousses and crackers and compotes and pastries. "Thank you," Sylvia said.

Over a second round of coffees and croissants, they talked over the schedule for the day for what seemed like the hundredth time, and as they were finishing, a tall, stout young man approached their table. His pale, smooth cheeks were splotchy with red, and Sylvia wasn't sure if it was from the cold outside or nerves at coming over to say hello.

As soon as Adrienne saw him, she rose from her chair and embraced him, bestowing the usual kisses of greeting. "Michel! How nice to see you outside the *boucherie*."

"I often stop here before I open. But I admit I never expected to see you here so early, Adrienne," he said in a low and gravelly voice that was older than his looks. Sylvia guessed he was probably in his twenties, though his voice sounded ancient.

"Michel, please meet my friend Sylvia Beach of America. She is opening an English-language bookshop on the rue Dupuytren today, and we are having a party later. You must come."

His face flushed redder, and he smiled widely, in an earnest way that broke Sylvia's heart a little. "English? I speak a bit, and read it, too," he said to Sylvia *en anglais*.

"How wonderful," she replied in her native tongue, wondering how this boy came to speak and read English. Oh, there were many mysteries to unravel at Shakespeare and Company! "And yes, you must come. It would be a pleasure to have you."

"Do you have any books by Siegfried Sassoon?"

"I do." Sylvia nodded, bursting with curiosity as to why young Michel the butcher would ask about the famous English war poet.

"I knew Wilfred Owen," he said quietly, and Sylvia understood. Owen had been an apprentice to Sassoon, and while many of his poems about the war had been published in journals, he didn't have any books to his name because he'd died in battle a mere week before the armistice was signed. Here in France, at twenty-five years old.

She nodded reverentially.

"He was a good man," Michel added, eyes flickering to the floor.

Just then, behind the counter of the café, someone dropped what sounded like a tray of cups and saucers. In a single sweeping move-ment, Michel grabbed his coat and pulled it over his head as he dove to the ground and huddled at her and Adrienne's knees. If the table were big enough, he'd have been under it.

Adrienne's eyes filled with water, and she gently put a hand on his back. "It's all right. It was only some glasses."

Slowly, he unfolded himself and stood to his full height, and this time, though Sylvia guessed he was likely over six feet tall, he looked like a small boy, embarrassed. "Sorry," he said. "Habit."

"I'll hold a copy of Sassoon's *Counter-Attack* for you," Sylvia said. "And I have something else in mind, too."

Michel nodded his thanks and went silently on his way.

"He's one of the nicest boys I know," said Adrienne, her voice thick with emotion.

"I can see that."

"We grew up together, not far from here. But that place, that world, doesn't exist any longer. It's been harder for him to accept than it has for me. He was comfortable in it, and I was not."

"You seem so comfortable in this world," Sylvia observed, think-ing to herself that she'd had to come all the way to Paris for the kind of easy, broad comfort Adrienne seemed to enjoy.

"Well, I created it, so I should hope so. I had help, of course. Rinette and Suzanne and my parents were always very supportive of my strange ideas."

Strange ideas. "You mean . . . ?"

Palms up and gesturing with each hand as if balancing a scale, Adrienne replied, "My bookish ways, the travel to London, the shop, and yes, even my . . ." Her eyeballs swiveled in their sockets, check-ing the crowd in the café, before she whispered, "Sapphism."

Lowering her own voice, Sylvia said, "Have you ever discussed it with them?"

"No." Her palms were out now, pushing the very idea away. "But I do not think Michel would discuss his girlfriends with his parents, either."

Sylvia laughed. "You're right. It's been much the same for me. In my family, I mean. My parents and older sister Holly don't ask me any difficult questions about men, and they have never suggested I get married. It's the same with Cyprian. But America is much less accepting than France. In New York, it would be a crime for me to love . . ." *You*, she almost said, but stopped herself in time. She didn't need to say more, though, because Adrienne understood without the words.

Nodding, Adrienne replied, "France is accepting on paper, in the law. And many families like mine accept their sons' and daughters' special friends. But otherwise . . ." She made a *not so much* wag of her hand.

"Well, the United States is struggling even on paper."

"It's a shame."

"*Oui.*"

Sylvia shook her head to rid herself of the sudden dark cloud that had descended on her. "Well, thank you for sharing your world with me."

Adrienne laughed. "*Chérie*, you are making it with me."

When?

She was finally starting to feel impatient.

Sylvia was sure she'd always remember the moment that she and Adrienne stood in front of Shakespeare and Company just before nine that morning, full from their indulgent breakfast, keys in hand, about to unlock the doors and throw open the shutters for the very first time.

"I know you're not supposed to open till ten, but . . ."

"I know, I can't wait, either."

There was a glorious quiet in that first hour while Sylvia looked around at her Blake drawings and Whitman pages, both framed and hung on a small patch of wall between her well-stocked shelves. Breathing in the leather and paper and ink, she thought with a chest full of smoke and pride, *This is mine. I did this.*

She hardly had time to think, *Will anyone come?* before "anyone" arrived, in the form of Rinette, Adrienne's sister, her husband Paul-Emile Bécat, and her lover Léon-Paul Fargue, the poet who had affectionately deemed the regulars in Adrienne's shop *potassons*, a play on *potasser*, meaning "to learn or study hard," using the inclusive "we" version of the verb, *nous potassons*, to mean their circle of friends. But *potasser* wasn't nearly as common a word as its synonym *étudier*, and so a certain exclusivity was embedded in the term. Sylvia was honored to be the only American *potasson*.

The rest of the day was a blur of people coming in and out of Shakespeare and Company. Her shop! Mostly it was the *potassons* who stopped by to say hello, procure a lending card, buy a volume or two, and promise to return for the party later. But there were also a healthy number of locals who came because they were curious. "I've been watching and wondering what something called Shakespeare and Company might be," as Monsieur Desautel, a neighborhood doctor, put it.

Once the sun had set and the autumn evening was dark, Adrienne and Rinette began bringing over the trays of food Adrienne had prepared. Sylvia marveled again at the quantity, the sheer bounty of it all, and wondered if this, as much as Michel's distress at the café that morning, was a kind of response to the war—an emphatic *oui, merci* to the fact that they could, once again, enjoy a bacchanal of food and drink.

She put on Cyprian's shoes and lit a cigarette, welcoming guests as they arrived. It was then that Michel appeared, greeting Sylvia like an old friend, with kisses on the cheek, and an apology for being late. "I was going to come earlier, but decided I should go home first and wash the entrails off."

"There is no such thing as late, and welcome! I have the Sassoon for you. But first, have a glass of wine."

Miraculously, so many people came to the party, the crowd of people eating and drinking spilled out into the streets. "When are you going to give your speech?" Cyprian asked her when the moon shone bright and the party was reaching a peak.

"Don't be silly. A speech?"

"Sylvia, you must say something," agreed Adrienne.

She swallowed and it was suddenly painful. Without giving her sister more time to think, Cyprian tapped a silver spoon to her wineglass, and the note sounded like a distant church bell, quieting everyone in waves until it was silent.

Too petite to be able to see anyone beyond who was standing in front of her, Sylvia looked around for something to stand on. Where was the damn stool she'd used to stack books on the highest shelves?

Adrienne charged forward with it, and set it down in front of Sylvia with a flourish. As soon as she stepped up on it, the crowd cheered. Instead of feeling excited, though, Sylvia felt deeply nervous. Glancing down, she saw Cyprian's shoes on her feet, then she flicked her eyes up and saw Adrienne's steady, encouraging gaze on her. She drew in a deep breath and said, "Thank you, everyone, for coming tonight. It means the world to me to see so many old friends, and to be meeting so many new ones . . ." *Why, oh why didn't I prepare for this?*

In an instant, she saw Michel and knew what she should say next. "One year ago almost to the day, America, Britain, and France signed a treaty ending a war the likes of which our nations have never seen. But *liberté, égalité, et fraternité* triumphed, and here, a place of exchange between English and French thinking, we get to enjoy the spoils of peace: literature, friendship, conversation, debate. Long may we enjoy them and may they—instead of guns and grenades—become the weapons of new rebellions."

A chorus of "hear, hear!" and "*salut!*" and "felicitations!" went up around them, and—flushed with jittery pride—Sylvia stepped down so that she could lose herself once more in the crowd.

As soon as she could find time, she tugged on Michel's sleeve and presented him with two books. "The Sassoon is a gift," she said, "and the Whitman is a loan, from the library. Return it when you're done with it. I'm curious to see if you like him."

Michel smiled a smile that would have melted any icicle from a New Jersey roof. "Thank you, Mademoiselle Beach."

"Sylvia."

"Sylvia." He nodded. "Don't give away too many books *s'il te plaît.* I want you to stay in business."

"I won't. Me too."

Had it not been for the pleasure of reliving the evening in excited chatter with Adrienne and Cyprian and Rinette, the cleaning up would have seemed to take forever.

"I told you it would all get eaten," Adrienne noted proudly as they wrapped up the very small, crumbly remains of the feast.

"Goodness, did you dare doubt my sister's culinary temptations?" laughed Rinette. "I'm surprised you escaped such questioning alive!"

Cyprian laughed heartily at this. "Sylvia's middle name is Question."

"My doubt had nothing to do with the quality of the repast," Sylvia said. "I just couldn't imagine that so many people would come."

"I could," Adrienne said with a lingering look at Sylvia that set her heart aflame.

Midnight found the two of them alone in the tidied shop, at long last. "Thank you, Adrienne," Sylvia said. "There aren't enough thank-yous in the world."

Adrienne took Sylvia's hand and looked at her, those pale blue eyes under the black brows, her lips a dark, delicious slash on her pale, cream-perfect face. So many contrasts. Sylvia thought she could look at Adrienne forever and never get bored. She wondered what Adrienne saw in her face.

To Sylvia's astonishment, Adrienne lifted her hand to her mouth and kissed the palm, then each finger, closing her eyes as if she were enjoying a favorite treat. Sylvia, too, closed her eyes, her skin tingling at each brush of Adrienne's lips and tongue. She had no idea so much *feeling* was in her hands, of all places. *Her hands.* When she dared open her eyes, she slid her hand gently so that it cupped Adrienne's cheek. She let her fingers weave into that mane of dark hair. Eyes open now, Adrienne leaned toward Sylvia and they kissed. It started slow and searching, and the sensation of Adrienne's lips on hers made every nerve in her body hum. Soon their eyes were closed and their arms were wrapped tightly around each other and the kisses became excavations; everything they hadn't known about each other before that night would be known then, it seemed. Their teeth clicked together, their sighs mingled, and their fingers began tugging at buttons and zippers.

Coats open to cool their bodies with the November night air, they managed to get from the store to Adrienne's bed, where they fell into hours of exploring that left Sylvia hot and spent and bruised. Adrienne was magnificent—firm beneath her smooth, soft skin, confident in every flick of her fingers, lick of her tongue. She inspired Sylvia to be bolder than she'd ever been before, slipping her hands under and between garments, limbs, folds, sating a hunger she'd been denied her whole life.

She'd never known what a joy it could be to be inside her own body. *This* was what they were all writing about. She couldn't remember the last time life had made books pale in comparison. Had it ever? Now that she knew, there was no going back.

CHAPTER 5

The wallowing hours she spent in bed with Adrienne after they each closed their shops gave Sylvia the sense that the world—or her world at least—was irreparably different. Even Cyprian noticed. Before she returned to America at the start of 1920 when her contract was up, she observed, "I've never seen you so *consumed*."

Falling in love with Adrienne even changed the way Sylvia read. Instead of awe and ache when she read passages about love and the cravings of the body, she felt herself part of that world, anointed into it by Adrienne. She could now truly feel in her veins the releases that Stephen Dedalus so feared and also longed for in *Portrait*. With a newfound appetite, she began reading and rereading the serialized excerpts from Joyce's new novel *Ulysses*, which she'd been perusing with interest in *The Little Review* for the past year. Once again, his story was set in Dublin, though Sylvia had read that Joyce hadn't been to his home country for years, and was an exile not unlike the hero of Homer's *Odyssey* on which *Ulysses* was so brilliantly patterned.

Joyce had brought Stephen along from *Portrait* and given him a friend in the form of older, more sanguine Leopold Bloom. Describing Stephen's and Leopold's every word, thought, and movement in minute detail as they went about living a single day—June 16, 1904— in the Irish capital, Joyce's new novel seemed to want to explode every protective surface of modern life as surely as grenades had blown up cities and trenches all over Europe. Whether his characters were sitting in an outhouse or discussing *Hamlet*, Joyce spared no detail, leveling the vulgar with the sublime. Here was a book that brooked no compromises, and was unwavering in its clear-eyed portrayal of Stephen's and Leopold's minds and bodies.

The novel's insistence on thorough, truthful detail was also what was sparking controversy in England and America, where journals containing its chapters had been seized by John Sumner's New York Society for the Suppression of Vice and labeled as obscene. Margaret Anderson had complained about it in her *Little Review* editorials recently, and Sylvia shared her outrage. She could understand why some readers might not want to follow Bloom into an outhouse, but to outlaw it? Readers needed to wake up to the book's shocking honesty as much as to the boldness of its prose, for in the book's very challenges lay its greatest truth: *the world as we knew it has ended, and it's time for something entirely innovative.* Joyce hadn't just done away with quotation marks, he sometimes flouted the conventions of sentencing and paragraphing altogether, in order to tunnel as deeply as possible into the minds of his characters—where, after all, grammar doesn't exist. It was truly a novel for their times. She wondered what a reader like Michel would make of it—would he identify with the ways in which *Ulysses* was remaking meaning?

She felt breathless and alive each time she looked up from one of the *Little Review* installments, and the letters she received from

America only reinforced her sense that Joyce's book was necessary. Her childhood friend Carlotta Welles wrote:

> *I cannot BELIEVE the Volstead Act goes into effect the first month of the new year. It's an absolute travesty, and absurd to boot. Goodness, everyone we know has stockpiled a generation's worth of liquor in their basements. Some people have even dug basements just to accommodate it all. How is that change for the better? When will they ever learn?*

And Mother said:

> *I cannot want to visit you in Paris, dear one. I fear this country has at last succumbed to its baser instincts. Greed runs rampant. Your father sermonizes about it constantly, but I suspect that the men leave church with their wives Sunday morning only to go to work Monday to pray to Plutus. Would that the Volstead Act aimed to curb avarice instead of drunkenness.*

Even Cyprian saw a similar set of problems:

> *I miss you, dear sister, and Paris, too. New York is full to the brim of hostility and fear. The establishment Irish politicians pretend their families were never immigrants while they lobby for tighter restrictions on the tenements, people are still afraid of catching Spanish influenza, and the post office is stealing journals and novels and shoving them in the incinerator. Anything even remotely interesting has set our countrymen to moral handwringing, and it's strangling all the arts, movies included.*

It appeared that the ruling class in America wanted to outlaw anything that offended its sense of decorum, and so a book, play, film, organization, activity, or person that smacked of vice or difference from a life one might find in the comforting illustrations of the *Saturday Evening Post* was in danger of being silenced. The irony was that the very suppression created more of what they feared—more anarchism and Marxism and protests and unrest—and it was books like *Ulysses* that sought to open minds rather than slap them shut.

Well, she intended to stock *Ulysses* when it came out in book form, and to encourage everyone to read the journals until it was. *In fact,* she vowed, *I'll do my best to promote all the writers in this modern project of honest writing.* Thankfully, their numbers appeared to be growing.

Everyone in the Left Bank knew of the eccentric writer and art collector from California, Gertrude Stein, whose collection of paintings by Cézanne, Matisse, Gauguin, and other masters from the last few decades was famous. Anyone who was anyone in bohemian Paris would eventually be invited to dine and talk about the new writing and the way forward for the arts. Picasso himself was a regular visitor, as was Jean Cocteau, who was also a fixture in Adrienne's shop. Sylvia wondered if Miss Stein would ever deign to enter her little shop; presumably, the American who'd long lived in Paris had devised ways to acquire books in her native tongue, and so she probably wouldn't need Shakespeare and Company. Still, Sylvia hoped that her growing reputation and common friends would be enough to lure her in. It would be a baptism of sorts.

"Madame Stein," Adrienne said with exaggerated deference when Sylvia expressed this wish as they peeled potatoes shoulder to shoulder at the kitchen sink. Adrienne was making her *gratin dauphinois* that night, and Sylvia's mouth was watering just thinking of it. "She keeps to herself, no? Or rather, she asks for people to come to her? She is not much of a *flâneuse*. This is what Cocteau tells me."

"I've heard the same. But I can dream, can't I?"

"Her approval would certainly confer a certain . . . gravitas to the store, it is true. And what about Madame Wharton? Would she also inspire other Americans to visit?"

"*Peut-être*. But she doesn't live in Paris any longer, does she? She's in an estate in the Oise, I believe, and she winters on the Riviera. She might be too la-di-da for a scrappy little store like mine."

"*C'est vrai*. When she lived in the seventh on the rue de Varennes, I would occasionally see her at events and she looked far more bourgeoise than bohemian."

Sylvia clinked her glass of Sancerre to Adrienne's and said, "*Vive la bohème*." They kissed, and Sylvia could feel it in every atom of her being.

Grande Dame Stein at last lumbered into her store along with Alice Toklas, on a warm June day in 1920. Sylvia saw immediately that Alice was Gertrude's foil in most ways: efficient to her languor, slim to her plump, fashionably bobbed dark hair to her gray, clipped helmet. Gertrude herself was an imposing figure, not just for her height and girth, which she wore well, but for her severe charcoal-colored dress and the way her ruddy cheeks seemed to be stuck in a perennial frown even when she smiled. Her dark eyes fixed on Sylvia like an eagle's.

"Good afternoon," Miss Stein said, making her way straight to the desk where Sylvia was sorting the day's mail, trying to think of a greeting that wouldn't be too obsequious, and wondering if Miss Stein could tell that she, too, was in a partnership with a woman.

Cyprian had once given her a monocle to put on for just these occasions, since her regular uniform of a skirt and jacket didn't say much about her one way or another other than that she couldn't afford modish clothing and she liked to dress sensibly. But she wasn't sure where the little eyeglass was. *Nothing to be done about that now.*

Sylvia reached over her smoldering cigarette in its tray to offer her hand, and said, "Hello. I'm Sylvia Beach. Please call me Sylvia."

"And I am Gertrude Stein. Gertrude." She shook Sylvia's hand firmly. "This is Alice Toklas. Alice."

Sylvia and Alice also shook hands and smiled politely.

"I have heard about your shop," Gertrude said with an appraising look around. "You certainly have a great number of books here. More than I expected."

Sylvia wasn't sure what Gertrude had expected to find at Shakespeare and Company, but she nodded and said, "Thank you. We do our best to keep the shelves full."

As if pulled by a magnet, Gertrude walked toward the books at the end of the alphabet. Sylvia saw the writer's eyes flicker toward her own books on the shelves and was relieved all of them except one were there. "I lent my last edition of *Tender Buttons* last week, and I'm awaiting new ones to sell."

Gertrude nodded a silent reply, then moved left to the earlier letters of the alphabet. Alice busied herself with the display of journals near the front window and picked up the latest *Dial*. After scrutinizing the shelves, Gertrude said, "You don't have any John Fox Jr. *The Trail of the Lonesome Pine* is a great novel."

Sylvia could hardly believe her ears. The Appalachian bestseller? Requested by her own country's foremost avant-garde, urban writer. She half thought Miss Stein was having her on. Was it because Gertrude herself was from the west of the United States, which seemed to Sylvia a wild, untamed expanse, as foreign sounding to her as

Madagascar? Feeling it the safest answer, Sylvia replied, "I'll be sure to order it."

"Excellent," Gertrude said heartily, folding her hands before her with a satisfied air. "Please tell me, Sylvia, what brings you to open this store in Paris? It is more, I assume, than our nightlife." *Ah, so I didn't need that monocle.* Sylvia had noticed that references among women to the city's nightlife very often described the scene that one could find on the Edgar-Quinet, or in the Pigalle and Montmartre neighborhoods.

Sylvia smiled. "I do enjoy the nightlife," she said. "But you're correct; it was more than that. I saw a need here in the city, and I wanted to fill it," she said, surprised at how simple an explanation it really was, despite the fact that the truth involved a hundred other moments with Adrienne, Suzanne, Cyprian, Mother, a lifetime of reading, and a childhood year spent in Paris that had changed her forever.

Gertrude nodded. "I toyed with the idea once myself, I admit. But I prefer writing sentences to selling them."

"Owning a bookstore is much more than selling sentences. It's putting the right sentences into the right hands." Like Michel, who'd loved the Whitman and come back for more. Sylvia was inching him ever closer to Joyce, Eliot, Williams, and other important new writers.

"Indeed," Gertrude replied doubtfully.

Sylvia noticed that Alice, still silent with her journals but hanging on every word, suppressed a smirk.

Fearful from Gertrude's short reply that she might have overstepped, Sylvia added, "And I feel nothing but gratitude for the writers who make the sentences. Sentences have changed my life." It was odd, she realized for the first time, but opening Shakespeare and Company had all but banished her youthful wish that she herself become a writer. It helped that her parents supported her endeavor;

both of them wrote letters expressing their pride and asking all sorts of questions about the running of the store.

"The sentence is undergoing great changes."

Sylvia almost burst out laughing. She agreed with Gertrude wholeheartedly, but it sounded so professorial coming from her mouth.

"I'm grateful for that as well," Sylvia said, employing her most solicitous tone. "I am a great reader of your work, Miss Stein— Gertrude—and believe your project with the English language to be extremely important."

"I see you carry all the journals I subscribe to."

"I try to stay current."

"And which is your favorite?"

A test.

"Oh, I couldn't pick just one. But I must say I'm partial to *The Little Review*."

Gertrude frowned. "Yes," came her drawling reply. "Miss Anderson has done well by many artists I admire, and the Man Ray photographs she reproduces are especially good. But now she's publishing that Irishman James Joyce."

"*Ulysses*, yes. It's too bad the post office in the United States keeps seizing the issues with his chapters in it. I'm never sure if I'm going to receive the latest installment." Though it was clear Gertrude Stein had a different opinion of *that Irishman*'s work, Sylvia couldn't help but show her enthusiasm; it gave her a little bit of the same thrill as passing notes in school.

"I may not like Joyce's pages, but I do agree that the American post office is out of line. Censorship is not commensurate with democracy. Or art."

"No, it is not." Sylvia smiled, glad to have something they completely agreed on.

"I think it's time I took out one of your lending cards," said Gertrude.

Sylvia set up just Gertrude, not Alice, with a card for the lending library, and after a bit more looking, her new patron checked out a copy of *The Letters of George Meredith.*

"Did you know he was nominated for the Nobel Prize *seven times* and never won?" Gertrude asked.

"Goodness no. Seven?"

Stein rapped her knuckles on the volume of letters and said, "I wonder if he has anything to say about that in here."

"Please let me know."

When Gertrude Stein and Alice Toklas left, Sylvia felt a tingle of excitement pass through her. A genuine literary celebrity had come to her shop! It was a banner day, and Sylvia felt positively light on her feet all afternoon and evening.

"That was how I felt when Romains came to my shop for the first time! Like I had arrived!" Adrienne exclaimed that evening as they shared another of her delicious meals: lamb chops accompanied by rice cooked with carrots. There was a salad of pickled vegetables and then a platter of cheese and Spanish oranges waiting for them as second and third courses. Sylvia was glad she wasn't hungry most of the day, as she couldn't possibly afford the new clothes that would be necessary if she ate as well as this from morning to night.

"It's almost embarrassing to admit how happy it made me," said Sylvia.

"But why?"

"Well, in my family, Cyprian was always the one looking for attention. And she got it. I was jealous sometimes, but had nothing to offer the world like she did. I would occasionally bask in her reflected glory, but I'm really more comfortable in the background. But in the shop, I feel I can have both—to be in the background, but also have one of my accomplishments noticed." She'd never admitted any of that out loud before, and she suddenly feared what Adrienne's reaction might be.

Adrienne tucked a thick lock of Sylvia's short hair behind her ear, and a current rippled through Sylvia. "Do not be afraid of your talents. You have so much to offer."

Why did Sylvia doubt this? Adrienne's talents seemed larger than her own, like a tree with more branches and deeper roots. She ran La Maison, plus she published an occasional journal and wrote essays herself. And she was an accomplished chef. Then, too, she heard Cyprian's musing from a year ago: *Adrienne strikes me as a woman with appetites, who might get bored easily.*

Nonsense, she told herself. Adrienne had been true to Suzanne, her store, and her friends for years. If only Sylvia could stop worrying whether she'd be enough for her.

CHAPTER 6

A t 8 rue Dupuytren, the early July sun needled her back as she unlocked the central door to her shop and then opened the shutters to reveal the books and magazines displayed in the large picture windows. She smiled to see her stalwart stack of *Leaves of Grass*, the new edition of *A Midsummer Night's Dream*, and Sherwood Anderson's collection *Winesburg, Ohio* alongside the journals. Her shop officially open, Sylvia busied herself by making her morning's second pot of coffee—the first having been shared with Adrienne at breakfast—in the little room behind the shop. Then, steaming cup in hand and fresh cigarette lit, she settled into one of the church-sale chairs whose jade-green upholstery had gone nearly white and threadbare with use where her rear end now rested, ledger on her lap.

How she hated accounting. It was not her forte—especially because, well, if she was being honest, business was not exactly booming. She squeaked by, but she was nowhere near being able to repay her mother. Adrienne told her to be patient, that she hadn't even been open a year yet, and her mother assured her over and over that

62

she never even expected repayment, but Sylvia couldn't help feeling nervous. She'd thought that Shakespeare and Company—a first of its kind!—would take Paris by storm. But after some initial fanfare, which had included announcements in most Paris newspapers and a few in New York and Boston, it had been more like a drizzle than a tornado.

She trudged through a few columns of sums, telling herself that if she finished, and everything was still quiet, she'd close up for an hour and visit Adrienne at La Maison. Tempting as this plan was, she was nonetheless thrilled when it was derailed by the arrival of Valery Larbaud. Jumping up from her chair and nearly knocking over her empty cup and full ashtray, she exclaimed, "Larbaud! I thought you were in Vichy until September!"

They embraced and kissed on both cheeks, and then Larbaud said, "I had to check on a few things at home, and thought I'd come in to see if you had Millay's latest, or anything new by Williams?"

"I don't have anything you haven't read already," she said, feeling that familiar buzz of satisfaction at knowing her trade, and flattery that someone like Larbaud should rely on her for reading advice. Much as she loved putting the exact right novel into the hands of a visiting stranger and then having that same person become a friend who returned for more books, it was a special pleasure to be the English-language reading concierge of Paris, as Ezra Pound had deemed her recently. Dear Ezra. He'd found his way to Shakespeare and Company as soon as he arrived from London, just a few weeks ago.

"Millay's next book hasn't reached me yet," she went on. *"A Few Figs from Thistles.* I hope it will be here soon."

"Do reserve a copy for me when it arrives," Larbaud said, picking up the latest issue of *Chapbook*, thumbing through it, and then pausing to read one of the poems. He sighed, then set it down. "Speaking of writers from abroad, I've heard that James Joyce is in town."

"How could you know that sooner than me?" said Sylvia, feigning horror. Though she did actually feel somewhat slighted. How could she not know this? And why hadn't he stopped by the shop? But then, she'd heard that Joyce read and spoke many languages. Perhaps he was content to read in French while in France. But he hadn't been to Adrienne's shop, either.

Then she thought, *What would I say if he* did *walk in that door?*

"Now, Sylvia, be patient. You know it's only a matter of time till he needs his own copy of *Leaves of Grass*," Larbaud teased with a glint in his eye. She was learning that few people understood why she loved nineteenth-century Whitman as much as the very modern Joyce or Eliot or Pound, whose poems she was growing to love more for his visits to the store. Larbaud understood Whitman, though. Come to think of it, so did Pound himself.

"Maybe I should send him a copy, compliments of Shakespeare and Company?"

"No, I think you should let it be the beacon that lights his way," he replied, and they both laughed.

Then, as if summoned by the sunlight itself, three more customers wandered in and began browsing, and it was time for her to don her shop owner's cap and help them find the exact book they were looking for, the volume they had no idea they needed but that might just change their lives.

Michel stopped by on a hot summer Friday when Sylvia was pining for a glass of American iced tea in her stifling shop and looking forward to the next day when she'd close early and head to Rocfoin, where Adrienne's parents lived in a charming cottage with a thatched roof. There, away from the noise and heat of the city, they could swim and pick wildflowers and read on patio chaises before sitting down to a delicious meal that was very often nothing more than for-aged berries with a locally made *fromage blanc*, baguette, *saucisson sec*, and a strong red wine made by one of the neighbors. Maman and Papa Monnier had welcomed Sylvia like another daughter, and she was so grateful to be able to escape into a family that felt so comfortable and familiar.

"Bonjour," Michel said with a broad smile on his face, which was streaked with sweat. His shirtsleeves were rolled up to reveal his tanned and hairy arms. "Sweetbreads," he said as he set a brown paper package on Sylvia's desk. He often brought by something for Adrienne to cook.

"Let me just pop it into the icebox," she said, hoping there was enough of the frozen block left to keep the meat fresh until closing. It appeared there was, and she touched her hand to it for just a moment's relief before hurrying back out to attend to Michel, who was flipping through her last copy of F. Scott Fitzgerald's *This Side of Paradise*. It was flying off the shelves; she'd barely been able to keep it in stock since it came out in March.

"Is this good?" he asked her. "My sister asked me to get it if you had it."

"It is," Sylvia said hesitantly.

"You don't sound convinced," he replied.

"I am. It's a masterful and promising first novel," she said, more enthusiastically than was necessary—though it was, after all, true. "And I'll be curious to hear what you and Genevieve think." Which was true as well. But. Sylvia went to the Joyce section and plucked a copy of *Portrait of the Artist as a Young Man* off the shelf and handed it to Michel. "I'll be curious to see what you think of this one, too. Fitzgerald's novel owes something to Joyce's."

He nodded. "Your recommendations have always been perfect, so I trust you."

They chatted a bit about their weekend plans, and when he said evasively that he was doing *rien*, the bold words were out of her mouth before she could stop them: "Nothing? Michel, you should be taking out every pretty girl in the neighborhood!"

At this, the usual splotches of red in his face joined together for a hot, embarrassed blush.

"Oh, I see . . . you are taking them out!"

"Not *every* girl. Just one. Julie. She's a ballerina I've admired for a long time, the younger sister of an old friend of mine. I finally got up the courage to ask her to dinner."

Sylvia beamed. "Good for you. If she doesn't like you, she's a fool."

Still blushing, Michel said, "It's hard, you know. To find what you and Adrienne have."

Sylvia was taken aback and felt goose bumps erupt on her neck. Her relationship with Adrienne was quietly accepted by everyone around them—so far as she knew, anyway. As with Gertrude and Alice, no one commented on them. Though she was aware that a casual observer might simply assume two women having dinner together were acquaintances or sisters, among their friends and local patrons who knew better, she'd yet to hear even a thoughtless slur.

But it was rarely *acknowledged*. Even her parents hadn't asked a single question when she wrote that she'd moved in with Adrienne on the rue de l'Odéon "for the company and to save on rent." But the embarrassment she felt before Michel was a pleasure. She felt seen.

"It is a rare thing," she agreed. "And yet, it seems to happen every day. Good luck with the ballerina."

"Thank you," he said.

The following Sunday found her and Adrienne in the sixteenth holding a bottle of sweating Bordeaux blanc as they waited for André

Spire or his wife to greet them at the door. It had been a long and hot journey on the metro, and beads of perspiration were trickling down Sylvia's back under her linen shirt. She wished they were in Rocfoin instead.

André threw open the door and greeted them with hearty *baisers* and *bienvenues*, ushering them into his large, light-filled apartment.

"Come in, come in. The Pounds have already arrived, as has Paul Valéry and Romains, and," he went on, dropping his voice to almost a whisper, "James Joyce and his family are here."

Sylvia swallowed hard; she wasn't supposed to meet Joyce *here*; he was supposed to find his way to her shop.

Adrienne, who must have sensed Sylvia tense up beside her, put a reassuring hand on Sylvia's arm and exclaimed, "*Merveilleux!*"

A pack of children boisterously chased each other and a cat through the rooms, and before she could say anything, Sylvia was handed a glass of white wine in exchange for the bottle she was holding, and shown into the sitting room where the women were gathered on the couches and chairs, fanning themselves and drinking the cold wine. On their way from the entry hall to the living room where the wives sat, they passed the library and she glimpsed Ezra, Romains, and—*was it?*—James Joyce himself, all shadowy silhouettes against the early afternoon sun. Normally Sylvia was annoyed when parties separated into gendered factions, but today she was glad of an opportunity to gather herself. Ezra's wife Dorothy introduced her and Adrienne to Joyce's wife, a woman with an imposing physicality, like one of the nudes climbing out of Rodin's marble. Except she was rosier, with a glorious mane of reddish hair haphazardly pinned up from her damp neck, and hooded eyes that had a sultry look to them.

"Mrs. Joyce," Dorothy called her. *Aren't we all on formal terms today*, reflected Sylvia as she lit a cigarette. Sylvia knew her name was still Nora Barnacle, as she and Joyce were not legally married. She'd heard that they had lived together as man and wife for years, but in an iconoclastic fashion that was in keeping with his writing, the couple had always refused to capitulate to social norms. Sylvia liked this about him, about them. After all, she and Adrienne could not marry even if they wanted to; she liked the idea of a couple who *could* get married flouting the convention.

Sylvia smoked silently while she listened to Mrs. Joyce effuse in her Irish twang about how glad she was to be among English speakers.

"I'm very happy to be in Paris, but of course we all speak better Italian than we do French." Her voice was throaty and feminine at the same time. "Since we arrived, it feels I've only spoken to the children. And you know how that is. Clean your teeth, brush your hair, have you gotten enough exercise? I'm practicing at the markets, though honestly I don't think it's because of my poor attempts at French that the men at the stalls always gave me the finest peaches and apples."

No, thought Sylvia, her eyes falling to Mrs. Joyce's ample bosom, her milky skin, and delicate fingers, *I don't suppose it is*. It was curious and refreshing, however, that the woman was so willing to admit it. Sylvia thought of the lustier passages in Joyce's work and wondered how much of Mrs. Joyce might have inspired him.

Then, clearing her throat loudly, Mrs. Joyce changed the subject: "I beg you all to tell me what we can do while we're here. And please, no literary events. I want Lucia and Giorgio to know there's more to life than books."

Curiouser and curiouser, thought Sylvia.

Dorothy and Adrienne launched into an impassioned list of theatrical ensembles, musical concerts, and art and sport lessons, and the men began to drift in, lured perhaps by the herbaceous and gamey scents of lunch coming from the kitchen. In a nearby room, a dining table had been beautifully set with silver, crystal, and low vases bursting with wildflowers.

Sylvia noticed Joyce wasn't with André and Jules and the rest, and thought perhaps this was a moment to meet him without prying eyes. On her way to the library, she was waylaid by wild-haired Ezra, who gave her a tight, tipsy hug and grinned at her assurances that his journal *The Dial* was doing well at Shakespeare and Company.

"I'm glad to hear all the effort's not wasted," he said in his gruff voice. "And did you receive the latest of Anderson's journal? I wondered if any copies made it out of the States alive."

Sylvia nodded. "I did. Ten copies, in fact."

"Excellent," Ezra said, a Machiavellian smile on his lips. Dropping his voice and his lips so that only Sylvia could hear, he said, "You know, I edit some of the more worrying content out of James's pages, but there's only so much I can do. Can't bleed all the life out of this movement just to keep John Sumner happy. Which is proving impossible anyway."

Sylvia loved this about Ezra: his prophet's willingness to state that he and his friends were in the vanguard of *a movement*, one that would set fire to everything and everyone that had gone before them and remake meaning from the ashes.

"Sumner does seem like an ogre," said Sylvia. "Like Comstock before him. I'm glad to be shod of him and his ilk here." Though was she really free of him? It occurred to her now that even in Paris she was affected by Anthony Comstock and his infamous act, which was responsible for censoring so much important writing, from Margaret Sanger's book about birth control to James Joyce's great novel. If the United States Postal Service, Sumner's favorite weapon of suppression, incinerated *The Little Review* before it could reach Paris, weren't she and her readers subject to the same censorship as those in New York? *For Pete's sake. Is there no stopping him?*

"I just hope he doesn't put Anderson and Heap in jail next time," said Ezra.

"*Jail?*" Sylvia could hardly believe it. Of course, she knew of this theoretical consequence of violating the Comstock Act, but jail seemed terribly extreme.

"Sumner's really frothing at the mouth this time, but he's not going to terrorize us into stopping," said Ezra, with equal parts glee and exasperation, though not a trace of actual fear. He sounded more like a general preparing to rally his troops.

"Bien sûr," she agreed. "But jail?"

He shook his head confidently. "It'll never happen. One of the best lawyers in New York is on our side. Remember the Armory Show? He helped put it together. He owns more Cézannes and Picassos than Stein, which is more impressive, really, because he's just a lawyer, not an artist himself. John Quinn. Irish parents. He loves Joyce."

"Sounds like you're lucky to have him," she said.

"We're lucky to have *you*, Sylvia." He smiled, and she saw the wine shining in his eyes again. "Keep stocking the hard stuff. I have a feeling more and more American writers will be finding their way to your store soon. It's shit to be a real artist in America these days."

Much as she enjoyed sparring with Ezra, she badly wanted to meet Joyce before lunch, so she told him she needed to find the loo before it was time to eat, and then hurried away.

There Joyce was, miraculously in the library, preternaturally still in a wooden chair. His long legs were crossed, and his large hands drooped from arms draped on the chair. Sylvia wondered if he'd ever played piano with those fingers, two of which had rings on them, on both hands. His head was almost perfectly egg shaped, and he was looking out the window at a leafy tree with two twittering goldfinches as if they contained the meaning of life.

Ignoring her nervous heartbeat, she stood just to the side of the window, cleared her throat, and said, "I understand you are the great James Joyce?"

Her words drew his interest, and she saw that the eyes behind his brass wire glasses were a glorious blue, except that the left iris was obscured by a milky film. Yet he didn't squint or struggle to see her, and in fact he unnerved her further by devoting the same attention to her as he had to the birds and tree outside.

"I don't know about great," he replied. "But James Joyce is correct enough. And you are?"

"Sylvia Beach," she said. "I have an English-language bookstore and lending library in the sixth. Shakespeare and Company."

A burst of laughter erupted in the other room, startling her.

She held out her hand to shake his, and when he accepted, rising for a moment from the chair, she was surprised to find that his seemingly strong, beringed hand gave such a weak shake, limp at the wrist.

"It's a pleasure to meet you Miss Beach. Your reputation precedes you, you know." He gestured for her to sit in the chair that was the twin to his, a foot or so away.

Heart thudding wildly, she perched on the very edge of her chair. "Please, call me Sylvia. And I'm honored to know you've heard of my shop. I do hope you'll visit soon."

"I try to model the niceties for my children, *Miss Beach*. I hope you don't mind."

Sylvia smiled. So this was why Nora was Mrs. Joyce. *The niceties*. Somehow, it was hard to imagine this effete, languid gentleman in marital communion with the earthy, shapely woman in the other room—or, for that matter, writing the scaldingly frank passages that had kept her awake so many nights. The mystery of this contrast intrigued her, and she wondered why it was impossible *not* to imagine that it was unimaginable. But there was something so mismatched about Mr. and Mrs. Joyce.

"Tell me about this shop of yours. I have been meaning to get there," he said, his tenor voice a lovely lilting mixture of educated Irish and Continental sophistication. Sotto voce.

"Well," she began, not knowing where to start or what part of the history would most interest him. "We opened last fall, at the end of 1919, and . . ."

"We?" he interrupted.

"Well, *I*, I suppose," she corrected herself, amazed he'd picked up on this pronoun. "Do you know Adrienne Monnier? Her store La Maison des Amis des Livres has been quite an inspiration to me, and she is such a help in mine, that I often think of Shakespeare and Company as *our* store."

Mr. Joyce nodded. "I haven't had the pleasure of visiting her store, but Messieurs Spire and Pound have already informed me that I must."

"You must."

"Then I shall," he said with a puckish smile. Another surprise.

"You know, Ezra—er, Mr. Pound—was one of my first, and still one of my few, native English-speaking customers. And he did more than purchase books and procure a lending card. He fixed some of the ailing chairs I have for people to sit in. Nothing wobbles in Shakespeare and Company because of Ezra Pound," she said with an amused smile of her own, for she liked to think about Ezra with a hammer in his capable hands.

"Dear Mr. Pound, always fixing something."

"Has he mended anything of yours?"

"My life."

"Goodness, that's quite a statement."

"It has the benefit of being entirely true. I'm published because of Mr. Pound. I'm here in Paris because of Mr. Pound. I am supported by patrons because of Mr. Pound. It's a pity Mrs. Joyce has no patience for him because he's a writer. Perhaps I should have introduced him as a carpenter."

"It would have the benefit of being entirely true," Sylvia said, and they smiled at each other, as if sharing a joke they'd been lobbing at each other since the nursery.

Before Joyce could reply, a dog barked from somewhere outside, an excited and friendly yapping that floated in through the open window. Joyce visibly winced.

"Are you all right?" Sylvia asked.

Laying a relieved hand on his chest, Joyce said, "As long as the beast is outside, as it seems to be. I was bitten by one, you see, when I was a boy."

And you never got over it, marveled Sylvia to herself. It said something to her about the kind of writer he was.

Then suddenly Ezra was leaning in the doorway saying, "I've been dispatched to call you to lunch, though I'm extremely glad to see the two of you have met."

"*Moi aussi, Monsieur Pound, moi aussi*," said Joyce, leaning on his ashplant cane to help him out of his chair, as if he was a much older man, not *Portrait*'s or *Ulysses*'s young Stephen Dedalus who also went about with such a stick. He hardly used it as he walked to the dining room, however.

She could barely make herself move to follow him. *James Joyce*. Her brief exchange with one of her most favorite writers had left her feeling as if the two of them had known each other for years. *Well*, she supposed, *I have known him for years—in a manner of speaking*.

Conversation at lunch was lively, and it became a point of comedy that Ezra kept trying to fill Joyce's glass with wine, and Joyce would reply, "Not before eight," with a glance at Nora, who nodded her staunch approval and sipped her own cup of water.

As was always the case in the homes of Adrienne's friends, it was a gathering of noisy equals, all the writers of varying nationalities unwilling to cede the floor but somehow all managing to have their say about the poems, stories, and essays in the recent journals. Sylvia marveled as she often did, at the strength with which Adrienne added her own voice to the conversation, and the respect with which everyone listened. In recent months, Sylvia had learned of herself that she was more comfortable discussing any topic, even books, in smaller groups; a few friends in her store was just right, whereas Adrienne was just as comfortable in front of a noisy, jostling mess of people. It was the unspoken reason they continued hosting readings at La Maison instead of Shakespeare.

Sylvia recognized a bit of herself in Joyce, though, who hung back and listened until he was asked to deliver an opinion. At which point, everyone paid close attention, which he clearly enjoyed; in fact, Sylvia thought perhaps he spoke with deliberate slowness to make sure every word he uttered was heard and understood, something she never would have done; she talked so fast, people often asked her to slow down.

After Joyce's particularly astute commentary on the latest poems by Yeats, Ezra joked, "Well, I suppose such erudition is what comes of not drinking with one's fowl." He said it good-naturedly enough, but Sylvia could detect the drunken irritation. She and Adrienne exchanged raised eyebrows across the table, and Sylvia wondered what this lunch, this official introduction of James Joyce into the Odéon circle, portended. If the excited buzz in her veins was any indication, it was going to be big.

Later, over brandy and fruit in their own apartment, their legs tangled on the couch as they sipped and read, Adrienne set her book down and said, "He is a *crooked* Jesus, isn't he?"

"Who?" Sylvia looked up and asked, genuinely confused, since

Ezra—whom she'd often referred to as a prophet—wasn't crooked in any way. You always knew where you stood with him.

"*Monsieur* Joyce."

"How do you mean?"

"Well, tales of his drinking are legendary, *non*? And yet he doesn't drink before eight? And his writing is bawdy, but his demeanor is so bourgeoise. His wife, though, *oh, là là*! She is magnificent."

"Adrienne!" Sylvia flushed hot to realize her lover had had the same kinds of thoughts about Joyce's wife that she herself had earlier in the day. It felt illicit somehow.

"Don't be jealous, *chérie*. You know how I love your *petit corps*. And anyway, Madame Joyce hates books. Another strange, crooked thing about him. How could a man of letters, a writer of his caliber, be married to someone who's never read a word of his writing?"

"Not everyone wants to share what we share," Sylvia said.

Adrienne rocked herself onto her hands and knees and moved forward like a cat so that she hovered above Sylvia, her face centimeters away. Dropping her voice she said, "And he is like Jesus because he seeks disciples. He was happiest when everyone was hanging on his every word."

Adrienne was right, but Sylvia didn't want to talk; she wanted the heat between them to make her lover forget the form of any other woman. Sylvia lifted her hands to Adrienne's breasts, the opposite of her own in their abundance, and gently traced the nipples through her blouse with the backs of her fingers. Adrienne closed her eyes and kissed her hard and searchingly as she dropped her hips and pressed them against Sylvia's. Like this, it was only the two of them in all the world.

CHAPTER 7

❧

It was awful, Sylvia, just awful. All New York was in chaos, with people running home, pushing prams and clutching children, shouting for their wives and mothers. Some men started running straight toward the danger—it was extraordinary. And moments before, it had been the most clear, blue, crisp day.

Even though the bombing was on Wall Street downtown, I could hear it all the way up near Union Square. The newspapers speculate that it was the work of the anarchists, but no one really knows. If it was the anarchists, who can really blame them? They are mainly immigrants, and immigrants are blamed for everything, which is just as much the fault of the people at the top who won't help the immigrants, and instead use them as the perfect scapegoats as they go about eating and drinking at the Waldorf as if there aren't real problems that need solving, which their money could actually improve. I can only hope the bombing gets the attention of someone important who can do something about the strife in the city . . .

Carlotta's letter made Sylvia queasy. She'd read about the September bombing a few weeks ago in a newspaper, and her first reaction then had been a surprising homesickness, a deeply felt wish that she could be physically close to her American friends as they recovered from the horror and indignity of the shocking act of violence. She hadn't wanted to trouble her French friends with her feelings because what was thirty-eight people dead in New York compared to millions dead in France, during the war? And since New York seemed so far away from 8 rue Dupuytren, the feeling had passed.

Now, though, reading the thoughts of a friend whose feelings and politics had long been so close to her own, the bombing felt very near. Carlotta's letter also tapped into the same feelings of injustice that the seizures of *The Little Review* did, the same feelings that the fight for women's suffrage had ignited when she was younger—perhaps because she'd been hearing similar complaints from her family and friends in letters since the start of 1920, and now from the mouths of expatriated Americans who found their way to Shakespeare and Company. All of these strains were starting to sound familiar, echoes and foreshadowings of the same theme.

Sylvia began to feel jittery with a need to *do* something, to rebel against the stodgy, censorious forces at work in America. Prohibition, Sumner's vice squad, anti-immigrant feeling, suppression of anarchist and other "foreign" ideas—it all seemed to Sylvia like part of the same overall problem with America. The problem writers like Pound were leaving to escape. *America's a shit place to be an artist these days*, he'd said.

But what could she do from Paris? Supporting banned issues of controversial journals like *The Little Review* was a start—when they reached her intact. Surely there was more she could do.

"Why don't you write something?" Adrienne suggested.

"I don't think I'd say anything more or different from what Margaret Anderson, and Ezra, and Larbaud and Spire are already saying. I want to *do* something." *Doing* was how she'd made the most impact in her life: knocking on doors, handing out blankets, tilling soil.

"More voices speaking against injustice strengthens the cause. More is always better in that way. And I'm sure you would say something different. You are you, not Pound or Spire."

Adrienne's faith in her made Sylvia simultaneously proud and nervous. Adrienne herself composed essays and poetry, and they were beautifully written and well received. She also published short works by their friends in Cahiers des Amis des Livres. She often left La Maison in the care of an assistant to spend hours with her books and typewriter, reviewing the latest novels or arguing for the equality of women in the lycées. It was a difficult balancing act that Sylvia didn't covet; she found she preferred to spend the whole day in her store with the books and book people. But she didn't want Adrienne to think she didn't approve of her choices.

"I know," she replied slowly and carefully. "And you could write the most effective essay about this, I am sure. I just don't . . . feel moved to write about it myself. But I do want to help make the situation better."

Adrienne looked at her a long time, and Sylvia wondered if somewhere in her mind she was comparing her to Suzanne. Suzanne had not written, either. Had that frustrated Adrienne?

At last Adrienne put her hand on Sylvia's and squeezed it firmly. "The right opportunity will come along," she said. "Just like the rue Dupuytren."

Was there anything she could do to speed it along?

About a week after Carlotta's letter, Ezra Pound stopped by. It was early October, and she hadn't seen him since the lunch at André

Spire's in July, although Joyce had become an almost daily figure in Shakespeare and Company, much to her delight. They could while away hours together in wordplay and banter about travel, books, and mutual friends. With him, her most mundane activities became literary: she took her cigarettes *smokingly*, Adrienne's macarons were *morsels of manna*, he entreated customers to read Whitman's *poems prayerfully* anytime she put a volume of *Leaves* in anyone's hands. He was every bit as brilliant as his writing suggested. More. There were moments when she had to remind herself that this was her actual, real life, that *James Joyce* was her friend, that he liked her well enough to come to her shop and spend an hour or two with her most days of the week.

Ezra's arrival in the shop was precious in part because of its rarity. Instead of engaging her about the latest books on display, though, he immediately set about testing the tables and chairs—which on that day was fortuitous, because she'd just acquired a new side table that had lain abandoned on a country road, and it needed repair. Within minutes of his arrival, he was lying on the floor, looking up at the underbelly of the antique, trying to ascertain the problem and solution to its wobbly state while he said, "Have you heard the latest on *Ulysses*?"

"No, tell me. It must be very recent, because Joyce was in just two days ago and didn't mention anything."

"Oh, he's known for at least a week."

"Known what?"

"There's going to be a trial."

"What?" *And he didn't tell me?* She felt hurt, like a child excluded from a game of tag.

Ezra came out from under the table to sit up and explain. "The day after the bombing on Wall Street, John Sumner lowered himself to entering the Washington Square Book Shop for the express purpose of buying the latest issue of *The Little Review* that has the Nausicaa episode of *Ulysses*. He then sent the vice squad to arrest Josephine Bell, who owns the shop, for selling pornography. And now she and the two editors of the *Review*, Jane and Margaret, are being brought up on obscenity charges in the New York courts. John Quinn is defending them."

"No."

"Yes." And with that, Ezra put himself back under the table, where he started prying something out with great effort.

Sylvia stood there, mouth open and fists clenched at her sides. At last she found words to ask, "Isn't Josephine Bell married to her business partner in the shop? Eggie Arens? Why wasn't he arrested, too?"

"He must not have been there when the police arrived." Ezra finally pulled whatever he needed loose with a grunt and a "Eureka!"

Sylvia doubted very much it was an accident that Josephine's husband had not been present when the arrest took place, nor was it an accident that it was three women who were being put on trial: Bell, as well as Margaret Anderson and Jane Heap. As enlightened as Ezra was about many matters, he wasn't much of a feminist, and she didn't feel like challenging him that morning. If there was one thing she'd learned campaigning for suffrage, it was that sometimes it was as important to shut up as it was to speak up. And there was also the place in her chest that was still smarting from the knowledge that Joyce hadn't bothered to tell her any of this. Was it because she was a woman?

Lighting a cigarette, she inhaled so deeply, she almost coughed. "And why did Sumner do this the day after the bombing? I can't imagine that was a coincidence."

"I agree. Sumner hates anything foreign. Anything real. Anything new. He's been after Joyce for ages, just for being Irish, if you ask me."

Of course. Because even though half of New York was Irish, they were *American* Irish. Tammany Irish. Now that they were in control, they couldn't tolerate where they'd come from. *Immigrants always seem to be to blame*, Carlotta had written. Ezra elaborated on that idea with something she hadn't thought of: "And anyway, Joyce looks far more Continental than he does Irish. Maybe even Russian. *A Trotskyite*. Ho-oh! God forbid. And his writing is so far above the head of someone like Sumner that I'm sure he can't help but hate it because he's just smart enough to realize he doesn't understand it."

He pounded a fresh nail into the table. When he finished, he sighed and said, "It doesn't help that Margaret and Jane once supported Emma Goldman."

The infamous anarchist. Goldman wasn't the one being blamed for the Wall Street bombing, however; that honor was going to Luigi Galleani.

"So Margaret and Jane are very much in the sights of those who still support the Sedition Act, like Sumner," Sylvia said. *Good lord, there are so many acts to keep people in line: the Volstead, the Sedition, the Comstock . . .*

Ezra nodded. "Add to all that the fact that part of Nausicaa is about masturbation, and we have all the small-minded prejudices of our homeland in a crucible."

Masturbation? It was shocking to hear the word spoken out loud, and so casually. Sylvia didn't think she'd ever said it aloud. But then she thought, *How old-fashioned of me*. This is one of the points of the new literature: saying things that had gone unsaid too long. Joyce used the word freely in his writing. *Masturbation*. So she countered, deciding that maybe her friendship with Ezra could survive the challenge, "I suspect the problem has less to do with Leopold than it does with Gerty being willing to show him her drawers. It's always the woman's fault, you know. *Madame Bovary. Anna Karenina. The Scarlet Letter. Sister Carrie*."

"It is," he grumbled, not looking at her.

Undeterred, and hoping his reticence could be overcome, she pressed, "Perhaps it's because our Joyce doesn't *blame* Gerty for Leopold's arousal that the episode is so troubling to some readers?"

"No doubt," he said noncommittally.

What a shame. She could see he'd decided to bite his tongue. This evasive quiet was what always seemed to befall men who actually valued their relationship with her. Clearly, they didn't think the friendship could withstand outright debate on issues of gender.

Though she was annoyed, she swallowed it back and searched for a way to return them to common ground as she finished her cigarette. "What is becoming of our country, Ezra?"

"It's in a very deep sleep from which no one seems to be able to wake it," said Ezra as he rolled out from under the table, stood, and attempted to tip it over. Which it did not.

"Thank you," she said, staring down at the table with arms folded across her chest. "Can John Quinn help stir the sleeping beast?"

"I certainly hope so, but he's complaining about it bitterly because he has a bigger *paying* case he's arguing in front of the Supreme Court."

"Goodness, I didn't realize he was in such demand. And what does our Mr. Joyce think about all this?" *Because he apparently doesn't want to tell me himself.*

"The man is a genius, but as blind as a child about these matters. As long as he can barely feed his family and write for hours every day, he's not bothered."

"Where does he get his money, anyway?" She'd been dying to ask this for a while but always felt it rude; today, though, she was feeling peeved enough to stick her neck out.

"Quinn sends him some, in exchange for early copies of his work. And there's Harriet Weaver."

"Mrs. Weaver? Harriet? Of *The Egoist*?" She knew the Englishwoman had been serializing *Ulysses* in her journal from London, as Margaret and Jane were from New York, but Ezra's comment made it sound as if her support of Joyce extended beyond that.

"One and the same. I set them up years ago. She's been his patron since *Portrait*. She inherited more money than she knows what to do with, and she feels it was all made by her forebears on the bloody backs of others, and so she's made it her mission in life to give away as much of it as possible."

Sylvia gave Ezra a sly smile. "Good thing she has you to help her find worthy causes."

"Isn't it, though?"

Just then the shop's doorbell chimed, and who walked in with a gust of chill October air but Mr. Joyce himself.

"Speak of the devil," exclaimed Sylvia. That cool morning, he was wearing his usual stiff wool overcoat with the collar up around his neck, shoes polished at the end of his long, slim legs, his mustache and hair neatly trimmed. He was a handsome man, Sylvia often thought to herself. So much more refined than disheveled Ezra, who with his mane of wiry hair and often unshaved jaw was actually more of a magnet for the women of the Latin Quarter. She'd heard rumors that he was sleeping with many more women than Dorothy, but she'd never heard anything of the sort about Joyce.

"I see no devil," said Joyce, looking around casually, his fair head swiveling slowly atop his coat-darkened form. "Unless Miss Beach has come by a dog since I was last here?"

"I wouldn't dream of it," Sylvia laughed, though she would have liked a little shop dog. Shakespeare and Company did have a shy black cat named Lucky whom Joyce liked to stroke when it deigned to curl up on his lap of an afternoon.

Leaning his walking stick against one of the bookshelves, Joyce came further into the store and unbuttoned his coat. Sylvia put a few more coals into the little stove at the back, feeling a clump of words in her throat, a demand that threatened to burst out of her mouth: *Why didn't you tell me about the trial?*

"Were your ears burning, sir?" asked Ezra, setting himself down in the very chair he'd fixed when the store first opened, close to a year ago.

"'Like a house on fire,'" Joyce replied.

"Washington Irving?" Ezra inquired of the quote, which was Sylvia's guess as well, from his *History of New York*.

"Thomas Carlyle, I believe."

"Typical," Ezra said with a shake of his head.

"Regardless, it's my eyes that are burning," said Joyce. "I've been at it since four in the morning."

"Goodness, when do you sleep?" Sylvia asked.

"Odysseus's worst trouble comes when he falls asleep," he replied musingly, eyes roving over the shelves of books.

Ezra shrugged at Sylvia as if to say, *See? What did I tell you?* Then he began chatting with Joyce in Italian, which irritated Sylvia, because her Italian was poor, and she couldn't quite follow the conversation. When she realized they were talking about the *Ulysses* trial, she finally interjected, "English, please. Or at least French. The fate of *The Little Review* concerns me since it's one of my bestselling journals."

Laying a hand on his chest, Joyce nodded and said, "Touché, Miss Beach. *Mie scuse.* You are right. Mr. Pound, *in inglese, per favore.*"

"I so rarely get to practice my Italian." Ezra sighed. "But very well. I was telling Joyce that he ought to write Quinn and explain in detail how to defend the book."

"And I don't think it's my place. I am not a lawyer."

"You're an *artist*. Who knows better than an artist how to discuss art?"

"Quinn has written me in no uncertain terms that the American courts are not interested in art. Only in whether or not my work is a reader's road to perdition. And I trust him to convince the judge that it is not."

Ezra blew out a frustrated gust of air and shook his head. "Fine. I'll do it. And Yeats is doing it. I wish you'd take more of a stand."

"'The first thing we do, let's kill all the lawyers.'"

"Damn it, Joyce, I'm not plotting against Henry the Fourth, I'm trying to help you."

Tickled at the irony of Ezra Pound and James Joyce hurling one of Old Bill's most famous lines at each other in her shop named for him, Sylvia saw both their points: Joyce wanted to leave the law to the lawyers, and Ezra wanted to make certain the lawyer did right by the art. But she hated to see discord between two of her favorite patrons. "It strikes me," Sylvia ventured, "that Margaret and Jane are also well versed on the subject of why *Ulysses* deserves to be published. They have each written movingly of its status as art. And art is not pornography."

"That would be great if Quinn could see them as anything other than two filthy Washington Squarites," said Ezra.

Sylvia felt in her belly a sensation like a stone breaking the surface of a pond. How had that phrase *filthy Washington Squarite* followed her all the way to Paris? For it was precisely what she and Adrienne would be called by residents of other, more conventional neighborhoods, if they lived on Bleecker Street instead of the rue de l'Odéon. And though she could tell Ezra was simply repeating what Quinn had said of Anderson and Heap, his lack of remorse in repeating it made her grind her teeth. "If he despises them so much, why does he defend them?"

"Because he has great respect for *him*." Ezra thumbed toward Joyce.

Sylvia lit another cigarette. "Well," she said, suddenly realizing that she'd had about enough of Ezra's blind spots. "I hope he prevails."

Turning her back to them, she busied herself with some shelving, and Ezra and Joyce returned to Italian for more chatting before Ezra left.

After a few minutes, Joyce surprised her by saying, "I hope we didn't offend you, Miss Beach. That I could not abide. You have been too kind and helpful for me to wish you anything but the best."

"Oh, I'm fine. But . . . I must admit I was surprised you hadn't mentioned the trial to me."

"I didn't want to upset you. I find it upsetting enough."

"I'm not made of porcelain."

Joyce smiled. "No, you are made of bronze."

She blushed, though it was only flattery. "That's a nice compliment, but the point is that I want to help, Mr. Joyce. And . . ." *And what? I thought we were friends?* She sounded like she was ten years old. "And that's it. I want to help."

"You help by providing my favorite diversion in Paris."

She wished his compliments were enough, but they weren't. She wanted to do something, wanted Shakespeare and Company to be more than a diversion. Wanted Margaret and Jane to be seen as more than *filthy Washington Squarites.* Wanted *Ulysses* to have as broad an audience as possible. So many things to want. Just two years ago, she'd wanted a bookstore. Now she had it and she wanted more? Was that greed or ambition?

Was there a difference?

※

"When one is invited to the rue de Fleurus, one goes," said Adrienne as she waved the flat card on which Gertrude Stein had scrawled an invitation to lunch, and then set it down on the table with an exasperated sigh. "Though I do wish she would speak a bit of *French*. She lives here, after all."

"Yes, she does treat Paris a bit like a backdrop, doesn't she?"

But Gertrude's staunch Americanness wasn't what troubled Sylvia about this invitation. They'd been to Gertrude's salon several times now, and Sylvia had noted each time how conspicuously absent *that Irishman* was from any conversation. Every writer, photographer, professor, and intellectual that Stein invited seemed to know enough not to bring him up in her presence.

Regardless, Adrienne was correct: an invitation to 27 rue de Fleurus was like being called to tea by Marie Antoinette, except that Gertrude and Alice resided not in a *grand palais* but in an unassuming Haussmann-era building made of the same limestone as Sylvia's and Adrienne's shops and their apartment, as well as the homes of pretty much everyone else they knew. No, it was the inside of Stein's apartment that made it a veritable bohemian Versailles. Her drawing room had a unique bifurcated quality: from about the height of a guest's chin to the wood floor was a darkly painted room populated by thick wooden antiques that served to anchor the flight of art above. Above one's head on the soaring white walls hung paintings that would one day glory in the most important museums of the world, if the trajectory of Picasso's career was any indication. As Gertrude herself was fond of reminding people, she was especially adept at picking winners. "Some people bet on horses. I on artists," she once said.

And so they went to lunch on a drizzly Saturday, and Sylvia was surprised to discover she and Adrienne were the only guests in attendance. Gertrude liked to hold court, and the two bookstore owners plus Alice were hardly that. Over sherry and candied plums and slices of a sharp, salty goat cheese, they chatted lightly about business and books, then recent films and plays, and the mystery of their summoning grew. Sylvia even began to feel a tightening of nerves in her shoulders as the soup course began, and wondered when Gertrude would at last show her hand.

"With a certain Mr. Joyce apparently taking up permanent residence in our city," she said, a brothy onion spoonful suspended in midair as the back of Sylvia's neck tingled, "I thought we should speak plainly. As women. And . . . as curators."

Sylvia suppressed a laugh by glancing at Adrienne, who was seated across the heavy dining table from her, and the irony of their hostess's words passed satisfyingly between them, for had there been writer couples in attendance that day, most of the *women* would have been banished to the wives' anteroom while Gertrude commanded the men—a practice that irritated Sylvia greatly on the other women's behalf. As non-wives, she and Adrienne were allowed into Gertrude's court, an exception that Sylvia liked to flout on occasion by decamping to the wives' couch, for she'd come to realize that the spouses very often understood more about their writer men than the writers themselves. It was Gertrude's loss not to speak to them.

"Well, you've certainly piqued my curiosity," Sylvia replied.

"*Moi aussi*," Adrienne agreed.

Alice watched intently from under her black brows.

"Have you met him?" Gertrude asked.

Sylvia sensed danger, for Gertrude must know that Joyce was a regular; she knew everything that happened among artists in Paris. "He's come in a few times," said Sylvia.

"And how is he?" Gertrude folded her hands in front of her mouth and waited for more than six words to escape Sylvia's lips.

Sylvia thought for a moment before responding with a perfectly true if serviceably pallid description, for she didn't want Gertrude to become Shakespeare and Company's enemy. "He seems extremely focused on his work, even though it hurts his eyes to write for so many hours at a time. And he's preoccupied with providing for his children and wife."

"And yet I hear he's itinerant? A different apartment every month? In Italy, too?"

Goodness, you know quite a lot about him, don't you? "Is that so different from other visiting artists?" Sylvia asked.

"It is," Gertrude growled knowingly and impatiently.

Sylvia tried to laugh this off. "Well," she said, "then I wonder why I spend so much time finding accommodation for writers fresh off the boat from America, who stay in hotels far beyond their means when they arrive. Why, just yesterday, I found a place in the sixth for a friend of Sherwood Anderson's."

"I marvel that you have the time."

"Our days are very full," said Adrienne.

Alice smiled slyly.

"I must admit," Gertrude finally said in the tone Sylvia's pastor father always took with a wayward pilgrim, "that I cannot see what is so new about this *Ulysses* everyone is talking about. I've read every installment, and though I can see allusions in every ejaculation, I cannot see true genius or originality."

Aaaaahhhhh. Sylvia understood now. Choosing her words carefully, she replied, "It's clear he has been influenced profoundly by your work, Gertrude. But surely you must see where your styles diverge."

"Where he goes farther than I have, you mean?"

"Not at all," Sylvia said. "He is merely on the path you cut." Would this little bit of partially true flattery be enough to satisfy her?

Gertrude sniffed, then looked up at the portrait of her that Picasso had painted not long ago, his gratitude for her patronage apparent in every meaty brushstroke. "I know that many in our circle think it strange I do not invite him here," she said, transferring her eyes from the Picasso to Sylvia. "Do you?"

Stunned by Gertrude's sudden candor, Sylvia could only be honest. "Yes."

The writer nodded. "Well, perhaps chance will bring us together someday. In Shakespeare and Company. Perhaps I shall discover I am wrong about him. Perhaps he is a great genius, a family man of integrity and grit. An exemplary human."

Gertrude's suspicions about Joyce struck an uncomfortable chord inside Sylvia. She'd defend his originality to her death, even in the face of Stein's work, and she relished his visits to Shakespeare, but . . . why had he not told her of the trial? There was something evasive, even dishonest, about that omission that nagged at her.

"But until then," Gertrude went on, "I shall not seek his company."

Sylvia thought she heard Alice exhale.

Later, in bed, after a few glasses of wine, Sylvia and Adrienne howled with laughter. "Do you think, if they ever bump into each other," Adrienne hiccupped, "that Gertrude will get out her crop, to tame him into submission?"

"I think she'll find him already cowed by another woman."

Adrienne wiped a tear of laughter from her eye. "Can you imagine what she'd say to poor Nora?"

"*Mrs.* Joyce," Sylvia corrected.

"*Oh! Excuse-moi!*"

"And I don't think Gertrude will dignify Nora's presence with so much as a hello."

Sylvia basked in the laughter with Adrienne, though her right side had begun to cramp. Once they'd calmed down, Adrienne observed, "I feel badly for her. She cannot see what true partnerships would gain her."

"She is used to protégés," Sylvia said with a shrug.

"I am glad our shops are meeting places of equals," said Adrienne, rolling onto her side and laying her hand flat on Sylvia's soft belly, which was slightly rounded below the navel from the three-course lunch. "I wouldn't trade our used books for any of the pictures on her walls."

Sylvia kissed Adrienne and felt the threads between them tighten. "Neither would I."

CHAPTER 8

⌒∾✾∾⌒

"The book's as good as banned now," seethed Ezra. "I don't know who I'm angrier at: Quinn or Joyce."

"You can't be mad at Joyce," said Larbaud in measured tones. "He's not finished. He can't be rushed."

"He's been working on the damn book for years. He won't be able to write any more at all if he doesn't let someone publish a private edition of this one before the trial, like Quinn suggests."

"I thought you were mad at Quinn, too?" Sylvia asked, lighting another cigarette off the one she was finishing because it was steadying her hand. Shakespeare was officially closed but no one could stand to leave, and although she was as outraged as Ezra for Joyce and his book, privately she was thrilled down to her toes that her store—*her store!*—was the home of this conversation in Paris. Adrienne had hurried over to join them on the rue Dupuytren as soon as La Maison closed that evening.

"I am," Ezra replied. "Because he made a stupid argument at the hearing. John Yeats has been writing letters for weeks explaining that what *Ulysses* needs, what *all* of us need, is a defense on the grounds

92

of truth and beauty. That Joyce's book can't be obscene because it's the Sistine ceiling. Dante's *Inferno*. Bosch's *Garden*. We should regard it with awe for its difficulty, not lump it in with peep shows and dirty pamphlets because it treats the human body with perfect, painful realism."

"No fig leaves on the penises of masterpieces!" cheered Robert McAlmon, who went by Bob. He was an American writer who'd shown up just recently with his new wife Bryher, an English writer. He'd quickly become the most popular man in Paris, and Sylvia suspected it had something to do with his deep pockets and the sharp, frequently mean wit that always seemed at paradoxical odds with his handsome, boyish face.

"Exactly," exclaimed Ezra, raising a fist in the air. "Instead, the philistine pleads that the book's *so ugly*, it can't corrupt. His idea for the private edition is a good one, but it's only because he doesn't truly believe the book can be saved."

"I don't understand," said Larbaud. "How will a private edition save the book?"

Ezra expelled a harried sigh and ran his fingers through the froth of hair atop his high, lined forehead. "Quinn's tried to convince Ben Huebsch to publish the book before it goes to trial, because then it will be a fait accompli; the book will already exist as a book and thus the trial of a *piece* of the book from a journal will be moot. Quinn also contends that certain kinds of scenes can exist in books that cannot exist in periodicals disseminated by the postal service, because the Comstock laws can only apply to smut that must be disseminated through the post office. But Huebsch is wary of that logic and has refused to publish the book. He's afraid he might wind up the one in jail."

"Ben Huebsch? The publisher who released *Sons and Lovers*? He's afraid of *Ulysses*?" asked Bob in disbelief.

Ezra nodded, distraught. "He also published *Portrait* and *Dubliners*."

"Are the disciples abandoning our Crooked Jesus?" whispered Adrienne in Sylvia's ear. With some reluctance, Sylvia had come to adopt Adrienne's nickname for Joyce. She could hardly say it was incorrect, and it felt good to have this kind of private language with her.

"Has anyone heard from Mrs. Weaver in England?" Sylvia asked, grasping at a last hope.

"She's gone to every printer on the island, and they're all too scared to print anything with shitting and fucking in it, even though the book is only incidentally about those things," said Ezra.

"Well, when you put it that way, I can understand their hesitation," joked Bob.

"Has anyone asked the Hogarth Press?" asked Larbaud thoughtfully.

Sylvia's heart expanded hopefully at the thought of Virginia and Leonard Woolf's little press in Richmond, England. The editions she carried from Hogarth were paragons of the new forms. Surely the author-printers responsible for *Two Stories* would be amenable to Joyce's daring novel; after all, they lived—or so Sylvia had heard—as freely with forward thinkers like Lytton Strachey and Clive Bell as did her little crowd in Paris. She also noted to herself with frustrated pride that it was all women who were the book's last hopes: Margaret and Jane, Harriet, and now perhaps Virginia Woolf.

"Harriet is going to speak to them," said Ezra, "but Eliot doesn't hold much hope. He's always thought the Bells and Woolfs to be ironically conservative."

Sylvia exhaled. Not unlike Gertrude.

"Bah!" Adrienne exclaimed. "I have no patience for these hypocrisies! How can the same people who conceived of the two most important art shows of the last ten years in London and New York be so closed-minded about writing that is trying to do the same work as their precious painters?"

"Do not forget, my dear Monnier," said Larbaud, "that London and New York were much slower than Paris to the new forms. Those paintings had been shocking us for years, and were practically ho-hum by the time they shocked the English. We must give them and the Americans time to catch up."

He said it kindly, even philosophically, but Sylvia completely understood why Ezra retorted, "We are not a heathen race, Larbaud."

"Of course not," Larbaud replied, unruffled. "It took your American Revolution to stir ours, after all, and ours was much longer in coming. I only mean that there is an ebb and flow to these things. Rebellions cannot be controlled and cannot be forced. They take hold in their own time."

"Tell that to Lenin," Bob said, plucking the lit cigarette from Sylvia's fingers and taking a long drag.

"Art is gentler than politics," said Larbaud.

"Would that it wasn't," grumbled Ezra.

Into this storm walked Michel, looking positively radiant with happiness and carrying a stack of books under his arm. He greeted Sylvia and Adrienne and the writers he knew with kisses on the cheek, set his books triumphantly on the desk, and announced, "I'm engaged! Julie and I will be married before the end of the year!"

Sylvia threw her arms around him and laughed as she shouted, "Felicitations!"

Ezra shook his hand and said, "The ballerina? Well done."

"Yes, she wishes she could have come tonight with me, but she has a rehearsal."

Sylvia had seen Michel and Julie, who was a lead dancer in the corps de ballet, many times since their first outing. She spoke very little English, and was shy in the store, but she had beautiful long reddish-blond hair, which seemed so old fashioned these days with everyone bobbing their locks to chin length—but, she said, dancers were required to keep their tresses long enough to pull back in a bun.

Bob clapped his hands to get everyone's attention and said, as if he were a town crier, "Thank you, Michel, for giving us a reason to change the subject and celebrate. I'll buy the first round at Le Dôme."

Cheers erupted in the store, all thoughts of fig leaves and trials and revolutions forgotten in this moment of heartfelt congratulations and optimism. Although Sylvia and Adrienne didn't often join the crowd for its late nights of absinthe and Pernod, they went along that evening. Under the soft glow of the Dôme's chandeliers, their group refilled glasses first with champagne and then with garnet-hued wines and passed around plates of buttery sole and crisp potatoes as the merry clinks of forks and knives against plates echoed off the glass windows and tile floors. Sylvia felt part of something grand that night, a wide river rushing forward from a past that had swept up the likes of Ben Franklin, Baudelaire, Picasso, Edith Wharton, and now Blake and Whitman along with Larbaud and Cocteau and Joyce and Adrienne and *Sylvia and her store*. They were all part of the same persistent current, like a river crashing over rocks and tree roots, picking up speed and often carrying away the things that threatened to hinder its flow.

⁂

Joyce's mood was as blue as the Paris twilight, which fell too dark and too early every night that December. "It's just not ready," he said of his novel, echoing Valery Larbaud as a light snow fell outside the windows of Shakespeare and Company. For once, perhaps because of the weather, it was just Sylvia and Joyce in the shop that afternoon. She had made a pot of tea, and the two of them held the hot cups in their hands. She put her nose right over the rim, allowing the steam to warm her chilly face.

"How can they convict an unfinished book?" he lamented.

"It does boggle the mind," she agreed.

"And what if they do?" he said, suddenly petulant. "It won't stop my writing it. Someone will publish it."

For the first time, Joyce's faith felt unfounded, and she was worried for him. Virginia Woolf had refused to open her press to *Ulysses*, effectively eliminating any possibility for publication in England, and all the New York publishers were waiting on the trial to decide how to proceed at this hazy juncture.

"Honestwise, I'm more distraught about Mrs. Joyce threatening to desert me and take the children with her," he went on.

Sylvia was taken aback by this personal disclosure, but her natural curiosity about the writer and his wife who rarely appeared at readings and dinner parties with her husband made her ask, "And where would she go?"

"Back to Ireland," he said, the gloom in his voice a match for the overall droop of his long limbs in the chair.

"Do you have family there? People who could . . . help you?"

"No one I'd take a farthing from," he replied, an edge of pride and anger in his tone.

Sylvia knew Joyce had been writing to Harriet Weaver with increasing frequency for funds. Which the saintly woman obliged. Sylvia had to assume Mrs. Weaver knew little of how Joyce spent her money, the moment at André Spire's luncheon when he hadn't imbibed because it wasn't yet eight o'clock a distant memory. Joyce had become a regular fixture with Bob and some of the other writers at the Dôme and the Loup; she'd heard one hilarious anecdote of Bob and Fargue delivering Joyce home early one morning in a wheelbarrow. Though perhaps those nights actually did begin after eight in the evening.

Sylvia prided herself on never judging Joyce or any of the others, just as she valued not being judged for who she was. Slow though his progress seemed, Joyce was spending untold hours on *Ulysses*. Most days when he turned up at Shakespeare and Company, he'd been at work for ages, at the expense of his health—he looked too pale and too thin, his eyes were worse, and all through the winter he'd been fighting a cough that sounded tubercular. His fingers perpetually felt like blocks of ice. She sometimes thought he came to the shop just for the warmth, like many of the other struggling students and aspiring artists who found their way to Shakespeare and La Maison and looked around for hours, making humble apologies for not purchasing anything. Sylvia had adopted Adrienne's generous stance on them: *You never know which of them might go on to become the next Cocteau. The next Proust.*

"Do you know what Margaret Anderson wrote me?" Joyce asked.

"Do tell."

"That the artist has no responsibility to the public whatsoever."

"I agree with her wholeheartedly," said Sylvia. "I also agree with Jane, who wrote a truly masterful essay saying that the only real question worthy of *Ulysses* is, 'Is it art?' And it *is*. Great art, at that."

"Well," he said, clearly enjoying the praise but glancing away. "Thank you for saying so."

Sylvia looked down at her full ashtray and wondered if she should have another; lately she'd begun to notice a yellow tinge on her teeth and on the middle and index fingers she used to hold her cigarettes. *Oh, just one more.* A moment of silence ticked by while Sylvia smoked, and Lucky padded out from under the table where he'd been lazing by the stove and went to curl up on Joyce's feet.

"I sometimes think," he said, so quietly she almost couldn't hear him, "that I am doomed to be an exile who always and forever writes about my home country."

"You are your own Odysseus, then," Sylvia observed. "Never quite able to get home. Always waylaid."

Joyce smiled. "And perhaps also wayward."

"Like all great writers *must* be."

"I don't deserve you. Or Harriet."

"Well," she said brightly, hoping to lighten the heaviness of the air between them. "I hope your *Ulysses* finds a home. The right and best one. Please keep me informed."

"I shall." He nodded.

If *Ulysses* could be freed from the stigma of pornography and anointed as literature, some of her own faith in her homeland might be restored. She'd write to her father and ask him to pray on it; while she didn't set any store by a man in the clouds directing immensely complicated human dramas, she found her father's faith comforting. Anytime she expressed doubt or sadness as a child, he told her to pray on her troubles, and promised he would as well. The solidarity made her feel stronger and more confident, and even if she didn't get the outcome she wanted, she felt better knowing she hadn't been alone in her wish. It reminded her of the comfort reading had always given her.

Joyce and his exiled novel needed all the help they could get. Sylvia vowed to be one of the people—one of the women, really—who helped see the novel to publication. *Ulysses* was a fight worth joining.

PART TWO
1921–22

And indeed there will be time
. . . for a hundred visions and revisions

—T.S. Eliot, "The Love Song of J. Alfred Prufrock"

PART TWO

1921-22

CHAPTER 9

J oyce was as good as his word and brought Sylvia whatever news
   he had of *Ulysses*'s adventures in New York as the winter of early
1921 trudged on—which is to say, he brought her nothing. Except for the occasional brief letter or telegram from John Quinn saying that he was doing his best and would have a verdict soon. Still, the fate of Joyce's book became a daily topic of conversation in Shakespeare and Company; her store was rapidly becoming the hub of all information. If someone had heard a rumor—which nearly always turned out to be false—they would bring it to 8 rue Dupuytren to deposit the intelligence with Sylvia, who could then disseminate it.

The biggest news was that no American publisher would come within a hundred feet of Joyce's novel, and so a private edition was now out of the question. If it was declared obscene by the judges of the Jefferson Market Courthouse in New York City, it would be a banned book with a grim future.

Joyce took to coming into Shakespeare and Company and saying to Sylvia with exaggerated excitement, "Guess!"

The first time he did this, his face alight with anticipation, she'd felt her heart go from a trot to a gallop and she said, "Innocent?"

When he'd replied, "Nothing!" she wadded up a receipt and threw it at him. On subsequent occasions when he got her hopes up, she just blew smoke at him with a stern look on her face and he'd laugh till he coughed.

In a curious turn of events, Sylvia began to see Michel's young bride Julie more often in the store. "I like to practice my English," she said when Sylvia asked why the girl came to Shakespeare and not La Maison, where the clientele all spoke French. "Also, Michel loves this store because you showed him many poets he loves. It is a way of being close to him, you see?" Sylvia smiled, her heart breaking with pride at this. Much as she enjoyed Julie, she missed Michel and wondered why he came so seldom now. Instead, he sent Julie to purchase books and deliver his special packages of meats.

By late February, Julie had become pregnant, and she fretted that soon she would have to stop dancing. "I love ballet," she said with glistening eyes. "It is the only thing that helped me when my father and brother died in the war, and my mother went to the convent. Ballet helped me support myself and Babette." Julie was sweetly proud of her little sister, who was now enrolled in the university and planned to become a teacher. "How can I just give it up?"

The best solace Sylvia thought she could offer was Jane Austen novels, the very best books she knew for portraying the joys of family life. She'd never tell Julie the truth of what she'd thought to herself about the baby and the dancing: *Thank goodness I'll never have to make the same choice.* She said, as convincingly as she could, "I am sure that motherhood will offer many other rewards."

"I am sure," Julie said resignedly. "But you understand, don't you?"

The girl was trembling with her need to be seen and heard. Sylvia took Julie's hands in hers and said, "I understand completely. And I suspect Michel would as well." Anyone who read that much had to be given to empathy.

❦

Sylvia's mother came to Paris in the first weeks of the new year and was positively rhapsodic about Shakespeare and Company. "My dearest Sylvia! What a marvel this is!" Clapping her hands together, Eleanor Beach flitted around the store, taking one volume down and merely glancing at it before her attention was pulled in another direction. *The Whitman pages are perfect! Oh, and the Blakes! Do you have any Rossetti?*

Without her father or sisters present, Sylvia saw her mother in an entirely new way. She was lighter, airier, always and almost about to blow away—and entirely absorbed in her own thoughts and pursuits. Sylvia thought that she might actually be able to kiss Adrienne right in front of her mother and Eleanor wouldn't even notice.

"Your mother is charming," Adrienne said at the end of a long day that had included a trip to the Rodin Museum *and* the d'Orsay. Though she was on her feet all day in the shop, Sylvia rarely felt her muscles ache like they did after walking in and between the museums and metro stations.

"Thank you for keeping us company. It was heroic."

"I enjoyed myself thoroughly. Eleanor knows so much about Paris and artists. I learned much from her today."

"She does like to lecture, doesn't she?" Sylvia's mother had given an especially long dissertation in front of *The Thinker*. Sylvia might have enjoyed it more if it hadn't been the fifth such talk of the day.

Adrienne laughed. "She does, but I like to learn."

So did Sylvia. And she loved her mother. So why did she feel so burdened by her behavior?

Eleanor threw herself into the daily life of the store, and Sylvia was thrilled to see so many things getting done in the gust of her mother's enthusiasm: re-alphabetizing, sweeping, dusting, and a total organization of her back room, which had lately begun to feel like a jumble of partially open boxes. "Thank you, Mother," Sylvia said, feeling both grateful and silly for not having completed any of the tasks weeks ago. Looking at the tidy room, she couldn't figure out why she hadn't been able to do any of this herself. Other things—customers, conversation—always seemed more pressing.

"I'm glad to see you still need your mother," she replied with kisses on Sylvia's cheeks. Then, more quietly, "It's nice to be needed."

There was something about her mother's tone in that phrase that broke Sylvia's heart a little. It made painful sense, though. Eleanor thrived on the lively chaos of hosting, and of meaningful, tangible work. *Like Adrienne*, she realized with a jolt.

And now that her mother's daughters were all grown, and none of them had children of their own who needed a grandmother, Eleanor was by herself much of the time. Her husband, Sylvia's father, had always been absorbed in his parish and his teaching; except for the social events required by his job, Sylvester Beach didn't need Eleanor for his thinking, preaching, and writing. And anyway, Sylvia always suspected her mother would rather talk about artists than God. She loved that about her.

When her mother left Paris after two whirlwind weeks to take a train to Florence, where she planned to visit one of her oldest friends who was living there, she left Sylvia with a store that was neat as a pin, and a heart that was confounded. It was easy not to think about her parents when she was away from them. But visiting with one of them made her miss them terribly, and also see them differently. Who was this woman who'd raised her? Perhaps it was time to get to know her in a new way.

That heartache was soon subsumed. News of the trial finally reached the rue Dupuytren, nearly a week after the decision had been handed down, which incensed Sylvia. Why hadn't that damn John Quinn bothered to telegram anyone? *Because he's mortified*, she had to assume. Instead it was an American tourist who came by with a days-old edition of a newspaper that revealed the verdict to her—before it had even been revealed to Joyce, she was sure, because she'd seen him just last night and they had discussed the lack of information.

And there it was in black and white: ULYSSES FOUND OBSCENE. GIRL EDITORS BAILED OUT.

Girl Editors. Could they be any more patronizing?

John Quinn's so-called defense was summarized in the paper exactly as Ezra had predicted: Quinn had tried to convince the judges that Joyce's writing was too difficult, confusing, and offensive in its portrayal of the body and desire, to inspire lust or corrupt anyone—especially not the most corruptible of readers, with whom the trial was apparently concerned.

What about readers who actually understand the book? Sylvia thought angrily. *They wouldn't be corrupted, either, because they would see its revolutionary nature, the staggering beauty in its sentences, and the humanity in its characters.*

Sylvia was tempted to burn the paper in the stove. She kept it only to show Joyce.

Fortunately, she didn't have to keep the pages long, as he arrived later that afternoon in high spirits. "An excellent day at my desk."

She hated to do what she was about to do, but she couldn't not tell him. So she handed him the newspaper.

Smoking nervously, she watched his eyes rove over the article, his expression stoic.

"Well," he said in an even tone, handing the paper back to her. "I'm glad this aptly named Mrs. Fortune of Chicago paid the bail for Miss Anderson and Miss Heap. I'd have felt much worse if my two most important publishers had had to spend any time in jail for me." *Crooked Jesus*, she heard in Adrienne's voice.

"I'm terribly sorry," Sylvia said. "This is a crime against literature."

"And yet the crime is mine, apparently." Joyce inhaled through his nose, long and slow and deep, his shoulders rising as if his whole body were inflating. Then he let it out, almost inaudibly. "My poor book."

"Aren't you angry?"

"At what?"

"Well . . . I'm angry at Sumner and the post office and the vice squad, and John Quinn for not coming up with a better defense, and those judges for being hopelessly illiterate."

"I thank you for your outrage, Miss Beach."

"You should be outraged as well!"

"But why? When you do it so well for me?"

She laughed, both amused and frustrated. "What are we going to do with you, Mr. Joyce?"

"The better question is what are we going to do with my book?"

The words were out of her mouth before the idea had even completely formed in her head: "Let me do it. Let Shakespeare and Company publish *Ulysses*."

It was as if every conversation, every book she'd ever read or shelved or lent, every framed page by Whitman and Blake, every conversation she'd had with Adrienne about Cahiers, every encouragement of her parents, had been pushing James Joyce's masterpiece to this very destination. Paris. Her door. Its very own Ithaca.

The smile he bestowed on her was whole and unfettered. "What a marvelous idea."

"Let me work on some numbers, and draw up some terms," she said, trying to sound calm and businesslike when what she felt like was a schoolgirl who wanted to burst out of the building and skip down the road. *I, Sylvia Beach, am going to publish James Joyce!* "We can discuss the details tomorrow."

They shook hands before the blessing eyes of Walt Whitman.

"I couldn't be happier, Miss Beach."

Sylvia hadn't felt this excited since the fall of 1919, knowing she would open this store and possibly, probably, be united with Adrienne. Her body was full of a burbling excitement it couldn't contain, so she bounced about the store, scrounging up a fresh notebook and pen as she smoked. Shakespeare and Company was about to right a great wrong, ensuring the publication of a tour de force that should be required reading, not a banned book. Adrienne had been correct, of course—the right opportunity *would* come along for her to effect change in the world, and here it was.

And, she admitted to herself, this venture would also put her store on the map. Everyone would know about Shakespeare and Company after it published *Ulysses*, ensuring the store's success, making it the kind of accomplishment that might outlive her.

It was dark when she finally lifted her eyes from the ink-damp pages of her journal where she'd written numerous equations hypothesizing profits and percentages and costs, and brainstormed ideas for marketing the book even where it had been banned. Especially there. The idea of thumbing her nose at John Sumner and everything he represented filled her with glee. The gas lamps outside cast shimmering light on damp sidewalks. It had rained. She hadn't even noticed. Collar up, she hurried home, relieved she wasn't too late for dinner. There was a wine shop not far out of her way, so she stopped in to purchase a *fillette de champagne*.

At home, Adrienne had the wireless on, and Cole Porter's "Old

Fashioned Garden" was crackling into the kitchen. Sylvia inhaled the scent of thyme and carrots and beef and thought she might just expire from happiness on the spot.

"Darling," she said as she handed Adrienne the cold *demi-bouteille*. "Shakespeare and Company is going to change the world. And once again, *you* are the inspiration—I need to know how you publish Les Cahiers."

Adrienne smiled and eagerly took the champagne from Sylvia's hands. "Tell me everything."

As Adrienne poured the golden bubbles into two coupes, Sylvia rushed through the details of her outrage about the trial's verdict, then explained her offer to publish Joyce's novel. "I had to do it," she effused breathlessly, "How could I not?" Holding up her glass, Sylvia said, "To *Ulysses*?"

Adrienne's eyes sparkled with surprise and pride and excitement, and she clinked the rim of her glass to Sylvia's so that the sound rang out above the cooking and music. "To *you*, my dear Sylvia."

They sipped. It was the best champagne Sylvia had ever tasted.

Over dinner, Adrienne explained how she ran the publishing side of her enterprise, starting with the printer Maurice Darantiere in Dijon, and roving over the correct number of copies to print, how to calculate profits, how to collect subscriptions from interested buyers, and how to share and distribute the proceeds. Sylvia took eager notes and asked many questions. When the clock ticked into a new day, her notebook was full of wrinkled pages, and her stiff fingers were stained black. It was the most beautiful mess she'd ever made.

When at last they rose from the kitchen table, limbs stiff and swallowing back yawns, Adrienne turned to Sylvia at the sink and said, carefully and tenderly, "I do worry about one thing, *chérie*."

"*Quoi?*"

"I must speak plainly." She hesitated for a moment, then said almost resignedly, "Our Crooked Jesus is very needy. He is bad with money, and other people's money, at that. He is a very great writer, but . . . I hope . . . Well, we must find a way to protect you and the store. I hope you don't mind my saying so. You might start by re-thinking the profits. Seventy-five percent is much to give him, and you will be doing significant work. You must consider what *you* are worth."

Adrienne's warning quelled some of her joy, but she knew her lover was right. Sylvia nodded. "I know it's true, though I wish it wasn't. I'll think about the seventy-five percent."

Adrienne kissed her lightly on the lips. "I will be here to help, if you need me."

"I always need you." Sylvia slid her arms around Adrienne's soft, wide waist, longing for more—skin, hands, folds, sighs, release. But Adrienne kissed her chastely on the cheek and pulled away.

CHAPTER 10

❧

The first thing that happened was that Gertrude disavowed her. Incredibly, she and Alice traveled all the way from their cozy apartment in the March slush, just to do it in person.

"I'd like to pull my lending card," Gertrude said.

"I'm sorry to hear that," Sylvia said, feeling her heart thud in her chest. This was a bad sign, if not unexpected. And despite it, she still felt extremely confident in her decision to publish *Ulysses*—it was the right thing for her, for her store, for *literature*. So many people had extended their congratulations, relief, and thanks, from Bob McAlmon and Bryher to Margaret Anderson herself, who wrote Sylvia a letter saying, "I couldn't be happier to know that the best bookstore outside New York City will be sponsoring this important work. When Joyce wrote to tell me of your offer, Jane and I rejoiced and popped open one of our last bottles of illegal bubbly in your honor." Their approval reinforced the feeling that she was doing the right thing.

Gertrude would come around. Surely. Anyway, making such a show of coming to Shakespeare and Company just to cancel her subscription, when it would have been easier to simply stop coming in, made Sylvia suspect that this was more of a tantrum than a lasting change of heart.

"The new American Library will serve my needs better, I think," said Gertrude.

Ah yes, Sylvia's new and only competitor in Paris, which had opened a year after her in the higher-class eighth, near the Champs-Élysées. But the library was so institutional and lacked the charm of her store. Anyone could see that. It was also much farther away from Gertrude than Shakespeare. Still, tantrum or not, the encounter left a tiny sliver of ice in Sylvia's heart.

She couldn't dwell on it long, though, as she had urgent tasks to devote herself to, chief among them assembling Joyce's pages and getting them ready for Maurice Darantiere, for a planned publication date of fall 1921. She never imagined that this part of the process would be such a challenge, but the pages of the manuscript were scattered here, there, and everywhere, scrawled in Joyce's nearly illegible handwriting—in fact, she wondered if his failing eyes made seeing so difficult that he assumed his penmanship was better than it was. But she was spending untold hours poring over his handwritten drafts and comparing them to issues of *The Little Review* and *The Egoist* and finding all sorts of discrepancies she had to run by him before she could begin the equally arduous task of typing them onto clean pages for Darantiere.

It didn't help that his work made such important use of punctuation, paragraphing, subheadings, and the like. Every *p*, *q*, comma, and semicolon simply had to be correct for *Ulysses* to be appreciated for the work it was. "It's so ironic," she said to Adrienne, bleary-eyed one morning as she sipped strong coffee and smoked, "that some of the very things I love about this book should be the things that will drive me to insanity."

Adrienne laughed. "You are stronger than that, *chérie*." Nudging a plate of toast and homemade jam toward Sylvia, she added, "Keep your strength up."

Some nights, when she heard the stroke of midnight and her own eyes hurt from concentrating, and Adrienne had already gone to bed, Sylvia wondered if the one-third profit she finally settled on keeping was enough. As quickly as she thought them, she shoved those petty thoughts away, though. Profit was not her motivation; she needed to cover her costs, but any money she made would go straight back into Shakespeare and Company. It was not her goal to enrich herself, and a perfectly timed letter from her father reminded her of this:

> *Midwifery is as essential to God's plan as creation, for without those brave and selfless souls who usher new life into the world, no one could prosper. Carry on, daughter. Your mother and I are very proud of you.*

Just as she was nearing her wit's end, Cyprian returned to Paris to shoot a film. "In the nick of time!" exclaimed Sylvia, giving her sister a tight hug at the entrance to the store. It was so good to see a little bit of home in the midst of the new chaos of her life; her sister felt like a life preserver thrown to her at sea.

Once she was settled in a hotel in Montparnasse, they met at the Loup and over an early spring pea salad, Sylvia poured out her troubles. "I've tried doing some of the typing myself, to put everything into a coherent draft for the printer, but I simply don't have the time. Can you help, dear sister?"

Cyprian, expansive and flushed with happiness at being back in Paris with exciting screen work to do, clasped her sister's hands and said, "I would like nothing more. I'm a whiz at typing, you know.

Back in New York, I had to take some secretarial jobs, and believe me, no one has worse handwriting than an accountant under pressure from Wall Street."

Sylvia put her hands on her sister's cheeks and kissed her forehead. "I'm so relieved. Thank you."

"You should also think about getting an assistant for the store, if you don't mind my saying so. You look positively frayed around the edges. When was the last time you got a decent night's sleep? When was the last time you brushed your hair, for that matter? And I'm taking you shopping tomorrow for a new frock."

"I can't afford a frock, Cyprian. Especially if I'm going to hire an assistant, which I must admit I'd been thinking of myself." She had—for weeks now. An unfortunate side effect of publishing *Ulysses* was that by comparison, the day-to-day running of the store had begun to seem prosaic. It was exciting to throw herself into a project for which she had to learn so much—the ins and outs of printing, writing to bookstores and collectors and other writers for subscriptions to the novel, composing notices for newspapers so that they would report on the progress of the book, thereby garnering them free publicity. Which, she was amazed to discover, they did! A handful of local reporters had taken an interest in Joyce's book because it was banned; her publication of the "obscene" novel was equally interesting because it was the first book of Shakespeare and Company. The story even lured an American journalist named Janet Flanner, who filed stories with the *New Yorker* from Paris.

"It's a pity you're such a tiny little bird, or you could borrow some of my clothes," said Cyprian.

Sylvia smiled. "I still have your red shoes from the store's grand opening."

"Have you ever worn them again?"

"Once. To a show at Le Chat Noir."

Cyprian shook her head. "You're impossible. If your store becomes world famous, you'll have to let me dress you."

"Why? So you won't have to be embarrassed by your big sister if she's photographed for *Vanity Fair*?"

"Exactly."

"If you can get *Ulysses* properly typed, we'll take a trip to Printemps."

Cackling like a vaudeville villain, Cyprian said, "It's a deal."

But Cyprian had hardly begun typing when she stormed into Shakespeare and Company in a tizzy, distraught and sobbing with crumpled pages in her hands.

"I can't," she wailed.

Though the last thing she wanted to do was comfort her melodramatic sister, Sylvia reminded herself that Cyprian was doing her a favor, so she put her arms around her shaking form and cooed, "Darling sister, how can I help?"

"You can tell this Crooked Jesus of yours that it's no wonder he's going blind. *I'm* going blind and I can't take it anymore."

The nerviness of her sister's tone was foreboding, and Sylvia found breathing difficult for a moment. Even her sister couldn't help her. *Who am I to publish James Joyce?* She felt like an amateur. Entirely in over her head.

Desperate, she tried to convince Cyprian to continue. "I'm so sorry it's such a challenge . . . Could I pay you more? . . . Think of the bragging rights with the artists in the cafés . . . Your name will be in the most famous book in the world!"

But Cyprian was having none of it. "I need to *sleep*, Sylvia. I've been getting up at the crack of dawn to do this, and look at the bags under my eyes! I'm an *actress* for god's sake. I can't *look* like this."

Sylvia recognized this truculence and knew this was the end of the line with Cyprian.

When Cyprian left, Sylvia slumped over her desk in the quiet store. She couldn't help wishing it were her mother that was in Paris rather than her sister.

"Sylvia?"

She startled and looked up. She had thought she and her sister were alone, but there was her friend Raymonde Linossier, who lived in the neighborhood and was one of her earliest and most consistent customers. As a female doctor with her own practice nearby, she was a rarity and someone Sylvia deeply admired.

"Goodness, I'm sorry you had to hear all that," Sylvia muttered.

"I completely understand the vagaries of the sister-sister relationship." Raymonde smiled, and Sylvia wanted to cry.

"Also, I think I might be able to help," Raymonde went on. "You see, my father isn't well, and I've been caring for him many hours a day in his home. I've been reading and reading and reading, but I could do with a change of pace now and again. Perhaps I could type some of Joyce's pages? It would be an honor."

Sylvia's eyes widened. "I could never ask you . . ."

"Let's not be snobbish, Sylvia. Just because I am a doctor doesn't mean I cannot type."

"It's likely to be very frustrating work, as you saw . . ."

"I'm tough. I was one of two women in my science classes in medical school."

Sylvia beamed. "Well, then, let me show you what needs to be done."

Another Florence Nightingale to the rescue of Ulysses.

✺

Winter thawed into spring and the snow melted into puddles in which pigeons gloried in bathing on sidewalks and street gutters. On one of the first warm days, a very young, very handsome, and unmistakably midwestern young man entered the shop. He had hair the color of boot polish and a trim little mustache Sylvia assumed he kept to add some gravitas to his soft, practically adolescent face. Thick but compact, his physique made her think of the athletic boys of her youth who preferred throwing balls to reading books.

And like a well-trained child who'd been brought to church, he took off his worn tweed cap when he entered the shop and set about examining the shelves of novels and journals. It was a busy morning, and Sylvia watched him out of the corner of her eye as she rang up purchases and recorded books her regulars checked out of the library.

At last, just after Sylvia lit a cigarette behind her desk, he approached her and said, "Are you Sylvia Beach?"

This never got old, no matter how many times it happened: when a young American like this already knew who she was, it was such a compliment. And she felt a fizzy excitement, sensing she was about to hear a great story about how this newcomer had found out about her and her store.

Smiling widely, she took a puff of her cigarette, then set it down and thrust out her hand to shake his. "I am indeed. Pleased to make your acquaintance, Mr. . . . ?"

"Hemingway," he said eagerly. "Ernest Hemingway."

Well, he wasn't anyone she'd heard of yet, but still she sensed a story behind his arrival.

"Where've you come from, Mr. Hemingway?"

"Ernest, please. And Chicago, with my wife Hadley."

"You'll have to bring her next time. And likewise, call me Sylvia. So. What lured you to Paris, and Shakespeare and Company?"

"I've been hearing for a year that Paris is the best place for a writer to work. And by best I mean cheapest. So I managed to convince the *Toronto Star* to pay me as a correspondent. But I'll be working on my own stories, too. Maybe a novel. And Sherwood Anderson told me about your store. He raved about it, in fact, but I must say even his praise didn't do it justice." He looked around appraisingly and gratefully. "I had no idea," he marveled.

"It's just books and chairs," Sylvia said, though this young man's wonder pleased her.

"And Walt Whitman's own pages," he remarked, going back over to the framed sheets and looking so closely at the penciled scratches that his nose nearly touched the glass. "Any place presided over by Shakespeare and Whitman is meant for greatness," he said, still looking at the words in the frame.

"Many people struggle to understand the pairing," she observed.

Tearing his eyes away from Whitman to look at her with a studious and serious look, he replied, "Not me."

Sylvia felt an instinctive kinship with this Ernest Hemingway from Chicago. She introduced him to Bob McAlmon and another recent American in Paris, the composer George Antheil, both of whom wandered in a few minutes later, and the men became fast friends. She had the sense that some missing piece had been found and put into place.

She set Ernest up with a lending card, even though he hadn't come with enough money to secure it. "I trust you'll be back," she said.

"Thank you," he said, as if she'd given him a new bike on Christmas.

"And if you haven't yet secured permanent accommodations, I don't mind telling you that the store can serve as your post office box for as long as you need."

"Sylvia likes being a French foil to the American P.O.lice," Bob quipped.

Ernest frowned. "Yes," he grumbled. "Sumner's postal service is no friend to writers, that's for sure."

"Are you aware of the travails of our friend James Joyce?"

"Of course. I'm a newsman."

"Are you on the lam for incendiary writing as well, then?"

"Hardly," he said, and Sylvia had the sense from Ernest's grimace that his lack of persecution was maybe something he wanted to remedy.

"You're young. You have plenty of time," Bob said in a rare moment of letting someone off the hook.

"Say," said their new friend with a consciously subject-changing grin, "were either of you in the war?"

"Air Corps," said Bob, though without any pride. "George here was too young, more's the pity. He was in New York fraternizing with the selfsame editor who was convicted for serializing *Ulysses*."

"Margaret Anderson is a great lover of music," said George worshipfully, and not for the first time Sylvia wondered what had happened between the two of them. She'd heard that Margaret was as happily paired with her coeditor Jane Heap as Sylvia herself was with Adrienne, but one never knew in this set.

"Also," George said, making his voice a bit more stern, "Margaret was *after* the war. *During*, I was studying with Ernest Bloch."

"I drove an ambulance in Italy," said Ernest, wisely ignoring the spark of tension between the other two men.

"Gruesome work, I heard," said Bob.

"It certainly didn't keep me from being wounded. Mortar fire." He pointed down to his feet.

"Let's have a look," said Bob.

Sylvia had seen plenty of war injuries, but observing a healed one in her store was a first. Ernest's scars were many and pink, a scattering of stitched lines like macabre confetti on his foot, ankle, and calf.

"It's a wonder you don't limp," she said.

He shrugged. "It's all on the surface. Didn't get to the bone."

The store's bell jingled and in walked Adrienne.

"Monnier!" Bob exclaimed with great warmth. "The pleasures of this day just continue."

"*Mon amie*," said Sylvia, waving Adrienne over, "this is Ernest Hemingway, who just arrived in our fair city from Chicago. He was showing us his war injury. And, Ernest, this is Adrienne Monnier, who owns a shop very like this one but for French literature, on the rue de l'Odéon. In fact, her store was open all through the war, and is the reason Shakespeare and Company exists."

He stood and put his hand out to Adrienne, who smiled and pumped it vigorously.

"I've heard of your shop," said Ernest in excellent French. "It was going to be my next stop today."

"I'm happy to hear it, Monsieur Hemingway. I could help you this afternoon, but we are closed now for lunch."

He laughed. "Closed for lunch. I do love France. Well, I hope to see you there soon. And please, call me Ernest." Then, abruptly, he pulled his cap onto his head and said, "If you'll excuse me, I should see if Hadley needs anything. I'll bring her with me next time, I promise. She's the best reader I know."

When he'd gone, Sylvia did something she rarely even considered doing: she shooed everyone out of the store, proclaiming that for once she was going to observe the extended French lunch break. Then, arms chastely linked, she and Adrienne meandered down to their favorite bistro, where they shared a decadent steak and a carafe of wine.

"You know, I'm ashamed to admit it," said Sylvia, "but I've been feeling a bit bored in the shop lately, wishing I could concentrate entirely on *Ulysses*. But today reminded me of how much *fun* the store can be."

"Why should you be ashamed? There are days when I watch the

clock and I would swear an hour has gone by, but it's only been three minutes. It's normal."

"How do you overcome it?"

Adrienne shrugged. "You plan for more exciting moments."

"But the best ones are unplanned."

"It might seem that way, but it's not true. Ernest didn't come to Shakespeare by chance. He came because of the experience you provide American writers in Paris. He'd heard of you. The more experiences you provide, the more interesting people you'll attract."

"I've always wondered about opening a little tea shop above the store. A place where writers can drink and work in peace, near a library if they need it."

Adrienne smiled. "I love it. You must do it."

Where would I possibly find the time, though?

"Someday," she said, and she felt equal parts excited and exhausted thinking of it, looking down at her plate so she wouldn't have to see Adrienne's reaction to her ambivalence.

CHAPTER 11

Raymonde's father made a sudden and almost miraculous recovery, which meant that Raymonde herself could return to seeing patients—but she told Sylvia not to worry about the typing because she'd found a replacement for herself in the form of Mrs. Harrison, an Englishwoman who'd come to the store a few times with Raymonde and was keen to do the job. Sylvia hardly had time to exhale before calamity struck, however. On one of the first warm days of May, Mrs. Harrison hurried into Shakespeare and Company wringing a well-used handkerchief in her red hands.

"Oh, Sylvia, I'm so sorry," she said with a trembling voice.

Though the other woman's expression struck fear in her heart, Sylvia replied, "No, no, I should be thanking you."

"You won't when I tell you what happened."

"I'm sure we can fix whatever it is."

Breaking down in tears, Mrs. Harrison hiccupped out the story. "I was nearly . . . finished . . . the Circe episode. It was so good, but . . . but . . . but . . . I left it out on my desk . . . I'm sorry, I never should have . . . because . . . because . . . *my husband* came home and . . . he read it, and he *burned it. Both copies*." At this, she completely dissolved into tears.

"Both? Your typed copy as well as Joyce's draft?"

Mrs. Harrison cried and nodded.

"Oh, for heaven's sake," Sylvia snapped. "What is it with men and this book?"

"I'm so sorry, Sylvia."

"It's not you who should be apologizing."

This made Mrs. Harrison cry all the more. If she hadn't felt so fiery with anger, Sylvia might have cried herself—not with sadness, but with wit's-end exasperation. Would *Ulysses* never become a book? Would her own failure be the ultimate one to damn it to obscurity?

Joyce hasn't even finished it, she reminded herself. They'd already had to push the fall publication to winter. Joyce had promised to finish by mid-January so that the novel could be published by his birthday, February 2. He'd be forty that year, 1922. Something about this goal seemed to spur him on—so much so that he rarely even came to Shakespeare and Company these days, so intent was he on finishing. Sylvia hoped his eyes wouldn't fail him before he finished; he told her that most days after he stopped writing he spent the rest of the day in bed with cold compresses on his eyes.

As Mrs. Harrison cried, everything about *Ulysses* felt doomed.

When Sylvia finally convinced her to go to Raymonde's office to calm down, she sat smoking despondently, and Joyce himself made one of his infrequent appearances.

"I have some bad news," Sylvia said as he leaned his ashplant stick against the shelves and lowered himself into the green chair. She explained what had happened to his latest pages.

"Well, I suppose you'll just have to ask John Quinn for his copy."

Sylvia blinked, racking her brain.

John Quinn's copy?

Ah yes. She remembered now. Joyce had been sending duplicates of his drafts to Quinn from the beginning; he was buying them as if they were objets d'art. Wasn't it Ezra who'd told her that months ago? She'd entirely forgotten. Now, remembering, the fact of it presented Sylvia with more questions than it answered. Joyce had enough time—to say nothing of enough productive eyesight—to copy out duplicates of his chapters? How different would Quinn's pages be from those that Ezra had edited and were eventually printed in *The Little Review*? Why was John Quinn purchasing Joyce's novel, when he'd effectively denounced it as repulsive in a court of law? She didn't see much point in asking Joyce any of these questions; she often felt that the less she knew of his process the better.

"Well, this is excellent news," she simply replied. Then, once he'd gone and a dried-out Mrs. Harrison had been reassured that all hope was not lost, Sylvia wasted no time in writing to the lawyer.

> *Dear Mr. Quinn,*
>
> *I'm Sylvia Beach, and I run Shakespeare and Company, an English language bookstore and lending library in the sixth arrondissement of Paris. First, let me extend my admiration for your attempts to ensure a future for our dear friend James Joyce's* Ulysses *in the United States—which is my home as well as yours, as I was born in Maryland and grew up in Princeton, New Jersey.*
>
> *I, too, am a great admirer of James Joyce. He has become quite a fixture at Shakespeare and Company, and his* Portrait *is one of my favorite novels.* Ulysses *just might supplant it, which is why I offered to publish it when it became clear that American publishers could not.*
>
> *Putting together a complete manuscript is proving difficult, however, what with the seizures and Joyce's own labored process.*

It's come to my attention that you have a complete copy of the manuscript. I would be greatly indebted to you if you could send me your draft. I would of course reimburse you for expenses, and send the pages right back to you after we record them.

I do hope that if any of your travels bring you to Paris, you'll stop by the store. It would be wonderful to meet you in person.

I send you many thanks and wish you well.

Yours truly,
Sylvia

A month ticked by and no reply was forthcoming. Three more typists came and went, to work on the pages after the missing Circe episode, and she managed to send Monsieur Darantiere the first sections for typesetting, noting that there was a blank space to be filled when some pages arrived from America. When Darantiere sent the first set of pages back to her for proofing, she opened the wrapped package with hands so excited they actually shook. She was a publisher! Oh, and they were beautiful. The paper was crisp and white, the ink fresh and black. She ran her hand over them, and they felt cool and smooth, and made the most soothing sound under her fingers.

Joyce came to the store a day or so after they arrived, and Sylvia handed them to him with an eager smile. "Aren't they gorgeous?"

His eyes were so watery these days, she couldn't be sure, but she thought she saw tears cloud his vision even more. "My, my," he said in a hushed tone as he gently thumbed through the pages.

"You'll want to take them home, I assume? To make sure they are correct?"

It took him a minute or two to reply, he was so mesmerized by the pages. Finally he cleared his throat and said, "Yes, thank you."

It was a warm afternoon, and Sylvia took her cigarette to smoke just outside the entrance to the store. Joyce joined her on the step, and the two of them looked up and down the rue Dupuytren together.

"Any Leopolds today?" he asked.

"None yet."

This was one of her favorite games, played many times with Joyce on this very spot, and also at café tables on the sidewalks of the carrefour: Which passersby looked like Leopold Bloom, Stephen Dedalus, Gerty MacDowell, and other main characters from *Ulysses*? Since Joyce never described them in a conventional sense, their game was based more on feeling, on an air carried by someone walking past. Stephens were generally young, hungry, and tightly coiled; Leopolds were closer to middle age, more languid and nourished; Gertys were confident, unafraid to meet a gaze or cast one herself.

"I saw a very fine Leopold by the *école* on my way here today, in a once fine but slightly fraying overcoat, tapping a rolled-up newspaper against his leg."

"Have you seen any other ashplant sticks in Paris? I keep waiting for that to become a trend."

"My dear Miss Beach, some affectations are too unique to be adopted by the common man."

She chuckled, then gasped. "Look! A Molly Bloom."

Joyce fixed his gaze in the same direction as Sylvia's, at the tall woman with a figure like the body of a guitar walking down the street with—of all things—a red rose tucked behind her ear, amidst her long chestnut tresses.

"Good lord, she's even walking from the direction of the theater. Perhaps she's also an opera singer?"

"She must be."

"A good omen." Joyce lived for the opera. He was as familiar with Mozart and Rosetti as he was with Homer and Tennyson.

"Very good," Sylvia agreed just as the woman passed by the two of them at number eight, without so much as looking at them, but leaving behind her a cloud of strong, rose-scented perfume.

"Speaking of good signs, Adrienne and I have already received twenty replies to our letters asking for subscriptions to *Ulysses*, and that's in addition to the dozen we already took down from our favorite customers in Paris. People are very excited to finally read the work in its entirety. Including William Butler Yeats." Just thinking about sending James Joyce's opus to writers like Yeats gave Sylvia a fluttery feeling. "In fact, given how quickly we're receiving replies to our queries, I wouldn't be surprised if we need a second printing right away."

They had agreed to print one thousand copies in the first edition, one hundred of which would be signed and printed on the finest Dutch paper and cost 350 francs, and another hundred and fifty would be on vergé d'Arches paper and cost 250 francs. The rest would be on regular paper and cost 150 francs. All the editions would be bound in a blue paper cover lithographed in the precise color of the Greek flag—at least that was the plan. She and Maurice Darantiere had yet to find a dye that was right.

"Have you heard from Shaw yet?"

"Not yet, but I'm sure we will." Sylvia wasn't sure why Joyce was so concerned about George Bernard Shaw's reaction to their personal letter and plea for a subscription; he hadn't even wanted to solicit the great playwright from his own country, but Sylvia had insisted. "He doesn't like me," Joyce had warned.

"I'm sure he won't let that stand in the way of buying your book."

"Want to wager? If he replies and he's kind, or he makes the purchase, you win and I have to take you for lunch at Maxim's. If he never replies, or if his reply reflects his true and negative feelings about me, you have to take me for lunch."

"I can accept those terms."

They shook on it. Joyce smirked and said, "I can taste the turtle soup now."

While they waited on Shaw, Joyce spent time with the page proofs from Dijon. In just a few days, he returned to Shakespeare and Company with the pages covered in scribbles and scratches and whole sections x-ed out.

The once clean, crisp paper had become soft and gray under his hand. Her heart plunged in her chest. "Goodness, I hope he can make all these changes."

"I'm sure he can. I made changes to *Portrait* at this stage as well."

Still, Sylvia had a feeling she ought to go in person to speak to Maurice. He was already doing her the enormous favor of printing the novel speculatively, without any money up front.

"You must take him to a very fine lunch," advised Adrienne.

"Just what I need, another expense." Until money from paying customers came in for the novel, she had nothing to spare.

"It will be worth it. Maurice loves good food and wine. I know just the place in Dijon."

"Come with me?"

Adrienne tutted, then kissed Sylvia tenderly. "Of course."

Sylvia nervously smoked one cigarette after another the whole train ride, feeling disgusted with her smoke-sodden fingers but unable to stop. Then, when they stood before the wiry, tall printer with the brilliantined crow-black hair, among the humming and clanking iron machines in his workshop, Sylvia's mouth felt as dry as ashes. He greeted Adrienne like an old friend, with an embrace and two cycles of kisses on the cheeks, and one cycle for Sylvia, whom he was meeting for only the second time. At their first meeting a few months before, when she'd explained to him that he would be printing a novel that had been banned in the United States, his eyes had lit up mischievously and he'd said, to her intense relief, "So the work will be very interesting, *non*? *Bon*. I am not afraid of the American courts."

Today he said, "To what do I owe the pleasure of my two favorite *libraires rebelles*?"

"Does Petit Cochon still serve the best boeuf bourguignon in France?" Adrienne asked.

"Indeed it does, but I feel their coq au vin has surpassed it."

"Then let's order both."

Over the beef and chicken, both of which were delicious but Sylvia was hardly able to stomach, she finally showed Darantiere the pages.

He frowned down at them. "You were wise to order the Bordeaux," he said.

"We know how time consuming it is to set the type, and we are terribly sorry to have to ask for this many changes," Adrienne cooed apologetically, and Sylvia was so grateful for her longtime relationship with the printer. "But Joyce is a genius, to put it simply. And this book will be famous. *You* will be famous, as the man brave and skillful enough to print it."

Darantiere looked carefully at each page, his expression unchanged. Finally he set them aside and said, "If this continues, the job will cost more."

"How much more?" Adrienne asked. She and Sylvia had discussed this inevitability and come to a decision about how much extra Sylvia could afford to pay.

Thank god for Adrienne, Sylvia thought as she haggled brilliantly with the printer. It wasn't long until she wrangled him down to the right number, and Sylvia finally began to relax, though her first bites of coq au vin were cold.

Some of the best breaks from *Ulysses* came in the form of Ernest and Hadley Hemingway, both of whom stopped by Shakespeare and Company regularly. One of the first things Ernest did was insist on taking Sylvia and Adrienne to a boxing match in Ménilmontant. Sylvia had never been there before, and when Adrienne whispered to her in the snug metro car that it was a neighborhood where only lowlifes lived, Sylvia felt as thought she'd entered an exciting movie complete with nefarious characters and illicit deeds. Squeezing Adrienne's arm, she whispered back breathlessly, *"Quel frisson!"*

"Tu es terrible," Adrienne whispered back, though she smiled and leaned into Sylvia as she said it.

"Boxing is a tremendous metaphor for life," Ernest said as they sat down, he and Hadley making a companionable foursome with Sylvia and Adrienne. The small audience was a fascinating mix of clean-shaven men in bespoke suits alongside working-class Parisians in their berets, many of whom seemed to be arguing passionately with each other and pointing heatedly to the glowing ring around which everyone was seated; there were also far more women than Sylvia had anticipated, many in fine clothes and coiffures.

Sylvia became as absorbed in watching Ernest watch the fight as she became in the fight itself. It was almost as though the young writer were attempting to puppet the men in the ring, as he moved his shoulders and arms, fists clenched and making small jabs in the air, as he alternately muttered and shouted tips from the sidelines: "Don't drop your guard!" "Fists Up!" "Duck, you fool!" "Wait! Let him come to you!"

Adrienne occasionally covered her eyes with her hands, then peeked between her fingers when noses gushed blood and chests were gashed. "Scratches," pooh-poohed Ernest. Sylvia found herself surprisingly drawn in, the hard-eyed determination of the men with their wrapped hands in tight balls in front of their faces, and the cheering and jeering of the crowd around the ring. The boxers were so light on their feet! Sometimes it felt like watching a dance at a cabaret.

Hadley appeared to be as invested in the match as her husband. When she noticed Adrienne's more squeamish attraction to the spectacle, she said to Sylvia, "I was like that the first few matches Tatie brought me to. Now I can't tear my eyes away."

Apparently, Ernest had also enticed Ezra to the ring, because the next thing Sylvia knew, she was hearing about the two of them spending long, sweaty hours at a nearby gymnasium as the younger writer taught the older the finer points of pugilism. Occasionally she'd think to herself that it was too bad Gertrude was missing out on the fun being had by the Americans of Shakespeare and Company because of her feelings about Joyce, who'd befriended them all, at which point Sylvia would remember that Ernest and many of the others attended the salon on the rue de Fleurus with some regularity. It seemed Gertrude had taken Ernest under her wing; it mattered less to the grande dame that *he* was friends with *that Irishman* than that she was. Sylvia wondered how Ernest felt about being a protégé, this hotheaded former ambulance driver who seemed intent on showing the older writers what *he* knew about boxing, journalism, war, and life.

One thing she knew, which thrilled her: she'd find out how all the dramas in the crowd played out, because her store was rapidly becoming the Latin Quarter's vault of secrets and ambitions, hopes and fears. It was even beginning to make a bit of money, which she'd sent to her mother as repayment, and her mother had immediately sent back with a letter saying, "What I gave you was not a loan, darling girl. It was a gift. I cannot wait to read *Ulysses* in full."

"Shakespeare and Company is doing so well," Adrienne would brag on Sylvia's behalf to her own parents at Rocfoin, or to anyone else who'd listen.

"It's all because of you and La Maison," Sylvia would reply.

"Nonsense."

Sylvia didn't know why Adrienne's unabashed faith in her made her feel so queasy. While she could see the ways in which her own heart and talents were present in Shakespeare and Company, she was also keenly aware of its origins and the ways in which Adrienne propped her up every day. What was Shakespeare without La Maison? A half dream, a twin missing its sister.

But.

As long as they were together, perhaps none of that mattered.

CHAPTER 12

Dear Miss Beach,

Thank you for your inquiry. I am aware of your offer to publish Ulysses, *which I've only been purchasing because I think someday it might be of value. The pages themselves leave a smell in my drawer.*

I must say I think your foray into publishing as misguided as that of the Misses Anderson and Heap—and Miss Weaver, too, if I'm to complete the list of women bamboozled into ruining their lives for Ulysses.

My pages from Joyce are something closer to an artifact than anything resembling a useful draft; however, I see from your letter that despite their unfortunate shape, they amount to the only complete version of the manuscript in existence. As such, they are already more valuable than they were when I purchased them. Thus, I am afraid I cannot risk sending them abroad, especially in the current climate of search, seizure, and censorship.

Regretfully yours,
John Quinn, Esq.

Indignation rose to her mouth in the form of some choice French epithets for John Quinn, Esq., when Adrienne burst into the store wearing a flushed, thrilled expression.

"Shakespeare and Company can move across the street from La Maison!"

"No." She didn't dare hope. *Truly?*

"Yes! Monsieur Bousset at number twelve is leaving in July."

"Bousset? The antiques dealer?"

Adrienne nodded vigorously and they hugged tightly, and the two of them danced around the store. They had spoken so often of how wonderful it would be for their complementary stores to be closer together—not only to make their own journeys back and forth simpler, but for their customers' sakes as well. In many ways, La Maison and Shakespeare were one entity, and being on the same block would only make that plainer.

"Well, this certainly brightens my day, which I needed," Sylvia said, handing John Quinn's letter to Adrienne.

She read it, then replied, "It will be John Quinn who is bamboozled, and this letter smells far worse than anything Joyce has ever written about the less delicate bodily functions. Don't let this imbecile shake you, *chérie.*"

Sylvia smiled and raised her left eyebrow in the way that had come to mean, *I wish I could kiss you right now.* But alas, there were customers in the store who were strangers to them.

After making plans to see the new space on the rue de l'Odéon, Adrienne left, and Sylvia composed a reply to John Quinn, because much as she didn't want to so much as dignify him with a response, she did need those pages—and soon.

> Dear Mr. Quinn,
>
> I understand your reticence to send such precious cargo overseas, and I am terribly sorry I find it necessary to press the issue—but you could well be the savior of Ulysses! I have another suggestion: My mother lives very near New York City.

Would it be possible for her to come and copy the necessary pages
in your offices?

With thanks and apologies,
Sylvia

Depositing the letter in the postbox, she held her nose and her breath, hoping he and her mother would both agree to the arrangement.

✿

As spring heated into summer, Sylvia started to get anxious about the move to rue de l'Odéon. Of course it was the right thing to do, and she couldn't wait to be across the street from Adrienne, but how on earth would she accomplish the move, run the store, and keep current with Joyce's considerable edits, which page by page threatened to make Maurice Darantiere quit? Though subscriptions and down payments from eager readers came steadily in, Sylvia found herself constantly short on cash for anything related to *Ulysses*, especially as the cost of printing rose with every revision Joyce made. On top of all that, Joyce's eyes seemed to be failing faster by the day, and Sylvia feared she'd have to delay publication again, no matter how intent he was on having the book ready for his February birthday.

One sunny, stuffy morning in June, Giorgio and Lucia Joyce charged into the shop, flushed from the heat and the exertion of apparently running all the way to the shop from Valery Larbaud's apartment on a leafy courtyard just off the rue Cardinal Lemoine, which he'd lent to the Joyce family while he was away at the seaside for the summer months.

The gangly teenagers attempted to explain their sudden presence but only talked over each other in a loud and confusing cacophony. "Come, come, you two," said Sylvia, ushering them into the back room so they wouldn't disturb the browsers who no doubt had no idea that these were the children of a great writer, perhaps even the very writer whose words they sought on the shelves.

"All right, Lucia, you first," Sylvia said, hands on her hips and ready to listen intently.

"Papa's eyes are hurting him terribly, Miss Beach. Mama's been up all night tending them," the girl said, gulping air between phrases.

"Papa said that if there is one person who can help him, it's Miss Beach," added Giorgio.

"I wonder that he didn't say Mr. Pound."

"Oh, he and Mr. Pound had a row," said Lucia solemnly.

Sylvia had a feeling that the disagreement would be temporary. She'd come to feel that the two men were like brothers, constantly spoiling for a quarrel but ultimately willing to set aside their differences in the interest of the shared blood in their veins—in their case, literary blood.

"And Mama thinks Mr. Pound doesn't have Papa's best interests at heart," added Giorgio.

Of course.

"I have an idea." Sylvia snapped her fingers. "Run along and tell your parents I'll come by soon."

They sighed with audible relief, and she sent them on their way with a madeleine each, though she suspected Giorgio would have preferred a cigarette.

The most pressing question was how to escape the shop for a few hours. She'd been meaning to hire an assistant for some time, as she'd told Cyprian, and moments like this drove the point home to her. There was a sweet Greek girl named Mysrine Moschos who'd come by the other day and industriously told Sylvia that she was looking for a job and would be glad of an opportunity to work with books and writers. Sylvia could ill afford such a luxury, which was why she'd been dragging her feet on the task of hiring anyone. And yet, she could ill afford not to. Especially with the move looming. And Joyce, she was sure, would say Mysrine's nationality was auspicious at this moment when she was also attempting to locate the exact color of the Greek flag for the *Ulysses* cover.

She took it as a sign from her father's god that when she telephoned Mysrine that afternoon to ask if she could come and look after the shop while she stepped out for a few hours that the young woman was standing at her door in less than ten minutes.

"Thank you so much," Sylvia gushed, after giving a brief tutorial on the lending system and how to record a sale. "If anyone asks for anything else, take down their name, address, and telephone number if they have one, and inform them I'll be in touch soon. Or ask them with apologies from me to stop by tomorrow."

"Thank you for the opportunity," said the cedar-haired girl with such keen confidence that Sylvia left her shop with a burst of gratitude in her chest that balanced the unease in her belly. Never before had she left Shakespeare and Company in the hands of anyone other than Adrienne, and she had a feeling that what she felt was something akin to what a new mother must feel on leaving her baby with a nanny for the first time.

Fortunately, the oculist Dr. Louis Borsch was in his office that afternoon and willing to see her on short notice. She'd met him a few months before, when an irritated tear duct had sent her to his nearby clinic for students and similarly underfunded patients, and he'd prescribed a drop that had brought her overnight relief. Even then, his skill had made her wonder about introducing him to cloudy-eyed Joyce, and so she'd made sure to write down his name and regular office address on the rue de la Paix.

What was more amazing, and flattering, was that Dr. Borsch

remembered her. "Of course I remember the enterprising American with the bookshop," he said when she introduced herself again. "I'm only sorry I haven't had a chance to patronize your establishment myself."

"I shall be there whenever you find the time," she assured him. "Today, though, you have an opportunity to help one of my most illustrious customers. James Joyce is an Irish writer of considerable acclaim."

He nodded and said, "I'm aware of his book *Dubliners*."

"I'm so glad to hear that. Well . . . you see, he has a terrible affliction of the eyes, which naturally disturbs his writing. It's gotten bad enough for his children to come to my shop this morning to implore my help."

"Has he another doctor?"

"He's had other doctors in Europe, and I think there's one here in Paris, but there must be a reason they sent for me and not him."

"Regretfully, I cannot pay a house call to a patient who isn't already in my care. But if you can get him here, I'd be happy to see him right away."

Sylvia hurried to the rue Cardinale Lemoine. After climbing the narrow wooden staircase, she arrived to find the usually light and airy apartment close and smelling of many sour and pungent body odors as well as antiseptic, even with all the windows wide open.

Mrs. Joyce's cheeks were red when Sylvia found her at her husband's bedside, changing a damp compress on his eyes. When she saw her at the door, she didn't alter her movements, but said in a tremulous voice, her Irish accent adding to the pathos of the scene, "Thank heaven you've come, Miss Beach. He's been in and out of sleep and in pain all night and day. I simply didn't know what to do. It's worse than it's ever been."

"Miss Beach is here, darling?" Joyce asked meekly, barely above a whisper.

"She is, my dear. Just as you said she'd be."

Sylvia was touched by this scene of domestic tenderness, and all her questions about the hitherto seemingly mismatched man and wife were suddenly and forcefully answered.

Sylvia crossed the threshold, feeling as she did that she was intruding even though she'd been invited. In a quiet, even tone she said, "I've been to visit a premier oculist. Dr. Louis Borsch. He trained in Vienna with the best surgeons and now spends much of his time helping those who couldn't normally afford services such as his. Like me, when I went to his clinic months ago." Sylvia had rehearsed this speech on her walk from the office, wanting to make sure to appeal to Mrs. Joyce's pragmatic side while also assuring Mr. Joyce he was getting the best.

"Will he be able to visit us soon, then?" asked Mrs. Joyce, holding her husband's hand inches above his chest.

"Unfortunately, he cannot make a house call before he's been officially engaged as Mr. Joyce's doctor," she said, layering as much regret into her tone as she thought prudent. "But if Mr. Joyce can stand and walk a bit, we can take a taxi the short distance to his office."

Like Lazarus—or perhaps more like their very own Crooked Jesus than ever—Joyce rose from his sickbed moments after hearing Sylvia's words. "Nora, my love, will you fetch me my coat?" he said, and Mrs. Joyce hastened to pluck it off a hook at the other end of the room and help him into it. His movements were those of a nearly or completely blind person who'd learned long ago to function with the help of others.

"You rest, now," he said, somehow knowing exactly where to deposit a kiss on his wife's forehead, which she received with closed, exhausted eyes.

Mrs. Joyce put her husband's hand into Sylvia's, and the two of them made their way down the stairs and into the dim late afternoon light.

Goodness, I hope Dr. Borsch is still in his office, thought Sylvia.

By some stroke of luck, he was. Sylvia wished heartily she'd brought a book with her—she was in the middle of *Three Soldiers* by a promising American writer named John Dos Passos, whom Ernest had recommended—so that she could entertain herself in the little wooden chairs of the still, spare waiting room.

At last Dr. Borsch called her in to join them in his tidy examining room, which had a great deal more instruments than the clinic to which Sylvia had gone when she first met him. She listened as Dr. Borsch explained the dangerously advanced state of Joyce's glaucoma, concluding that "although an operation might fix it, I wouldn't advise it. The risks are too high. Any number of things could go wrong, and I'd like to keep watching this develop, and see if with time and care we can help Mr. Joyce without anything as invasive as surgery."

"Thank you, Doctor," said Joyce, in the hardest Irish accent Sylvia had ever heard him use, his long-fingered hand on his heart. "My last oculist in Zurich felt that surgery would be the only way forward if I ever had a bout of iritis as wretched as this. So I'm grateful for your more conservative prescription."

"Doctors do disagree," said Dr. Borsch judiciously. "I wouldn't blame you if you wanted a third opinion."

"The opinion of Miss Beach's doctor is more than good enough for me," he said, and Sylvia felt gratitude double the size of her heart.

Which reminded her for the first time in hours: How was Mysrine doing? How was her store doing? Worry gave her goose bumps and made her refuse the tea and biscuits Nora offered her when she delivered Joyce back to Larbaud's apartment.

But she needn't have worried. It had been a slow afternoon, and Mysrine had taken messages and rung up sales exactly as Sylvia had described. She'd even dusted the shelves. Sylvia hired the young woman on the spot. "I'll see you at ten tomorrow morning."

Her first employee. Such an accomplishment!

But when she told Adrienne about her day and its successes at dinner, she'd narrowed her eyes at Sylvia and said, "I am very glad you have hired an assistant, but . . ."

Sylvia let a moment or two slip by, watching Adrienne struggle to find words before saying, "What is it? You know you can say anything to me."

"But I have already said it."

"What?"

"That he is a very great writer but not . . . a great man."

Was that what she'd said? When they first talked about her publishing *Ulysses*? Sylvia remembered Adrienne's warning as more . . . charitable. The frustration now plain on Adrienne's face made Sylvia nervous.

"Does it matter if he is a great man?"

Adrienne shrugged and made that infuriatingly French *pfft* sound with her perfect lips. "Not to anyone other than us."

"Does it?" Sylvia truly wasn't sure if it did. Or why.

Adrienne hung her head and shook it. Then, dragging her eyes to Sylvia's, she said, "It doesn't have to."

Sylvia was genuinely confused. Was it possible that Adrienne was jealous? But she knew she'd never been attracted to men. She was consumed with a need to reassure her love.

Reaching out her hand and tucking a lock of dark hair behind her ear, then using her thumb to stroke Adrienne's cheek, Sylvia said, "No one could come between us. Not in my heart."

Adrienne closed her eyes and kissed her, then whispered, "It's not your heart I fear, *chérie*." And even though Sylvia wasn't sure she understood Adrienne's point, she was relieved the conversation seemed to have reached a conclusion. Kissing Adrienne with more intention, Sylvia vowed to think more on the matter, and make sure nothing came between her and the woman who had changed her life for the better.

❧

John Quinn's next reply contained a surprise. *I simply cannot part with the pages, but I shall be in Paris to see the new Picassos at the end of the month and will bring them with me.*

Well, thank you, Picasso, thought Sylvia. *Joyce and I owe you a great debt.* Thinking of the Spanish artist reminded Sylvia of Gertrude, and she decided to jot off a note of hello in the hopes of starting the process of wearing her down, killing her with kindness.

Just a few days after Quinn's letter, Sylvia received another from Margaret Anderson of *The Little Review*, in response to a query about which bookstores in America would be most amenable to carrying Joyce's banned novel. Anderson replied with a cleverly annotated list of shops, and Sylvia found herself laughing and feeling as though the other woman were standing right there in Shakespeare and Company, telling her these tidbits of American publishing gossip instead of scrawling them with a fountain pen. Her thoughts on a shop in Chicago were especially funny:

> *The owner is typically middle western in his preference for overdone steak but this can be overlooked in light of the fact that he relishes to the point of violence blood in his literature.*

At the end of the long missive, she added:

> *I have heard that John Quinn will be in Paris soon. I hope for your sake he avoids you, as his opinion of you isn't much higher than his opinion of me or Jane. He's a terrible snob and*

hates Washington Square—my dear home!—with a passion he
reserves for anything not entirely sanitized and homogenous. I
once overheard him refer to my own street as a urinal. A urinal!
I believe what he meant was a toilet, as women don't use
urinals, but why quibble with a man like that? It's a good thing
I have a healthy sense of humor. But I suppose I'm being an
ungrateful wretch, as he did take our case pro bono. One can
only wish he'd actually listened to us about how to defend Joyce's
book. Oh well, I am happy to pass the baton of those problems to
you. I hope you don't mind. It's not as bad as I've made it sound,
and I sense that you, too, have a superior sense of humor. Which
you'll need, ho ho.

Sylvia immediately penned a reply of thanks and reassurance: "I shall enthusiastically carry the baton to the finish line, and I'm so grateful to you and Jane for the legs of the race you've completed in such style."

The remainder of June rushed forward at a considerable clip, what with overseeing Joyce's appointments with Dr. Borsch; exchanging pages with him, the typists (the most recent of whom was an excited and very pregnant Julie), and Darantiere; and preparing the new location of Shakespeare and Company on the rue de l'Odéon—shelves had to be built, scrubbing had to be done, paint had to be applied, books moved, and questions fielded. The weeks of paying two rents nearly doubled the number of cigarettes Sylvia smoked in a day out of nerves and fear of bankruptcy.

Adrienne refused to let Sylvia buy any groceries or pay for anything when they went out. Still, she was on her last few hundred francs. She wasn't even sure how she was going to pay Mysrine in a week or two.

"I feel terrible about not contributing more," Sylvia said as she and Adrienne ate another simple meal of omelets and salad.

"Everyone needs help sometimes," Adrienne said. "And it will all be worth it to have you on the Odéon. Together, we will be able to help even more writers, which will ensure the success and solvency of your store. Soon you'll be able to open that tea shop as well."

"I hope so."

"Why do you doubt so much?"

Sylvia sat back in her chair, looked at her partially finished meal, and said, "Have you ever wondered if you were doing the right thing?"

"With La Maison? No, never. It has brought me more happiness than anything else in my life. It's brought me friends, and literature, and you. I thought you felt the same way about Shakespeare." There was a petulant, impatient edge to Adrienne's voice.

"I do," Sylvia assured her. "I'm just worried about the money, that's all."

"The money will come," she said emphatically. "And in the meantime, do not worry about relying on me a little. I love you, *chérie*. I am happy to help you."

No one other than her mother had ever expressed a sentiment like that to Sylvia, and it gave her a gasping pain in her heart. She missed her mother. Was it even right to depend on Adrienne this way?

⁂

The day John Quinn turned up, unannounced, at 8 rue Dupuytren, Sylvia was very glad that Ernest and Bob happened to be there to help her carry boxes between that address and her new one at 12 rue de l'Odéon, which smelled thrillingly of sawed wood, fresh paint, and the bouquets of lilies and roses brought to her by excited friends like Michel and Julie, Raymonde Linossier, and George Antheil.

The tall, handsome lawyer with the meticulously clipped hair and clean-shaven face handed a sheaf of papers to Sylvia and said, "I'd like these back before the week's end."

With an enormous sense of relief, she skimmed the familiar lines in Joyce's hand, flipping through the pages until she saw it—*yes*, the lost Circe episode was there! "The end of the week won't be a problem," she replied.

John Quinn put his hands on his belt and frowned. "I hope your new store is larger than this. You really sold books here?"

"Indeed, it's quite a bit bigger," said Sylvia, trying to stay positive but feeling the anger that she'd shored up from reading each of his letters.

"Good. We can't have Joyce published by such a small institution."

"So his book is repulsive but large?" Bob interjected without looking at Quinn, stacking one box atop another. Ernest was on the other side of the room, packing as much as he could into another box while he listened and smirked at Bob's vulgarity.

"I'll thank you not to remind me of the trial," said Quinn. "It was a grave disappointment."

"For all of us," said Bob, lifting the boxes and carrying them out of the store as Sylvia stifled a laugh.

"I'll overlook his sarcasm in light of his labors," Quinn said.

"Oh, he's always delightfully sarcastic," said Sylvia.

"He's a favorite of the editrixes, is he not?"

"Miss Anderson and Miss Heap? I believe so."

"They would be right at home here," Quinn said. "I'm surprised they haven't come to visit."

"I hope they will someday, but I understand they don't make much money with their journal."

"Because they keep making absurd choices."

Such as to accept your counsel?

"In fact, Miss Beach," he went on, "I hope you won't make the same mistakes that they did. You must keep Joyce in line. I understand he's troubling you with endless revisions?"

"Oh, it's no trouble at all." It was such a pleasure to lie to this man.

"Ezra says otherwise."

"Dear Ezra likes to look out for me. He's like a brother that way, which is nice because I only have sisters."

"It seems to me that Joyce needs a firm hand to steer him on the right course. I'll say something to him."

"You can say anything you like to Mr. Joyce, but please don't say anything on my behalf. We get along quite well, and I approve of his work on *Ulysses*. As his publisher."

Quinn folded his arms over his chest and looked down on Sylvia from his considerable height. "You sound just like Margaret Anderson."

Sylvia lengthened her posture as much as her petite frame would allow and replied, "I take that as the highest praise."

"I think you'll find that Sylvia knows exactly what she's doing," said Ernest as he heaved a box onto his shoulder, startling Sylvia; she'd forgotten he was in the room with them.

"Would you like to come with us to our new location?" she chirped to John Quinn, heartened by her friend's defense. "Perhaps you'll feel better about things on l'Odéon."

He followed Ernest and Sylvia into the searing summer sunshine and looked around at the neighboring shops appraisingly. It wasn't a neighborhood with art galleries and fine restaurants, thought Sylvia, which was surely what he was used to in Paris. The Latin Quarter was much more like Washington Square, and Sylvia remembered what Margaret had written about Quinn's opinion of that part of New York City. *A urinal.*

"Much better," he pronounced the larger store with its new shelves and swept floors, using a wrinkled handkerchief to mop sweat from his high forehead.

Sylvia shook her head and told herself to be glad he'd brought the missing pages of *Ulysses*. She had to hide her laughter behind her hand when Ernest put a box in Quinn's hands and said, "We could use another set of strong hands. Can't have the women doing all the lifting, can we, sir?"

※

Shakespeare and Company squeaked by with fewer than twenty francs in the kitty after she paid the final rent on Dupuytren and the second installment on her new Odéon location.

And though it gave her a crook in her neck, she had to tell Mysrine that she couldn't pay her that week. "I promise to pay you double next week."

"I understand," the girl said. "I have seen the ledger, so I know."

"Thank you," Sylvia whispered thickly, guilt ridden—though she knew she'd done nothing wrong. Not exactly. She'd been turning down invitations for drinks and dinners for weeks because she knew how much money she'd have to spend on those nights at the Dôme or Monocle. She hardly had time anyway, as she was spending long hours organizing the new shop. "I wish I could, but I'm too busy" had become a chorus for her. Every night she lay down in bed, her back and legs and arms sore from the bending, lifting, and pushing.

When a substantial check from Bob's wife, Bryher, arrived in the mail from Italy, where she was traveling with H.D., Sylvia almost broke down in the store in tears of shame and gratitude. The amount was ostensibly for three copies of *Ulysses*, but Bryher had far overpaid, and in her letter she acknowledged as much:

> *Sylvia, dear, I lost your letter saying how much each copy costs, so if I haven't paid enough, please let me know. If, on the other hand, I've sent too much, I refuse to hear a word about it.*

When Bob came into the store a few days later, she took him aside and whispered, "Thank you."

His smile was broad and unfettered. "We publishers need to stick together, eh? I think you're doing an amazing thing. And I believe in karma."

She threw her arms around him and hugged him tightly, swallowing down the threatening sobs. He squeezed her to him in return.

"Might I recommend a *convenient* marriage like mine? A spouse with a large trust is capital, if I may say so."

Sylvia laughed and brushed a few tears away from her eyes. "You may, Bob. You may say anything you like." *Though I happen to know your marriage is more complicated than convenient.* She could hardly keep track of the competition between Bob and Bryher and H.D.; the three of them swapped beds like it was going out of style.

"I always do, don't I?"

Laughing harder at this and hugging him again, she said, "Thank goodness. And I'm sure your Contact Editions will be a huge success." Bob's own publishing venture, backed by Bryher, was coming along nicely; William Carlos Williams had already promised his next book of poems, and Ernest was considering a book of stories.

Though most subscribers to *Ulysses* wouldn't pay in full until they received their copy, Sylvia was heartened to see more and more orders from their local French and American friends as well as—exhilaratingly—writers and other important figures abroad like T. S. Eliot, T. E. Lawrence, Winston Churchill, and Wallace Stevens. Even American publishers like Ben Huebsch and Alfred Knopf, who'd refused to publish it, wanted one of her Paris editions for their private collections.

And at last they heard from George Bernard Shaw, who wrote a long letter to Sylvia explaining why he would not be purchasing

Ulysses, because he'd read parts of it in the journals and concluded that it is "a revolting record of a disgusting phase of civilization," and that even though "I have walked those streets and know those shops . . . I escaped from them to England at the age of twenty." In his and Joyce's shared home country of Ireland, he proclaimed, "they try to make a cat clean by rubbing its nose in its own filth," which appeared to be Joyce's project in his novel. But Sylvia's favorite part of the letter was its conclusion: "I am an elderly Irish gentleman, and if you imagine that any Irishman, much less an elderly one, would pay 150 francs for such a book, you little know my countrymen."

Joyce read and reread the letter amid the boxes of books and bric-a-brac that she and Mysrine had been unpacking all day in the new address on the rue de l'Odéon.

"It appears you owe me lunch," he said.

"I don't know about that," said Sylvia. "His letter might be full of criticism, but he obviously thinks you're a writer of enough note to spend this much time explaining why he won't be buying your book. Also, it's hilarious." She'd been giggling over his turns of phrase all morning. Striking a theatrical pose with one arm overhead, she attempted a thick Irish accent in a gruff voice to say, "I am an Irish *gentleman*. Hem-hem. Gentleman, I say."

Lucky the cat jumped out of one of the boxes and then padded over to Sylvia, who laughed and scooped him up and touched her nose to his, and said, "Lucky, what do you say to Mr. Bernard Shaw, Irish gentleman?"

Joyce smiled. "You sounded just like him."

"And yet we've never met."

Fondling Lucky in the soft fur between his ears, she said, "Lunch it is, then. Maxim's, correct? Except it will have to wait until my funds replenish."

"I am the soul of patience."

"We have other victories to toast as well," she said, feeling light of heart for the first time in weeks. It helped to have Joyce in the store, to remember that he was real, his book was real and a masterpiece, and she was going to publish it. "Larbaud wrote me that he is hard at work on the French translation and hopes to do a reading at Adrienne's in the fall, and . . ." She paused for maximum dramatic effect. "Monsieur Darantiere is hot on the trail of the perfect Greek-flag blue for the cover! One of his associates in Germany claims to have the perfect dye, and he needed to go there anyway on business so he said he'd investigate."

"Saint Cajetan is smiling down on us."

"My saints are a bit rusty, having been raised Presbyterian."

"Patron saint of good fortune. And Argentina."

She laughed. "Does that mean Argentina is full of people with good luck?"

"Perhaps Mrs. Joyce and I should go and find out. I have read that it is a beautiful country."

Though she was loath to do it, she said, "To return to the subject of Darantiere, I think I should warn you that all the revisions you're making have increased the printing costs substantially. I don't mind for myself, but I do think you should know that there might not be any profits if all the subscription money goes toward resetting the type."

He sighed—Sylvia had noticed lately he was a great sigher—and replied with a shrug, "It's more important that it be right than we be rich."

Her thoughts exactly.

Though, in that case, why had he wagered lunch at Maxim's?

CHAPTER 13

~❖~

In the week between the Fourth of July and Bastille Day, before Paris was drained of every last friend who headed to the cool of the seaside or mountains for the long, hot remainder of the summer, Shakespeare and Company reopened in its new location across from La Maison des Amis des Livres.

Valery Larbaud returned to Paris from Vichy for the occasion, and all of Sylvia and Adrienne's closest friends came to raise a glass of champagne and wish her well as the shadows lengthened on the street, and a breeze blew down from the Théâtre de l'Odéon. The block was so crowded with French and American writers and readers, artists, musicians, locals, and expatriates, "one could be forgiven for mistaking this for a new exhibition at the Louvre," twittered Adrienne.

They clinked glasses and Sylvia said, "You've outdone yourself," glancing over at the table groaning under the bounty of summer fruits, beautifully trimmed and cut into little animals, or arranged like flowers; many cheeses and breads and *saucissons* and salads, and the pièce de résistance, an enormous two-layer cake in the shape of two books: *The Autobiography of Benjamin Franklin* and Walt Whitman's *Leaves of Grass*. Sylvia had heard Adrienne cursing at the fondant many times in the last two days, and she'd had to store the final products in Michel's freezer, but they were stunning. "Thank you," Sylvia whispered with as much suggestion as possible in Adrienne's ear.

Cyprian was in her element, bestowing her long-lashed attention on only the most famous of the guests. Hadley and Ernest held hands and laughed and talked with everyone, as Ernest filled glasses with golden wine from chilled bottles and informed everyone, "I finished another story last week!" Julie waddled about, holding her back to support her protruding belly, though Michel looked anything but happy, his eyes tired and his posture slumped. Sylvia didn't want to pry, but hoped one or both of them would visit her soon so she might ascertain what was happening and whether she could help in any way.

Bob got drunk quickly, and Bryher, who'd just arrived in town, barely sipped her champagne. Both of them watched with jealous eyes as the vivacious dark-haired H.D. flirted with everyone else, oblivious to her two lovers' reactions—and to Ezra's, as he too had once had a youthful dalliance with the poet. The spectacle made Sylvia all the more grateful for the steadiness of her love with Adrienne. They didn't stay up until quite one in the morning anymore, but they talked and laughed endlessly and knew precisely how to please each other in bed; Sylvia treasured the moments when Adrienne's breathing grew ragged and raspy, her fingers pulling hard on Sylvia's hair as pleasure pulsed through her body.

Mrs. Joyce handed Sylvia a lovely pot of coral-colored geraniums. "For your front step," she said. "And thank you for Dr. Borsch. He is an absolute lifesaver. Mr. Joyce is so much more relaxed in his care."

"You are very welcome. I am relieved as well."

"Now if only I could get him to teach again."

"I hope he won't need to teach once *Ulysses* is published," Sylvia replied.

Mrs. Joyce shook her head. "Teaching is a *respectable* profession."

Sylvia laughed to herself to note how much alike Mrs. Joyce and John Quinn sounded in their stalwart conventionality—and yet how tangled they each were in the life of one of the least conventional of writers.

Joyce came over and slid his arm around his wife's waist and offered her a glass of ice water, and the way she leaned on him reassured Sylvia that no matter what Nora said, her love was unwavering.

"Congratulations, Miss Beach," he said, surveying the cheerful scene before them, "on your very own Stratford-on-Odéon."

She clapped her hands and gasped. "What a wonderful name!"

Even Mrs. Joyce added, with an approving nod, "There is something of the Globe about it."

If that wasn't a baptism, she didn't know what was.

Adrienne coined an equally delicious term for their little strip of Paris: Odeonia. Sylvia loved both of them, the way her lover's and her writer's names sounded in her ear and felt in her mouth as she said them.

Stratford-on-Odéon.

Odeonia.

Adrienne's had the benefit of being the same in English and French, and while hers had a timeless, mythical quality to it, Joyce's yoked the French and American stores into something as important to the history of letters as the writer for whom her shop was named.

She noticed, however, that while Sylvia used both nicknames interchangeably, glorying in them both, Adrienne never used Joyce's term. And he never used hers.

Shortly after the opening, Paris emptied out, and replies to her queries about *Ulysses* dried up—temporarily, she hoped—while people enjoyed their summer holidays. At least she had a free summer retreat of her own to visit: Adrienne's parents' house in Rocfoin, where they decided to stay until September. She closed the store until her return to save on expenses; Mysrine would occasionally check on things, sort the mail, and fulfill requests while forwarding correspondence that required Sylvia's attention. Sylvia had just enough money left from Bryher and the sales she made at her opening to stay afloat a few weeks.

Out of the city, Sylvia tried to fill her days with as many physically taxing activities as possible: long hikes through the woods and hills, chopping wood and fetching water, exploring nearby towns with their Roman and medieval ruins, and reading, reading, reading for hours at the end of every day. She found that if she wasn't tired enough at night, she woke in the darkness with her heart racing and a damp spot on the sheets where her body had lain. *Is Joyce all right? How are his eyes? Surely Dr. Borsch or Mrs. Joyce would contact me if he took a turn for the worse? Will he finish in time for the February release? What will I do if I run out of money? Am I out of money already—what if my sums weren't correct? What if Gertrude never comes back to the store? Will the Greek blue from Germany be right? What if it's not?* And on and on. She could be up for hours worrying and speculating, then the next day would feel like a forced march until she accidentally fell asleep in the shade with a book on her lap before dinner, and the whole process would repeat itself.

"Sylvia, you must stop worrying like this," Adrienne said one morning as they lay in bed, listening to the birds greet the sun.

"But I've put everything into Joyce's book. What if it fails?"

"What if it does? You'll still have Shakespeare and Company, and Odeonia is much more than *Ulysses*."

"I just don't want to fail."

"I know you don't. And it won't. But if it does, the failure will be his, not yours."

She wasn't so sure about that.

⚜

Returning to Paris in September, she felt as though she could breathe freely for the first time in weeks, knowing she would soon be among the many friends who would help her make sure *Ulysses* didn't fail. On the Monday morning she threw open the creaky shutters to her store and immediately saw a new arrangement of books and journals for the window in her mind's eye, she felt the knots in her shoulders loosen.

She was assembling that very display, taking care not to get cinders from her cigarette on the books, when Joyce arrived twirling his ashplant stick and looking finer than he had in ages. They hugged in greeting, and he asked to hear all about her holiday, which she obliged as much as she could before being unable to help herself: "Now you must tell me what's happening with *Ulysses*."

"Well, I spent most of August in bed, so much so that the calluses on my fingers from holding the pen began to heal. But do not fear, my dear Miss Beach, for I was thinking about *Ulysses* the whole time, moving it around in my mind, piece by piece, and imagining the way to end it. Then miraculously, about a week ago, I woke up able to see. As if I'd drunk the water at Lourdes. I took out a fresh piece of paper, filled my pen with ink, and began writing. I don't know when I've ever written so much or so quickly."

"Have you been doing it in the sun? Your skin looks so brown and healthy."

"Indeed. There is the most lovely bench in the courtyard of Larbaud's place, and I found it perfectly conducive to writing. Until that bitch dog chased me off. Fortunately, she was very regular, and I learned to go to the Dôme to finish around three in the afternoon. By six, I was usually joined by Mr. Hemingway or Mr. McAlmon."

"Sounds like a perfect week."

"Today I eschewed the Dôme for you, as I thought I heard a whistle in the air that sang of your return."

"Oh, it had nothing to do with the letter I wrote you last week?"

"Nothing whatsoever."

They grinned at each other, and Sylvia felt light and happy. "I've missed you. Let's see if Molly or Leopold is out today, shall we?"

"Let's," he agreed, and they went to the entrance to look out.

Adrienne happened to be sweeping her own front step, and she waved. "I just saw Buck Mulligan go by!"

"Buck! We haven't seen him in ages, poor old chap," said Joyce.

"Glad to see you out and about," Adrienne observed from across the street.

"Never better," he said.

Adrienne cocked her head and gave Sylvia a look that said, *See? All is well,* and Sylvia kissed her index and middle fingers and waved the *baiser* across Odeonia.

Autumn's pace was as brisk as the weather, and for more than just Sylvia. Larbaud was so busy he couldn't continue with his translation of *Ulysses,* though he promised to finish the essay he was writing about the novel for the illustrious *Nouvelle Revue-Française,* part of which he'd give as a lecture at La Maison later that fall—though, ironically, it was that deadline that was keeping him from the translation. "Please forgive me. I love Joyce's work too much not to give it my fullest attention. And I have a suggestion for you in any case. What about Jacques Benoist-Méchin?"

"Well, he's not you, but he does do lovely translations," Sylvia replied, relieved that Larbaud had solved this problem for her so she wouldn't have to give it any more thought. Benoist-Méchin was a regular in Adrienne's store, an honorary *potasson*, so Sylvia had known him for years. He was quite young, but gifted with languages—he spoke and read French and English and German like a native in each tongue. In some ways, he was a better choice than Larbaud, though she'd never say that to her friend.

"I am honored you would consider me," Benoist-Méchin said to Sylvia in Shakespeare, holding his beret in his nervous hands. "Joyce's work is revolutionary."

With a hearty American handshake, Sylvia said, "I couldn't be happier you want the job. I can't lie, though, it won't be easy."

"Even better."

What a relief. Someone who wanted to rise to the challenge!

With nearly all one thousand of Darantiere's first planned print run sold to a combination of individual readers and rebellious American bookstores, Sylvia had lately turned her attention to reviews and—she could hardly believe it—smuggling.

"I'm about to become a bootlegger," she said to Adrienne, Larbaud, Rinette, and Fargue at a dinner party in October. "Though perhaps a better term is booklegger!" She laughed uproariously but alone, and she quickly realized that her French friends didn't get the pun. "A bootlegger sells illegal liquor in America," she explained, "so a *book*legger sells illegal books."

"Ahhhhhhh," they sighed and laughed approvingly.

"I can't use the post office," she mused. "Though for individual buyers, I can use a private postal service once the books are over the border. The question of how to supply the Washington Square Book

Shop and others like it with the stacks they've ordered is another thing entirely."

"Once they have the book, how will they sell it? They can hardly put it on display," asked Fargue.

"I assume they'll have some covert way of letting certain customers know they have copies in a back room. But that, as they say, is not my problem."

Fargue rubbed his hands together and said with a wicked smile, "What a wonderful story unto itself. *The Banned Book and the Bathtub Gin*." He pronounced the title in heavily accented English, to the general amusement of the group.

Even with Mysrine to help, the new store was so busy, it kept Sylvia from thinking enough about the smuggling problem. Not only was there the book business and library, but Shakespeare and Company had become the central hub of all tourist and expat information on Paris for the hundreds of Americans visiting for any length of time, from a week to a year or more. Every day, her friends brought more friends, and strangers arrived with letters of introduction or her address scribbled on a napkin or scrap of paper. They came for everything from mail services and accommodation requests to information on the opera, ballet, and museums.

They also came to spy. Sylvia came to know the furtive look well: while pretending to read a book or journal, the Americans' eyes would roam far from the page, inspecting every face in the store in search of James Joyce, who was a regular in the shop as they'd no doubt learned from one of the many articles popping up in French and American publications about the progress of the Irish writer's banned book.

To her private delight, Joyce was often in plain sight, sitting on the green chair or in a corner of the library room. She would never, ever offer him up to a stranger, and forbade Mysrine from greeting him by name when the store was busy. Since he was in on the joke, Joyce started to arrive with little more than a wink in Sylvia's direction, and a twitch of a smile when he heard a couple say to each other, "I wonder if James Joyce is here." Sylvia wished they'd look less and buy more, but sales were up just enough to set her mind at ease. *As long as he can finish the book by January*, she told herself.

Amazingly, though she had a new baby at home, Julie continued to keep pace with Joyce, typing his pages as he produced and revised them. Sylvia was still worried about her and Michel, however. The sadness she'd seen in his face back in July hadn't disappeared. Adrienne reported that while he smiled and joked in his *boucherie* as he always had, there was a hollowness to him that hadn't been there before. Sylvia tried to ask Julie if everything was okay, and even offered to give her a break from the typing, but Julie's only reply was "I need this, Sylvia. Michel works so much, and he sleeps so poorly. Well, I suppose we both sleep poorly with little Amélie crying in the middle of the night, but he has bad dreams that wake him up as well."

"Bad dreams?" Sylvia hoped this wasn't too intrusive a question.

"Of the war," Julie said.

"I'm sorry. Does he still read Owen and Sassoon? Very often it helps to feel less alone."

"Constantly," she said, looking sad and lost herself.

"You'll tell me if there is anything I can do, won't you?" Such inadequate words, and yet they were the only ones.

"You can keep me busy," Julie replied with a vehemence that surprised Sylvia.

"I shall," she promised. "And I can give you this." Sylvia went to her store shelves and plucked off *Little Women* by Louisa May Alcott, then handed it to Julie. "This is a gift. For you. She is America's first great woman writer, and this is a wonderful story of four sisters making their way in the world."

"Thank you." Julie's voice was hoarse, and little Amélie began crying in her pram. Startled, Julie bent over the baby, cooing and tenderly running a finger up and down her daughter's little round cheek. "Thank you," Julie whispered again before pushing the pram hastily out of the shop and into the street, leaving Sylvia to wish there were something more she could do.

CHAPTER 14

❧

"Last night was really something," Ernest said the afternoon of December 8 in Shakespeare and Company, looking a bit worse for wear, though he wore the hangover well on his dark, handsome face. Sylvia was tired, too, though she hadn't stayed out as late as he had. Everyone had gone to the Dôme in a celebratory group after two exhilarating hours when 250 friends and admirers had gathered at La Maison to hear Jimmy Light, one of the American crowd, read from *Ulysses*, then listen to Valery Larbaud explain the novel's genius and its contribution to French and American literature. It had been heady stuff, with all their friends, old and new, present for this French debut of Joyce's novel. Sylvia and Adrienne had left Joyce, Ernest, and about a dozen others still drinking at midnight.

"And to think you'd been such a skeptic about the evening." She loved ribbing Ernest. He'd become like a brother or a cousin to her. She didn't mind his teasing, either.

"Can you blame me? You threw a debutante ball for a novel written in English, not for the novel itself but for a very small piece of a

French translation, in a bookstore for French books, when the English bookshop and the novel's publisher is right across the street. And you thought I was the crazy one?"

"It worked, though, didn't it?"

"It did. You and Adrienne make everything work."

"Well, we wanted to recognize Joyce's integration into the local literary community. You and he are rare birds here, you know, speaking the language and befriending Larbaud and Gide and Benoist-Méchin. So many of the Americans and Brits keep to themselves."

"Their loss."

"*Oui.*"

Ernest frowned. "I'll admit last night made me damn jealous, though."

Sylvia laughed. "Ernest, Joyce is almost twenty years older than you."

"Yes, and he was nearly ten years older when he published *Dubliners*," he added so quickly Sylvia could tell he spent quite a bit of time thinking about writers and the rates of their success, measuring himself against them—which reminded her of Eliot's Prufrock and his coffee spoons. *Well, why not? Ernest is a competitive man; likely the comparisons inspire him to work harder.*

"Hadley mentioned to me the other day that the stories you're writing now are superb. Truly fresh and exciting. That's the important thing."

"I hope so. It's tough, you know, being here with Stein and Joyce and Pound. I want to write well and say something new, but it's hard to feel that's even possible with them around."

"I think it's *better* if you're doing something other than what Joyce and the others are doing." *That's what I could never figure out—how to be Sylvia Beach in the face of Chopin, Whitman, and Joyce.*

"If you say so. You're one of the few people whose opinion really counts to me."

"That means a great deal to me."

The two of them went about their separate business in the store for a few minutes, then it dawned on Sylvia that this young boxer, journalist, former ambulance driver, man of the world far in excess of his actual age, just might be able to help her with a problem that had been steadily growing in her mind.

"Ernest," she said quietly, for there were few other people in the store. "I wonder if you could help me with something."

"If I can, I will."

"I need to figure out how to smuggle Joyce's book into the United States. First I have to get them across the border, then I have to get the copies safely into the hands of people who have paid good money for them. The reputation of Shakespeare and Company is at stake."

"It's a wonder you don't say *your* reputation."

"Oh, I'm not nearly as important as the store."

"I heartily disagree." He smiled. "But that's exactly why I'd do anything I can to help you. I think I might know someone. Give me until after the holidays."

"Thank you so much."

"Merry Christmas, Sylvia."

"Merry Christmas, Ernest."

☙

Nineteen twenty-one came to a fitting end. While Cyprian partied with her theater and film friends in Paris, Sylvia spent a quiet holiday with Adrienne and her parents in the country, where roaring fires and spiced wine brightened every cold night. They made their way through a mountain of books they'd been meaning to read from under piles of blankets on the couch, sometimes accompanied by

Mousse, the family sheepdog, who added his body to their tangle of legs, warming their limbs with his heavy, hairy form.

"I wish I could get a dog for Shakespeare and Company," said Sylvia, idly petting the curls on Mousse's head.

"Of course you can," said Adrienne.

"But our Crooked Jesus is afraid of dogs."

"The best way for him to overcome his silly fear is to befriend a dog."

"Perhaps. . . . but not until after *Ulysses* comes out."

"*C'est vrai.* It would be a mistake to disturb his final burst. For *your* sake."

Burst was the right word for it, for the marks he made on Darantiere's pages looked like an explosion of words and symbols. Even Julie had begun to flag—"Now he really may as well be writing in ancient Greek!"—and Sylvia had to bring on one last typist to help in the first weeks of 1922, bringing the total to more than a dozen.

Joyce was so consumed, he rarely came to the store, and when Sylvia went around to his apartment to collect and deliver pages, she usually found him alone. "Where is Mrs. Joyce? Lucia? Giorgio?"

"I have no idea" was his invariable reply.

"Have you eaten?"

"I think . . . perhaps . . . yesterday." At which point Sylvia would head to the neighborhood *boulangerie* and *fromagerie*, and bring back two loaves and some hard cheese that wouldn't rot if he forgot to put it in the icebox; Julie told her that Michel had sent some cured meats to the Joyce house on the same theory. One time, Sylvia stood and waited while he finished a sandwich and a tall glass of water in front of her.

His eyes were watery, red, and inflamed, but he continued to work. As far as she could tell, all he did was write and sleep. Ernest and Bob hadn't seen him at the cafés since the reading. "Damn impressive," Bob observed. "I'm glad for the man, but it does mean I'll be out fifty francs."

"Pardon?"

"There's a pool on whether he'll finish by his fortieth," explained Ernest.

"I see." In spite of her own concerns for the book and its writer, Sylvia found this highly amusing. "And how did you bet?"

"I changed my wager after the reading, which Bob here kindly allowed me to do the one time. I didn't think there was any way Joyce would finish until I saw the look on his face when Larbaud called him a genius seventy times."

"There's nothing like flattery to spur a man on," Bob said.

Sylvia laughed and shook her head. "I think it's more than flattery."

"Flattery never hurts," said Ernest. "By the way, Sylvia, I have a lead to discuss with you on the matter you raised before Christmas."

"Excellent! Stop by tomorrow?"

"Wouldn't miss it."

✾

"I'm sorry, Mr. Joyce, but I cannot let you add one more word," she finally said, less than a week before his birthday. He'd come all the way to Shakespeare and Company to make the request, which she supposed showed just how much he wanted to change the manuscript, but she'd begun to feel that his changes had less to do with genius and more to do with mania, compulsion, and even a fear of actually finishing. Maybe Bob would win the pool after all. Someone had to stand between Joyce and himself. "To make more changes at this point would virtually ensure that this edition makes no money, and might even cause Monsieur Darantiere to quit. Please, please don't ask me to do it." Her voice quivered with anger and fear. She hated that it had come to this.

"It's only on the last page," he begged, his voice ragged with fatigue and despair. "It won't cause anything else to be reset."

Sylvia's heart beat in her throat, and her head throbbed.

She closed her eyes and breathed, then asked with her eyelids still shielding her, "How many words is it?"

"Three. The last three. Please. Sylvia."

Deeply, she sighed. "All right, yes. I'll ask. But I can't make any promises."

"Thank you," he gushed, looking and sounding on the verge of tears.

She would never publish anything else. Ever again. It was too painful.

On the first train from Paris to Dijon on February 2, 1922, Sylvia nodded off with her forehead on the cold window. Given how excited she was to be on this errand, she was amazed to realize how tired she was. The elderly woman in the seat next to her actually had to shake her gently awake a few minutes before the train arrived in Dijon.

The first thing she did in Maurice's shop was to hand him a hamper with the finest Bordeaux she could afford, two jars of Adrienne's jams, and the nicest *saucissons* Michel had been able to donate. "You've been kind to Julie when I couldn't be myself," he'd said appreciatively and apologetically. "This is the least I can do."

The printer smiled at her when he saw her, even before she handed him the basket. "It is done," he said.

The relief she felt was so overwhelming, she found herself sobbing in Maurice's arms within seconds. His embrace was solid and strong, and he held her until she didn't have any tears left. "I'm so sorry," she said.

"Don't be. You put your whole heart into this, as did Monsieur Joyce. We do not always have control over our hearts."

"I feel so lucky to have been on this journey with you." *This odyssey*.

"As do I," he said. "Come, let me show you the first copies."

Into her hands, he placed a book as heavy as a brick. The thick, creamy paper within was hand cut at the edges, and it was bound in a blue the precise color of the Greek flag—a hue that in book form called to mind the lapis of illuminated manuscripts, the Mediterranean, and *pâtes de fruits* all at once. It was one of their hundred and fifty best editions, and it was absolutely beautiful. When she opened it, the book let out a satisfying crack in greeting, and when she saw the words on the pages unmarred by pencil edits, her eyes welled up again.

"Look at the title page," Maurice said in a hushed tone.

Treating it with the care she would a newborn, Sylvia went to the page and saw Shakespeare and Company printed there beneath ULYSSES and Joyce's name.

She couldn't look at it longer than a second. It was too much to take in all at once.

Snapping the book shut and holding it to her breast, she said, "I don't know how I'll ever be able to thank you."

"Well," he said, "that's why you're paying me so handsomely."

And they laughed together at the absurdity of that idea.

By contrast, on the train ride home, Sylvia felt like she was on fire. She *could not wait* to put the book in Joyce's hands, for she'd come away from Dijon with the only two copies in existence thus far, and one would make the finest birthday present in the history of birthday presents. Practically sprinting out of the Gare de Lyon under gray skies pregnant with snow, Sylvia indulged in a taxi to take her as quickly as possible to Joyce's latest flat on the rue de l'Université, drumming her fingers on the book all the way.

Mrs. Joyce greeted her at the door, and Sylvia held up the book without words but with an enormous smile, and the other woman inflated with a grand sigh and said, "Well. Come in, then."

"Who is it?" Mr. Joyce called from the kitchen, Sylvia guessed.

Giorgio caught sight of Sylvia and the book in the entrance and replied to his father, "Your birthday present!"

Sylvia's pulse thudded through her body, all the way to her fingertips and earlobes. Putting the book behind her back, she stepped silently into the apartment. She and Joyce met in the hallway, and as soon as he saw her, he put his hand on his heart and raised his eyebrows behind his glasses.

As slowly as her own excitement would allow, she brought the book around her body and held it in front of her chest.

Giorgio let out a *whoop!* of a cheer, and Lucia—who'd put her head into the hallway from the bedroom—gasped with pleasure. "Oh, it's beautiful, Papa."

Joyce's hands shook as he took the book from Sylvia. He gazed down at it reverentially, at the white title and his name on the front cover. "Is it . . . really . . . ?"

Sylvia put her hand on his elbow and tightened her grip just a bit. "Your *Ulysses* is home at last."

He let out a labored sigh, and she could hear all the wet, raw emotions he was trying to contain. "Thank you, Sylvia."

"It is my absolute honor and pleasure," she said, meaning every word. She'd taken a gamble, and it had been the right one. It had all been worth it. This moment, this book, this writer, this city. Stratford-on-Odéon.

Odeonia.

Her very own mythical Ithaca.

The novel brought more notoriety to her store than she had dared allow herself to imagine. On February 3—a Friday, which was a busy day in the slowest of weeks—she put her copy of *Ulysses* in the window of Shakespeare and Company, and word spread through the Left Bank like wildfire. Every one of her regulars came to admire it, and dozens of others she'd never met before clambered for a look at Joyce's banned book, most of whom also signed up for lending cards or purchased other books.

Notices about the book's arrival also appeared in no fewer than three weekend newspapers, and so the following week brought flocks of Americans, English, Parisians, and even a few stray Italians and Germans to her door. Joyce stopped by every day around midmorning, and on the first day when Larbaud and Fargue and the Pounds and the Hemingways were there, it felt like a party with Joyce as the jolly good fellow; Sylvia reflected at one point how like Gertrude he suddenly seemed, though she and Alice were notably and predictably absent from the fun.

Not only did new customers pour in every day, but she was flooded with letters from admirers and cynics alike; she could tell which was which from the first sentence and didn't bother reading the disagreeable ones; unless they were from another famous writer, they went straight into the bin. Her favorite of that genre came via Ezra Pound, who'd apparently continued to hound George Bernard Shaw to purchase the book. At last, fed up, Shaw had sent Ezra a postcard with a picture of Christ being entombed as Mary his mother and Mary Magdalene cried, and Shaw had written "J. J. being put in his tomb by his editresses after the refusal of G. B. S. to subscribe to *Ulysses*." It was Joyce who brought the postcard to the shop, and he and Sylvia and Mysrine laughed so hard tears leaked from their eyes, and Sylvia clutched at a sharp stitch in her side.

A few industrious writers even sent her requests to consider their misunderstood novels for publication, to which she replied that much as she wished she could consider their manuscripts, her schedule was full to bursting with *Ulysses* and Shakespeare and Company. She was surprised to find that she didn't even feel an impulse to publish other writers' works. Shakespeare and Company would remain a bookstore first, and a publisher of James Joyce second. Those were more than enough.

CHAPTER 15

❧

Once Maurice began sending crates of the novel to 12 rue de l'Odéon, including the regular edition, Sylvia began to put in motion the plan that she and Ernest had concocted to smuggle *Ulysses* into the United States—a process that would actually begin in Canada, where Sylvia had paid the rent on a modest apartment in Toronto for one Bernard Braverman, an old war compatriot of Ernest's who had once been the editor of *The Progressive Woman*.

"I know him!" Sylvia had told Ernest as they whispered the details of their plan in the back room of Shakespeare and Company.

"You do?"

"Well, we exchanged letters once. His journal was friendly to articles about suffrage and the emancipation of women, and at the time I was campaigning in Washington, DC, and writing the occasional essay on progressive subjects, so I sent one to him for publication. He declined, but extremely politely. I couldn't be happier that he is the one who will now help *Ulysses*."

"What a damn small world this is. What made you stop writing, though?"

Shrugging, she said, "It was never for me."

"If you could let it go so easily, I guess that was true."

"You'll never let it go."

"Never. It's the only thing."

"Shakespeare and Company is my thing." Saying it out loud, it felt right and true. It *was* her thing. And it was *her* thing.

"Thankfully for the rest of us."

So it was that in the damp, chilly spring of 1922, Saint Barney, as Joyce christened him, received boxes containing hundreds of copies of *Ulysses* in Canada, where it was not illegal—boxes packed by Sylvia, Mysrine, and sometimes even Joyce himself, who was hopeless with the glue and paper and always seemed to leave the store covered in the sticky goo, which he swore he enjoyed peeling off in the evening.

Every single day for weeks, Bernard stuffed a copy into his pants or jacket and then boarded a ferry that took him to Michigan, where he deposited the book in a hotel room in Detroit. Once he'd accumulated enough, he sent them to the correct addresses through the American Express.

It was a slow and painstaking process, and Sylvia began to receive letters of complaint from the more impatient and disgruntled of her subscribers: "Mrs. Wilcox received hers last week, and since my money's as good as hers, I have to wonder where mine is." And so on. Then there was the day a telegram from Bernard himself arrived that read

BORDER AUTHORITIES SUSPICIOUS NEED TO SPEED UP
ADDED HELP DON'T WORRY WILL UPDATE

Sylvia smoked an extra half a pack of cigarettes when that arrived, and spent much of the evening coughing as she and Adrienne dined on a cold supper of cheese and bread and fruit because she was arriving home so late every night, and Adrienne had been working on an essay of her own as well as publishing a translation of Whitman by Larbaud for *Cahiers*. She couldn't remember the last relaxed evening they'd spent together, uninterrupted by work.

"*Chérie*," Adrienne said, and Sylvia could hear the hesitation in her voice as she went on, "perhaps fewer Gauloises would be good for you?"

"To say nothing of my teeth." Sylvia sighed. "It's just so hard. I've tried to smoke less, but . . ."

"It is a compulsion."

"Oh, it's much more than that."

Adrienne frowned, and Sylvia wondered how long she'd been harboring these thoughts about her smoking. Pretty much everyone around them smoked, including Adrienne herself on occasion, but as with cocktails and absinthe, some of their circle overdid it. Gauloises were her vice, as surely as wine was Joyce's, and Sylvia knew it—quietly, to herself. She'd begun to notice that when she smoked more than her usual pack in a day, her head felt painfully tight, and no matter how much water she drank, she went to bed thirsty; then she'd be further punished by getting up to relieve herself seven times in the night.

Unable to contemplate giving it up, or even to discuss it further with Adrienne, she cleared their plates and changed the subject: "Do you think the books will all get to their destinations safely?"

"I hope so, but no one can be sure. You've done absolutely everything you possibly can. The only thing you can do now is pray."

Sylvia raised an eyebrow.

"Ask your father to pray, then."

They laughed together, then Sylvia made tea and took out their precious tin of chocolate, where Adrienne hoarded only the best, darkest bars to be enjoyed after supper.

"I'm also worried about piracy," Sylvia said, nibbling a square that should have tasted sweet, but instead tasted smoky. "*Ulysses* seems ripe for it, just like *Sons and Lovers*. I don't know if Lawrence made any money from that book. I wrote to John Quinn to make sure our novel is copyrighted, and he assured me that its publication in *The Little Review* had already imparted a copyright, but something about that doesn't quite add up to me. And if *Ulysses* is copied and sold without permission, and it isn't copyrighted, we'll have no recourse."

"One problem at a time. Let's make sure our copies get to safe harbors first. And why shouldn't we believe Monsieur Quinn about the copyright?"

"Ezra said he's not sure if Quinn is right. He said it should be cataloged with the Library of Congress." She sipped her chamomile tea and felt it cleansing the ash from her tongue.

"Can a banned book be cataloged?"

"I have no idea. I've asked, but Quinn won't even bother answering me."

"Is there any way to stop the piracy of a book, even if it is copyrighted?"

"Probably not." Sylvia folded her arms on the table and slumped forward.

Adrienne twined her fingers into Sylvia's hair. "If a storm comes, we'll decide how best to weather it. There's no use in worrying now about something that might not happen."

Adrienne moved her hand suggestively from Sylvia's hair to her neck, sliding her fingers under Sylvia's collar so that she could move her hand freely over the muscles and bones of her back and shoulders. It had been a while since she and Adrienne had made love, and this solicitous gesture sent all the atoms in her zinging. Soon they were kissing and tugging at blouses and buttons and bloomers. When they were naked in bed, Adrienne told Sylvia, "Close your eyes, and do not open them no matter what."

Then Sylvia heard her get up from the bed and leave the room. Her heart raced and her eyes fluttered open. *What is she doing?* After some mysterious sounds in the kitchen, Adrienne padded back into the room, and Sylvia shut her eyes tight and tried to relax into the pillows.

"Where did you go?"

"Shhh. Keep your eyes closed."

Then Sylvia felt something cold and soft on her breast. It felt like a finger, but . . . not. And she smelled something sweet. Vanilla?

"What. . . . ?"

"Shhhh." The cool, slippery, sweet finger traced a pattern on her breasts and torso, and Sylvia felt both incredibly aroused and shocked. *What is she doing? Is that . . . custard?*

Then she felt Adrienne's mouth, her warm lips and tongue, retracing the patterns made by her finger, and the sensation was . . . well, she no longer cared what Adrienne was doing. As long as she kept doing it.

⁂

Sylvia mentally washed her hands of John Quinn for good when—true to character and his distrust of any woman who'd tried to help Joyce—he found an alternate means of smuggling his own fourteen copies of *Ulysses* into the United States. He sent an errand boy to Shakespeare and Company to collect his stash and arrange them like ham and cheese between two Cézannes he'd purchased from a gallery, all of which was to be wrapped tightly and shipped to New York. As soon as the boy left Shakespeare and Company with his book sandwich, Sylvia slammed the door behind him and shouted, "Good riddance!" to the confused expressions of the five patrons who fortunately didn't know her or the situation at all.

Saint Barney's contraband books continued to arrive, however, and slowly Sylvia started to receive more letters of thanks and congratulations than queries and criticisms. From their friends in England like Eliot, they heard little other than praise and awe:

Where does literature go from here?

Such daring! We will be reckoning with that final monologue in Molly's voice for generations . . .

I was moved to tears and other less mentionable emotions by the inner tumult of Stephen and Leopold's minds . . .

Not only are Joyce's words art, but your volume should be in a museum! Truly, it is bookmaking at its finest. Congratulations, Sylvia!

Sylvia had never received more than a handful of compliments from close friends and family on anything she'd ever accomplished before. But this avalanche of praise and thanks . . . well, nothing could compare to the moment she held the book in her hands for the first time, but the cumulative effect of so much applause made her feel relieved, smarter, and somehow taller, all at once. Combined with the new stage of sexual experimentation she'd embarked upon with Adrienne, Sylvia suddenly felt giddy half the time. The other half of the time, she found herself wondering, *How did Adrienne think of doing that? Am I creative enough for her? Am I enough for her? Am I doing enough for* Ulysses? *For Shakespeare?*

She voiced some of these concerns to Cyprian, who said, "Jesus, Sylvia, you work all day and never come out with me at night. How could you be doing more?"

Translation requests from all over Europe started coming in, and Sylvia was working with Harriet Weaver on an English edition that had to be printed in Dijon and would serve as the second official edition of the novel, because all the printers on "this tiny, provincial island," as Harriet put it, had refused "the greatest novel of our time." By the end of March, all 750 copies of the regular edition had sold out.

Reviews surfaced as well. The very first was in the *London Observer* a month after the book's release, and Sisley Huddleston proclaimed that "its very obscenity is somehow beautiful and wrings the soul to pity." At first, Sylvia worried about Joyce's reactions to the reviews, but he took them all in stride. In fact, it became a game in the shop, especially after the novel was roundly criticized in London's *Sporting Times*, of all places, where Joyce himself was called a "perverted lunatic" even though he was "a writer of talent." Then, under a massive headline reading SCANDAL OF JAMES JOYCE'S ULYSSES, the paper had listed all the handicapped horses for the season.

"Well," said Joyce, "I'm glad to know my book ranks up with the Derby in the estimation of Englishmen."

After that it was "What column are we in today, Miss Beach? Jockeys or Artists?" They kept a running tally of Jockeys (less than favorable reviews) and Artists (favorable reviews). Very often what was offered as criticism was read by Sylvia and Joyce as praise.

"This review says that '*Ulysses* is a bible for exiles and outcasts,'" she said.

"Hear, hear," said Joyce, punching his ashplant stick in the air.

"Amen," agreed Adrienne.

"Precisely," added Larbaud.

Just as often there was a mix of praise and criticism.

"Edmund Wilson in *The New Republic*, after comparing you to Flaubert at some length and finding you wanting, concludes that 'for all its appalling longueurs, *Ulysses* is a work of high genius.' And that it 'has the effect at once of making everything else look brassy. Since I have read it, the texture of other novelists seems intolerably loose and careless.'"

"Brassy, eh? I'd take that over leaden," offered Bob, who was in that morning asking for advice on his Contact Editions.

"All right, then, I think overall Wilson is in the Artist column," Sylvia said, making a mark in chalk on the little board they'd stashed behind the desk for this game. "Who's next?"

In April, she arrived to open Shakespeare and Company in the soft yellow light of morning, and found a disheveled and morose Joyce sitting on her front step with his ashplant stick tossed to one side and his head in his hands, elbows on knees.

"Goodness, how long have you been here? It's chilly," she said, helping him up, then opening the door. As soon as they were inside, he sat in the green chair and began sobbing.

It wouldn't do to have customers coming in at that moment, so she relocked the door and kept the shutters closed, then knelt by her friend. "I'm sure we can fix whatever it is," she said.

He mopped his face with a wet, well-wrung handkerchief, and choked out, "Nora's gone."

"What?"

"She left for Ireland yesterday. With the children."

Goodness. Sylvia knew his wife had long threatened to do just that, but she'd always assumed that was all it was: a threat. A threat that often succeeded in reminding her husband of what was really important in his life so that he reined in his drunken antics for a while. It seemed curious that now, of all times—when *Ulysses* was doing so well, and Joyce's career had taken a turn for the better—she would leave.

"I'm so sorry," she said, for there seemed to be nothing else to say. "But surely she'll come back?"

"She says she won't. And I *can't* live there again. She knows that."

"Give her some time," offered Sylvia, whose experience of Cyprian's moods and also Adrienne's grieving had shown her the power of time. The problems of Michel and Julie did not bear this out, though, she considered with worry. Time since the war seemed to have worn Michel down, and there was something about having a child that had brought out the worst in him. Julie still wouldn't share any details with her, so it was hard for Sylvia to puzzle out exactly what was happening—all she knew was that the smiling, voracious reader who'd been intent on battling his demons alongside Sassoon and Homer and Whitman had vanished.

But, Sylvia consoled herself, since Nora wasn't shell-shocked like Michel, it seemed likely that Joyce was dealing with a case of familial woe that would be receptive to the healing powers of time and even distance. "She'll miss you," Sylvia added as compassionately as she could.

"And Dr. Borsch thinks I might need surgery after all," he moaned. "It appears that my teeth problems might be aggravating my eye problems."

"Goodness," she sighed, feeling her own limbs tensing up with some of the writer's overflowing anxiety. Teeth problems? What teeth problems? Were they the reason he often ordered soup for dinner? "Let me make some tea," she said, as much because the hot drink would be a comfort as because it would give her a minute to think about what to say, and how to help her poor dear James Joyce, whose life seemed to be coming apart.

But when she came out with a tray laden with strong tea, milk, sugar, and a pack of the ginger crèmes she knew he loved and so she stashed in a special cupboard in the back, all she'd come up with was "Let a month pass, and if she hasn't returned to Paris, we'll talk about how to entice her to return. In the meantime, let's make sure we get you into the best health possible for when she does return."

He sighed a great deal as he dressed his tea, sipped it, and dunked the cookie in the liquid to soften it, which prompted Sylvia to ask, "What's wrong with your teeth?"

"Abscesses. So common with the wretched state of dentistry in Ireland." He pronounced the name of his home country harshly.

Sylvia nodded, and watched the labored way he ate the soaked ginger crème, moving it around in his mouth without really chewing it, and then finally, slowly, swallowing the bite. He ate two more cookies like that, and drank down three more cups of tea, as Sylvia felt her own heart ratchet up its speed, her shoulders knotting themselves, her palms and fingers feeling sticky with sugar and perspiration. She wasn't sure why his tragedy should affect her so much, but it did.

Talking assuaged the anxiety, at least in her, so she started describing her plans for the next edition of *Ulysses*—a one-sided conversation that mainly consisted of her babbling away while he nodded and occasionally thanked her. When he didn't do more to respond, she opened the shutters and then turned her attentions to the first customers to her store. Working also settled her, focusing on books, numbers, and other tangible things. He left shortly before lunch with George Antheil, who told him of a quartet that would be playing in the Jardin du Luxembourg. "Music was my first love," Joyce said to George. "I used to sing quite well."

"Do you still?" inquired George.

He shook his head as if it were the saddest thing in the world.

"Let's be cheered by some quaint concertos," George said.

Joyce nodded and leaned heavily on his ashplant stick as George shot Sylvia a look that said, *I'll take it from here.* When they were on the Odéon and out of sight, everything in Sylvia relaxed.

Later that evening she picked at her dinner distractedly as she explained about Joyce and Nora to Adrienne.

"It's very sad for him," Adrienne said, "but I can't say I blame her."

Even though Sylvia had sometimes thought to herself how difficult Joyce would be to live with, Adrienne's reaction still surprised her. "Why?"

"He says he's devoted to her, but it seems to me that they live different lives. She does not care for books. He is obsessed with his own. They rarely attend events together."

This observation plucked an uncomfortable string inside Sylvia. "It must be awful to love someone as much as Joyce loves Nora, and not feel it reciprocated."

"On the contrary, I think she loves him deeply. I think she doesn't like to feel ignored."

Sylvia nodded slowly. "But he is such a genius."

"Geniuses are not always good husbands."

Lighting a cigarette and taking a long drag, she said, "I hope she comes back."

"*Moi aussi.*" Adrienne hesitated, then added, "But if she does not, remember that this is not your problem, nor is it your fault."

"How do you do it?" Sylvia asked.

"Do what?"

"Keep things . . . so separate."

Adrienne shrugged. "I remind myself all the time that my friends, even those I love with all my heart . . . I remind myself that they are not me. I am Adrienne, and I have my own life to live."

"My father used to say that we were put on earth to serve."

"It is possible to serve without losing oneself."

Sylvia nodded, knowing that Adrienne was right, but wondering in her soul, *Who is Sylvia Beach without James Joyce and* Ulysses? It was hard to untangle them. Shakespeare and Company had become famous and successful because of his notorious book; it was what had finally allowed her to accomplish something that felt independent from Adrienne and La Maison. She loved to think of herself as the book's savior, even though she recognized that this very feeling was not altogether pure. But it was true. And what did that say about her, and what she stood to lose?

PART THREE
1925–31

*The artist, like the God of the creation, remains within
or behind or beyond or above his handiwork,
invisible, refined out of existence, indifferent,
paring his fingernails.*

—James Joyce, *A Portrait of the Artist as a Young Man*

CHAPTER 16

"Happy Bloomsday," Sylvia chirped to her first customer on June 16, 1925, using the term she'd invented the previous year to commemorate the day on which the myriad, epic events of *Ulysses* take place. Teddy, the gray-haired terrier who'd adopted the store, whom Sylvia had adopted in return, yapped cheerfully as if repeating his master's salutation.

As it happened, her first customer was Ernest, looking bright-eyed and clean-shaven on the hot summer morning. He smelled of sunshine, soap, and the rising steam from the sidewalks that had been rinsed by street cleaners hours before. "Happy Bloomsday indeed," he replied, stooping to scratch Teddy behind the ears. "I've already written most of a story today."

"My, my, aren't you productive."

"Have to be as productive as possible before we leave for Spain."

"Ah yes, Pamplona. The bullfights. Lady Macduff?" Sylvia chuckled. Lady Duff Twysden was her real name, but she could never hear it without thinking of *Macbeth*, and so she couldn't resist the pun. Teddy trotted off to find Lucky, who lived full-time in the store, whereas the little dog bedded down with Adrienne and Sylvia every night. Canine and feline got on well enough during business hours, and Lucky did a tremendous job of keeping Teddy away from Joyce when he stopped by—for which the writer was very grateful, and resulted in his rechristening the tenacious cat Lancelot.

"The very same," replied Ernest, who squatted to get a better look at the *W* shelf.

"Will you be at the party later?" she asked, referring to the first—annual, she hoped—Bloomsday party to be held that evening at the Joyces' fine digs on Square Robiac near the Eiffel Tower. Shortly after Nora's reluctant return from Ireland, Joyce had found them a spacious and lovely place with grand windows and an especially lovely belle epoque facade. Joyce had confided in Sylvia, "I had to do something to make sure she stays this time. Make our lives more respectable. No more moving about." Hearing him say these words had filled Sylvia with unexpected relief of her own.

The past two years had felt like a Pax Odeonia. Sylvia commissioned a third edition of *Ulysses*, she and Adrienne began translating poetry together, lately embarking on a French version of Eliot's "Prufrock" for a new journal Adrienne was launching out of La Maison, *Le Navire d'Argent*. They also discovered a new favorite vacation destination in Les Déserts, where they gloried in sunshine and long walks and wildflowers and being entirely away from the relentless pace of their lives in Paris, where more and more Americans were coming to stay. Whether they were single aspiring writers or young families eager to make a fresh start, they came to Shakespeare and Company as soon as they disembarked, smelling of excitement, nerves, and lunch on the train. Tired of repeating the same information again and again, Sylvia had written out a three-page welcome document full of recommendations for restaurants, hotels, churches, and theaters, from which hundreds of newly arrived Americans fervently and gratefully scribbled down insider tips. Bob's Contact Editions had gotten off the ground and had published Ernest's first book in 1923, *Three Stories and Ten Poems*, to great acclaim. Meanwhile, the Joyces set about decorating as they had never before, with wallpaper, Persian rugs, and heavy, dramatic drapes. It cost so much that Harriet Weaver actually mentioned it in one of her letters to Sylvia about her English edition of *Ulysses* and other matters of Joyce business: "I was under the impression that Paris was inexpensive to live in, which made it more attractive to the young artists—but that cannot be true if Mr. Joyce's recent housing expenses are to be believed!"

Ernest sounded the same note now as he slid the latest volume of Williams's poetry across the table toward Sylvia and her ledger. "You don't think Joyce has gotten too big for his britches in the seventh? With his view of the tower and all?"

"It's still in walking distance of here," Sylvia said, lighting a cigarette. "And all his friends are in the fifth and sixth. Visiting him will be like going abroad."

Laughing, he replied, "No one has ever had a truer friend than Joyce has in you, Sylvia."

"I hope many of my friends could say that of me."

"And we do. In fact, Hadley's planning to make your favorite American chocolate cake for the party as a token of our gratitude."

"Now *that* is a cause for celebration."

"Say, has Scott finally met Joyce?"

"Not that I know of, why?"

"Just curious."

Right. The two American writers had met in the spring at one of the popular Montparnasse spots—the Dingo, maybe—and according to everyone who was there, Ernest Hemingway and F. Scott Fitzgerald had started arguing right away, about everything: books, bars, midwestern cities. It was hardly surprising. Though Scott was only three years older than Ernest, he was three novels ahead of him—well received at that—and this was something Ernest could not abide. Sylvia had watched him studiously ignore the constantly replenishing stacks of *This Side of Paradise*, then *The Beautiful and Damned*, and now *The Great Gatsby* as his own slim edition of stories and poems sold merely respectably.

It didn't help that just a few months ago, Ernest had missed an offer letter from Scott's editor Max Perkins at Scribner's that was waiting for him in the pile of mail Sylvia held for him at Shakespeare, while he and Hadley and their little son Bumby were in Austria, where he'd signed a contract with the smaller house Boni & Liveright. The publisher he'd accepted would do right by him, Sylvia knew, but she'd watched as his face darkened and he'd crumpled Perkins's letter, growling to himself about "my own goddamn impatience. Hadley was right, as usual."

"I've heard he and Zelda are off to the southern coast soon anyway," she said, not minding that this information would only reinforce her friend's less charitable image of the Fitzgeralds, that they were spoiled and shallow. Though Ernest wasn't entirely wrong, Sylvia still found Scott and Zelda to be lively and entertaining when together, and Scott to be charmingly awkward and modest when alone—it had taken him ten minutes to finally get around to introducing himself to Sylvia when he came to the store, and when he did he'd said with wide, boyish eyes, "I can't quite believe I'm meeting the famous Sylvia Beach."

"Typical," Ernest mumbled.

A torrent of piano notes rained down on them from George Antheil's apartment above the shop. Things had gotten so busy, she'd given up on the tea shop idea and rented the upstairs space to the composer, which supplemented her income in a way that cost her little time and energy.

"He's at it again, eh?" Ernest said with a mix of amusement and exasperation.

"Every day!" Sylvia sang over the music. "Someday, Shakespeare and Company might be better known as the home of the composer of the *Ballet Mécanique*." With the symphony being heard in previews around Paris, young and handsome Antheil was gathering quite a following for himself, none more vocal than James Joyce, whose eyes continued to give him never-ending problems while his ears were mercifully intact and always in need of filling.

"God in heaven, I hope not," Ernest said. Then, almost as if he could admit it with the music to smother his words, he said to Sylvia, "I don't think Hadley much wants to go to Pamplona this year."

"I'm sorry to hear that . . . but maybe she'll change her mind when she arrives? I know how she's loved your previous visits."

"I hope so."

Sylvia had sensed tension between the Hemingways in the past year, and especially since their return from their ski holiday in Austria; their formerly easy, expansive way with each other, all holding hands and sloppy kisses on cheeks in the day and lips in the night, had given way to a stiff formality. One of them always seemed to have Bumby in arms or on hip as a soft, smiling shield. She couldn't remember the last time the couple clutched their sides laughing in the shop. It made her sad to think of them.

Much as Sylvia loved her Stratford-on-Odéon, it didn't seem to have the same effect on marriage that it did on art. Lasting unions like the Joyces', however volatile at times, were rare—so perhaps they were right to make a home in the seventh, away from parties like the one to which Bob had taken her and Adrienne the week before, with many guests wearing nothing more than paint, and not even bothering to find a private corner for sex when the impulse struck. It made Sylvia queasy to think back on how Adrienne had stared at two women wrapped suggestively in a threadbare sheet that pulsed rhythmically with their lovemaking. Sylvia was satisfied with their sex life and the ways in which it had deepened in intimacy and a certain amount of daring, but Sylvia was always uncomfortably aware that it was Adrienne who tended to introduce the variety and novelty. Sometimes an experiment would end in a fit of laughter, but it was always just the two of them in the room. Watching Adrienne watch the exhibitionism at the party made Sylvia fear there were hungers in her she could not sate, which reminded her uncomfortably of Cyprian's warning to her when Suzanne was still alive.

"Hadley loves you, Ernest."

"Sometimes I don't think I'm worthy of it."

"I'm sure you have nothing to fear," she said, though she wondered what weighed on his conscience heavily enough for him to reveal such a fear to her.

So many competing desires.

"I'd rather hoped to see Mr. Pound while I was here," said Harriet Weaver over tea and meringues expertly made by Adrienne that sultry July afternoon. The three women were sitting on folding chairs in the little cobblestone courtyard of the apartment Harriet had hired for her stay that summer. A breeze riffled the leaves on the branches above them and cooled the perspiration on the back of her neck, exposed beneath her recently trimmed hair. Even Teddy was too hot to beg or play, and had lain down for a nap in the shade.

It was a lovely place a few minutes' walk from the place de la Contrescarpe, very near Valery Larbaud's apartment on the Cardinal Lemoine, and Sylvia was pleased to have been able to secure it for the woman to whom she'd always felt so linked, much as their lives were entangled with Joyce's. Amazingly, this visit was their first time meeting face-to-face. Sylvia looked forward to introducing Harriet to Margaret Anderson and Jane Heap, who'd moved to Paris "forever!" the theatrical Margaret had pronounced after her first week of parties and meals in Montparnasse. Their visit to Natalie Barney's urbane and highly intellectual salon sent her into an orbit of joy. "Why have I not come here before?" she kept asking.

"Ezra seems to be enjoying Italy so much, I wonder if we'll ever see him here again," said Sylvia. "More's the pity. I miss him and Dorothy."

"Perhaps I should extend my sojourn and pay them a visit," Harriet said idly. She sipped her tea, and though Sylvia hadn't been in her presence long, she could tell the other woman was searching for the right words to say what was really on her mind. Adrienne, still shy about her English among native speakers, closed her eyes and slouched down in her seat, allowing the breeze to cool her upturned face.

As she waited for Harriet to get around to it, Sylvia eyed the Englishwoman's severe gray dress—though it was linen, it was long sleeved and buttoned up to her neck, and Sylvia wondered that she was not positively dying of the heat. Her own white cotton blouse had short sleeves, and she'd eschewed stockings that morning for bare legs under her linen skirt, but she was still uncomfortably warm.

"Do you not think," Harriet said at last, in a tone so searching as to be pleading, "that perhaps our Mr. Joyce drinks . . . too much?"

Adrienne's lips twitched into a smile. Even she, Odeonia's resident gourmet and connoisseur of fine wines and brandies, had wondered this about Joyce—among others of their friends, including Ezra. Sylvia's answer to the question was always the same, and she delivered it to Harriet now: "Very much so. But there is nothing in the world we can do about it. Nora has tried everything, including leaving him for Ireland."

"Good for her," Harriet huffed. "I approve. But she came back! What did that show him?"

"That she can't stay away. That she loves him as he is."

Harriet frowned. "What romantic nonsense, Sylvia!"

"Don't you and I continue to help him despite his flaws? And we're certainly not in love with him." *His work, maybe, but my heart belongs to Adrienne.*

The corners of Harriet's mouth turned down more. Sylvia knew how many times the Englishwoman had pleaded with Joyce to be more temperate—in all things, not just alcohol. Writing, music, and money, too. The days he received such admonishing letters from his patron, he'd come into Shakespeare and grumble, then go treat whoever happened to be there at eight o'clock to a fine meal at the Deux Magots.

But Harriet never cut him off.

She sighed. "Yes, I suppose we do," she agreed.

Adrienne's mouth fixed itself into a thin line.

"I understand your frustration, Harriet," said Sylvia, tapping a cigarette out of the slim silver case Joyce himself had bought for her as a Christmas present. "I'm constantly advancing him funds for the next editions of *Ulysses*, and even loaning him money from the store"—though she'd never admit it, even to Adrienne, those loans often went unpaid and were "forgiven" on one occasion or another, like Bloomsday or a birthday—"but I feel strongly that my place is not to meddle in his life. My job is to help him do his work, and then get it into the hands of readers. After all, look at what *Ulysses* has already done! No one can ignore it. Even writers like Virginia Woolf who originally purported to hate it have been powerfully influenced by it. Have you read *Mrs. Dalloway*? It uses his style of interior monologue. *Ulysses* is the most inescapable book of our time." She lit her cigarette and inhaled, feeling the hot smoke singe her lungs before she blew it out and took a cooling sip of lukewarm tea.

"I agree," said Harriet with conviction. "Although . . . I do wish I . . . *understood* his most recent work better."

"*Work in Progress*, you mean? Or the poems?"

"The poems seem harmless enough. Not his best work, but I can see how he'd want to write something simpler following *Ulysses*. No, I mean *Work in Progress*. I can barely parse much of it, and what I can understand reads to me as mean-spirited. *Ulysses* was expansive. It broadened our view of Homer's original, of humanity itself. This new work . . . does not. For me. Does it for you?"

Though her eyes were still closed, Adrienne had knitted her brows together. She hadn't read Joyce's most recent and extremely complicated writing, and Sylvia could see that Harriet's view of it concerned her.

"I don't think he's written enough of it for me to judge," Sylvia replied, which was exactly what she'd been telling herself since she'd read the first pages he'd shown her.

"Well," Harriet said, "I find that comforting. And perhaps you're right and it's never our place to judge."

Later, though, as Adrienne banged restlessly around the kitchen, assembling a simple supper of vichyssoise and bread as the sky turned from aquamarine to cooler amethyst, she demanded of Sylvia in her most strident French, "Do you really believe that? That it's not our place to judge?"

"Adrienne, *mon amour*, I am no critic or poet myself. Not like you are. You know that."

"Don't flatter me, Sylvia. You sell yourself short all the time. You're doing it now."

"I don't think I am. I just don't aspire to criticism. You do. That's wonderful. I support you in that. And I enjoy the translation work we do together, though it's nothing compared with the undertakings you bravely take on." Adrienne had been working even harder lately on *Le Navire d'Argent* and had engaged Auguste Morel to translate *Ulysses* for future issues, since young Jacques Benoist-Méchin, who'd done such a marvelous job for the French debut in 1921, had to leave the project for other, better-paying work. Soon Larbaud would also publish an essay on Walt Whitman, and Adrienne was working on one about Gide and Valéry. The long hours strained her, keeping her away from other pursuits like cooking that usually relaxed her. Sylvia was trying to be patient and wait out the worst of it, as Adrienne had done for her in the thick of the *Ulysses* publication.

"You translate some work on your own as well," Adrienne argued, with a surprising vehemence in her tone. "And translation is a form of interpretation. Even Pound thinks it's an art unto itself."

Teddy poked his head into the kitchen to see what the fuss was about.

"Why are you so upset with me today?"

Adrienne shook her head as if to clear it, then said in a much softer tone, "I . . . I just worry about you giving others more than you need to, and not keeping enough for yourself. Look at Harriet. She gives Joyce everything and . . . what has she to show for it?"

It was true. Harriet's life did seem to revolve around Joyce. "I have Shakespeare. And you." Sylvia stepped forward and wrapped her arms around Adrienne's soft, abundant middle, then kissed her salty, damp jaw, neck, and ear, feeling her relax very slightly. "And we have Teddy. Isn't that proof enough that I am not completely ruled by our Crooked Jesus?"

Adrienne slid her arms around Sylvia, and they kissed.

"Adrienne . . ." There was a question that had been burning her throat ever since that damn party. And this frustrated outburst from Adrienne was forcing it out at last. "Are you . . . happy? Is there anything you need that we don't share? That I am not giving you?"

Adrienne closed her eyes and tapped her forehead to Sylvia's and seemed to be considering how to reply. At last she said, "No. Except I wish you'd ask the same question of yourself. Not if I am giving you enough, but if you are giving yourself enough."

"I must be, since I'm the happiest I've ever been." Which, she realized, was both true and not at all an answer to Adrienne's question. "I'll think more about it." She kissed Adrienne and slipped her hands under her blouse. "I promise."

CHAPTER 17

❧

"Darling, it's so good to see you!" her mother cried breathily, kissing Sylvia repeatedly on her cheeks and then hugging her so tightly, she lost her breath.

Sylvia wanted to return her mother's affection and enthusiasm more heartily, but Eleanor Beach's sallow cheeks and bloodshot eyes, her stringy hair and paradoxically smart skirt and jacket, which further betrayed the reason for this unexpected reunion, made it impossible for her to do more than hug her mother perfunctorily and say, "I'm so glad you're here, Maman."

Then, to one of the stern-faced *gendarmes* watching the display, Sylvia said in clipped, professional French, "I paid at the front. May I take her home now?"

He nodded wordlessly, and Sylvia linked her mother's arm with hers, and they walked out of the chilly, noisy police station together as Sylvia made pointed eye contact with every officer who met her gaze; her mother kept her eyes fixed on her leather shoes with the fashionable buckle at the toe.

That bloody buckle. Why is it, Sylvia wondered, *that the people I love most in the world care so much for . . . things? Well, except for Adrienne.* Joyce, who'd practically begged for extra money to take his family north to Belgium for a cooler summer vacation, had just shipped home care of Shakespeare and Company a small Renaissance painting that must have cost a small fortune. And now here was her mother, caught stealing a brooch and scarf from a boutique on the Champs-Élysées! She hadn't even told Sylvia she was in town. *And Adrienne and I have to scrape together every penny we have just to take a few weeks in Les Déserts, where we sleep in a barn, for Pete's sake!*

She wasn't jealous. She didn't want things. She cared only for the health and happiness of her loved ones and the store. But the impulse of those loved ones toward false, material happiness did sometimes make her want to spit.

She felt all the more grateful for Adrienne, whose great earthly indulgence was food, which at least she and Sylvia could enjoy together. And those weeks with her in the rustic barn at Les Déserts, tending and harvesting their own vegetables and hiking winding paths into the hills burned gold by the summer sun, had been some of the best of her life. For once, she had been reluctant to come back to Paris.

Sylvia led her mother underground and into the metro, where they sat shoulder to shoulder as the train clacked and screeched and swayed, watching silently as well-dressed Parisians, still tan from their summer holidays, entered and exited, reading newspapers or chatting with friends. Back in the heart of the fifth, they alighted into the bright early fall afternoon, and Sylvia brought her mother to a little café with three sidewalk tables, ordered them each a café crème and a flan, and finally asked, "Why?"

With an almost petulantly thrust-out lower lip, her mother shrugged. "I wanted them."

Their coffees and flan arrived, and Sylvia was grateful for the distractions of the clinking and arranging of stoneware and cutlery.

"Holly wrote me that the boutique is doing well," she said, referring to the little import shop in Pasadena, California, that her mother and sisters had opened recently. Well, mainly Holly and Eleanor; Cyprian came and went between the shop and Hollywood, where she auditioned for every movie she could—usually to be bitterly disappointed. Holly had written that their store, which specialized in European housewares, did quite well out west, where European luxury seemed "more removed from the landscape here than the Orient." Less charitably, Cyprian had written, "These farmers wouldn't know style if it bit them on the balls so we can sell them anything, and at a high price, too."

"It is," her mother replied, licking a dab of milk foam from her upper lip. "But not well *enough*."

"Ah."

It was useless to ask about Father, who'd paid a much more conventional visit to Sylvia earlier in the summer, as he was stopping in Paris on his way to the eastern countries on some mission work, where he still was now, in fact. Why had he not mentioned that his wife, her mother, was not herself? Had he not noticed? If he had noticed, why had he left her alone? Why was her mother not planning to meet him on the continent? Questions swirled and made her feel unsteady.

"How can I help?" she asked her mother. Her favorite question. If she could only find a way to *help*, things would be better.

Her mother swallowed a bite of flan and sighed. "It is too late for me, Sylvia. I am old, I've lost my figure and my beauty. The only thing that brings me joy is *looking* at beautiful things. It's not enough, as it once was, to go to a museum or a market or a *vista* like they have in California and enjoy them from afar. I need to *have them on me*. It's as if wearing a beautiful bracelet, or a dress, confers some of its properties to me." She sighed again. "Or maybe I am fooling myself.

Maybe it's just that when beauty is close to me, *on* me, I can forget for a moment that I am no longer beautiful."

Heart aching, Sylvia closed her hand over her mother's on the cold surface of the little round marble tabletop. "I'm so sorry, Maman. I know I'm your daughter, but I see you very differently. You're hardly old! And you're healthy. Reread Balzac and take heart from the elder courtesans. Or look at Edith Wharton or Gertrude Stein still holding court here in Paris."

"I'm poor."

"Since when has that ever stood in your way?"

"Every day of my life."

This was a stunning revelation. Had her mother really always felt so restrained? How had Sylvia herself not noticed that? She wondered what Holly and Cyprian thought, and made a mental note to write to both of them right away.

"Please stay with me for a few days," she pleaded. "Adrienne is a marvelous cook. We'll eat well, and you'll enjoy the characters who come in and out of my shop. And we can do some proper shopping. Maybe get you a chic new haircut?"

Eleanor Beach shrugged.

It was a start.

⁂

"George is in Africa?" Julie asked.

"Good god, why?" Joyce asked.

"Antheil?" Bob chimed in. "No wonder it's been so quiet in here."

"Yes, George Antheil, and yes Africa, but no one really understands why," Sylvia reported to the group, though even as she said it, she began to understand why the composer had gone to the southern continent. The amazed pondering that Sylvia saw on the faces of her shrewdest friends would certainly get him and his *Ballet Mécanique* some attention.

Sure enough, word spread quickly. The same papers that had reported on Joyce's progress on *Ulysses*, then Sylvia's publication of it, now reported on rumors of the composer's whereabouts, stoking conversation and interest in all the cafés and bars that fall. *Where is George Antheil? Why has he disappeared just before the scheduled debut of the full* Ballet Mécanique *and promised* Second Symphony? *Is he as unhinged as his bizarre music suggests? Is he researching tribal rhythms he'd use in a new piece for the scheduled spring concert? Is he music's Gauguin?*

Even Sylvia, his volunteer publicist and mail collector, received precious little firsthand information. At first she delighted in reporting the rumors and general interest. But as fall darkened toward winter, and the talk turned uglier—*Maybe he doesn't care about his audience. How can a so-called genius be working on a great symphony in Africa? Has he gone to the Heart of Darkness?*—she sent him a letter pleading with him to come home soon.

It was all too much. As 1925 hurled to a close, she began to feel as overwhelmed as she'd felt when she was juggling Joyce's edits and the first subscriptions for *Ulysses* in late 1921. In addition to George's antics, there was the usual Joyce business to attend to—accounting, planning for future editions, overseeing translations, organizing his medical bills and doctor's visits, listening to him fret about his prospects because even Ezra Pound didn't seem to like *Work in Progress*. And recently two new problems had emerged: a Samuel Roth of New York City appeared to be serializing a pirated version of *Ulysses* in America, with a promise of publishing a full edition of the novel in the near future. And Joyce's daughter Lucia, who'd recently discovered a dance studio she adored, was behaving more and more erratically and causing her father and mother to argue about the best way to care for her.

On top of all this, Sylvia was trying to take Adrienne's advice and carve out time for one of her own dreams: a Walt Whitman retrospective with displays of his drafts in his own hand, first and later editions of his books, photographs, portraits, letters, and the like. For once, her own correspondence with the descendants of the venerable poet's former patrons and friends, not to mention a handful of museums in possession of his artifacts, outpaced her correspondence on Joyce's behalf. Or perhaps that was because she was allowing the Joyce correspondence to pile up as she worked on Whitman. Joyce, a devout lover of the American poet, was fully supportive of the endeavor and offered to help however he could. He'd even taken to greeting her as "O Captain, my Captain!" when he entered the store.

Not long after her mother's shoplifting, on a crisp fall morning as Sylvia composed more descriptions of the Whitman ephemera and her mother and Mysrine helped customers, shelved, and organized the front room of the shop, Julie came in with little Amélie on her hip, looking forlorn. Sylvia's mind immediately went to Michel, and she wondered about his mental state, for Woolf's heartbreaking *Mrs. Dalloway* had set Sylvia's mind on a morose line of thinking about the sweet-faced butcher: he was so like Woolf's character Septimus Warren Smith, the traumatized Great War veteran. Julie was typically a locked box about Michel, but that morning Sylvia decided to broach the subject, saying in the privacy of the library room, "Are you all right, Julie? How is Michel?"

Tears glistened in the young woman's eyes, and she swallowed wetly, unable to respond. Amélie played with her mother's hair and babbled.

Sylvia touched Julie's arm lightly. "There are people who understand what he's been through, who could perhaps help him."

Julie cleared her throat, and said in a gravelly voice, "He would never consent to analysis. He thinks they are witch doctors." It was clear that Julie didn't agree, and that she'd already tried to convince Michel to see such a doctor. "The poetry is his best antidote."

"Is there any way for me or Adrienne or any other friend to help him, or convince him to talk to someone?"

She shook her head. "One of his best friends from childhood has tried. His mother has tried. I have tried."

Sylvia's heart felt like a heavy water pail in her chest. "Is there anything I can do to help *you*, then?"

"You already do. And Adrienne, too. Your shops . . . they are like Elysium for us."

Coming into the library almost on tiptoe, Sylvia's mother looked at Amélie and said in playful French, "Who might this be?"

Julie, brightened by the interest in her child, nudged the girl toward Sylvia's mother and said, "Tell her your name."

"Amélie," the girl muttered with her fist in her mouth.

Eleanor smiled widely. "What a beautiful name. I'm Madame Beach."

Amélie turned her large blue eyes to Sylvia, took her wet hand out of her mouth to point at her, and said, "Madame Beach."

"Mademoiselle Beach," Eleanor corrected her with a wink. Then, patting her own chest, she repeated, "Madame Beach."

Thoroughly confused, Amélie looked at her mother and said, "Maman?"

Julie laughed and said, "You may call her madame or mademoiselle, *petit lapin*."

"Bien sûr," Eleanor agreed, taking obvious pride in having cheered the melancholy Julie. "Sylvia, would you mind if I took a short break to take this lovely child for a walk and macaron?"

Amélie's eyes became even bigger, and she looked to her mother for permission.

"What a special treat," Julie said. Then, looking at Sylvia's mother, said, "Merci beaucoup, Madame Beach."

"*You* must call me Eleanor," she said. Then she took Amélie's hand and led her out, asking in soft tones if she had ever heard of a naughty rabbit named Peter.

The whole tableau moved Sylvia, and she felt a lump form in her throat. She'd never wanted children for herself, but she suddenly and ardently wished she could give a grandchild to her mother. She wondered if Holly ever would; she was the most likely candidate, as Cyprian grew less and less patient with men, especially what she described as the "unrefined cowboys" of California.

Sylvia had been wondering why her actress sister stayed out west instead of trying to get onstage in New York or Boston, and then a reply to her letter about their mother arrived.

> *Mother's been unhappy for the last year, which is part of what keeps me here, despite the lack of roles for me. She and I share many traits, in particular a love of European luxury, and so arranging the shop together is a genuine pleasure. Holly's best with the books, and so we three make a good team. Dad's useless, I don't mind telling you. He's always teaching or at the church or away doing his mission work. It seems like he's not interested in anything we're doing, and frankly, the feeling is mutual.*

Holly's letter wasn't much more comforting:

> *Mother and Father don't get along as well as they used to. There's little laughter when both of them are home, and Dad just doesn't understand the store at all. "Why don't you do something more meaningful, like Sylvia?" he's always asking us. Don't*

worry, though, dear sister—no one holds your success against you!
We are all so proud. But Dad does seem to wish all of us would
find our own Odyssey to embark upon. He can't see that we have!
We're happy in the store—I'm sure you can appreciate that.

The letters depressed Sylvia, not only because of the unhappy facts they relayed, but also because there was so little she could do about any of it from Paris. The best she felt she could do was to help her mother rest and enjoy herself before returning home—which she seemed to be doing, especially in her surprise bond with Amélie, whom she saw almost every day. Eleanor would relieve Julie's maternal burden for a few hours, returning to Shakespeare as delighted as Amélie, who radiated simple joy after their trips through the Luxembourg Gardens, or to a puppet show, or a pony ride, or to eat a Breton crêpe smothered in strawberry jam. Sometimes Julie would run errands, and other times she'd collapse into the green chair, read, and doze. It seemed that everyone in that triad was getting something elemental that they needed.

Tearfully, Eleanor left in late November for a buying trip in Germany and Switzerland, but she returned soon enough with happy, ruddy cheeks and laden with gorgeous, delicate trinkets from the Christkindl markets: tiny wooden trees with golden balls, stained and blown glass ornaments, painstakingly carved and painted crèches. With blushing, hubristic fanfare, Eleanor presented one of almost everything to Sylvia and Adrienne, and to Julie and Amélie. The rest she shipped to the store in Pasadena, in the hopes that some of it would arrive in time to be sold this very Christmas season, though she'd purchased enough for the following year as well.

True to the speech she'd given Sylvia after her arrest, the very near proximity of beautiful, festive items revived Eleanor Beach, as even their several trips to the Louvre had not. Sylvia noticed a slim gold cuff on her mother's right wrist and hoped it had been procured with cash and not stealth, but she didn't have the heart to inquire. It was like the exquisite square painting that hung on Joyce's wall near the window with its glimpse of the Eiffel Tower; the picture was an intimate interior scene, a representation of a window itself, through which one could see a sliver of sea and ships. It was so like Joyce to hang that picture near his own window, his own room with a view. A quote, an echo, a dialogue.

Though she hated to admit it, and she felt bad for Julie and Amélie, Sylvia was relieved when her mother boarded the first of many trains and ships that would take Eleanor back to California in time to celebrate Christmas with Cyprian and Holly and her father in the western sunshine. In contrast, she and Adrienne went to the familiar thatched cottage in Rocfoin to celebrate with the Monniers. They made a present of the crèche, because there was barely enough space for it in their little apartment on the Odéon, while it was given pride of place above the mantel in the Monnier living room, beside the glowing tree they decorated on Christmas Eve. For a glorious week, they listened to carols on the wireless and drank mulled wine and ate the most delicious ginger cookies Sylvia had ever tasted. Teddy and the Monniers' huge dog, Mousse, wrestled and snuggled like long-lost siblings.

As she fell asleep those last nights of 1925, Sylvia felt that something had shifted in her relationship to Paris. Her heart was still there; it was still the place she loved best in all the world; but something in these country retreats tugged her away. It was like the restlessness she'd felt everywhere else in her youth, the restlessness that had always brought her *back* to Paris. Feeling its tingle again was unsettling.

It must be Mother. And this Samuel Roth character, she told herself as she tried to focus instead on Adrienne's gentle, consistent breathing beside her. *May 1926 bring more peace.*

CHAPTER 18

Sylvia buzzed from guest to guest as the crowd spilled from her shop into the street on the mild April night of the opening of her Walt Whitman exhibit. Eliot had come all the way from England, Ezra from Italy, and her parents from the West Coast of America. Even her most dogmatically modern literary friends had come to the party, if not to toast Whitman—because as Eliot pointed out, what need does Old Walt have of their celebrating when he sounds his barbaric yawps loud enough from the pages he wrote—then to support Sylvia and celebrate each other. Curiously, it was her original Paris friends and clientele, the *potassons* from Adrienne's store, who were most enamored of Whitman. And Joyce, of course. Just when she thought she couldn't take any more of his complaining about his eyes and money, he'd turn up at the store reciting "O Me! O Life!" or "What I Heard at the Close of the Day" with a fist full of daffodils, and she couldn't be irritated any longer.

"Pity Gertrude couldn't make it," said Ernest. "She might be the only American in Paris not here tonight."

"Don't be disingenuous, it doesn't suit you," Sylvia replied with a grin, for she knew of Ernest's recent break with Stein. Though she didn't have the details, she knew there had been some sort of rift between them, and she couldn't say she was surprised. What with Ernest's hot head and his ego, and Gertrude's intolerance for anyone who dared to dissent from her in any way, it seemed inevitable. And while Sylvia was relieved to know that she and Joyce weren't the only people Gertrude was willing to excise, she also felt genuinely bad for her. It was only herself and Alice she hurt with her recalcitrance.

"Disingenuous? Me?" Ernest asked wickedly.

Ever the gadfly, Ford Madox Ford passed by with a bottle of champagne and refilled both their glasses before moving on to the next clutch of people, and Ernest and Sylvia spent a few minutes reliving their adventure to the final of the six-day Vél d'Hiv bicycle races earlier in the month. The sound of the cycles and cheers of the crowds inside the Vélodrome had been loud and invigorating. "I've been meaning to suggest that you sponsor a Parisian writers' boxing tournament," Ernest said.

Sylvia laughed. "Just what I need, writers with knuckles too bloodied to write!"

"I think Thornton and Ezra are in good enough shape," he said. "Joyce would get a pass because of his eyes, of course."

She shook her head, "I don't know how you find the time, Ernest!"

"I don't know how others don't," he replied. "And nice dodge, Sylvia."

She ducked in the way she'd seen his favorite boxers do to escape a punch, and he chuckled and then clinked his glass to hers.

Next she found herself sucked into what seemed like a conversation from five years before. Ezra, Larbaud, McAlmon, and Joyce were locked in an intense discussion about the fate of *Ulysses*.

". . . and Quinn was simply wrong," Ezra was saying as she joined them.

"I'm having déjà vu," she said. "How could he be wrong again, from the grave?" The lawyer had died suddenly, close to two years ago; he'd only been in his midfifties and everyone was surprised.

"His mistakes about the copyright still haunt us," Ezra grumbled. "Which is how Samuel 'The Pornblisher' Roth can pirate *Ulysses* with impunity."

"Pity Quinn's too dead to regale with his wrongness," said Bob.

"I did worry about this very issue to Quinn three years ago, when I asked if I should have a copy cataloged with the Library of Congress. He assured me that *The Little Review* chapters would suffice to cover its copyright." Sylvia shook her head. "There was no arguing with him, and so he wouldn't help."

"I rue the day I ever trusted him," said Ezra.

"Who else were we to trust?" she asked. "It wasn't like other lawyers were lining up for his job. I seem to remember that Margaret and Jane asked around." Sylvia glanced around to see if she could see the two editors, but couldn't find them in the crowd.

"Let's not forget that he was a great collector, and patron," Joyce pointed out. "And at the time, he seemed to want the best for the book."

"Do you have a plan for fighting the pirated edition?" Ezra asked Sylvia.

"Not yet," she said, annoyed that this topic was overtaking her party for Whitman. "But we do plan to fight it. It's a source of income for both Joyce and the store. We can't just have Roth siphoning off what's rightly ours."

"Exactly," said Joyce, nodding.

"Well, if you need anything, please let me know," Ezra said, as if offering to fix one of her creaky chairs or tables. She noticed, though, that he shot Joyce a kind of scolding look, and wondered if she even wanted to know what it was all about.

Excusing herself to say hello to Sara and Gerald Murphy, but in fact to get away from the rain cloud of a conversation, Sylvia drifted off. From across the store, she glimpsed her mother kissing Julie, Amélie, and Michel goodbye, and her father watching with tender eyes. She was glad he was accompanying her mother on her upcoming buying trip to Italy, even though he had work of his own to accomplish there as well. She thought it was best if her mother wasn't alone, though Cyprian's recent letter on the subject intruded on her peace about it: "Mother just seems moodier when Dad is around. Less able to relax and be herself." Sylvia had been so busy these past days that she hadn't been able to gain much insight into the relations between her parents when they were in town together. But surely her mother was better off now than she'd been in the fall? She looked it, anyway.

As Sylvia made her way over to her parents, Ezra stopped her and said quietly, "You know that Joyce contracted with Roth to publish pieces of his *Work in Progress* last year in *Two Worlds* journal?"

Sylvia shook her head, and felt that same sense of exclusion she'd felt years ago when Joyce hadn't kept her up to date on the trial of *Ulysses*. It was his prerogative to serialize his writing in the United States, but she did wish he'd run the idea by her.

Ezra leaned in closer and with narrowed eyes said, "Roth's been hounding Joyce for *Ulysses* for years. And I wouldn't put it past Roth to have sent him a contract that implied more permission than simply publishing bits of that *Rag in Progress* he's writing now. Nor would I trust Joyce to have read the document carefully enough to have stayed out of such a trap. Roth's a snake and Joyce a lamb. Don't say I didn't warn you."

"I consider myself duly warned," she replied, feeling her blood get hot, flushing her cheeks and making her neck itch. "Thank you, Ezra."

Oh, Walt. How did you stay so optimistic as—of all things—a writer?

🐚

"It sold how many copies?"

"Twenty thousand."

"In its first year alone?"

"Apparently."

Joyce slumped into his chair, and Sylvia stood beside him with a hand on his shoulder. "*The Great Gatsby* isn't *Ulysses*. Not even close," she said. "It's not even a bestseller at that many copies."

"It could well become one." Joyce looked at Sylvia pleadingly. "Do you think *Gatsby* will last? You've always said *Ulysses* will last."

"I don't know," she said, unable to be anything other than truthful, even with her favorite writer, because Fitzgerald's novel did have something special about it. True, it aspired to be a popular novel, and it was not even in the same league with Joyce's tour de force. Any yet. It sparkled. It was moving. It tapped into something essential about being American. There was something Whitmanian about it. "I do know that there has always been plenty of room in literature for both the avant-garde and the commercial. It doesn't have to be a competition."

Joyce didn't reply. A minute or so ticked by, and then he said, "I missed him the last time he was in Paris, but I've seen pictures of him everywhere. He and his wife are beautiful. Magnetic, I've heard."

"Yes," she said carefully. "He and Zelda are charming."

"Ernest met him, and told me that one of the reasons Mr. Fitzgerald wanted to come to Paris was me. He said any city in which *Ulysses* could be written and published was for him. I wasn't sure if I believed it. What does the great F. Scott Fitzgerald need of Leopold and Stephen?"

"How can you say that? We all need Leopold and Stephen. Any writer worth his salt has to reckon with them."

"You mean that?" Joyce looked at her with his one milky, bespectacled eye, and the other behind a black patch.

"Of course I mean it," she said.

"Have you ever thought about opening a branch of your store in New York?"

This was such an abrupt change of topic, Sylvia had to shake her head and say, "Pardon?" to make sure she'd heard him correctly.

"New York," he repeated. "I was thinking the other day, it might be easier to fight Roth from his side of the Atlantic."

"But my home is here." *What's he talking about? Is he joking?*

But he wasn't. "It would only be temporary. Just long enough for you to set up shop in America, vanquish Roth, and begin publishing my work there."

"But . . . *Ulysses* isn't any more legal in America now than it was four years ago."

"Perhaps we could find another, better lawyer than Quinn to fight for it again. That's next to impossible from Paris, as we discovered last time."

Breathing hard against a rising panic in her chest, Sylvia considered for a moment what to say. "I'm not sure if I ever told you this, but my original idea for the store was to open a French-language bookshop like Adrienne's in America. But rents in 1919 were already too high. They've only gone up since then. My mother and sisters had to go to Pasadena, all the way out west in California, to open their boutique, and California is just as far from New York and publishing as Paris."

He frowned. "I can see you're not interested in my idea, even though it could be just the thing to fix our problems."

"It's not that I'm not interested, it's that I see it creating as many problems as it might solve." *And it would throw my life into utter chaos.*

He shrugged in a pouting manner; *I disagree*, it clearly said.

"We will find a way to fight Roth," said Sylvia with conviction. She wasn't sure how, but she would. She had to. She was smuggling hundreds of copies of the novel all over the world, in the face of the Comstock laws, John Sumner, and the post office. Samuel Roth wasn't going to stop her.

But Joyce's lack of reply was what pushed the words from her mouth: "Mr. Joyce, did Roth publish part of your *Work in Progress*?"

His head snapped up in such surprise, Sylvia felt the wind knocked out of her.

Then, returning to himself and waving a lazy hand, he said, "A chapter or two. He wanted more, but I saw him for the swindler he is."

"I wouldn't blame you, you know, if you'd corresponded with him. Especially if he was offering you a handsome sum." She was leaving the door wide open for him to be honest with her.

"You are my publisher, Miss Beach," he said firmly. *Conversation over.*

She wished she felt more reassured.

CHAPTER 19

"But of course Antheil is the musical Joyce," Margaret Anderson proclaimed at Le Monocle, Margaret and Jane's favorite haunt, particularly because Jane dressed like so many of the all-female clientele, in a three-piece suit. And many of the others wore feather boas and sequined headache bands like Margaret. Making an effort for their new friends, Sylvia had donned her sister's red shoes and a black dress, and Adrienne wore an old suit of her father's that fit her surprisingly well.

Earlier that night they'd been at the riot that was George Antheil's *Ballet Mécanique*'s premiere at the Théâtre des Champs-Élysées. As the sixteen automated player pianos ground through their Braille-like reels of notes, and the orchestra played its sporadic and dissonant score, the audience of music-loving Parisians and expatriates stood, threw fruit, and booed, inspiring the other half of the audience to stand and cheer. The audience's brawl became louder and rowdier than the boxing matches Ernest brought them to.

"True enough," agreed Jane, leaning back in her woven chair and taking a drag from her slim cigar. "Both of them are prepared to piss everyone off for the sake of art."

· "But it's more than reception, darling," Margaret enthused. "It's also *musicality*. I don't know if you know this," she said to Sylvia and Adrienne as if divulging a state secret, "but I got my start in music. I was a symphony-goer long before I was a reader. And Joyce's gift for playing his work *in my ear* was one of the first things I loved about his writing. Isn't that right, Jane? Haven't I always said that Joyce's musicality is what will make his work last?"

"You have," said Jane with a sage nod. "Though of course as *I've* always said, that ignores the fact that what most people respond to in his writing is its style, the way it appears on the page. And its dirty qualities. And its at times deathly boring realism. And its habit of exposing every dark and wicked secret our minds have ever harbored."

"Which are all acts in his symphony!"

Jane blew a puff of fragrant smoke at Margaret and smiled adoringly. Sylvia had the impression that she and Adrienne were seeing a routine the couple was accustomed to performing. "I don't see why it can't be both," Sylvia suggested, "musical *and* literary."

"Oh, Sylvia," Margaret laughed, finishing the last of her Côtes du Rhône, "you're no fun at all."

Adrienne, who was quickly exhausted by any conversation related to Joyce, changed the subject. "So tell us, Margaret, more about Antheil's work from a musical perspective. I do not have the same background as you. I enjoy music but have no formal training."

"Well! Neither did the philistines throwing perfectly good peaches at the stage! They would have been ever so much better in a pie. A pie would have restored order in their lives. Or a *tarte*, I suppose. Regardless. As you no doubt heard, as everyone heard, George's music simply tells us that harmony is over. That beautiful music that lulls us into the illusion that life has meaning and order is a lie."

"I am tired of this line of argument," said Adrienne testily, "which we hear all the time about the new writing and the new music, just as we heard it about the new painting a generation ago. How could one piece of music negate centuries of beauty? Beethoven's Fifth? Chopin's piano concertos? Bach's fugues? The new art does not negate what came before! No. It's an opening, a garden gate, revealing a path to what comes next."

"Marvelous," exclaimed Margaret, puffing on her cigarette from the other end of its elegant bone holder. "Adrienne, you should write something for *The Little Review*."

"*Peut-être*," Adrienne responded noncommittally, and Sylvia was amazed—as she often was—at Adrienne's je ne sais quoi, her ability to command attention and then wave it off, as if she didn't need to keep it, for there was plenty more where it came from.

☙

Once the excitement of the Whitman exhibit and the *Ballet Mécanique* died down, it seemed that the rest of 1926 was swallowed whole by Sylvia's legal battle with Samuel Roth. She learned more about copyright law and piracy in publishing than she ever dreamed she might, and every detail of it was so dull that she wouldn't have visited it on her worst enemy. Every day, after poring over documents dense with type, she'd collapse on the couch in her apartment with Adrienne, occasionally hoping one of her migraines might come on so she'd have the excuse not to read more of it the next day. But then a migraine would emerge, and she'd be felled by it so painfully, she regretted her stupid wish with every fiber of her being. And the headaches did seem to be coming more frequently than before. She wasn't sure if she could ascribe that to the difficulty of the reading, the exacting correspondence with the lawyers in Paris and New York, or the overall stress of the battle.

To add insult to injury, Joyce brought up his New York shop idea again, and when he continued arguing with her about it, suggesting that she should at least try to find an affordable space, she'd finally said, "Mr. Joyce, my life is here is Paris. I do not want to live in New York."

"You can always come back."

"But I don't want to leave at all."

"Not even to save our book?"

"I do not believe that my living in America will save *Ulysses* from Mr. Roth. It will only make me miserable, being away from everyone and everything I love."

"Miss Beach, please, you must know that the last thing I want is for you to be miserable."

"Then please discontinue this line of inquiry," she said with more force than she ever took with Joyce. With anyone. She wasn't even sure where it had come from, this decided tone that implied, *Stop upsetting me right this minute.*

Joyce, too, appeared taken aback. With a glance at his pocket watch, he said, "Mrs. Joyce is expecting me," then gathered his coat and ashplant stick and walked out of the store, leaving Sylvia with blood coursing noisily in her ears.

"Good for you," said Mysrine, startling Sylvia so much, she gasped and put a hand on her chest.

"Heavens, Mysrine. I'm sorry. I forgot anyone else was in here."

"I tried not to disturb you, and I tried not to listen, but . . . he was badgering you, Sylvia. It wasn't right. Especially not after all you've done for him."

"You sound like Adrienne."

Mysrine smiled. "That's the finest compliment I've received in a long time."

✳

The new unease in her relationship with Joyce didn't make it any easier to withstand the odious letters from Roth and his legal team, which referred to her as a mere secretary and, worse, called her openly misogynist names like "vicious virago." "It just goes to show," she wrote to her sister Holly and also her old friend Carlotta, both of whom she'd campaigned with for suffrage, "that although the law might have changed, feelings have not. What a long way women still have to go."

There were skirmishes in the battle that were satisfying, however. Ludwig Lewisohn, German by descent but American by growth and training, a novelist with a clear head and crusading spirit who'd recently fallen in with the expat writers she'd begun referring to as the Crowd, presented Sylvia with a draft of a letter one day at Shakespeare and Company. "We are writing to protest the grotesque theft of a great work of literature, *Ulysses* by James Joyce," he'd written, "which has been appropriated by the pirate Samuel Roth as if it were a treasure on the high seas." It was meant to be signed by as many writers and intellectuals as possible before being submitted to every newspaper in America that would print it.

Tears threatened when she read the letter in her shop that chilly, drizzly fall morning. "Thank you," she whispered to Ludwig, who only smiled at her.

"My dear Sylvia, it's the rest of us who should thank you, with more than just words. With action. This is only a small token of my own gratitude for all you've done for us American writers in Paris."

She was amazed. Here was a peripheral member of the Crowd, little more than a stranger to her and yet a subscriber to her library and a customer in her store, picking her up off the floor and dusting her off. The lump in her throat made it so she could hardly speak.

"I think we should have MacLeish read it for legality," Ludwig went on, and Sylvia nodded.

"Thank you," she rasped.

And off he went to find Archibald MacLeish, lawyer turned writer. Just like that. She'd become so accustomed to depending only on Adrienne, her partner in all things, and Mysrine, whom she paid, that it was unfamiliar and disquieting to depend on someone else. Someone unexpected.

But also, what a relief.

The letter and the signatures it attracted acted as a splint on her fractured relationship with Joyce. He began coming into Shakespeare and Company with an almost childish excitement, as he had in 1922 when the reviews and subscriptions arrived daily and they made a game of reading them aloud, volleying names and phrases around the store like verbal tennis balls.

"Truly?" he'd say. "Mr. Wells pledged his name for my book?"

"For your book and for independent thought and publishing," she'd say, and Joyce would raise an invisible glass in toast.

Everyone signed. All of the Crowd, obviously, but also Somerset Maugham, E. M. Forster, the esteemed physicist Albert Einstein, and the Italian playwright Luigi Pirandello. Even George Bernard Shaw.

CHAPTER 20

On March 14, 1927, just over a month after *Ulysses* turned five and Joyce forty-five, Sylvia turned forty. Though she hadn't planned anything to celebrate, her friends had other ideas in mind. It started with Adrienne serving her coffee and her favorite *tarte aux prunes* in bed, then Bob stopping by the store with a carton of her favorite indulgent brand of cigarettes, a few of which they smoked together while leaning on the frame of the windows of the store as the late winter sun warmed their faces, hands, and coats and they talked about his estrangement and likely divorce from Bryher. Ludwig gave her a rare edition of *Songs of Myself*, and Julie, Michel, and Amélie came by with a pound of venison and a cake frosted in red, white, and blue, "The colors of both our flags," Julie said proudly. Michel had seemed better the last few times she'd seen him, and his easy smile was its own gift.

Joyce showed up with forty roses in varying shades of pink and red, and declared that Mysrine wouldn't mind running the shop while he took her and Adrienne to lunch at the Ritz. As Sylvia was trying to stay awake after that luxurious midday meal, Ernest and the stylish Pauline Pfeiffer, whom he seemed intent on marrying before the ink was even dry on his divorce from Hadley, arrived in the late afternoon with tickets to a prizefight. And so her birthday ended with beer and soft, Bavarian-style pretzels and much cheering and booing. On their way home, she and Adrienne stopped at a gelato shop and licked cones full of chocolate, lemon, and vanilla goodness.

"I like Pauline," said Adrienne, "though I miss Hadley."

"Yes," agreed Sylvia. "I feel the same way. And . . ."

"And?"

Standing at the window of their apartment, Sylvia looked down the street at her own shop, which was shuttered after a festive day of friends and books, and tried to articulate what she was feeling. "Well, it's just that Ernest's divorce and his new marriage . . . It has nothing to do with us, and yet, it feels like a sign, or an omen. Things feel different in Odeonia than they did eight years ago, don't they?"

"I know what you mean," Adrienne said. "Many changes I like. The Americans who have come here have brightened the city and our lives, and the exchange of ideas with our French friends has been marvelous. But . . ."

"The parties."

"The drinking."

"The divorces."

"The jealousy."

Adrienne joined Sylvia at the window and looked out into the dark night, the deserted street. A gas lamp lit the sidewalk a few yards down from Shakespeare and Company, casting a warm yellow glow on the gray pavement, the creamy stone of the building. It looked like a picture, a moment frozen in time and already fading dustily into the past.

Sylvia wanted to say to Adrienne that despite all that was changing around them, her feelings for her remained unchanged, but the words clogged in her throat. Instead she breathed in Adrienne's ear the way she knew she liked, hoping. Eyes closed, Adrienne turned toward her and kissed her, and Sylvia tried to lose herself in the press of their bodies, but couldn't, quite. A part of her was still standing at the window, looking out, and wondering what else was going to change.

⁂

"Mother's gotten so depressed," Cyprian said. They were sitting at a sidewalk café on the Carrefour de l'Odéon having coffee and cigarettes. Her sister was in town on a vacation from her duties in California, and Sylvia was thrilled to see her.

Her sister's pessimism about their mother was surprising and worrying, however. Sylvia had felt encouraged by Eleanor's recent letters to her, in which she gregariously reported on the people who came in and out of their store. She also sent weekly letters to Amélie, always colorfully decorated with paint or crayon designs. "Her letters have been contented enough. Maybe she's a bit up and down these days?"

"More down than up, I'd say."

"It seems better when she's not alone."

"She has Holly," Cyprian said defensively, and Sylvia regretted her words—she hadn't meant to accuse Cyprian of leaving their mother, because she knew that Holly and her father were both with her now. Aggressively stubbing out her cigarette and blowing out a stream of smoke, Cyprian said, "You'll see what I mean soon. She's planning to come on a buying trip in a month."

"Another one?"

"It's the only thing that keeps her sane. I think she's running away from Dad."

"They seemed happy when they were here together for the Whitman exhibit." But Sylvia remembered with a pang of guilt that she hadn't paid close attention to her parents then.

"They know how to put on a good show. You know he gets mad at her for what he calls 'lavishing money on our spoiled daughters'?"

"Really? Dad?"

Cyprian nodded. "I've heard him say those exact words."

"He's never expressed anything like that to me."

"Nor to me, not directly anyway," Cyprian said. "He seems to save it all up for Mom."

"I wish I could have seen or heard some of that. Any of that, when they were here."

Cyprian shrugged. "What would you have done? What can any of us do? The die's been cast for all of us. And anyway, how much attention could you pay them with everything you're juggling?" Sylvia heard acknowledgment there, but envy, too. It was strange, how the tables between them had turned. A decade ago, it had been Sylvia who wished she could be Cyprian. And now, increasingly, it was Cyprian who wished she could be Sylvia. Her sister had all but given up on going to pointless auditions in Hollywood, and though she was still a beauty, age was beginning to show in her face and figure. Sylvia recalled what her mother had said about the costs of age, and how similar Cyprian had always been to her; it made Sylvia glad that her mother had sympathetic company in Cyprian, but it also worried her that Cyprian herself might someday find herself as unhappy as their mother.

They each smoked another cigarette in silence, sipping coffee between puffs, and Sylvia reflected to herself how much more she smoked with her sister around. As they were ashing the last of them into the glass dish on the table, a large, shiny brown bus came to a squealing stop across the street and a few yards up the rue de Condé, toward Saint-Sulpice. Out filed a stream of clearly American tourists with brand-new cameras, spit-shined walking shoes, and fashionable hats they'd probably picked up that morning at the Galeries Lafayette.

"What the . . . ," Cyprian marveled, her mouth open.

"Haven't you heard? The sun *only* rises in the fifth and sixth. More and more of these tours are arriving all the time," said Sylvia.

"And you can't make them go away?"

Sylvia heaved a weary, conflicted sigh. "It's hard to say no to their money. I've sold more books to buses full of them than I used to sell in a year."

"But they're so . . ."

"Bright-eyed and bushy-tailed?"

"Cloying."

"I've missed you, sister."

"Well, with *that* for company, I can see why."

"Between you and me, they're not *that* different from the American writers who have come and gone for years. Stein rarely associates with anyone other than other Americans. Djuna, Scott, Eliot, Pound—they've all been like a club. Joyce and Ernest are rare in their command of the French language and their friendships with other actual Parisians. Which is probably why I love them both so much." She reached for another cigarette, then stopped herself. She didn't want to feel so thirsty later, and she'd also noticed that too many could bring on the auras of a migraine, a throbbing rainbow that wanted to wrap around her like a boa constrictor.

"Well, not everyone can go native like you," Cyprian replied, her narrowed eyes still fixed on the group from the bus who appeared to be discussing which way to walk. "Still, our friends who have visited here the past few years are different from *them*. How long will they be here? A week? Two days? Just so they can go home to the middle west and say they came to Paris, spotted a famous painter or writer, ate at a restaurant they read about in *Collier's*, tee-hee about dipping their tongues in absinthe, and oh, wasn't the red wine the best they've ever had."

"Don't forget buying books at Shakespeare and Company."

Cyprian rolled her eyes. "I never had you down as such an opportunist."

"Shrewd businesswoman, you mean."

"Well, I suppose it's for a good cause. You *are* keeping the real writers afloat."

"I try."

"You do more than try . . . I'm jealous, you know."

Sylvia was flabbergasted at this admission and had no idea how to reply. But her sister saved her the effort. "I do have some good news of my own to report, however. I've met someone who makes California tolerable."

"Do tell," Sylvia exhaled, relieved.

"Her name is Helen Eddy. She used to act like me, but now she gives tennis lessons to little children. She's always tan and magnificent." Cyprian's eyes sparkled. "I've decided I'm too old to pretend to be anything I'm not."

"Good for you," Sylvia said. "I'd love to meet her someday."

"You might have to leave Paris to do that. Have you ever noticed how many people come to visit *you*? When can you take a trip to us?"

"I hardly think that's fair," she replied, feeling defensive, though, after all, what Cyprian said was true. She'd just never thought of it before. Nor had she ever felt a strong enough pull from the United States to want to return. "People come to Paris because they want to come to Paris."

"And they want to see you. Don't you want to see us? Where we live? How we live?"

"Yes of course," said Sylvia, but inside she could tell this wasn't true. Shoving that aside, she said, "Tell me more about this Helen Eddy."

※

Despite Ludwig's letter and the 167 signatures protesting the piracy, Roth persisted in publishing his version of *Ulysses*.

"So he's published an illegal version of an already illegal book?" Bob said. "And it's selling like hotcakes?"

"Well, he's not above marketing it as smut," Sylvia replied.

"Genius," he said, half seriously.

Sylvia didn't know how she was going to find the time to battle Roth any more than she already had. There just didn't seem to be enough hours in the day—which, she said to herself, was another kind of answer to Cyprian's question of why she never visited the United States. She was organizing so much: Joyce's volume of poetry, *Pomes Penyeach*, was already with Darantiere, as was the sixth edition of *Ulysses*, and she was putting together promotional materials for both little by little every day; she was organizing a volume of criticism on Joyce's *Work in Progress* for publication in about a year; the French translators of *Ulysses* were squabbling, and requests to translate the novel into even the smaller European languages like Czech and Serbian were coming in. Joyce continued to hurt his eyes with hours of candlelit toil, which Dr. Borsch continued to advise against.

Every time she heard Roth's numbers—that he'd sold a hundred, a thousand, seven thousand copies of his cheap, fraudulent *Ulysses*—she couldn't help but tally up the money she wasn't making, money he was swindling from her and Joyce.

There were days when she wanted to quit, when she heard the siren song of that empty barn in Les Déserts calling to her.

So when Adrienne said to her one blissfully lazy Sunday morning,

"I think we should look into buying a car, to make it easier to go to Rocfoin and anywhere else we want to escape to," Sylvia practically jumped up from the couch where they were reading the newspaper and shouted, "Yes!"

In a week, they were the proud owners of a little blue Citroën. They drove it off the lot in a state of what Sylvia could only describe as unabashed glee, honking the horn, singing, "Wheeeeee!" and waving their scarves colorfully out the window. They took turns driving it, not straight home, but out to Versailles, where they walked about the gardens making jokes about eating cake in their fabulous new vehicle before hopping back in and looping up past the Eiffel Tower, honking madly as they passed the Joyce residence and wondering if anyone there noticed or cared, before finally winding their way to the rue de l'Odéon. The sun was setting on a glorious June evening.

"I haven't had that much fun in ages," she panted as they sat in the car a little longer, not wanting to leave its firm and fragrant leather seats, or stop looking at the picture view of their Odeonia from the black-framed windshield.

Adrienne reached over and twined her fingers into the hair at the nape of Sylvia's neck. "We need to have more fun."

"How can you sound so serious when you're talking about fun?"

"Because it is serious. You've been getting too many migraines. Doing too much for Joyce. It's time to do less. Enjoy your own life more."

Adrienne's words made her feel defensive. "You're busy, too," she replied.

"True." Adrienne nodded, then tightened her grip on Sylvia's hair. "I plan to start saying no more myself. But it will be easier for me because I don't have one person and his whole family entirely dependent on my industry."

"He's not entirely dependent on me."

Adrienne tipped her head down and raised both brows. "If he's not, then he should have no problem if you refuse his requests."

She knew Adrienne was right. Today she'd felt so free, as free as she felt in Les Déserts, or in Rocfoin, when she was *away* from Joyce's relentless requests. She felt lighter, happier, more amorous. More herself. Today she'd felt again like the young adventuress who'd come to Paris ten years ago, stumbled into A. Monnier, and fallen in love with a store and a life.

"I'll try," she said, and it was as much a promise to Adrienne as to that self from ten years before. Still, the idea of saying no to Joyce filled her with anxiety. *I should be able to balance everything better*, she replied to herself. *I'm not giving my mother grandchildren, after all. But I can give her, and Dad, another kind of legacy to be proud of.*

She also reflected that the young woman who'd come to A. Monnier all those years ago was in love with reading and the writing of James Joyce. It was a *privilege* to be his publisher, and his success was inextricably linked to that of Shakespeare and Company, which had become synonymous with his outlaw masterpiece; her store had changed literature. No, she couldn't give up on him or his book. Especially not now that Cyprian had told her that their father resented the ways in which his wife helped their daughters. She simply couldn't let him, them, any of them, down.

CHAPTER 21

The concierge from the hotel babbled in such overexcited, incoherent French that Sylvia had to hand the receiver to Adrienne so that a native Parisienne could parse the words. The only bits she caught absolutely were *Madame Beach*, and *lettre*. Then she watched and listened while Adrienne nodded, gasped, and listened with increasingly wide eyes. Though she said the requisite *bon*s and *merci*s, Sylvia could tell from her grave tone that nothing she was hearing was good, and by the time she hung up, Sylvia was a wreck of nerves and had already lit a second cigarette.

"*Chérie*," Adrienne said softly, "your mother is dead. At the hotel. She's left a long letter."

"Dead? With a letter?" Though Adrienne was now using words she could understand, Sylvia still couldn't make sense of them.

Until it dawned on her.

A letter. A long letter.

"How did she do it?" Sylvia whispered, the horrible, unbidden image of her mother hanging from a bedsheet flashing to mind.

"Pills."

Hand on her chest, Sylvia started heaving—or hyperventilating, or sobbing, it was impossible to tell which. Somehow Adrienne got her to the nearest place to sit. Were they in the kitchen? Bedroom? She had no idea, and no memory of it later. Nor did she form any specific or coherent memories of the next hours, for it was all a collage of jagged, black impressions: going to the hotel with Adrienne; seeing her mother rigid in the bed, vomit on the floor and pillows; ignoring a cup of tea while she made arrangements for a coroner to write a report and a mortician to collect the body. It was late June, warm and bright. Wedding season.

She would dream about those hours in the weeks—and years—to come. When she woke up in the middle of the night, shaking and drenched in sweat, the sheets sticking to her clammy skin, she'd think of those boys in Serbia who would climb into trash cans to feel safe when a loud noise startled them. She thought of Michel, whose sleepless nights Julie refused to talk about. Now she, too, had a wound too deep to excise, so deep it touched her bones, arteries, veins.

A pound of flesh she'd inadvertently bartered for her life.

I'm so, so sorry, Mother.

If only I paid closer attention.

If only I heeded Cyprian's warnings.

If only I spent more time with you.

If only I showed more understanding. More tenderness.

If only I had more time.

She seriously considered not even telling her sisters the truth. Suicide was a deeply private decision, and the letter her mother had written had been addressed only to her.

"And she did it here, in Paris," Sylvia said to Adrienne early the next morning. She could feel a migraine coming on, a tightness at the back of her skull that would become a brutal fist in hours, and even though she felt like she might throw up at any moment, she sipped coffee and smoked. "She could have done it in California. Maybe she didn't want anyone else to know."

"It is a compliment, in its way," Adrienne said.

"And a curse."

"All tragedies contain a gift."

Suzanne. There had been a time when not a day went by without Sylvia thinking of Adrienne's lost first love. But lately . . . well, she couldn't even remember the last time Suzanne had come to her mind, and now here she was again, her ghost hovering in the room.

"How often do you think of her?" Sylvia asked.

"Less often. And now, completely without regret."

The fist was squeezing her brain, and a fresh wave of tears was coming on, but an old question she'd carried around with her for years floated to mind, and it was out of her mouth before she could stop it. "Why did Suzanne get married?"

Adrienne's light blue eyes darkened with the old sadness. "Her parents believed that his family's money could help her get the medical care she needed."

"So she had to spend her last months in a marriage of convenience?" The indignity of it!

"He was kind to her, at least. He'd loved her for years. It nearly killed him that he lost her so quickly."

"So all his money couldn't help in the end?"

"It was too late. She'd refused to marry for too long." Sylvia heard the phlegmy guilt Adrienne was swallowing down. "I should have told her to marry him years before. But I was selfish."

"You are the least selfish person in the world," Sylvia said.

"No, *chérie*, that is you."

Sylvia laughed bitterly. "Then why did my mother kill herself?"

"There is nothing you could have done to stop it."

How can you possibly know that? "And Suzanne loved you so much, she never would have listened to you about marrying earlier, even if you told her to," Sylvia offered, because it was the truest thing she could think to say.

"That's what I tell myself as well."

Just before she opened the store, Sylvia sent a telegram off to her sisters and father in California.

MOTHER DIED TODAY FILLED WITH SADNESS LETTER WITH
MORE TO COME ALL MY LOVE SYLVIA

Later, at the end of a hollow day, sitting at her desk at home, she explained more. "Mother took too many pills," she wrote, and quoted from the part of the letter where Eleanor Beach had expressed a wish to be buried in Père Lachaise Cemetery in company with Oscar Wilde and Frédéric Chopin and Honoré de Balzac, among a litany of reasons she was too exhausted, embarrassed, and sad to go on living, pointing fingers at no one but herself—none of which Sylvia quoted or paraphrased. She had very nearly been caught shoplifting again. "I'm mortified," she'd written. "My love of worldly beauty is a moral failing, and I'm so grateful to you for not telling your father about the last instance, for I fear he'd never forgive me—not as much for the act itself, as for the underlying reasons for the act, about which I feel utterly hopeless." The last thing Sylvia wrote was that her mother's final sentences conveyed how much she'd miss her family.

Her own woefully inadequate letter complete, Sylvia slipped into the stuffy darkness of the bedroom and wrapped herself around Adrienne, who held her tightly all night.

CHAPTER 22

~∙◊∙~

The fourth of July was two weeks shy of her mother's death, and a Monday. Despite a few days in Rocfoin the previous weekend, where Adrienne's profoundly French family had attempted to cheer her with American treats like apple "pie," which was really a *tarte aux pommes* with extra sugar, and a dish called "chicken à la king" that Adrienne's mother had found in an American magazine. It tasted reassuringly creamy and bland on Sylvia's tongue, and she enjoyed the puns the family—which included Rinette, Bécat, and Fargue—bandied hilariously about the patio table: *poulet à la roi, poulet à la Louis, Phillip de le Volaille, Charles d'Pintade, poulette à la reine, poulette de Toinette.*

The buoyant mood was short-lived, though. Sensing her ennui, Teddy began following her around like a shadow, always jumping onto her lap as soon as she sat anywhere, and she found that stroking his warm, soft fur had a soothing effect on her nerves. She detected Joyce biting his tongue at this behavior as he looked suspiciously at her and Teddy out of the corner of his better eye. The day after she'd told him about her mother—the true details of which she made him swear to take to his grave—he'd brought her the most beautiful arrangement of lilies she'd ever seen. The day after that, three days before he was to leave for his family vacation in Belgium, he'd sat in the green chair and said, "What are we to do about Roth?"

The very question made her bones ache. "I don't see there is much more we can do than what we've done."

He looked down at his graceful hands, his immaculately pared fingernails. "Mr. Huebsch, now of Boni and Liveright, has written to me about publishing *Work in Progress*. Unlike Miss Weaver and Mr. Pound, he seems to like what's he's seen of it so far. As you know, I've thought for some time that an American publisher would be in a better position to vanquish Roth, and I wonder about offering *Work in Progress* to Mr. Huebsch."

The whole center of her body contracted painfully. "But we have been discussing its publication by Shakespeare and Company for more than a year. And there is the volume of criticism about it which is already underway."

"And I want you to continue with that. The criticism."

He was looking at her with such innocence, such openness.

"Mr. Joyce, how can Mr. Huebsch help you with Roth if he doesn't publish *Ulysses*?"

The length of his pause before he replied, "I have a hunch," made Sylvia wonder what he was trying to avoid telling her. She was too spent with grief to inquire further.

Then when a letter from Roth's venomous lawyer arrived the morning of July 4 in the evening post, accusing her of standing in the way of great business and great men, she found herself sobbing uncontrollably in the back room of Adrienne's store. "I can't," she barely uttered. "I just can't anymore."

Guilt. It weighed like an anvil on her chest.

If only.

If only she hadn't been so focused on *this*, this pointless merry-go-round with Joyce about Roth, about his eyes, about his finances, maybe she could have helped her mother. Maybe they would be at the Rodin Museum that very day. Together.

She looked into the deep pools of Adrienne's understanding eyes and thought, *This was what you meant about worrying I might give more than I needed to.*

Well. This was a fight she couldn't win. Even Ernest advocated throwing a match when a fighter knew he'd been bested. "Better to save his strength for another day," he often said.

Sylvia returned to her own shop's back room, and with a pen that got lighter with every word, she wrote a reply to Roth and his lawyer saying she was dropping her lawsuit. Then, she wrote to Joyce in Belgium.

> *My dear Mr. Joyce,*
>
> *I hope this letter finds you and your family well and enjoying cooler weather in the north. Adrienne and I continue to take the Citroën for excursions outside Paris. My true reason for writing, however, is to tell you that I am afraid I can no longer tolerate the ad hominem attacks of Roth and his lawyer, who makes John Quinn look like an avenging angel. You are free to pursue this fight if you choose, and if it includes signing a contract with an American publisher for* Work in Progress, *so be it.*
>
> *In the meantime, I shall carry on as planned with* Ulysses VI, Pomes Penyeach, *and our book of criticism. I look forward to seeing you again when we are both well rested in September. Please give my best to Mrs. Joyce and the children.*
>
> *Yours most sincerely,*
> *Sylvia*

It was nearly a month before she received a reply, a month consumed by hours spent with Julie readying the pages for *Pomes* and writing to other writers and intellectuals friendly to Joyce's work, like William Carlos Williams and Eugene Jolas, asking for contributions to their planned volume of criticism.

Then there were the medical bills. Dr. Borsch wrote a very kind note saying that Joyce had not paid any of his bills since 1925. Horrified, Sylvia immediately wrote a check out of Shakespeare and Company funds, jotting down somewhere that the amount should be deducted from his next advance on *Ulysses*, knowing full well in her mind that she would forgive the debt, like all the others. But she couldn't help but read Joyce's reply letter through the sooty lens of that bill:

My dear Miss Beach,

Mrs. Joyce and I are well, thank you. Lucia is so afflicted by melancholy she is difficult to coax out of bed even by the afternoon. The only thing that cheers her are dance performances, which of course we are happy to indulge. Though as you know, I prefer opera.

I was distressed to receive your letter informing me that you've given up on our battle with Roth. I fear that your recent tragedy colored your view of it, and I hope neither of us have cause to regret it later. I shall certainly take up the mantle, and I sincerely hope signing with an American publisher does not become necessary, since they were hardly on my side when I was a lowly writer of condemned "obscenity" and you were my rescuer. I hope I do not quickly forget my debts.

I have enclosed a list of requests regarding the French translation, as well as thoughts pertaining to Pomes, *and several bills I neglected to pay before I left—could you please write them out of my account with you? My most sincere thanks and apologies.*

My best to Mademoiselle Monnier.

With kindest regards,
James Joyce

His list of tasks was three pages long. The day she received it, she was tempted to ball it up and toss it in the wastebasket, but she looked up from it and around the books and pictures lining the walls of her shop. Her eyes rested on the bright blue stack of *Ulysses* volumes that still sold so well, and had made her shop the subject not only of newspaper articles all over Paris and New York, but *Vanity Fair* and *New Yorker* and *Saturday Evening Post* features as well. Those tour buses Cyprian had so reviled that she secretly didn't mind were coming to see her shop as much as the Paris of *The Sun Also Rises*, the novel that had finally evened the score between Ernest and Scott—a rivalry she felt privileged to be party to. Besides, it wasn't just tourists who came to her shop, it was real writers as well.

It was hard to stay angry at the writer who'd brought all that into her life.

She showed Mysrine the list, and they divvied up the items, and made a plan of action that would still allow both of them to go on holiday by August. As the hot days dragged by and Sylvia and Mysrine made progress toward vacation, Sylvia endured two more migraines and some delicate correspondence with her family. First there was the letter from Cyprian, who was convalescing in Palm Springs after being diagnosed with an asthmatic disorder:

I wish I could say I was surprised, but this seems to be the natural outcome of Mother's melancholy in recent years. I hope

*she is at last at rest. I am sure you are not, however, and I am
sorry you've had to cope with the details alone. I do find it
curious she should do it in Paris, and not here, her true home . . .*

Holly's communication was more earnest, and less suggestively
hostile:

*I simply don't know what to do. I miss her every day and every
hour. The store was never my idea nor my passion, but Mother
used to make it fun. She was such a grand hostess, and such a
big-hearted lover of beautiful things and kind people. The store
became like a dinner party she was constantly throwing (when she
wasn't shopping for it). It's a chore to keep it open without her.*

*Meanwhile, Freddy has become more and more persistent. I'd
become comfortable with the idea of being a spinster—if not an
entirely chaste one, I don't mind telling you—but now with
Mother gone, the idea of closing the shop, getting married, and
traveling is quite appealing. I love him. We have a very good
time dancing and walking through orange groves. I'm sure I'm
too old to have children, and that suits me fine. I wonder if a
marriage later in life could be happier than one made earlier,
which requires all the angst of growing up together while also
growing little people together . . .*

Her father wrote little other than "I miss your mother dearly.
Who else would love me in spite of my failings?"

For the first time, Sylvia wondered if Gertrude's term *lost generation* might apply to her. She often heard arguments in the shop about
this label, which Ernest had made famous in the epigraph of his
novel. Writers and tourists alike were either proud to be thought lost,
or offended to be accused of it. The arguments were rarely nuanced,

and she never entered the fray. *Lost generation* had always struck her as a contrivance of sorts, like those bespectacled eyes of Dr. T. J. Eckleburg's looking out over the ash heaps in Scott's *Gatsby*.

But that stifling July evening, as the sun set fire to the sky and a flaming golden light flooded the rue de l'Odéon and Sylvia sat with the correspondence from her sisters and father in her shop that was empty of customers because everyone had gone to the seaside, she thought, *Lost means gone, or unable to find*. It struck her that her mother had indeed been lost; she was always trying to get back to her dream of Paris, and unable to get there to stay; and it was more than Paris as a city, it was Paris as a concept of the bright, beautiful life she'd always wanted to lead, and felt she had led for a brief moment thirty years before. Sylvia had *found* her dream, and was living it— but that was thanks in large part to the money, books, and love her mother had sent her in the last decade. Odeonia would not be possible without Eleanor Beach.

Can it go on without her?

Can it go on without Joyce?

Am I enough to sustain this dream?

Or am I, too, lost?

The questions made Sylvia feel restless, like she needed to *do* something. If she'd been in Les Déserts, she'd have gone outside to chop some wood, then marinated in the exhausted twinges of her shoulders and arms the rest of the evening.

It was getting late, but there were still hours of sun left in the long Paris twilight, so Sylvia shuttered her store and walked briskly on the busy sidewalks of the quarter, then through the Jardin du Luxembourg, her eyes filling with the showy colors and delicate textures of midsummer petunias, begonias, and roses. Among those planted beauties, she found the flower merchant she was looking for, a toothless woman named Louise who'd lost both sons in the war, whom Adrienne had introduced Sylvia to years before, instructing her to buy flowers *only* from her. Her cart near the palace was small, but she always carried the finest, longest-lasting blooms. Eleanor's favorite were pink peonies, which were copious in late spring, not midsummer, but miraculously Louise had a single bouquet of them that evening. "They grew slowly, in the shade," she explained, when Sylvia marveled at their presence.

Then she hailed a cab, one of her mother's favorite luxuries, and enjoyed the little tour of Paris she got from the open window: past the Sorbonne and then over the Seine on the Pont de Sully with Notre-Dame Cathedral just to her right, then northeast and circling the Place de la Bastille, all the way into the twentieth arrondissement, where Père Lachaise Cemetery sprawled leafy and green, with arcades of trees shading countless gray tombstones, temples, and memorials. The light had turned silver by the time she got out of the car and passed through the break in the high stone walls that encircled the cemetery. The place was something of a maze, and even though she'd been there for the burial just a few weeks before, Sylvia feared she might not be able to locate her mother's small grave. Fortunately, though, she found it with no trouble.

I'm never lost in Paris.

Thanks to you, Mother.

She set the peonies down on the earth before the stone with her mother's name and dates of birth and death, then felt a breeze ruffle her hair and cool her neck. Breathing as deeply as she could, she wondered why, precisely, she'd come. To deliver the flowers, of course. What she wanted, desperately, was to speak to her mother. But she felt strange talking to her, even silently, in her mind.

So she sat down near the flowers, putting her hand on the cool dirt that was already sprouting grass, and thanked her mother again. Then she sat for a long while, as she wished she had done with her mother when she was alive, as the day ended and the moon rose in the sky.

CHAPTER 23

I n a cruel moment of irony fit for a Dickens novel, just as the sun
began to break up the clouds and cold in the early spring of 1928,
and she and Adrienne began to plan Sunday jaunts in their Citroën,
Sylvia felt a stabbing pain from her right temple to her jaw when she
took her first sip of coffee one morning. She'd been ignoring little
spasms in her cheek and forehead for a few weeks, but this was on an
entirely different scale—and different from her migraines, too.

"You cannot work today," Adrienne said.

"But Mysrine is away."

"Again? What's happened to that girl? She's never there anymore."

Holding her hand to her cheek, Sylvia wondered the same thing.
It seemed to her that Mysrine had been taking off a bit more time
lately, but Sylvia had been so consumed with everything else, she
hadn't paid it much mind.

"What about Julie?" Adrienne asked. "Just so you can see the
doctor."

"Good idea," she said, with enormous, mumbling difficulty. Amélie would be happy to play with Larbaud's toy soldiers, which normally Sylvia kept in a glass box to protect them from other children's curious, clumsy hands, but Amélie was careful and deliberate, and so Sylvia often let the girl play with the little toys in the back room.

"I'll fetch her. You put a warm water bottle on that side of your face." And with a peck on her other cheek, Adrienne hurried to Julie and Michel's place.

Hardly an hour later, sitting in the waiting room of the clinic's office, Sylvia felt ridiculous. Her face felt fine. She ventured a smile at the elderly woman in the seat across from hers, and . . . nothing happened. No pain. She was tempted to get up and leave, when a nurse called her name.

A doctor she'd never met before, a woman of about her own age with long raven hair laced with gray, which she wore unfashionably long and wound into a bun at the nape of her neck, asked her a series of questions about the pain, and then told her she had a condition called facial neuralgia.

"It is very rare," the woman said with a small, regretful smile.

"Unlike my migraines," Sylvia said, indulging in a rare moment of self-pity. The last thing she needed was another ailment.

"Migraines?" the doctor asked with something almost like excitement. "I have a very good friend, a colleague, who has had tremendous luck in treating them." The doctor scribbled a name and phone number on a sheet of paper. "Please contact him. He has worked miracles."

Sylvia took the paper, and said, "Thank you. And what about this facial . . ."

"Neuralgia. Yes. Unfortunately, there is no cure. But the attacks are usually very short, like the one you had this morning. Over time, they might become more frequent, I'm afraid. But you are young, and so I hope the progress will be slow. And the regimen for your migraines could also help the neuralgia."

Back on the street in the damp, chilly air, Sylvia lit a cigarette and felt the smoke warm her chest. She knew what this doctor would say: cut back on the cigarettes to help the migraines. Dr. Borsch, an eye doctor for heaven's sake, had already given her that much free advice.

Any other "regimen" she thought she could cope with—long, hard walks, plenty of fresh fruits and vegetables. Even requiring earlier bedtimes, and not taxing her eye muscles by reading late into the night. All of that she was willing to do, and had already intuited were good for her, as she never felt better than she did after a long stay at Les Déserts or Rocfoin, where plenty of time outside, less reading, and more sleeping were hallmarks of her routine. Thanks to Adrienne, she ate well all year round, though winter was always a time of rich sauces and hearty braises, which Sylvia had noticed did not agree with her in the same way as summer's lighter fare. But it was impossible to purchase fresh tomatoes and roquette and courgettes to eat in their natural states after October. By the end of February, the only raw vegetables to be had were the sad carrots and beets and turnips remaining in the root cellars, and the last of the preserved fruits whose syrupy sweetness seemed to leach out all the nutrition. By this time of year, even a great cook like Adrienne had no choice but to douse everything in butter and salt.

But give up smoking? That felt like the end of something, no matter how thirsty it made her or how it discolored her teeth and fingers.

It was hard to know, in any case, how many of her problems were due to smoking, or diet, or age. That summer she'd noticed a dramatic uptick in the number of conversations about aches and pains among her friends. It used to be that only Joyce complained endlessly about his eyes. But recently, Mrs. Joyce added her voice to the chorus, with fretting about her cycles; Larbaud complained about his joints, Bob about his back, Fargue about his lungs. Even vigorous and relatively young Ernest had a leg bandaged from a cycling accident.

"We've all been in quite a state," Sylvia observed to Adrienne after one especially maudlin dinner, where everyone drank too much to medicate one ill or another. "Do you think we're getting old?"

"Pish," she replied, "it's too much wine, if you ask me." Then, leaning close to Sylvia, she whispered in her ear, "And I don't intend to let age stop me in any way."

They made love that night, but Sylvia felt outside herself, watching rather than feeling Adrienne's body against hers. Something had been missing inside her since her mother died, and she felt it most strongly at times she ought to have been feeling great intimacy.

During the day at Shakespeare and Company, she was able to burrow into work and ignore her woes. She hoped that the detachment she was feeling was temporary, a passing thing like the attacks of facial neuralgia or migraines, but after too many days of feeling exhausted even after many hours of sleep, she realized she had to change something. By sheer dint of will, she cut her smoking in half and started taking long walks through the Jardin du Luxembourg every evening between shutting the store and either entertaining dinner guests with Adrienne, or attending a party elsewhere.

She began to feel better, at least in her arms and legs and lungs, but that fall, when the new batch of students flooded the quarter with the first of the foreboding breezes, Sylvia felt all of her forty-one years. Even the doctoral students looked hopelessly young. It seemed impossible she'd ever been twenty-two like them, so soft cheeked and clear eyed. It scared her that she recognized in her own weariness an echo of her mother's complaints. *It is too late for me,*

Sylvia. I am old, I've lost my figure and my beauty. What if she'd inherited Eleanor's inner turmoil? And if she had, was it possible to escape it?

🐚

"Did you know that Joyce is thinking of hiring a ghostwriter for *Work in Progress*?" Adrienne asked in the dark. Sylvia had just been about to fall into a deep sleep, but Adrienne's restless tone told her to shake it off and respond. Her pulse sped up with nerves about where this conversation would go.

"He's mentioned it," she replied.

"Have you told him it's out of the question?"

"I suggested that it might not be the best idea."

"It would be the height of dishonesty! The idea that a reader who loved *Ulysses* might buy his next novel and be fooled like that turns my stomach."

"I agree, Adrienne, but what can I do?"

"Nothing, of course. He listens to no one."

"And anyway, I'm not even publishing it, so it's not my integrity at stake this time." Saying this out loud filled her with relief. "If Shakespeare and Company's name were to be on the book, I would argue with him more forcefully."

There was a long silence, during which Sylvia felt her heart practically beat through her chest before Adrienne finally said, "I think Shakespeare would be twice the store it is now without him."

"But how? He is one of the biggest attractions."

"I think you'd be surprised, Sylvia. I wish I could help you see the Odeonia I see without him."

Sylvia felt seasick with loneliness. For her, it was both Odeonia *and* Stratford-on-Odéon, not one or the other. "I know our stores balance each other, Adrienne. They are two halves of a whole, especially for our French friends. But for my American customers, Shakespeare is an island unto itself." It was the first time she'd said it aloud: her store was something apart from Adrienne's. Instead of filling her with pride, though, tonight it made her feel marooned.

"I do not see why that means you should cater to the whims of that . . . man. The way you serve him, it's no different from marriage. Open the tea shop above the store! Fulfill a dream of your own, *chérie*."

"This is my dream," she said, her voice shaking. Publishing *Ulysses*, helping Joyce, running Shakespeare and Company—all of it made her feel necessary.

"But is it enough?"

"Yes," she replied. It wasn't a lie; not exactly. But it did feel incomplete.

Sylvia found herself avoiding the topic of Joyce with Adrienne, just when she needed her sage counsel most. But Adrienne had lost her ability to be impartial about him. The idea that he might not actually write all of his next novel was the last straw for her. He'd lost all integrity in her eyes.

Though she'd never dream of asking for secrecy, Sylvia was relieved beyond measure that Adrienne kept the information confidential. Among their French friends, Adrienne would complain openly of Joyce's greed and vanity, but never his dishonesty—out of respect for Sylvia's reputation as his publisher, she had to assume. After one dinner party at which Adrienne had gone so far as to call him Midas, Larbaud helped Sylvia wash and dry the dishes while Adrienne continued in animated conversation with Fargue and a number of other guests, and he asked in a low, sympathetic voice, "How do *you* feel about Joyce these days?"

Her friend's unexpected sympathy brought a hot rush of tears to her eyes. Sniffling them back, she said, "He's trying my patience, I cannot deny that."

He nodded, drying a heavy soufflé dish that had contained the rich and delicious first course of Adrienne's meal. "What do you think?" she asked, suddenly desperate for his answer. "Is he so different from the man we met in 1921?"

Larbaud thought about this, set the soufflé dish down, and took up a saucepan. "We have all changed, of course. And in aging, habits and thoughts that once were small become large. We settle into ourselves. This is happening with Adrienne, and with Joyce."

"And their habits and thinking have become ever more opposed."

He nodded. "I am sorry, Sylvia. This cannot be easy for you."

"I love them both," she said, a sob clotting her throat. "I don't want to choose."

Larbaud set down the pan, and put a hand gently on Sylvia's back. "I hope you never have to."

"But? I sense there's something else you want to say."

"If I may . . . Adrienne loves you fiercely."

"And Joyce does not."

"He loves you as much as he is capable. None of that lessens how much you love each of them, however. I understand that."

Sylvia wiped her damp nose on her sleeve, then set her head on Larbaud's shoulder and wished her heart desired simpler things.

CHAPTER 24

n the summer of 1931, correspondence about Joyce's novel began to make Sylvia feel like she was standing in a rainstorm with no umbrella or galoshes.

> *Dear Miss Beach,*
>
> *I am writing on behalf of Mr. Bennett Cerf regarding the novel* Ulysses *by Mr. James Joyce. We have received a copy of your contract with Mr. Joyce, and we are well aware of the time and effort you have spent publishing this Work. We understand that you have gone through many trials in the publication, translation, and dissemination of this Work, including but not limited to fighting piracy, the post office, and ignorant readers and reviewers. Please understand we hold you in the highest regard.*
>
> *The price of $25,000 to release you from your rights to the Work is too high, however; furthermore, we have explained something similar to Mr. Joyce about his request for 25% royalties and a $5,000 advance. Please also understand that we will have to embark on an expensive and time-consuming legal battle to*

remove the ban on the Work in the United States. We are
confident that the mood in the country and courts has shifted since
the trial of 1921, and it can be done, but not without some trouble.

Mr. Joyce appears willing to negotiate, and we hope you
will rethink your position as well, in the interest of this great
masterpiece.

Yours most sincerely,
William Bates

It was such an irony. After years of insisting they didn't need a formal contract, the previous year, Joyce himself had demanded that Sylvia sign a simple one-page document assigning him 25 percent of royalties for *Ulysses*, and giving her the power to accept or reject an offer from an American publisher: "The right to publish said Work shall be purchased from the Publisher at the price set by herself, to be paid by the publishers acquiring the rights to publish said Work." The written arrangement felt fair, and after he'd taken *Work in Progress* elsewhere, Sylvia had felt deeply reassured by the power Joyce had given her to veto offers by other publishers. At the time, she'd assumed it would never come to this.

The only reason she was considering any offers at all to buy her out of *Ulysses* was that an American publisher could potentially make the novel legal in the new, humbler post-crash America. At least, that was what Ezra and Joyce and Ernest and Bob all thought, because Cerf and a handful of other New York City publishers had been wooing Joyce with convincing arguments about more liberal courts and savvier legal representation. Ernest had added, "And it's because *you* published it first, Sylvia. You're the one who showed everyone the novel could find an audience and not corrupt it."

She wanted, first and foremost, for the book to succeed. She believed that it would continue to be the most important novel of the twentieth century—people would look back in the 1950s, '70s, and '90s and see that it changed literature for the better. Close to a decade after her first edition, it was already proving true: she was fond of pointing to William Faulkner and his *As I Lay Dying* and *The Sound and the Fury*, both of which he wrote all the way in the American south, in Mississippi for crying out loud, for proof of *Ulysses*'s reach and influence.

Equally, though, she had to look out for herself and Shakespeare and Company. Twenty-five thousand dollars was just barely a fair price for an American publisher to buy her out of her rights to a decade of her life and her future livelihood. They were getting the finest crown jewel of literature, after all! But given their silence on receiving her offer, three editors—Ben Huebsch, who'd moved to Viking, Laurence Pollinger of Curtis Brown, and Bennett Cerf of Random House—all men, of course, seemed to think otherwise.

Fine, let them. Inside her stirred the young feminist who'd once campaigned for women's suffrage and felt the injustice of women being held back from everything important. Even Harriet Weaver, whose willingness to rescue Joyce every single time, had written to Sylvia in solidarity, saying, "It's about time the men of publishing recognize what you've done for *them*." Adrienne had said vehemently, "You're worth every centime and more, *chérie*."

She needed to stay confident and strong.

> *Dear Mr. Bates,*
>
> *Thank you for your letter. I understand that you will have to bring* Ulysses *to trial again and that it is no small matter. I thank you for this valiant effort and hope you will prevail.*
>
> *Please understand, however, that I am just as much a publisher as you, despite the disparity in our sizes. I, a single*

person, have been doing the jobs of editor, agent, production manager, printing expert, assistant, publicist, and sales team. As you point out, I have also had legal troubles on behalf of Ulysses and its author, and these have had to be paid for, sometimes out of the coffers of my other business, the bookstore and lending library Shakespeare and Company, not out of the royalties from the sales of Mr. Joyce's writings.

You are also asking to buy me out of my rights to this novel, which might be written as a simple phrase in a letter like this, but is quite complicated in actuality; the repercussions of its sale are many for its publisher. My investment in Ulysses is not limited to the Paris edition, but includes foreign rights in more than a dozen countries, critical works about the novel, and—this reason cannot be overstated—the business it brings to Shakespeare and Company. This business is incalculable and to lose it during this ever-worsening Depression could be catastrophic for an institution in Paris that many of your own writers have called home.

I speak of writers like Sherwood Anderson and Thornton Wilder, whose bestselling novels will, I am confident, more than foot the bill for the new trial of Ulysses until Ulysses itself is able to repay the debt a thousandfold when you bring it out in an affordable edition and market it to every reader in America. Not to mention the large sum I am sure you'll make when a London publisher purchases the rights from you.

What Mr. Joyce decides in this matter is his own affair. Whatever he might agree with you for an advance now pales in comparison to what he will make in royalties when you bring the book out in mass scale, and Mr. Joyce is well aware of this. He is one of the shrewdest writers I've ever met in financial matters, and I include in my circle of friends and acquaintances

*virtually every published writer of the past decade. I stand to
make nothing from future royalties and thus cannot afford to
compromise at this essential juncture. I thank you for your time
and understanding.*

> *Sincerely,*
> *Sylvia Beach*

Heart thudding as she finished typing, Sylvia panted as if she'd
just chopped wood. What she couldn't say in these letters, or aloud
to anyone she knew, is that as much as she wanted *Ulysses* to go into
the world and succeed wildly, a part of her hoped that Cerf said no.
Is this how parents feel about their children? God, she wished she could
ask her mother.

My dear Mr. Pound,

Whatever you may think of my Work in Progress—*which is
stalled in any case because of the burden the fight about* Ulysses
*has placed on me—I hope you might see your way to supporting
Stephen and Leopold once again. You were their first champion,
and you understand them better than anyone. I think now you
might also understand better than anyone the corner the women
in my life have boxed me into. Miss Weaver with her tight fists
and pleas for temperance disguised as concern for my health;
Mrs. Joyce with her elderly body as needy as ever and her
demands about our children; our new landlady Fraulein Merck,
who refuses to let us pay rent even a day late; and worst of all is
Miss Beach, who believes she has some ownership in a novel she
did not write, and inhibits me from making my future living
because of this unfounded notion. Only my darling Lucia suffers
as much as I do.*

I think Miss Beach might listen to you if you would only write her a line or two. You've published works and let them go—encourage her to do the same, I beg of you.

Mrs. Joyce and I have had quite enough of the damp in this terrible English city and have such a hankering for Italy, you might just see us soon.

With deepest gratitude,
James Joyce

Dearest Sylvia,

What terrible news I hear about Ulysses, *though I wish I could say it's surprising. Jane and I always found Joyce to be a writer of genius but not integrity, and that novel seems to curse every woman involved with it, including the characters! It still stings my heart to remember poor Gerty so maligned in the Jefferson Market Courthouse by those pea-head judges who couldn't even bring themselves to acknowledge the sex of the publishers of the chapter. Women, they said, couldn't understand such writing; it's too difficult. Even when John Quinn, who was certainly no friend to women, pointed out that Jane and I were indeed female, they would not deign to look at us sitting before them.*

It seems that the book brings out the worst in men, its writer included. I'm sorry, Sylvia, and wish I could offer more than my solidarity, and you have that in spades. Please also give my best to Adrienne.

Wishing you all the luck in the world,
Margaret Anderson

CHIN UP THE WORLD IS FULL OF BASTARDS AND
EVERYONE KNOWS YOURE NOT ONE OF THEM TAKING YOU
TO DOME NEXT MONTH ERNEST

Dear Jim,

I'm afraid there is a difference—and a rather large one at that—between publishing short works in a journal as I have, and publishing many editions of a novel, as Sylvia has. And didn't you ask her to sign a contract? I never would have advised that, but here you are and you must honor it, else be no better than the women you deride. Sylvia's one of the sensible ones. Perhaps she'll come up with a solution.

—Ezra

Dear Miss Beach,

We regret that we cannot publish Ulysses *under the current terms. We hope you reconsider.*

Sincerely,
William Bates

Dear Mr. Joyce,

Much as Random House wants to publish your important novel, we simply cannot do so under the terms set by Shakespeare and Company. If you have the funds to purchase the rights from Miss Beach at the price she is asking, I am sure we can come to

*an agreement between us on royalties. Given your contract, I
don't see another way.*

   Please keep me apprised of your progress.

*Yours in hope,
Bennett Cerf*

"Have you heard from Joyce directly?" Larbaud asked. Sylvia was
sitting on the wooden chair in his flat on the rue Cardinal Lemoine,
where Joyce and his whole family had stayed that summer of 1921 as
he furiously and blindly finished *Ulysses*. Today her French friend was
bundled in sweaters and blankets on a chaise a few feet away, although
it was a mild early fall day. It seemed he could never get warm enough.

"Not a word." Joyce had been in London for months, at last marrying Nora in the Kensington Registry Office to secure his line of
inheritance for his children.

"I hope his silence means he is consulting thoughtful advisors."

"Like Léon-Paul? Eugene Jolas?" Both of whom ran his errands
and agreed with every word that came out of his mouth.

"Good point," he sympathized.

"The last time we spoke, he did say he'd written to his agent in
London to see if there might be a way through this. He said I deserved to be bought out of the rights."

"I wonder how much influence the Depression is having on Joyce
and the American publishers?"

Sylvia snorted a laugh. "Joyce with Harriet's bottomless purse,
and the American publishers with huge books like *A Farewell to
Arms*, Dos Passos's latest, plus the usual Agatha Christie novels and
now these Nancy Drew books for children? Hardly." Just saying all
that aloud strengthened her resolve.

"Surely fewer people are buying books."

"Yes, and I'm taking the brunt of that in Shakespeare and Company because it's a shop for expatriated bohemians, not a big store in New York catering to the people whose money never seems to run out. But all that really means is that publishers won't be taking any risks for a while. They'll only publish sure bets, and *Ulysses* is that. They will make a packet from it. And truly, I don't care about the money for myself. I feel almost . . . unclean . . . discussing *Ulysses* in those terms. I love the novel." She patted her heart. "I love it. But I love my store just as much, and I have to protect it.

"You know," she went on, clearing her throat, "our old friend Samuel Roth has brought out another edition of ten thousand copies. *Ten thousand.* Ernest wrote me that he'd seen them at the Gotham Book Mart."

"I imagine that only makes the matter feel more urgent to Joyce. And I know you don't want to sacrifice your friendship with him over this."

She nodded. Yes. Somewhere in all of this was the wretched truth that she had to choose between her relationship with the book and her relationship with the writer. How that was possible, when she'd seen them—and loved them and supported them—as one and the same for a decade, was too excruciating to think about.

Larbaud looked tired. Standing and closing the distance between them, she set her cool hand on his hot, damp forehead, and he closed his eyes.

"I must get home," she said quietly. "But I'll be back soon."

He nodded.

How she wanted to go home and crawl into Adrienne's soft embrace, but that was out of the question because of Adrienne's feelings about Joyce and the American publishers, which only made the longing more intense. Larbaud set his head heavily on his pillows, and she knew it was time to go.

CHAPTER 25

⌒⋘⋙⌒

"N ame's Kelly, Patrick Kelly. Please, though, call me Paddy."

Sylvia shook the hand of the pink-faced Irish boy with the heavy Dublin accent—for he truly was a boy; there was no other word for him. If he'd finished university already, she'd be surprised. "Pleasure to meet you, Paddy. Call me Sylvia."

It was a slow day in the store before the holiday rush was underway—at least, Sylvia hoped the holiday rush would eventually get underway—and Paddy puttered around the shop along with three other customers. Mysrine was sick, Julie was helping log in a shipment of new books while Amélie completed some schoolwork, and Sylvia was tackling her least favorite task, ledger balancing. She'd already procrastinated long enough by reorganizing her catalog of library cards—so many of them had gotten out of alphabetical order, or had been misplaced around the shop. Library cards were one of her favorite chores, however; it was like looking through a scrapbook or photo album, poring over this or that patron's cards and remembering what they had checked out and what had been happening in his or her life then.

The ledger was distinctly less fun and so she welcomed the distraction when Paddy approached her again at the desk. "Forgive me, Sylvia, but aren't you also the publisher of *Ulysses*?"

The hairs on the nape of her neck bristled, and Teddy trotted over to her and sat expectantly at her feet. Young Paddy was a poor liar, and she could tell he already knew the answer to that question. But she dutifully answered, "Shakespeare and Company publishes James Joyce." Then she leaned over to fondle Teddy's ears, which was soothing.

Mushing his flat cap in his nervous hands, he blushed and laughed. "I'm sorry, Miss Beach, but I did know that. You see, I've recently made the acquaintance of Mr. Joyce himself. I've read every word he's ever written, and feel he's my own voice, you know?"

Poor kid, she thought. It was immediately obvious that he lacked the intelligence and poise of Samuel Beckett, her favorite of these Irish aspirers who made pilgrimages to her shop.

"I love his work, too," she said to nervous Paddy.

"You see, though, and I hope you don't think me insolent because I have nothing but the highest esteem for you, Miss Beach, but I have heard there are some American editors interested in publishing *Ulysses*? And making it legal where now it is banned?"

"That's true." The hairs began to irritate her neck.

Julie glanced up from her work to take note of their new guest.

"It's just that it would be so . . . good, if that were to happen. Then all my family in Boston would be able to buy it."

"They can buy it now," Sylvia said. "I haven't had any trouble placing it in American bookstores recently. Officially it's still banned, but my impression is that the authorities now look the other way. Piracy is the bigger problem now." *Even in Japan*, she reflected, thinking of the letter she'd received from a legitimate publisher in Tokyo who'd complained of the problem.

Paddy shrugged, his right ear tipping toward his right shoulder. "Yes well, maybe. But the blue edition is expensive for working folk like my cousins, and I've told them not to buy the pirate as that's stealing just the same as picking Mr. Joyce's pocket."

This is a very strange conversation. She wanted it to end as soon as possible. Mustering a half smile, she said, "I appreciate that, Paddy, as I am sure does Mr. Joyce. The questions about the American publishers are very complicated, however, and I am sure you can appreciate that they are also confidential. Please let me know if you need any help finding anything in the shop or the library." She then directed her eyes at the ledger, though the numbers swam like fish before her. Teddy yapped and wagged his tail, asking for another pat.

"Of course, of course. Forgive me again." Paddy frowned down at the dog.

He returned to looking at the shelves, and Sylvia and Julie exchanged a *when will he take the hint and leave?* look. She was just getting the numbers to settle down on the page when Paddy approached her one last time, cap on and seemingly ready to leave without buying anything or taking out a library subscription. "It just seems like the book should be available to everyone, you know?"

She wondered how he'd managed to gather the courage to steady and lower his voice like that, for with those parting words, he sounded far older and savvier than his boyish face implied.

☙

Paddy started turning up every other day at Shakespeare and Company, running errands for Joyce. "He's even hand delivering me letters from him," Sylvia dared to remark to Adrienne, who shook her head and visibly bit her tongue.

"He included this note for you in a longer letter to me." Paddy handed her the envelope. He'd clearly been instructed to wait until

Sylvia finished reading because he waited around expectantly while she busied herself with a box of journals that had just arrived.

Finally he said, "Aren't you going to read it, Miss Beach? I can add a reply to my own letter to him."

"I'm busy right now, Paddy, and I know Mr. Joyce's address in London. I can also afford stamps."

She avoided further eye contact with him and made herself as occupied as possible. At last, he left.

The next time he came, Adrienne was in the store. She'd dropped by to bring Sylvia a stack of volumes that had been misdelivered at La Maison, and Sylvia introduced them.

"It's an honor to meet you, Madame Monnier," Paddy said, doffing his cap and making a ridiculous bow. "I've heard a great deal about the closest and most intelligent advisor of Miss Beach."

Was that derision she heard in "closest and most intelligent advisor"? Sylvia thought she heard the echo of John Quinn's "filthy Washington Squarite" in there. Had Joyce resorted to small-mindedness in his anger at Sylvia, or was this Paddy's opinion seeping through his rehearsed lines?

Adrienne must have heard it, too, for she pressed her lips into a thin line. "Sylvia does not need advising. She is the finest shop owner and librarian in Paris."

"I meant no offense, Miss . . . I mean, Madame Monnier, I only—"

"Only Joyce is ridiculous enough to use madame and miss with us, Paddy. You may call me Adrienne or simply Monnier as is the French literary custom. I'm sure Sylvia has also instructed you to call her by her given name."

"Oh, but I couldn't, I—"

"Because Joyce told you what to call us and you are an obedient little puppy."

"Now, Madame . . . I mean, Adrienne, there's no need to be insulting."

"I like dogs, Paddy, I meant to insult."

Sylvia felt as though she were watching one of Ernest's boxing matches. Occasionally, even though everyone knew who would win, it was thrilling to watch the champion bludgeon his opponent.

As if summoned by the naming of his species, Teddy jumped gently up Adrienne's leg, and she bent over and effusively played with his ears and kissed the top of his head.

Paddy curled his lip.

Sylvia almost burst out laughing.

Then, as if he'd heard a bell ring the end of the round, he donned his cap and said, "A pleasure, Adrienne. Monnier. Miss Beach, I'll see you soon, I'm sure."

As soon as the door closed behind him, the two women swooned with laughter. They laughed so long and hard, a stitch formed in Sylvia's side, and she had to sit in the green chair. Teddy leaped into her lap and yapped happily.

"Yes, Teddy, we love dogs," she said, stifling a fresh bout of laughter.

Steadying her breath in the nearby wooden chair, Adrienne closed her eyes and slouched as if she'd just enjoyed the greatest of pleasures. A hot flood of love and admiration filled Sylvia.

Grateful that no one else was in the store at that moment, she said, "*Je t'aime*, Adrienne."

Adrienne reached her hand out and took Sylvia's in hers. "I love you, too, Sylvia. I hope we scared that horrible weasel out of here for good."

"I don't think weasels are as smart as dogs."

Which set them laughing again.

The incident gave Sylvia and Adrienne a way of talking about

Joyce and Paddy in a humorous way, which significantly lightened the subject between them. Jokes and wordplay about puppies and other animals abounded, including what became a marvelously heretical category of puns about their Crooked Jesus and pets. "Perhaps Jesus should have had a dog to set upon Judas." "Messiahs and their mollycoddled mountain dogs." As they inched closer to Christmas, Adrienne found a few small dog figurines and added them to the crèche in Rocfoin.

One of them was a rottweiler, and her father inquired, quite innocently, "Don't you think that one might eat the lamb?" At which Adrienne and Sylvia howled with laughter, much to the consternation of both Maman and Papa Monnier.

Unfortunately, like the cliché of the bad penny, Paddy turned up at Shakespeare and Company again, and he seemed to have found a backbone during his absence.

"My cousins tell me that Roth's edition is selling well during the holiday season. Mr. Joyce is greatly aggrieved."

"As am I," she replied. Apparently Joyce was in close contact with this boy. Though she knew it was ridiculous to think of a book this way, she glanced at the stack of blue *Ulysses*es and thought, *You'd never do this to me.*

"It just doesn't seem as though you care, Miss Beach. The one thing you can do to save *Ulysses* and Mr. Joyce is to allow an American edition."

"I *want* there to be an American edition. But I also want to be treated with respect." As soon as she said it, she regretted it. Any words she spoke were an invitation for Paddy to respond.

"Who is not treating you with respect? Surely you don't mean Mr. Joyce. Doesn't he send you flowers every year to commemorate the edition you published? Doesn't he remember you on your birthday? Didn't he just send you a beautiful gift from Harrods for Christmas?"

How do you know that? "I'm not in the habit of discussing gifts with anyone, let alone a stranger."

"Come now, Miss Beach, surely we are more to each other than strangers by now."

I don't like to say what we really are to each other. As if on cue, Teddy growled at Paddy.

The boy drew in a deep, put-upon breath. "For instance, I feel we know each other well enough for me to tell you that Mr. Joyce is suffering mightily because of your pride."

She would have laughed at the notion of James Joyce *suffering* in London, dining at Brown's and the Savoy, if she hadn't been so rattled by the idea that Joyce was telling Paddy to say these things to her.

Clenching her teeth, she replied, "True friends can disagree without it ending the relationship. So if you are my friend, Paddy, I ask that you recognize that we have a difference of opinion, and leave it alone."

"Of course," he said. But she knew it wasn't the last she'd heard on the subject from him.

Admitting to herself that Paddy was simply Joyce's megaphone undid something inside Sylvia. It was like there had been a tightly wound ball of rope in the center of her body and someone had come along with a knife to slice one piece and it was slowly unraveling and expanding inside her.

There was only one person she could imagine talking to about this pain, the one person who would let her say everything she needed to say without argument or suggestion. Leaving her shop in Julie's hands in the afternoon before the early sunset fell on Paris, Sylvia hurried to the Jardin du Luxembourg and purchased a lovely poinsettia from Louisa and, fearing the cold, took a taxi to Père Lachaise, though usually she took the metro to save money.

In the three years since her mother's death, Sylvia had surprised herself by becoming a regular graveside chatter. Once a month or so, she'd purchase flowers from Louisa—always peonies when she had them—and venture to Père Lachaise at sunset, which was a harder trick in the winter months, but still she managed it. On the longer spring and summer days, when there was plenty of light and time, she might take a long, meandering route to her mother's stone, past the memorials to Proust, Molière, and Jacques-Louis David, whose stark, beautiful painting of Marat had been one of her mother's favorites, though she had only seen it in photographic reproduction, never in person at the Royal Museum in Belgium. How Sylvia wished she had taken a trip to Brussels to see it with her.

She always brought a thick wool blanket that she folded many times to separate herself from the cold, damp earth, and tucked her legs beneath her. That day at the end of 1931, she pulled her coat around her as tightly as she could and still shivered.

"I don't know how to let it go," she told her mother, speaking only in her mind. "The friendship or the book. They are the same. To me, at least. Apparently not to him. And finances are terrible, at both shops. Adrienne said something about selling the Citroën the other day, and I don't know if we can bear that. I know it sounds silly, as it's only a car, but it's also the location of so many good memories. It would be a tragedy to sell it. Like kissing the memories goodbye. And what will happen to Shakespeare if it's no longer the home of *Ulysses*? No longer its Ithaca? What will happen to it? To me?" The words were tumbling out now, louder and faster, almost warming her up. Almost, for she was starting to feel numb in her toes and fingers. "What are we, me and my little shop that you helped me open, what are we without our *Ulysses*?"

It wasn't a memory of her mother's voice she heard in reply, but Adrienne's: *I wish I could help you see the Odeonia I see without him.*

Sylvia looked down and saw that her ungloved right hand had been scratching the cold soil and her fingernails were black with it. When had she even taken off the glove? After shaking out the dirt as much as possible, then putting the glove back on and wiping her drippy nose with the handkerchief she always kept in her left coat pocket, she pushed herself into a standing position with some difficulty. She hadn't had an attack of facial neuralgia in some time, but her joints were screaming their age this winter. And she thought she was feeling the tingle of a migraine, too.

"Send me a sign, Mother," she said aloud. "Something to let me know what I should do."

The sun was low in the sky, and the bare branches of the trees made haunting, complicated patterns on the violet sky, like a scene from Poe.

"Goodnight," she bid Eleanor Beach.

She wasn't a superstitious woman. So it was impossible to explain, even to herself, why she'd asked her mother for a sign and why she then proceeded to watch for one everywhere.

She waited.

The Christmas season of 1931 was disappointing. Some of her oldest and best customers stopped by to wish her well and even bring her homemade cookies or wine, to chat about holiday plans or the state of the world, and then apologize for not purchasing their usual stack of books for family and friends: he had lost his job; her pay at the lycée had been reduced; we're going to have to return to America; my elderly mother needs care and we'll have to leave Paris to give it. Even Michel handed Sylvia a packet of meats half the usual size, his eyes wide with regret. "I am sorry, Sylvia, but people aren't buying as much so I'm not stocking what I usually would." Curiously, Michel seemed to have revived as the economy slumped, and correspondingly Julie smiled more and sparked with increased energy.

She tried to take all this in stride, though the parade of noncustomers made her think that she should hang on to *Ulysses* and the money she was asking for it, rather than let it go for less.

"I think we should sell the Citroën while there are still enough people with money to buy it," Adrienne said one quiet night as they lay in the dark after a simple dinner of soup and baguette, which they both ate while reading.

"Yes, I agree. But . . . it will be so hard to let her go."

Adrienne slid her hand over the table to Sylvia's, and laced their fingers together. "There will be other cars."

The next day she received a letter from Joyce in the evening post.

My dear Miss Beach,

I hope the holiday season at Stratford-upon-Odéon is as cheerful as it's been in happy years past. Mrs. Joyce and I miss the tree in the corner amongst the books, and the excellent cider you sometimes brew to take the chill out of the coldest afternoons.

I wish I could report that things are well with us, but Lucia seems worse in this wretched city—how could she not?—and my darling Nora is coping with health troubles of her own. A doctor has told her she'll need a hysterectomy before long. We are getting a second opinion. My eyes are . . . well, they are my eyes. I haven't had a chance to go to Switzerland for the planned procedure because I've been so needed here in London.

In less than two months' time, our Ulysses *will be ten years old, and its writer will be half a century. Both are almost impossible to believe, except that I feel all of those fifty years in every joint and fiber of my body. I can hear a clock ticking out the hours, days, years that I have left. I don't want to waste them. I've begun writing again.*

I hope that as this year ends, and with it Leopold and Stephen's decade, you might find it in your heart to release us. I shan't be able to finish Work in Progress *if I am so distracted by the fate of* Ulysses, *which is synonymous with the fate of my family. With my wife and daughter requiring so much in the way of medicine and care, I need to put myself in a position of security so that I can pay the bills without worrying, and I truly believe Cerf and his Random House can do that for me. Please, Sylvia, reconsider your position, for me.*

With deepest affection,
James Joyce

Almost as soon as she'd finished reading the letter for the third time, which had the effect of making the knot in her body expand to the point of suffocating her from the inside, Paddy entered the store.

She'd been about to close.

The early winter night was ink dark, and a light snow had begun to fall—big, white flakes shimmering to the sidewalks under the glow of the gas lamps. She longed for the comfort of the cider Joyce had described in his letter, but she and Adrienne had decided not to offer the luxury except on Christmas Eve this year. Before reading the letter, she'd been looking forward to a hot meal and a glass of red wine with Adrienne.

Paddy's entrance let in a gust of cold, wet air. "Good evening, Miss Beach," he said cheerfully. "Goodness, there is nothing like Paris during Advent."

"I'm sorry, Paddy, but I was just about to close."

Teddy trotted in from the back room at the sound of the door and the smell of the snow, took one look at Paddy, and then wandered over to Sylvia and flopped at her feet.

"I won't delay you long," he said, approaching the desk.

It occurred to her that he'd never bought anything, in all the times he'd come to Shakespeare and Company. Not a single book.

His eyes were a glacial blue. Had she ever noticed them before? And his hair raven black. *Quoth the raven.* Poe again.

He fixed her with those eyes and said, "This is my last try. I have to return to London in a few days. But I just want to ask one last time why you're standing in the way of James Joyce and his great novel? I'd venture to say it's the greatest novel of this century."

"The century isn't even a third over yet." *I just can't bring myself to agree with anything he says, even if I think it's true.*

He shrugged. "I said venture. It's a guess. What's not a guess is that you *are* an obstacle. It's clear to everyone who cares about Joyce, except you."

Sylvia met his gaze and searched for a reply. Nothing she could say would convince him, or Joyce himself. Even knowing that Paddy would soon be leaving brought her no relief. Joyce would simply send someone else in his stead.

I'm expendable to him.

After all I've done.

Sylvia felt truly and thoroughly angry at him for the first time. *I'm no different from Harriet or anyone else in his life. He's no Odysseus, fighting to get home to Ithaca, true to his Penelope and Telemachus. He might be able to write about such characters, but he isn't one himself.*

I've been wrong all along.

At that moment, even though the store was completely still, the only sound or movement Teddy snoring lightly on the ground, one of the Whitman pages her mother had sent her when the store first opened on the rue Dupuytren fell from the wall to the ground. The glass within the frame that protected the poet's scribbles cracked on contact and made a pretty chime of a noise.

Teddy startled and barked. Paddy didn't flinch.

If that wasn't the sign she'd asked for, she didn't know what was.

Thank you, Mother.

"Fine," Sylvia said, immediately feeling the knot inside her dissolve, "Joyce can have his precious book. Tell him Merry Christmas."

PART FOUR
1933–36

I celebrate myself, and sing myself,
And what I assume you shall assume,
For every atom belonging to me as good belongs to you.

—Walt Whitman, "Song of Myself"

CHAPTER 26

〜⚬〜

"Happy Thanksgiving," said Carlotta's husband James Briggs, holding up a glass of Bordeaux in their sunny apartment in the sixteenth, where Sylvia and Adrienne had been celebrating this American holiday for the past three years, since her dear childhood friend Carlotta Welles had finally decided to marry. Waiting to find the right match had been wise. James was lovely, and Carlotta was clearly in love with him, a widowed banker with a strong sense of joie de vivre who'd managed to keep his fortune despite the paroxysms of the market. He was well-read and enjoyed theater and travel, and together they'd taken up residence in Paris—which was more than a consolation to Sylvia as so many of her other American friends seemed to be leaving.

Carlotta had always adored Thanksgiving, and even in Paris she managed to find the right ingredients for a traditional turkey and stuffing feast. Ever excited to try new dishes, Adrienne, too, had come to love this day that was all about food and gratitude. Thus she'd become an enthusiastic participant in the American holiday, contributing her own decidedly French version of sweet potatoes, whipped practically into a mousse with butter and dark sugar. Her favorite item on the buffet was the pumpkin pie, which she never offered to make herself—the ultimate compliment to Carlotta's cooking.

"Let us give thanks to Kentucky, the thirty-third state to ratify the Twenty-First Amendment," James went on, and glasses clinked all around.

"How many more of your states need to agree for the law to pass?" Adrienne asked.

"Three more for a total of thirty-six," Carlotta answered, "Which is three-quarters of our forty-eight states."

"I've heard Pennsylvania will be next," said James with eyebrows raised and his glass in the air.

"Then this absurdly titled Great Experiment will be over," said Sylvia.

"Indeed. The number of people who have died as a result of this ill-conceived Prohibition is staggering," said James grimly.

"I admire your country for attempting to make such lofty ideals the law," said Adrienne, "even if in this case it didn't work. And then, to be able to admit one is wrong . . . that is a difficult thing for any one person to do, let alone a whole country."

"You are a great apologist for our nation," said James warmly. "You almost make me want to live there again, but then you would not be there."

"Cyprian actually suggested that we move to California," laughed Sylvia.

"Not until we move back as well! Which we have no plans to do," said Carlotta in a warning tone.

"Don't worry," assured Sylvia. "France is our home. I haven't even set foot in America in close to twenty years." She remembered that long-ago conversation with Cyprian, who had encouraged her to visit, but once their mother was gone and Carlotta had moved to France . . . any impulse she might have felt to cross the ocean evaporated.

"California sounds as exotic as China to me!" Adrienne said.

"What, 'The Jumping-Off Place'?" hooted James, referring to Edmund Wilson's recent essay about San Diego as the nation's leading city of suicides. Sylvia, too, had devoured the essay, and it had made her think in new ways about her mother. After all, Pasadena wasn't that far from San Diego. Was the commercialism and desolate, sublime beauty of the landscape really and ironically conducive to thoughts of ending one's life?

"Oh, darling, you're such an eastern snob," Carlotta said with an affectionate hand on his arm.

"I suppose I am," he said, kissing her on the lips.

Sylvia looked away from them, and from Adrienne. After a long—too long—celibate period, they had tried to be more amorous recently, but something wasn't working. It wasn't easy, thrilling, and comforting all at the same time, as it had been when they were younger. She couldn't figure out why. Surely after so long together, intimacy should at least have been comforting. But what Adrienne's body needed seemed to have changed, and Sylvia didn't know how to please her any longer; she had the sense that Adrienne might want to try new things, but Sylvia didn't have the energy or inclination. Though her facial neuralgia had improved, her migraines were worse, and lately her period seemed to last for weeks and leave her weak and sleepy. The best antidote was time outdoors, gardening and chopping wood in Les Déserts or Rocfoin.

She didn't want to think about any of that today, however. Today she wanted to wallow in the embrace of friendship and familiar foods.

"Aren't you waiting on another decision from America?" Carlotta's question interrupted her thoughts.

"Yes," said Sylvia. "Judge Woolsey just heard the case for *Ulysses*, and he's taking the week to deliberate."

"Woolsey's a good man," said James. "I took a class he taught at Columbia. Always struck me as fair-minded and liberal without being reckless. He'll make the right call."

"How do you feel about it?" Leave it to an old friend like Carlotta to ask the hard question.

"Of course I want the book to succeed. And if Judge Woolsey rules in its favor, doors will open for others. D. H. Lawrence, for instance. And Radclyffe Hall. And this young Henry Miller who's become quite a regular in the store."

"I'll be amazed if the ban isn't lifted," said Carlotta. "All that hand-wringing censorship from twenty-one seems positively quaint now."

Sylvia nodded. "*Ulysses* hasn't even been seized in years. In fact, Bennett Cerf's lawyer, Morris Ernst, actually had to go down to the New York customs office himself to *request* that the officers impound a copy of my edition, in order to trigger the legal events that would bring the novel back to the courts."

"Oh, this?" Adrienne frowned with mock disdain as she picked up a nearby paperback, pretending to be the border official talking to Ernst—a little show she often put on for friends when they told this story. "This book comes through all the time. We don't pay it any mind." Then she flung the book over her shoulder as everyone laughed.

"But it is bittersweet," Sylvia admitted. "I love the book, and I have such fond memories of working with Joyce to publish it. But my life seems . . . calmer . . . without it." Drawing in a fortifying breath and smiling at Adrienne, she added, "And Adrienne was right all those years when she told me the store would do better without it."

"You worked very hard to make sure of it," Adrienne said, putting a warm hand on Sylvia's.

It was true: she had worked hard, and she was proud of what she'd accomplished in two years: doubling her library memberships and increasing her sales with a little extra advertising. To her surprise, traffic didn't decrease without *Ulysses* and its writer, who had stayed well away from Odeonia since his return to Paris from London. In fact, Shakespeare and Company's reputation as the hub of expatriate literary life in Paris had only grown, and some friends like Gertrude and Alice—who'd long ago taken to inviting Sylvia and Adrienne to the rue de Fleurus but rarely attended events on the rue de l'Odéon—had begun frequenting the store again. But the real boon, financially at least, was that Sylvia no longer advanced Joyce any funds or forgave any of his loans. Shakespeare and Company was solvent and secure without its Crooked Jesus.

Still, though, part of her pined for those early days of the 1920s when everything felt like a thrilling new adventure.

Apparently sensing her friend's complicated tangle of emotions, Carlotta said, "There are many memories yet to be made."

"Many," Adrienne agreed.

"I'm sure you're right," she replied. They had to be.

※

If new memories were to be made, it would be in part because Paris itself was being remade by a whole new kind of artist in the Left Bank. These days, instead of running into ten Americans she knew when she went for coffee or a glass of wine at the Dôme, Sylvia was much more likely to sit down and talk about Spain or Germany with one of the many refugee artists from those countries who were fleeing Franco or the increasingly draconian Reich—in particular the anti-Semitism and anti-intellectualism that made so many, like their new friends Walter Benjamin and Gisèle Freund, feel unsafe.

Benjamin and Gisèle were in many ways the epitome of the rue de l'Odéon crowd: he a philosopher and writer, she a photographer and teacher. Even the fact that they were in self-imposed exile from their own countries made them like the Americans of the 1920s. But the America of 1920 or even 1927, however conservative and isolationist, was not menacing in the way that the Germany of 1933 had become. Calvin Coolidge was hardly Adolf Hitler, and John Sumner was nothing compared to this Joseph Goebbels who was controlling the German media. Americans had been escaping to drink and write and love freely, and they frequently returned to their homeland; in fact, they were going home in droves these days. These German artists were escaping persecution and assumed they would never return to the country of their birth. They despaired of seeing sisters, brothers, cousins, and parents ever again.

These new expatriates' eyes were rimmed with the violet of worried, sleepless nights, whereas the Americans' had been red and bloodshot from hangovers—nothing some baguette, coffee, and a glass of juice with champagne couldn't cure. This difference imparted a new darkness to the cafés and shops and parties in the Latin Quarter and Montparnasse. And yet these political exiles seemed determined to live life to its fullest—*in true Whitmanian form*, Sylvia liked to think to herself. She and Adrienne attended dinner parties and readings, concerts and lectures as often as they ever had.

Adrienne was in her element as a hostess, assembling guest lists for dinners with maximum intellectual stimulation, then trying all manner of recipes from a fresh batch of cookbooks, as well as experimenting with ingredients and methods for exotic dishes she'd learned at other homes. Truly, the meals they ate in the tiniest apartments these days were as astonishing as the stories of their hosts—goulash, spaetz-le, stuffed cabbage, and fresh yogurt with honey to accompany tales of public ridicule, store closures, and vandalized temples.

But after a few weeks' long cycle of work and socializing, Sylvia would feel an intense need to escape. Most of the time, Adrienne accompanied Sylvia to Les Déserts, but something in her had also become more vibrant in the presence of so much restlessness and need. It was more than the cooking. Sylvia wished the new Paris could bring them together, but instead it made them crave different kinds of comforts. She wanted to eschew some of the socializing and take more long walks or even classes with Adrienne—the horticul-tural courses in the Jardin du Luxembourg that she'd heard about sounded appealing, but when she mentioned them to Adrienne, she'd laughed. "I'd sooner butcher a side of beef than plant pots of flowers," she replied.

"I don't just *want* to spend time outdoors," Sylvia said, "I *need* to. The fresh air and exertion have done wonders for my headaches and neuralgia."

"That is wonderful, and I hope you continue to do it," said Adri-enne, taking up a carrot and beginning to peel it. "We don't need to do everything together."

But we always have. Sylvia picked at a loose thread on a napkin.

"Take the gardening class! I'll love having you bring home beauti-ful flowers." Adrienne punctuated her statement with a kiss on Syl-via's cheek before going back to her carrots.

"All right, I will," Sylvia said.

When she did, she was surprised to find she didn't miss Adrienne as she memorized the names and uses of various native plants, learn-ing how to coax delicate green life from tiny brown seeds buried in dirt.

CHAPTER 27

❧

"**Y**ou're looking well," Sylvia observed as Joyce leaned his ashplant stick against a shelf and settled into the green chair as if it were four years ago. Sylvia felt anxious with him in the store, and patted her pockets for a cigarette to steady herself, but they were empty because she was trying to cut back. She picked up a pen and twiddled it.

"I'm *looking*," he said, "that's the major difference."

When was the last time she'd seen him? Six months ago, maybe, when he'd breezed in with Samuel Beckett for a book and left before she could inquire how he was doing. It was midsummer now, and he'd been in Zurich for a few weeks, at last having his eye operation there because Dr. Borsch had passed away. Though there was a patch over his eye, Joyce's face had better color and shape than it had in years. She assumed it was the effect of the Swiss hospital, which she understood was surrounded by lovely verdant hills and wildflowers, encouraged time outside, and fed its patients well. No doubt better than the rich sauces and red wines of the Parisian establishments he favored.

"Have you heard about the progress of *Ulysses* in America?" he asked.

How can he sound so casual, as if I'm just any reader or admirer? "I have," she said carefully, "and congratulations on Woolsey's decision."

"Yes," he said musingly, almost distractedly. "I was pleased with it. As was Mr. Cerf. He articulated what you and the Misses Heap and Anderson always said about the book, which is that the novel is art. You and they were the first to stand by it."

She couldn't help it; even after everything, his compliment made her heart swell with pride. She and Margaret and Jane were indeed the first. There was something in that, being the first.

"No one else seems to understand just how much Judge Woolsey's words mean to me. I thought you might."

My god, he sounds lonely. It struck her for the first time that maybe he hadn't been enjoying his exile from Stratford-on-Odéon. For so long she'd felt mainly anger and betrayal when she thought of Joyce, but that day she felt pity and sadness.

"I do understand," she said. "His words meant a great deal to me, too." The day she read the decision in an American newspaper at the Loup, she'd had to brush tears from her eyes. "In writing *Ulysses*, Joyce sought to make a serious experiment in a new, if not wholly novel, literary genre," Judge Woolsey had written, then he'd gone on to describe in detail all there was to admire about the book.

"But I understand," she went on, "that it's still stuck in the courts?"

"The US Attorney is appealing," he said, his voice still remarkably even, practically disinterested. "But Mr. Cerf tells me that Judges Learned and Augustus Hand will be friendly toward our book."

Our book. His and Cerf's? Or his and mine?

"Well, I wish you all the best." And she meant it; she could feel it in her swollen, tender heart.

"Tell me some news of yours."

"Oh, it's just been the usual here, really," she sputtered, not knowing what piece of the store's lively year she should share with him; it felt like they hardly knew each other any longer. "Ernest comes and goes as always, though I sense things with Pauline might not be all roses. Adrienne and I have made good friends of Walter Benjamin and his young photographer friend Gisèle Freund. Oh, and Henry Miller's a regular here now. Believe it or not, he has the same literary agent as Gertrude."

"The Minotaur of the Latin Quarter?" he said, raising his voice and sounding more animated. "I've heard her latest book is a sellout, designed to make money and nothing else."

"*The Autobiography of Alice B. Toklas*? I thought it was very good. And not everything that's popular is a sellout."

"I hardly hold it against great artists who *become* popular after great suffering. But to *change one's style* just to be accessible?" He shook his head and tutted.

"I'm not so sure that's what she's done," Sylvia said, wondering if this was the first time she'd ever disagreed with Joyce about literature, and so freely. What she'd never say to him was that she suspected readers had simply become more accustomed to prose like Stein's—and his. It wasn't as shocking as it had been in the years after the war. Likely it was time for others to come along and shock people. This young Henry Miller, perhaps. So she simply said, "There might be a mellowing of the original Stein in *Alice*, but it's still recognizably her."

Joyce shrugged, letting the matter drop.

They were both quiet for a moment and then, as if waking from a dream, he looked around and said, "Where's Teddy?"

"He died last year."

"I'm sorry, Miss Beach. I know how you loved him."

"I did. Thank you." There was the lump in her throat again. Anytime she thought of her loyal little shop dog, it returned.

"It would seem that everything we love moves on."

Tears needled her eyes. This time she needed the damn cigarette. "Excuse me," she whispered, then hurried to the back room of the store and opened the drawer where she kept an emergency pack, fearing it might be as empty as her pockets. But—*ah!*—there was a mostly full pack. She lit one there, at the counter, and took a deep, steadying drag, then proceeded to finish it in under a minute. She walked back into the shop smoking a second slowly and more thoughtfully, to see Joyce readying himself to leave by putting on his hat and looking around for his ashplant stick as if he didn't know exactly where he put it, where he'd been putting it since the store moved to this location more than a decade ago.

He found it, then leaned on it and looked right at Sylvia with his one decent eye. "It was a pleasure seeing you, Miss Beach."

"You, too, Mr. Joyce."

He nodded and left, leaving her to chain-smoke for the next hour, migraines be damned.

A few days later, a bicycle messenger brought her a small clay statue of a terrier with a red fabric cord tied around his neck, from which was dangling a little brass bell with a cheerful ring. In the dog's slightly open mouth was a card, which she opened. Stifling a sob, her watery eyes swam over Joyce's nearly illegible scrawl of the last stanza of Tennyson's "In Memoriam."

I hold it true, whate'er befall;
I feel it, when I sorrow most;
'Tis better to have loved and lost
Than never to have loved at all.

"Three times higher?" Adrienne's eyes were wide and disbelieving.

Sylvia nodded and swallowed a gulp of wine that burned her smoke-raw throat.

Her rent, long so affordable, was being tripled.

"I have to make money, too," the landlord had written in the letter he'd sent her. He lived a few blocks away, so he was obviously too ashamed to come and give her this news in person.

"Bah." Adrienne began clattering around noisily in the kitchen. After taking sufficient stock of the cupboards and icebox, she proclaimed, "And we have nothing good to eat."

"I'm not hungry anyway," said Sylvia.

"Gauloises are not dinner."

In less than an hour Adrienne performed the magic trick that Sylvia had come to see as the hallmark of a great chef: making what seemed to be discarded ingredients into a delicious meal. In this case, a single onion and two potatoes became a fragrant soup, accompanied by formerly stale bread that Adrienne transformed into a hearty toast with a tiny bit of butter and Gruyère.

Sylvia wished she could taste it all better.

"What am I going to do?"

"To start, you're going to stop paying rent here on the apartment. I can manage."

Sylvia opened her mouth to protest, but Adrienne put her hands up between their faces and said, "I don't want to hear it. And I am sure some of our friends will help with Shakespeare."

"I can't ask them to help me that way. The store needs to grow its business somehow. But how? The selling portion is already dwarfed by the library portion, and no one has any money to spare these days."

"We'll think. I am sure more of my regulars could be persuaded to take out a subscription across the street, especially when they discover what's happening."

"Shakespeare and Company has always been a *provider* of charity, Adrienne."

"I know, *chérie*. But these are new days."

No sooner had they finished dinner than their bell rang, and both women startled. "Who do you suppose it is?" Sylvia asked.

"I have no idea. It's close to ten." Adrienne peered out the window down onto the street. "It's Gisèle. I hope nothing is wrong."

"Invite her in," said Sylvia. It was strange—late-night guests used to be quite common, when everyone was younger. There had been a long fallow period, and now they were seeing more and more of this new crop of young artists after dinner. Sylvia had to admit it annoyed her, though it didn't seem to bother Adrienne in the slightest.

Adrienne bustled downstairs and reemerged moments later with Gisèle, who said, "I am so sorry to intrude," her French burdened by her German accent, though her voice was smooth and low. It made sense with her dark eyes and hair, a tumble of tight curls she kept short and in check with a great deal of pomade. Her arms and legs were long and thin, accentuated by the high-waisted trousers and white blouses she favored. Tonight she wore a navy-blue sailor's coat as well.

"Nonsense, you're not intruding," said Adrienne as she filled the kettle to make tea. "I told you to stop by if you ever needed anything. Please sit."

Gisèle shrugged out of her coat and hung it on the back of one of the wooden kitchen chairs, then sat with a heaving sigh. "I received a letter from my mother today. Things are only getting worse in Berlin, and my parents refuse to leave. Also, Walter is depressed again. I didn't know where to turn."

For quite a while, Sylvia had assumed Walter Benjamin and Gisèle were lovers, as they were often together in the store, and it was clear they'd known each other for years and enjoyed each other's company immensely. But lately Gisèle had begun turning up at the store with other women, whom she touched in suggestive ways—a lips-on-the-ear whisper, a lingering hand on a back—and Sylvia had begun to wonder if Gisèle might be flexible in her attractions like Bob or Bryher or Fargue or Cyprian.

"Can you convince your parents to join you here?" asked Adrienne.

"I've tried many times." Gisèle held the cup in both hands and blew steam off the top. "I don't know how else to convince them that Berlin is dangerous for them now. They think I am being a silly girl."

"You are anything but silly," Adrienne said with indignation, at last sitting in one of the chairs along with Gisèle and Sylvia. She picked up a linzer cookie and nibbled it. Gisèle mirrored her. There was something unsettling about seeing Adrienne and Gisèle together, though Sylvia couldn't quite put her finger on why.

"It's hard to convince parents of anything," said Gisèle. "They always think they know better."

Am I old enough to be Gisèle's mother? Sylvia found herself wondering. She was about twenty years older than the photographer, who was twenty-five, so it was possible. Adrienne was five years younger than Sylvia, which had always seemed like nothing. In fact, Adrienne had seemed older than her in many ways, having opened La Maison years before Shakespeare and Company, during the Great War. Suddenly, though, her forty-one seemed at least a decade younger than Sylvia's forty-six, not only because of Gisèle, but also because of the midlife ailments Sylvia couldn't seem to shake.

Gisèle exhaled dramatically. "And what of Walter? He is so low it scares me sometimes. He might be in more danger from himself than my parents are from the Nazis. At least, right now."

This revelation made Sylvia feel sick, and she wondered, as she had often over the years, *What signs did I miss that Mother would kill herself?* Now she added, *What signs did I miss that this girl is not missing in Walter Benjamin?*

Adrienne put a hand on Gisèle's, and said quietly, "If he wants to do it, there will be no stopping him." Then she looked at Sylvia and gave her a small, remorseful smile.

With a set jaw and clear eyes affixed to her cup, Gisèle nodded. Sylvia's heart throbbed at Adrienne's discreet validation of her own daughterly helplessness. There was a deep well of reassurance in this, an acknowledgment of their bond, their shared past and secrets. Gisèle Freund and these other late-night intruders, Sylvia thought with conviction, had much life to live before they formed relationships as intimate and lasting as theirs.

CHAPTER 28

꧁⚜꧂

August 8, 1934

ULYSSES DECISION UPHELD

Judges Learned and Augustus Hand of the US Court of
Appeals have upheld the decision of Judge Woolsey from
the end of last year, in a two-to-one vote with Judge Mar-
tin Manton dissenting. Citing Woolsey, the Judges Hand
agree that the book "does not, in our opinion, tend to promote lust" because "the erotic passages are submerged in
the book as a whole."

The ruling of the appeals court is important, but a
mere coda in the literary world, which made Woolsey's
decision a part of the canon itself, as it was printed in every edition of Mr. Joyce's novel, which began selling in
January of this year, just a month after his decision was
made. This staggering speed can be accounted for by the
nimbleness of Random House's Bennett Cerf. Within the

hour of Woolsey's decision, he ordered the typesetters to begin work.

Woolsey, who read Joyce's tome in its entirety, declared that "in spite of its unusual frankness, I do not detect anywhere the leer of the sensualist." He went on to declare the novel "a serious experiment" in which "Joyce has attempted—it seems to me, with astonishing success—to show how the screen of consciousness with its ever shifting kaleidoscopic impressions . . . affects the life and behavior of the character which he is describing." Furthermore, "It is because Joyce has been loyal to his technique . . . that he has been the subject of so many attacks and that his purpose has been so often misunderstood and misrepresented."

On reading Woolsey's decision, Joyce himself proclaimed, "Thus one half of the English-speaking world surrenders."

Today, *Ulysses* is entirely free in the home of the brave, and the way is paved for other works of literature to be daring and experimental without fear of censorship. More than that, there appears to be an appetite for such writing in these trying times: in just three months on the shelves, Cerf reports that *Ulysses* sold 35,000 copies.

Though she'd read summaries of the news in letters and cables to Les Déserts, Sylvia hadn't been able to lay her hands on full print articles until she returned to Shakespeare and Company in September and read the many copies of articles that friends had saved for her and delivered in person as soon as she turned the lights back on. Many of them wrote versions of "of course you knew this already" (Ernest) or "typically, a man needed to say it for it to be true"

(Cyprian), or "I couldn't be prouder of my daughter for being *the first* publisher of this famous novel" (her father).

Consuming the official news and more letters all at once, as she drank coffee and tried with clenched teeth not to chain-smoke in the back room of the shop while Julie manned the front, was almost too much for her. More than once, her eyes spilled over with tears and she gasped a combined laugh and cry at the well-wishing, brimming with pride and grief and love and gratitude and relief.

In the mix of letters was one from Holly, announcing that she and her husband Fred had adopted a baby boy in England—they had enclosed a picture of the precious little thing in a bonnet and wrapped in a blanket so that all one could see of his actual self was a squishy face, eyes closed. Still, this was her first and likely only nephew! And he was entirely unexpected. Holly was a few years older than she was, and Sylvia had assumed that the Beach sisters would live childless lives that were productive in other ways. But with their Pasadena store closed, and the world so uncertain, Holly had decided that a family was the surest road to occupation and security. Meanwhile, in Palm Springs, Cyprian lived contentedly with Helen Eddy, breathing the desert air that was supposed to cure all manner of ills.

Sylvia looked at the photograph of her sister's baby, and felt—as she had gazing into the faces of so many children over the years—a gush of warm affection and happiness for its mother, and awe and wonder at what the child itself might become. The next Joyce? Antheil?

And that was all. Occasionally her fondness and curiosity about a loved one's new baby would be tempered by a foreboding at the limitations the child might place on its mother, or a fear that he or she could grow up to be unmanageable like Lucia, or sickly like Suzanne. This picture, though, of her *nephew*—oughtn't it to inspire more in her? An intense desire to hold it? A stirring in her own womb? A regret that her own life would be childless? But she felt none of those things. Her life was full. She couldn't imagine introducing a child into it, a living being wholly dependent on her. Shakespeare and Company was its own kind of progeny.

As was *Ulysses*. Though the newspapers gave all the credit for the triumph of *Ulysses* to five men—three judges, Cerf, and his lawyer—the letters of her friends and family reminded her of the truth.

"Gisèle has been practicing her portraits, and they are marvelous. I keep telling her to do a series on the writers of Odeonia," said Adrienne to their friends who had gathered around the dining room table for a meal it had taken close to a week of shopping to prepare, for she had to make frequent stops at all her favorite grocers, waiting for them to stock certain items she used to take for granted—butter, sugar, Roquefort, chicken. Even seasonal fruits and vegetables were difficult to find; she had to be there right when a delivery of pears arrived to get five of them, all underripe and requiring days of coaxing and care to ripen properly in the kitchen. "Cooking has become like a hunt," she observed. But it was all worth it when she set her perfectly roasted, sautéed, and whisked dishes before their vocal and appreciative friends. That night it was Carlotta and James, Gisèle and Walter.

"James and I were just talking about having our portraits done, weren't we?" Carlotta put a hand on her husband's arm and turned to Gisèle. "We may not be writers, but we could certainly pay you. Would you consider it?"

"It would be my pleasure," said Gisèle.

The young woman had become a fixture in the two shops, and she even purchased books now and again with her meager salary from the Sorbonne, where she taught a few classes. The way she tended to shy and brilliant Walter Benjamin touched Sylvia, particularly since it was clear to her now that, if they ever had been lovers, they were no longer. Gisèle had settled right into the lesbian scene of the Left Bank, making herself a regular at Natalie Barney's salon, which Sylvia and Adrienne themselves had dropped in on more often in the twenties. But Gisèle and Walter were more like siblings: she was able to gently tease him, cajole him into dinners and other social events he might have otherwise avoided, like their little party that night. He was mostly quiet, but seemed amused by the company and generally at ease.

"Wunderbar," he said of the suggestion to take the Briggses' portrait, adding, "but I also agree with Adrienne that you should be taking photos of the writers. There might be limited time to do such things."

"But usually artists wait to be asked to *take* the picture, to be commissioned. It was even true for painters. Are you suggesting I ask the writers if I may take their photos?"

"Why not? You are an artist yourself," said Adrienne. "It's no different from seeking a model, and I know that painters frequently propose portraits to certain subjects."

Gisèle was quiet, thinking.

"I can understand your hesitation," said Sylvia. "It's the same in the store. I don't like to push or pry, and prefer to let people come to me. If they want something, they will ask. On the other hand, I believe in artists and their projects, and would do anything to help promote them, so if you feel shy about asking certain writers, I'm sure I can help in that regard."

Adrienne beamed at Sylvia. "Exactly! As will I. Let us do the asking."

Benjamin patted his friend's knee under the table, and said, "What wonderful friends we have in Paris."

Carlotta clapped her hands together with an enormous smile and added, "And when the pictures are in the Anderson Galleries, we'll be able to say we were there when the series was conceived."

James kissed his wife.

Talk wandered to the sorry states of the economy and Europe, as it always seemed to, and then to the states of La Maison and Shakespeare and Company.

"I'm doing all right," Sylvia demurred.

"Sylvia, we have a banker here. You should ask questions," Adrienne said.

"He's a friend," Sylvia corrected her, feeling her face hot with embarrassment—though she was hardly sure why, since Carlotta was one of her oldest friends, and she already knew about the dire straits of Shakespeare because of inflation, Americans leaving Paris, and the rent increase. All her gains of the early thirties lost, Sylvia was barely making ends meet, had let Mysrine go, and she rarely paid Julie except in free books and the occasional gift, though her friend insisted she liked helping in the shop regardless of salary.

"I have wondered about this," James said delicately. "Have you thought about incorporating? Selling shares? I'm sure many patrons of the arts would love to say they owned a bit of Shakespeare and Company."

"But wouldn't that mean Sylvia wouldn't own it any longer?" Adrienne asked.

"Correct. Not entirely."

"Well, then, that's out of the question," Adrienne said to the emphatic nods of Gisèle and Benjamin. Silently, Sylvia agreed. She could never sell Shakespeare and Company.

"And this selling of shares is what got the world economy in this mess in the first place," Benjamin said.

James smiled good-naturedly. "In some ways. But I also happen to think it's what will get us out."

"After your new president's New Deal has a chance to take hold," said Benjamin.

James shrugged. "I hope Roosevelt's plans work. We're certainly in uncharted territory here. But the economy can't be said to be up and running again until the stock market is healthy. And that will mean buying and selling shares."

This time Benjamin shrugged. Clearly they disagreed, but neither man thought economics was worth fighting about tonight.

"I appreciate everyone's interest in Shakespeare and Company," said Sylvia. "And, James, maybe we could sit down and have a talk about my options? I hope there might be something I can do other than selling pieces of it."

"I'll do some thinking and inquiring," he promised.

It wasn't the heady, boozy dinners of the twenties, and she didn't envy the young artists making their ways in the Paris of the thirties, but Sylvia went to sleep that night feeling hopeful. She and her store were established and respected; there was real comfort in that. They'd weathered other storms together. What was one more?

CHAPTER 29

"Why do you look so low?" Jean Schlumberger asked her one night in 1935 after a celebration at Adrienne's store for the first issue of her new journal *Mesures*.

"Do I? I'm sorry," Sylvia replied, forcing a smile. "It's such a festive evening."

"You're not fooling me," he replied. "Tell."

"I received word today that Shakespeare and Company cannot apply for French government assistance because I am American." She felt ashamed even admitting she needed the help, but she was also exhausted from the effort of hiding it.

"But that is absurd," Jean said, sounding genuinely outraged.

"What is?" Paul Valéry asked, joining them along with Jules Romains and André Gide.

Jean explained, and Gide shared his outrage, saying, "Your shop and Adrienne's have become more important to Franco-American relations in Paris than any treaty, statue, or speech. It is the place where we meet and exchange ideas. We cannot allow the English-language half of this partnership to suffer."

"I quite agree," said Paul Valéry. "It's criminal that Sylvia is not eligible for a subsidy from our government, so essential has her shop become to *us*, the French, to say nothing of the expatriates who come and go and spend money at French establishments."

"Certainly you have done more than this Mary Ryan in Ireland who merely teaches French on a tiny island, and who was just awarded the Legion of Honor," said Jean.

"I read about her," said Sylvia. "And she is more accomplished than you give her credit for. She's the first woman in England or Ireland to be made a full professor at a university."

"That explains a great and unfortunate deal." Jean folded his arms over his chest and frowned down at the floor.

"What if . . . ," Romains thought aloud. "What if Sylvia hosted a series of exclusive readings in her shop, and charged for them? Like theater. I'm sure all of us would be happy to read from our works in progress. And I'm sure her famous American friends would do the same, isn't that right, Sylvia?"

Snapping his fingers, Jean looked up excitedly, and Sylvia nodded in agreement. Something was taking shape, something that just might save her beloved shop—and it was fitting somehow that it was her French friends, the original *potassons* of La Maison des Amis des Livres, who would think of it. After all, they were the permanent residents. Even the Americans who loved Paris were transitory, and those who stayed, like Gertrude and Alice, had never applied the "when in Rome" theory of living abroad. Sylvia wished her dear friend Valery Larbaud were there to participate in this plan, but he was convalescing with family in the country.

"Perhaps instead, the readings should be free and available to members who pay a sort of subscription," Jean suggested, "above and beyond the library membership."

"But they would not own part of the store?" clarified Sylvia.

"Of course not," Jean replied. "They would be friends of the store. Patrons."

"Speaking of Sylvia and patrons," said Adrienne, adding herself to the discussion, "an American literary agent stopped by last week to ask if Sylvia would write her memoir." Adrienne's pride at this offer was getting embarrassing; she brought it up at every opportunity.

"I said no," Sylvia said, clearing her throat.

"But why? It would be an important work! A personal history of one of Paris's best decades," Romains said.

"He told me I would have to downplay the rivalries and bad feelings, and I didn't want to have to feel I was being censored from the start." She'd had enough of censorship for one lifetime. But part of the truth, one she couldn't even share with Adrienne, was that she still felt too angry at Joyce and the other men he'd colluded with to be able to write about him with any fairness. Adrienne, she was sure, would advise her to use that anger as fuel—not necessarily to embarrass Joyce but to get words on the page. Truthful words.

In the brief time she'd considered writing the memoir, Sylvia had wondered if perhaps the real truths of life were best left to fiction. It was safer for everyone involved.

"If someday you want to write your memoir, then I shall be first to purchase it," said Gide, "but if you never do, so be it. Shakespeare and Company is a great work of art unto itself, one that anyone would be proud to have produced."

"Thank you," said Sylvia, feeling both embarrassed by and proud of all the praise.

Jean clapped his hands and then rubbed them together with appetite. "In the meantime, let us begin the Friends of Shakespeare and Company."

She could hardly sleep that night for the planning, but she didn't feel tired the next day. In the middle of the night, she began scribbling ideas down in preparation for the lunch Jean promised to have with her to draft an initial appeal to potential Friends—he was emphatic that it should come from him and the other French writers and not Sylvia herself. "To keep your charming humility intact," he'd said.

Looking around the shop that morning, she didn't feel sad, as she had the past months, when she feared losing it. But . . . there were a few items she thought she could stand parting with. "Julie," she said, "how much do you think that Blake drawing might fetch?"

Looking up from the ledger, Julie fastened her eyes on the drawing and raised her brows. "I don't know. But . . . well, I suppose it's like selling one's grandmother's pearls, is it not? Very sad, but necessary. Perhaps someday you can gain it back."

Sylvia began a catalog of papers, pictures, and manuscripts she thought could be sold to keep the shop afloat. *If the Friends bring in enough members*, she told herself, *I can stop the sale. Best to be ready.* The hardest items to consider putting on the list were the ones that had been with her from the first days, like the Whitman pages and the Blake sketches. Almost as difficult were the Joyce items she thought would be quite popular: an early draft of *Portrait*, when it was still called *Stephen Hero*, and the letter signed by so many famous writers and thinkers—Albert Einstein! His signature was still incredible to her—in support of *Ulysses* and against Samuel Roth's piracy.

Once word got out about the Friends of Shakespeare and Company, thanks in large part to Janet Flanner's article in the *New Yorker*, offers to help poured in. In fact, Marian Willard, who'd been a favorite customer in the twenties, wrote and offered to form a New York City chapter of the Friends. It felt laughably predictable that the American members were largely women of means who wrote large checks out of their substantial bank accounts, whereas her French members were men or couples who paid the three hundred francs for their two-year membership.

Though it was all very encouraging, Sylvia still went forward with her sale. In the first week after she sent out her catalogs, Bryher wrote and said she'd purchase the Blake drawing for a thousand dollars, "on the condition that it continue hanging exactly where it is in the store," which made Sylvia laugh so hard with surprise and gratitude, she practically cried.

What a contrast to the letter Joyce wrote her:

> *My dear Miss Beach,*
>
> *It's come to my attention that you intend to sell some of the papers I've given to you as gifts over the years. While I would never suggest that they are not yours to do with as you like, may I say that it pains me to know that my favorite publisher is being driven to such ends. And, truly, I never meant for the world to see my early pages—consider, please, what an embarrassment it would be to me.*
>
> *Yours sincerely,*
> *James Joyce*

Since he'd written the letter from his fine apartment in the seventh rather than coming to the store to make the request in person, Sylvia had to assume that he actually did feel the papers were not truly hers but he was too proud to admit it out loud, face-to-face. She waited for the familiar anger at his attempt to make her feel guilty, but the emotion never surfaced, and she hoped this meant she was making progress in her heart regarding the writer. Her goal was to feel nothing about James Joyce. Or, at least, to stop feeling the searing anger.

There was something clarifying about the process of selling these old items and at the same time embarking on a new project—as if

Shakespeare and Company could be remade, as if she were closing one great book and beginning another.

☆

Torrential spring rains flooded the city. The Seine rose dangerously high, and there were days when the rue de l'Odéon looked like a river itself, with streams of water rushing down from the theater at the head of the street, down into the carrefour, which looked at times like an urban pond, with bistro tables and chairs sometimes floating down a side street. When the sun finally emerged, it shone down hot and sticky on the drenched city, and Sylvia was able to resume the long walks she'd been taking through the vast parks and gardens, which improved the migraines and heavy periods she'd been enduring of late.

"It is good to see your step lighter," Adrienne observed one evening as they sipped glasses of cold white wine and nibbled on cheese and cherries.

"It's good to feel lighter." Sylvia glanced over at the window box of geraniums she'd planted just two weeks before that were already bubbling over with coral and fuchsia. True to her word, Adrienne had been effusive in her enjoyment of Sylvia's developing horticultural skills—almost to the point of embarrassing her by lavishing praise on the flowers to any dinner guest who so much as mentioned them. But then, Adrienne had always been so sure of Sylvia's talents. And wasn't that something Sylvia loved about her? Yes, maybe she could admit that now. Why had it been so difficult for so long?

"I have a little secret," Adrienne said, suddenly looking girlish.

"Oh?"

"Some of the *potassons* have banded together to nominate us for the Legion of Honor!"

"No!" The thought made Sylvia light-headed with delight.

"Yes!"

"But how do you know?"

"A little bird twittered in my ear."

"Come now, Adrienne."

"Jean told me. But you mustn't let on that I told you. He called us the presiding goddesses of Franco-American relations." She took no pains to hide her pleasure in being referred to as a deity.

"Goddesses?"

"Don't be so surprised, Sylvia! Look at us!"

Both women burst into unbridled laughter; they were shiny faced and ripe from their days' labors, their wrinkled skirts and blouses damp from perspiration. "If we're goddesses, I'd hate to see a mere mortal," Sylvia managed to say between cackles.

"Well," Sylvia said when she finally got a hold of herself. "No matter what the Legion decides, it is a great compliment."

"It is." Adrienne nodded.

As quickly as the laughter had come, tears rushed in. To be recognized in that way by her French friends . . . it was too much.

"Do not cry, *chérie*." Adrienne poured them each more wine and then clinked her glass to Sylvia's. "What is it Tennyson wrote in his 'Ulysses'? 'Tho' / We are not now that strength which in old days / Moved earth and heaven, that which we are, we are."

"'One equal temper of heroic hearts / Made weak by time and fate, but strong in will," Sylvia said, though the emotion in her throat would not allow her to speak the last line.

But the smile Adrienne gave her was poetry enough.

CHAPTER 30

꩜

The night of Saturday, June 6, 1936, had the feel of a wedding about it—it was a celebration, as well as one thing ending while another began. Friends from all times of her life were present for her, for Shakespeare and Company, and for T. S. Eliot's reading of *The Waste Land*: Ezra, Joyce, Carlotta and James, Julie and Michel, Larbaud, Valéry, Schlumberger, Gide, Margaret and Jane, Gertrude and Alice, Samuel, Walter, Simone de Beauvoir and Jean-Paul Sartre, and even Ernest and his new girl Martha Gellhorn, a journalist he'd met in Spain and clearly fallen hard for. (*Oh, Ernest*, Sylvia wondered, *will you ever learn?*)

It was the fifth reading of the Friends, and the first by an English-language writer, following readings by Gide, Valéry, Schlumberger, and Jean Paulhan. Each and every one had been a success, with sixty chairs crammed into the library of Shakespeare and Company filled by the nine p.m. start time, and attendees holding cups of wine they sipped while the writer *de la nuit* read from a work in progress.

It was hard to tell what was truly the main event: the hour of sonorous and theatrical literature, or the buzzy reception afterward, where the audience-cum-partygoers toasted the author, the Friends, and Odeonia as they feasted on delicious treats prepared by Adrienne and Rinette. Talk would very often turn to the fate of France in a Europe that seemed to be changing daily, with a war being fought in Spain, and a dictator in Germany whose promises were "no more than toilet paper," as Gide put it. But somehow, even those conversations, on those nights, had the feeling of reverie to them, buffered as they were by the ethereal quality of the twilight and the shelves of books that stood protectively between them and the outside world.

Eliot, who'd arrived from London that very morning, claimed not to have a new poem in the works as he was between plays and so planned to read his longtime Shakespeare and Company bestseller, *The Waste Land*, which had been published in 1922, just a few months after her edition of *Ulysses*. Sylvia wondered if Joyce remembered that year as clearly as she did. Sitting in the audience beside Nora, his fingers laced in his lap, his face was inscrutable.

The place was packed to the gills, with stragglers standing sardine-like in two makeshift rows at the back. Gisèle was there with her camera, as she seemed to be everywhere these days, taking pictures of famous writers and artists just as Adrienne and Sylvia had made happen after their Thanksgiving promises of a few years before. In fact, Gisèle was making quite a name for herself—another success story of Odeonia that Sylvia was proud of having had a hand in creating.

Since she'd hosted a few of these readings already, and this was the last of the first season, Sylvia was feeling relaxed and happy that night. All her favorite people seemed to be in one place; the only people she might have wished could be there were her parents and sisters. But she'd had a lovely graveside visit with her mother earlier that day, and she was considering a trip to California to see her father and sisters. Gertrude had recently returned from a victory tour around the United States, lecturing and reading to audiences that numbered in the hundreds—"But never more than five hundred," she'd told the group gathered in her salon with such false modesty Sylvia thought she heard Gertrude herself laughing at the back of her throat. Hearing jaded Gertrude Stein speak with such naked enthusiasm about the vast western sky, the skyscrapers piercing the blue above New York, and the storm clouds hanging over Washington had given Sylvia the first hankering she'd felt in ages to see the country of her birth.

A new adventure. What a marvelous thought.

Though she was tempted to go on talking to all her guests about this and that, like it was the busiest and most festive holiday in her shop, by nine it was time to begin. Jean Schlumberger took the makeshift stage and brought everyone to attention with the cheerful clink of a spoon to a wineglass.

After Jean introduced Eliot and the audience roared their anticipatory applause, the room fell utterly silent. Sylvia felt a fizzy excitement, though she'd read this poem hundreds of times. She'd even translated it into French.

Eliot cleared his throat and stammered, "Well, goodness, you're my friends, so you'll have to accord me less respect than *that*," and everyone laughed again.

And fell silent again.

Like a pastor on Easter morning, Eliot solemnly and joyfully opened the first edition of his poem that Sylvia hadn't been able to part with in her sales, and began with his dedication to Ezra Pound, at which more cheers erupted. Ezra stood and took a bow, and Eliot smiled broadly and replied, "There we are," then continued with those first now-famous lines about April, ". . . mixing/ Memory and desire . . ."

That was the crux of it, wasn't it, Sylvia thought. *Mixing memory and desire. How had he known that as such a young man? We were all so young in 1922.*

Sylvia closed her eyes and let Eliot's words wash over her, and it was like reading the poem for the first time. It felt, even after fourteen years, startlingly new and fresh and alive. When he came to the end, "These fragments I have shored against my ruins . . . Shantih shantih shantih," there was a heart's beat of silence before she opened her eyes to see every sitting person rise to their feet in a din of cheers and claps and whistles and stomping feet. None more enthusiastically than Sylvia herself from the center of the crowd, where she couldn't even see Eliot on the little dais, until suddenly a path was being cleared for her, and Eliot was holding out his arms to her, welcoming her up with him, eyes bright and shining. Hardly knowing what was happening—part of her was still inside the poem, in that shadowy ancient world he'd conjured in the Paris night—she walked toward Eliot, who put his arm around her shoulders and turned her to face the audience whose noise boomed louder, which she wouldn't have thought possible until it happened.

Profoundly uncomfortable, pummeled by the percussive clapping, Sylvia couldn't bring herself to make eye contact with anyone in front of her and so let her vision go blurry. Managing a smile that emerged from a mortified but also deeply grateful place inside her, she held out her hands and clapped at her friends.

"To Sylvia!" shouted Ernest, raising his glass and whistling.

"To Shakespeare and Company!" someone else yelled, to more appreciative whistles.

"To you," she responded.

Recalling the night of Shakespeare and Company's opening,

when Cyprian and Adrienne made her speak, Sylvia vowed not to speak that night even as she felt the same level of pride and joy she'd felt on that exuberant occasion. This occasion spoke for itself.

Once the ovation wound down and everyone refreshed their glasses and plates, the sound in the room returned to a low, resonant hum, and Sylvia felt comfortable again. She enjoyed gliding from one conversation to the next, and about an hour in, she found herself face-to-face with Joyce. Just Joyce. She couldn't remember the last time it had been just the two of them in a room full of people.

He presented her with a box wrapped in luminous silver paper with a white satin ribbon. "Please accept this wholly inadequate way of thanking you for making it possible for *Ulysses* to conquer America, and now Britain."

Sylvia felt her cheeks and ears get hot, and she couldn't seem to move her hands to accept the gift. "It's your book, Mr. Joyce. Publishing our eleven editions was gift enough." *Maybe, finally, after all this time it was.*

"And this was its first and still truest home. Stratford-on-Odéon. It wouldn't be what it is without this place."

Yes. His words meant so much to her, still. "Stratford is the truest home of *Ulysses*? Surely you're mixing your metaphors," she tried to joke, to deflect. Her ears were still on fire.

"I gave up searching for an approximation of Ithaca years ago." There was that sadness again, that remorse.

Clearing her throat, she pressed on with more levity. "I understand congratulations are in order. I read that the book sold thirty-five thousand copies in three months! That's better than *Gatsby*! And more than I ever sold, of all our editions combined."

"Regardless, Random House is not Shakespeare and Company." He took her hand in his—had he ever done that before?—and pressed the wrapped box into it. "Any gift is woefully inadequate to repay you, but it would mean a great deal to me if you accepted this one." He hesitated, leaning on his ashplant stick, then said, "There's something I always wanted to ask you."

"Goodness, please do."

"Why did you never publish another book? I know Lawrence asked you to do *Sons and Lovers*. And perhaps you could have helped *The Well of Loneliness*."

She'd been asked this so many times over the years, and all the answers she'd heretofore given—Ulysses *keeps me busy enough; the store takes up too much time; Shakespeare and Company is a one-writer house*—sounded suddenly and woefully incomplete.

"I suppose because I felt the injustice of what was done to your book the most fully. All the other banned books that needed help came after. I liked taking part in a first and only of its kind. *Ulysses* and Shakespeare and Company." Both top-notch firsts and onlys. If she couldn't admit this ambition to Joyce, she couldn't admit it to anyone.

"They are . . . of a piece, aren't they? The book and the shop?"

"A diptych."

"A two-part opera."

Sylvia laughed. "How old-fashioned of us."

"Thank you, Sylvia. For everything."

"It has been a great pleasure, James."

Eyes roving over the familiar shelves, he added, "I am so glad this magical place has so many friends to protect it." Then, before she could reply, he turned and went to find Nora.

The box he'd put in her hand weighed nothing. She couldn't imagine what might be in it. Curiosity got the best of her, and she slipped into her back room to open it. Inside was a royalty check from Random House in New York City, made out to Joyce, which he'd signed over to Sylvia.

These fragments I have shored against my ruins indeed.

Shantih.

Maybe such peace was possible after all.

AUTHOR'S NOTE

Sylvia and Adrienne were made knights of the Legion of Honor, the highest award for service that France bestows on its citizens and military officers alike—Adrienne in 1937 and Sylvia in 1938. And though my book ends in 1936, close to twenty years after it began, because I felt it told the story of her life as bookseller and publisher most satisfyingly, Sylvia lived a long life, all of it in Paris, until 1962, when she died at seventy-five years old. Here are some highlights of those years.

First, as they say, some bad news: Sylvia and Adrienne broke up in 1937. Adrienne took up with Gisèle Freund while Sylvia visited family in America, and as a result Sylvia moved herself into the apartment above her store that had once been occupied by George Antheil. Then, in 1941, during the Nazi occupation of Paris, a German officer tried to purchase a copy of *Finnegans Wake* and Sylvia refused to sell it to him. I think there is a marvelous poetic irony to this: Joyce gets her in trouble one last time, even from the grave (for he died earlier that same year). The German official was furious at Sylvia's refusal and told her that he and his men would come back later to close her shop.

Now here is some better news: A group of dedicated friends helped her move all the books to the fourth floor of her building, dismantle the shelves, and paint over the Shakespeare and Company sign, effectively eradicating any evidence of the shop and foiling the Nazis' efforts. The books stayed successfully hidden until the end of the war, and she donated many of them later to her old competitor, the American Library in Paris.

Not content with the shop's closure, the Nazis took Sylvia to an internment camp in the French resort town of Vittel. Thankfully for her, it was nothing like the concentration camps. As the camp for mostly Americans and British citizens who'd refused to return home, it still functioned much as a resort, and the German propaganda machine used it as a false example of how all their camps were run. Sylvia had to stay there for only six months, because Jacques Benoist-Méchin, one of the original translators of *Ulysses*, who had become an important officer in the Vichy government, intervened on Sylvia's behalf and she was able to return home—another truly poignant example of how the friendship she extended to the writers of Paris came back to help her in a pinch.

Though she survived the war, and there is a terrific story of Ernest Hemingway striding down the rue de l'Odéon right after the liberation of Paris in 1945 to "liberate Shakespeare and Company," Sylvia never reopened the store. Sylvia's biographer, Noël Riley Fitch, says that she told her friends, "One should not do anything twice." I suspect her reasons ran deeper than that. I suspect that once the store was closed, she was able to see it with some distance, as the great work of art that it was, her own *Ulysses*.

I also suspect she didn't want to do it all again and have it pale in comparison to the first remarkable experience that began in 1919. So, pioneer that she was, she embarked on new adventures instead. She wrote her memoir, *Shakespeare and Company*, which I recommend in particular for her charming account of Hemingway's liberation of the store and then the cellar at the Ritz.

I also suspect that Sylvia's reverence for those early years is what allowed her to reestablish a relationship with Adrienne, even after her partner's romantic betrayal. Though there is no evidence that the two women became lovers again, they remained very close friends, sharing dinners and the details of their daily lives, especially after Gisèle escaped to Argentina in 1942 (she returned to Paris after the war, as yet another friend, and enjoyed quite an illustrious career as a photographer). Unhappily, though, Sylvia lost Adrienne in 1955. After being diagnosed with Ménière's disease and suffering hallucinations as a result of the vertigo, Adrienne decided to take her own life, a loss that Sylvia never quite got over, perhaps because it reminded her of how she'd lost her mother.

Sylvia does not dwell on these sad episodes of her life in her own memoir, and to celebrate her life in the spirit she herself left behind, I tried not to, either; instead I tried to explore her life in a way that would show why she might become an older woman who wanted to keep the spotlight on the happy times.

It was her book that first introduced me to her story when I was in college. An English major obsessed with the 1920s, I found a used copy in one of the open bins in front of the bookstores of Telegraph Avenue in Berkeley, California, and I immediately read it and loved it. I'm amazed it took me a quarter of a century and two previous historical novels to realize she deserved her own fictional treatment!

Sylvia's *Shakespeare and Company* is a slim volume, especially considering what an enormous life she led. And as Fitch often points out, there are many passages she drafted but left out or revised for the reading public who, she was keenly aware, would be extremely interested in the famous writers who had become characters in her own story. In every instance, she chose to be affirming and affectionate about her friends and colleagues—but the fact that she altered her own story for her autobiography was liberating to me. I felt it gave me permission to do the same.

Writers of historical fiction, especially biographical fiction like *The Paris Bookseller*, are asked all the time, "How much of this is real?" Every writer's answer to this is different, and the Author's Note is the hallowed place where we all get to explain the ways in which we departed from the historical record. For me, though, the problem with this approach is that I've never wanted to burden this chatty little essay with all of my many, many mea culpas.

But I do think readers deserve some answers. This time, I thought I'd tell you what's *real*, and then say without apology that everything else is a figment of my imagination—which I hope will save us all a lot of time, angst, and ink.

So. What's real?

One reality, which I suspect many readers will find surprising—as did I in my research!—is the openness of the gay lives portrayed in the novel. The postwar years were immensely complicated socially, which I tried to dramatize throughout. On the one hand, conservatism was the norm—in America, Prohibition had outlawed alcohol, anti-immigrant feeling was at an all-time high, and censorship was rampant under the Comstock and Espionage Acts, as the censorship of *Ulysses* itself demonstrates. This conservatism affected both straight and queer life. On the other hand, I was delighted to discover, this was also a time of remarkable freedom, when gay speakeasies and cabarets in cities like New York and Chicago flourished, for the alcohol was as illegal as gay acts of love, but the artists and intellectuals of the time embraced both. Paradoxically, conservative and liberal tendencies often existed side by side, as in the very real character of John Quinn. In Paris, however, the social liberalism of American cities was augmented by legal tolerance, for same-sex relations had been decriminalized since the French Revolution, which had made the capital a haven for gay lovers for more than a century.

In addition, my research revealed an essential and surprising point: the closet as we understand it today is a recent construct. In fact, as one of the foremost scholars of LGBTQ+ history, George Chauncey, points out in a *New York Times* op-ed that accompanied the release of his seminal work *Gay New York*, "The systematic suppression of the gay community [in the later 20th century] was not due to some age-old, unchanging social antipathy, nor was it a sign of passivity and acquiescence by gay people. Anti-gay forces created the closet in response to the openness and assertiveness of gay men and lesbians in the early 20th century." While Sylvia—and Adrienne, Margaret, Jane, Gertrude, and Alice—might not have been "out" in the twenty-first-century sense, these women took their identities and lifestyles for granted in a way that LGBTQ+ people all too often cannot today, ironically and tragically.

To the best of my knowledge and research, the essential dates are accurate: the openings and closings of the store, the war, the publication dates of all of the books mentioned, the trial dates, the deaths, and the dates of Sylvia's travel.

Along these same lines, all the major events pertaining to her publication of *Ulysses* are accurate. February 2, 2022, will thus be the centennial of her very first edition of Joyce's novel, which she accurately foresaw would alter the course of twentieth-century literature. She also relinquished her rights to the novel a decade later so that Random House could use its considerable resources to make the book legal—something that eventually brought her genuine satisfaction, because all she ever truly wanted was what was best for the book and its author. I tried to imagine the roller-coaster ride of pride, joy, and anguish she felt in her personal and professional relationship with Joyce, which was necessarily bound up in her role as his publisher.

Except for Julie and Michel, the major characters and their spouses are real; if you google them, you'll find them. And the ways in which the characters are intertwined are also grounded in reality.

One minor but important character is a fictional composite: Patrick "Paddy" Kelly is an imagining of Joyce's many helpers, one of whom was a real person named Padraic Colum, whom Joyce dispatched to convince Sylvia to relinquish *Ulysses*.

Aside from the major dates, I did not consult diaries or letters to make sure that a certain character definitely would have been in Paris on a particular day. If they were in Paris that year, that was good enough for me. Nor did I consult weather reports for specific days. If it suited my narrative to have it rain on a particular day, it rained. (Though there really were torrential rains and flooding in the spring of 1935!) Occasionally, for the sake of narrative tension, I would slightly alter dates—for instance, John Quinn actually visited Paris twice, once when the shop on rue Dupuytren was open, and a second time after it had moved to the rue de l'Odéon; but I had him visit only once, in the summer it moved, so he could at least see both locations, which is the essence of what happened; also, he actually sent photographs of his pages of the Circe episode, but not without all the back-and-forth I describe. I also had Joyce stay away from Paris in 1931 a bit longer than the five months he actually took to marry Nora in London. And because true Hemingway aficionados will want me to confess, I admit I had him arrive on the scene about six months earlier in 1921 than he actually did.

Let's talk a little more about the characters and their actions, since the characters—understandably—are what readers get most attached to and want to know of their trials and tribulations. *What's real?* I'll be the first to admit that I did not read every letter, biography, or diary entry available to me for the major characters in this novel, in part because I never would have actually written my own book (yes, there really is a staggering amount of information on this particular cast of misfits). Also, since the novel is from Sylvia's point of view, the essential thing, it seemed to me, was to capture what she thought and felt about the people in her life. But I chose to write the novel in the third person because I wanted readers to see things that Sylvia might not, so I read as much as I could—enough to help me create characters of my own, who would work for the story and also preserve what I perceived to be the essence of the real people.

Note how many squishy, interpretive words were in that last paragraph. Because there is simply no such thing as The Real James Joyce, or The True Hemingway, or The Actual Adrienne Monnier. They are dead. The only thing writers can do is interpret their lives. As Hilary Mantel said in her brilliant BBC lectures, readers of historical fiction "are not buying a replica, or even a faithful photographic representation"; rather, we are "buying a painting with the brushstrokes left in." What a beautifully put distinction. The only thing I'd add is that when we read historical novels, we are interpreting the author's interpretation—so together writer and reader venture even further away from any actual "truth" of what happened.

All that said, I tried my honest and humble best to imagine what it would have been like for Sylvia to live her remarkable life in Shakespeare and Company. I tried not to make any actual mistakes, and at the end of this note, I've included a bibliography of the most important books I read. I was also able to integrate some of my own life experiences into this novel, since as a young aspiring writer I worked at an independent bookstore in Brooklyn, New York, that was a hotbed of literary talent just like Sylvia's shop—famous writers like Mary Morris and Paul Auster were regulars, and all of us who worked there were apprentice writers at various stages in our careers. Years before that, I worked in the conservation department of my university's library. My past in the stacks certainly predisposed me toward Sylvia's story, and it gave me some insight into the day-to-day workings of a place like Shakespeare and Company, as well as an abiding appreciation for the life-changing power of the books we put into the hands of readers. Nothing pleased me more than a return customer who wanted to know what he or she should read next.

Sylvia's other papers reside in the Princeton University Library. In fact, just in 2020, as I was finishing my manuscript, Princeton launched a fantastic website called the Shakespeare and Company Project, for which all of Sylvia's receipts and library cards have been scanned and cataloged and put into a searchable database so you can look up, say, what James Joyce checked out in 1926. The project has a variety of other marvelous twenty-first-century learning tools that I think Sylvia herself would have embraced, and if you're loath to leave this world as you read these final words, I encourage you to go there and explore.

You can also visit another Shakespeare and Company bookstore in Paris. It's a ten-minute walk from the original, and it was founded as Le Mistral by another bookselling American, George Whitman, in 1951. He changed the store's name to Shakespeare and Company in 1964, William Shakespeare's four hundredth birthday, and as such it is very much an homage to Sylvia's original, with plaques and information about Sylvia's shop all over the shelves. The store houses wandering writers, who are called Tumbleweeds, and although I didn't have the pleasure of being one, many other writers you've heard of have been, like Dave Eggers and Anaïs Nin.

The current owner of Shakespeare and Company is George Whitman's daughter, whom George named Sylvia. Appropriately, this latter incarnation of the store also realized Sylvia Beach's dream of an adjacent café, and if you sit there and sip your tea, you can look across the Seine and enjoy a spectacular view of Notre-Dame Cathedral— which I had the pleasure of doing while I was researching this book.

I felt as lucky as any of the writers in this novel getting to be a writer in Paris, gazing at the Gothic cathedral that was undergoing major repair after the fire of 2019, reminding me that art very often emerges from ashes.

ACKNOWLEDGMENTS

I wrote most of this book during the COVID-19 pandemic, when being unable to see my friends and family live made them feel all the more precious to me. I was constantly moved by the creative ways we found to be together anyway, even if it was on a screen—in fact, one of the gifts of 2020 and 2021 was getting to participate in the book tours of friends who lived across the country, celebrations I never could have been part of without the double-edged sword that is Zoom.

And it was bookstores and libraries like Shakespeare and Company that made those events possible, gamely rising to the occasion and shifting their events, recommendations, ordering, and book clubs online so that readers could continue to connect with writers they already loved and discover new ones. In no small way, the remaking of bookselling and -lending that took place around me while I wrote inspired my conception of this novel.

So thank you, bookstore owners and your staff, librarians, volunteers, publishers, publicists, marketers, bookstagrammers, and everyone else who rolls up their sleeves every day to make sure the right books land in the right readers' hands—this past year and every year. Though *The Paris Bookseller* might be about a famous store and famous writers, the daily practice of reading is a humble, deep, and incremental process; reading promotes empathy, helps us relax, shows us the world, educates us. You are the ones who make this life-changing activity possible.

I'd also like to thank some specific people who had a direct hand in the making of this book, because as romantic as the image of the writer in a garret scribbling into the night is, the fact is books aren't made that way. Many trusted reader-writer friends delved into drafts of this book, gave me spot-on feedback, brainstormed with me, and held my hand when the going got tough: Lori Hess, Heather Webb, Alix Rickloff, Christine Wells, Cheryl Pappas, Renee Rosen, Elise Hooper, Evie Dunmore, Danielle Fodor, Kip Wilson, Diana Renn, Kelly Ford, and Mary Garen. Sarah Williamson, research partner in crime, we'll always have Paris. Fellow Lyonesses, our virtual watercooler is one of my favorite parts of the job. And a special thanks to Kevin Wheeler—your insights and your belief in me, and your willingness to talk things over again and again (and again!), mean more than I can possibly express here; all the laughing helps, too.

Kate Seaver—I feel so lucky that you're my editor. Your trust, suggestions, and support are game changers, especially for this book. Thank you.

Kevan Lyon, Agent Extraordinaire. Thank you, thank you, thank you for your patience, positivity, and advocacy. I am honored to be one of the pride.

Taryn Fagerness and Tawanna Sullivan, I'm so grateful for all your hard work in selling *The Paris Bookseller* overseas! It's a special thrill to know that readers as far away as London, Madrid, Milan, and even Rio de Janeiro will read translations of this novel—which is so much about translation—in their home countries. For the UK

ACKNOWLEDGMENTS

and Australian editions, I'd like to say a special thanks to the team at Headline Review, particularly my editor Frankie Edwards, who believed in this novel and steered it so gracefully toward publication. Helen Windrath and Ellen Harber—I so appreciate your work on the business side. Alice Moore and Cathie Arrington: your covers are stunning and sophisticated! Hannah Cawse, thank you for the wonderful audio edition. Tina Paul, Rosie Margesson, Becky Bader, Chris Keith-Wright, Frances Doyle, Anna Egelstaff, and Izzy Smith—thank you for all you do to land this book into the hands of readers.

Berkley Dream Team in the USA—you take such amazing care of me! Claire Zion, thank you for being so enthusiastic about Sylvia's story; knowing you were behind this book really spurred me on. Ivan Held and Christine Ball, thank you for your vision and leadership. Craig Burke and Jeanne-Marie Hudson, I'm so grateful for your expertise and championing—I have learned so much about the whirlwind of book publishing from you and your teams.

Mom and Dad, you have been the best example of lifelong reading, fun on holidays, and unconditional love a daughter could ever ask for. And Elena, you're my best girl and best thing. I have been truly blessed in the family department.

Last but never least, readers, thank YOU. No matter what volume you pluck off a shelf, you keep the dream of reading alive. And that's what this is all about.

SELECT BIBLIOGRAPHY

Anderson, Margaret. *My Thirty Years' War.* New York: Horizon Press, 1969.

Banta, Melissa, and Oscar A. Silverman, eds. *James Joyce's Letters to Sylvia Beach, 1921-1940.* Bloomington: Indiana University Press, 1987.

Beach, Sylvia. *Shakespeare and Company.* Lincoln: University of Nebraska Press, 1991.

Birmingham, Kevin. *The Most Dangerous Book: The Battle for James Joyce's Ulysses.* New York: Penguin Books, 2014.

Fitch, Noel Riley. *Sylvia Beach and the Lost Generation: A History of Literary Paris in the Twenties and Thirties.* New York: W. W. Norton, 1985.

Hassett, Joseph M. *The Ulysses Trials: Beauty and Truth Meet the Law.* Dublin: Lilliput Press, 2016.

Hemingway, Ernest. *A Moveable Feast.* New York: Scribner, 2010.

Joyce, James. *Dubliners.* New York: Penguin Classics, 1992.

Joyce, James. *A Portrait of the Artist as a Young Man.* New York: Penguin Books, 1992.

Joyce, James. *Ulysses: The 1922 Text.* Oxford: Oxford University Press, 2008.

Monnier, Adrienne. *The Very Rich Hours of Adrienne Monnier.* Translated by Richard McDougall. Lincoln: University of Nebraska Press, 1996.

Tamagne, Florence. *A History of Homosexuality in Europe: Berlin, London, Paris, 1919-1939.* 2 vols. New York: Algora, 2004.

Walsh, Keri. *The Letters of Sylvia Beach.* New York: Columbia University Press, 2010.

ABOUT THE AUTHOR

Kerri Maher holds an MFA from Columbia University and founded *YARN*, an award-winning literary journal of short-form YA writing. For many years a professor of writing, she now writes full time and lives with her daughter in Massachusetts where apple picking and long walks in the woods are especially fine.

She is a budding Instagrammer at @kerrimaherwriter, and you can also find her on Facebook at @kerrimaherwriter and on her website, www.kerrimaher.com.

From Ancient Rome to the Tudor court, revolutionary Paris to the Second World War, discover the best historical fiction and non-fiction at

Visit us today for exclusive author features, first chapter previews, podcasts and audio excerpts, book trailers, giveaways and much more.

Sign up now to receive our regular newsletter at

www.HforHistory.co.uk